ALWAYS COME HOME

Inspired by a True Story

"Until global mental healthcare practices are changed; until we admit that psychiatrists do not possess the only valid insight into a patient's condition; until that day we will continue to endanger the very people we are tasked to heal."

Dr. Anne Tenbrooke, Clinical Psychiatrist

STORYLINES
ENTERTAINMENT LTD

Tom Richards

By the same author

Fiction for Adults

Dolphin Song

Fiction for young adults

Hotfoot

Hotfoot 2: Lucky's Revenge

The Lost Scrolls of Newgrange

The Den Adventure

Non-fiction

A Survivor's Guide to Living in Ireland

Always Come Home is the author's
second novel for adult readers

About Always Come Home

The Story's Premise: Accused of stealing $3million and attempting suicide, David Bloom is admitted to a psychiatric unit against his will. Misdiagnosed and prescribed incorrect medication, he will be released only if he silences the ghosts of his past and proves his sanity. But with release pending, and his ghosts still beckoning, he is forced to go back to a home that only exists in his wild imagination.

In 1982, on rural Bere Island, Ireland, 17-year-old DAVID BLOOM promises a future of happiness to loving girlfriend DOLORES. However, their plans shatter when his mother ROSE commits suicide. Blamed by his father HECTOR for negligence, David escapes his father's unjustified accusation and haunting feelings of shame by fleeing to America.

Years later David, now in his late 40s, has unsuccessfully masked his internal conflict by submerging into the frantic pace of American. Now a partner in a New York investment firm, wed to socialite LAURA, and with loving daughter RACHEL about to be married, David lives a pressurized life. David is hit by two events which shake him to the core: first, the accusation by business partner GARRETT LEDBETTER that he has stolen $3 million. The second, a letter received from an Irish solicitor informing him of his father's death, triggering past shame.

Overwhelmed, at Rachel's wedding rehearsal David has a breakdown. Laura accuses him of being an alcoholic, a thief and liar. Rachel refuses to allow David to attend her wedding. Confused, hurt, and becoming psychotic, David flees back to Ireland. There, for the first time in years, he re-enters his boyhood home. Delusional, he sees his dead mother and father and realizes he is mentally unwell. However, he becomes convinced that he can cure himself by confronting the delusions. When he meets Dolores, he begs her to help. Though still hurt by his abandonment, she agrees.

David relives the night his mother died. He sees Rose and re-experiences his father's rage. He orders his mind to banish the ghosts of his past. But they will not leave him. David is deeply disturbed when discovering they actually react to his pleas to let him prove his father was wrong: he was not responsible for his mother's death.

In New York, Rachel tracks her father to Ireland. With Laura, she journeys to County Cork because they know David can no longer help himself and are determined to do it for him.

Always Come Home is the author's second novel for an adult market.
What Readers Say:

Tamara Curtin Niemi

Always Comes Home hit so many notes. First my mom is schizophrenic, currently in a mental correctional facility in the US and will likely never leave; second Mikhail Bulgakov was the subject of my PhD dissertation, so the blending and travelling between two worlds was a familiar vehicle, and oh, that frustration of the system really screwing people and their friends and family too.

Patrick Bloom

My son suffered from a simple nervous breakdown. He was mis-diagnosed as being a threat to himself or others and thrown (illegally, in my opinion) into a mental health facility I would rather not name. There, he spent over 2 months while I fought the system to have him released. I was so tired and angry, I was the one who needed treatment.

Always Comes Home resonated with me. It demonstrates how those we love are never listened to: not when others believe they are mentally sick. Thank you for this book. You give me hope that the system CAN BE CHANGED AS IT MUST BE. Not only where I live, but ALL OVER THE WORLD.

To Hector & Rose and Mad, Loving Alternatives
& to Anne Tracey, Beloved Friend

Bantry General Hospital Psychiatric Unit
Bantry, County Cork, Ireland
Psychiatric Assessment

Name: Bloom, David Sex: M

Date of Admission: 2 May

Status: Involuntary Admission

Reason for Admission:

Nationality: American / Irish(dual)

Residence: Long Island, New York

Other Residence (if any): Bere Island, County Cork, Ireland

Next of Kin: Laura Bloom (44)
Status: SEPARATED

Children: Rachel Bloom (22)

Parents: Hector and Rose Bloom
Status: DECEASED

Other Family or Significant Relationships: Unknown

Medication on Admission: none

DOB: 21 March 1970 **Age**: 48

Initial Diagnosis: Alcoholism/Bi-Polar

Clinical Psychiatrist: Dr Paul Cutter

Mental Health Act 2001 (Harm to self or others)
Place of Birth: Ireland

Phone: Unknown

Phone: Unknown

Residence: Long Island, New York

Residence: Long Island, New York

Residence: Bere Island, County Cork, Ireland

SECTION ONE

FAMILY HISTORY &
BACKGROUND CLINICAL NOTES

Lecture Extract 'The Silent Scream' Dr. Anne Tenbrooke,
Consultant Psychiatrist St. James Clinic, Dublin

"Mental illness is the scourge of society. The World Health Organization estimates one in four people suffer tragic mental health disorders including anxiety and panic attacks, Bi-polar, schizophrenia, alcoholism and substance abuse, eating disorders, depression…the list is relentless. These illnesses have one thing in common: they destroy lives.

"The numbers suffering from mental illness are increasing rapidly and I warn you: no one is immune. Anyone can break no matter how strong they appear to be. However, much of society refuses to discuss mental illness due to its stigma of embarrassment and shame. That unwillingness impacts patients because it quashes the often-silent screams of those who suffer.

"Tragically, those screams remain unheard due to the mis-directed care many mainstream psychiatrists apply.

"Patients are often misdiagnosed leading to improper treatment. Subsequent drug therapies can result in sometimes harmful outcomes.

Involuntary admission to mental health units strips civil liberties, leading to immense suffering by treating patients as prisoners. All of these can strangle the voice of hope from the very people we are trying to heal.

"Professionals such as myself continue to press for better methods that lead to recovery for those suffering from mental health issues. By doing so we will learn to listen to—and decode—the silent torment which can be tragically misunderstood.

"If we do not, these patients will remain shrouded in darkness, their cries for help misinterpreted. Their lives silenced forever."

1

I can no longer trust. Not the doctor. Not my wife. Not my daughter. Not my business partner. Not what I see or hear. Not even myself. Especially not myself.

My hands shake as I type and I sweat enough to soak the bandana I wear around my neck. And always there is the ticking. Ticking, ticking, remorseless ticking. The metronome of a past that fills my head which no one else can hear. I fear it will never be silenced.

I had to beg them for this laptop. The doctor worried I'd hang myself by the electric cord. I'm not brave enough to commit suicide. If I was, I would have done it years ago. I said to Doc, the prick, trying for a bit of irony, "If you think I'm going to off myself you're crazy." He didn't even cut a smile.

But when I told Doc I thought writing about it would help, he agreed. Reluctantly. He lets me write two hours a day. I don't even have an Internet connection. When time is up, they take it away and I stare at the ceiling or stagger out to the courtyard to play with the other defenseless prisoners.

God I want out.

When they think you're nuts you have to live by their rules. Particularly if you're in a Psychiatric Unit against your will. It's called Involuntary Admission which gives the people who used to love you the legal right to lock you up.

The way it works is simple: you're sitting in the bedroom of a Bere Island Bed and Breakfast, out in the middle of nowhere. You're recovering from a fire that almost killed you. Most of you hopes you'll be left alone. Then someone knocks on the door. You think it's the owner. You open it, finding your daughter Rachel. You see your wife, the woman you've been married to for over twenty years. Both grin like they've found a long-lost puppy. At first you want to grab onto 'em and never let go because you think they've come to rescue you from your misery. But you soon realize their sunny smiles are bullshit.

Your loving family steps aside. A group of people you've never met (imagine three goons from the psychiatric unit and a no-nonsense female police officer) storm into your room. One of the Psych guys asks in an ugly, take-no-prisoners voice:

"Are you Mister David Bloom?"

And you'll say, "Who the fuck are you?"

Then the female cop, a member of Ireland's Garda Siochana, a law enforcement organization you've always trusted because you've never been in trouble, will command, "Mister Bloom, pursuant to section thirteen of Ireland's Mental Health Act Two-Thousand and One your daughter, with the agreement of a GP, has requested an Assisted Admission. You are now being removed to the Bantry Psychiatric Unit."

If you're still in your pajamas like I was, the goons will force you to get dressed despite the uninvited audience. I've discovered that standing naked in front of your adult child, both hands covering your privates, is hugely humiliating. You'll scream at the cop and goons, suggesting they're violating your human rights because you did nothing wrong. Their response is inconceivable: "Mister Bloom if you don't calm down we'll restrain you," and the cop rattles the cuffs hanging at her belt which scares you shitless. Then they grab you, marching you out the door where you meet the B&B owner who happens to be a family friend.

He can't look you in the eye because he thinks you're dangerous, a nut job, or both.

Did I say standing naked in front of your daughter was humiliating? Try being frog-marched through the B&B dining room where tourists and people from the small village you grew up in are having breakfast.

There's nothing quite like it.

Then they throw you in the backseat of a van, a goon at each shoulder, and drive you away. And there's not a Goddam thing you can do about it.

When I got to the Unit they had to drag me in. I struggled and cursed and told them I was going to sue. Then I realized if I kept it up they could hold me against my will until hell froze over. So I decided to shut-the-fuck up. When they asked my name I kept my mouth shut. When they offered to lend me a change of clothes I refused. The jeans, shirt, and runners I wore stunk of smoke. An EMT gave them to me, rescued by a thoughtful fireman. They were my badge of honor and damned if I'd hand them to those bunch of nut cases.

A pair of male nurses marched me to a ward. Six single beds lined four concrete walls. The paint was chipped. Three barred windows let in dull morning light. An old fella wearing torn pajamas sat on a bed in the far corner. He rocked back and forth muttering to himself. It was one hell of a reception.

One of the male nurses—a lad twice my size with the frustrated face of a castrated bullock—showed me a bed, told me to take a seat and stay quiet. He must have been deaf because I hadn't said a word since I stopped yelling. I sat on stained sheets and waited. My head pounded like it wanted to explode. I realized I was rocking on the bed just like the old fella. I was sure the muttering would come later.

Then bollocks came back. He towered over me, forearms ribbed like steel cable, and asked if I wanted to meet my shrink, Doctor Paul Cutter. Like I had a choice? I still think Doc's the biggest ass ever born.

When Nurse Bollocks led me into Cutter's office, he was sitting behind his desk. He never moved or offered a hand. He was reading some paperwork. Mine, I suppose. While he ignored me I scanned the rat hole he called an office. Framed degrees from English universities hung all over the walls. I wasn't impressed. I guess he wasn't bright enough to get into an Irish university. Unsurprising because what Irish college wants a gobshite?

He looked up with little bug eyes I'll never forget. The guy couldn't have been more than thirty. I wondered if I was the first patient he ever treated. Later I learned I wasn't half wrong. His appointment as the Unit's Psychiatric Consultant was the first real management job of his career. I hoped it would be his last.

"Mister Bloom?" he asked in an arid voice I hated as much as his colorless eyes. I refused to respond.

He studied my shirt. A faded short-sleeved red Polo Laura had given me years ago. The top pocket was torn. I pawed a cheek and a vagrant's two-day stubble. I wondered how I looked to Doc. Sane? Crazy? Delusional? Ridiculous?

Cutter consulted his paperwork. "How are you feeling?"

When I still said nothing, his chubby cheeks turned bright red. "Your heart rate and respiration are elevated, as is your blood pressure. Do you feel faint? Dizzy?"

Sure I was dizzy but damned if I'd tell him. He sat back in his big important chair and studied me like a bug. Then he struck the top of the desk as hard as he could. BANG! I spooked like a four-year-old kid about to get a whipping.

"Good," the doc said. "I have your attention. Mister Bloom, I'm here to help you, do you understand? Mister Bloom, do you understand?"

Fuck him if he was going to treat me like a half-wit. I turned my back on him.

"Do you want to tell me what happened?"

I shook my head. Just a bit. Just enough to tell him to drop dead.

"Do you want to tell me why you were angry at your daughter's wedding rehearsal?"

Who told him that? Nope, I wasn't going there. Tell *him*? *He can go on to fuck.*

"Do you want to tell me why you started the fire? You could have hurt yourself or someone else, Mister Bloom."

Fuck off, you little fuck! I did not start a fire.

"You're going to have to talk to me at some point." He smiled a patronizing 'I'm better than you' smile, leaning in to me. "Remember, Mister Bloom, I'm the fellow holding the keys."

A pounding heart made me realize what I was up against. I decided I'd better cooperate if I ever wanted to get out of this hell hole.

"How long am I going to be here?" My voice was raspy from all the smoke I'd swallowed. Was it only yesterday? The day before?

"That's up to you," he said in a manner way too smug. "I have a legal obligation to give you a psychiatric evaluation. If you won't talk to me how can I do that?" Pouting lips tried to look as innocent as a choirboy. It didn't work.

"How are you sleeping?"

"I sleep fine."

"Would you say you're eating enough?"

"I eat fine."

"Do you have thoughts of harming yourself or others?"

"Someone already asked me that."

"Do you?"

"If I did you're the last one I'd tell. But I don't." The prick frowned. I guess he didn't like my honesty.

"Are you on any medication?"

"No."

He studied me then asked, "I'm told you're under extreme pressure at work. A few weeks ago, you worked well over one hundred hours."

"I was busy."

"Wouldn't you say working over a hundred hours in a single week is a little excessive? Perhaps a little … manic?" He took off his rimless glasses to inspect me closer.

He didn't understand. Everyone in the City works over a hundred hours a week. I should have known where this was going but I'd never been in a Psychiatric Unit.

"I don't think so. I take care of things. In a hundred hours I get more done than most people. I'm not manic." He scowled. "Whatever my wife told you is wrong. I've had some problems but I can take care of it."

"So you don't need help?" Then the bastard said, "Mister Bloom, maybe that's why you drink too much."

The words stung. I broke into a sweat.

"Who told you that?"

"Your wife. Your daughter confirmed it when you were admitted."

"I don't drink."

"Your wife and daughter are still in town. Do you want me to ask them again?"

I couldn't say a word.

"They also tell me you're seeing things."

I sensed I had to be very, very careful. "Like what? I don't see things."

"But what about your dog?"

"I don't have a dog. Not anymore."

"Then perhaps you're hearing things? Are you hearing anything now?"

Just your whining voice you shit, I wanted to say. But I didn't. Nor would I tell him what I saw. Or what I heard and keep hearing. Who knows what's real anyway? Him? I folded my arms and stared hard at the floor.

"Mister Bloom, you're going to have to give me something to go on for an evaluation. What happened back in America? At the wedding rehearsal for instance?"

Hot shame crept into my cheeks. I figured I'd better say something. "I just… I didn't mean to. Everyone snaps sometimes."

"But not everyone attacks his business partner." The fecker looked again at his notes. "Garrett Ledbetter, wasn't it? You struck him in the face. Repeatedly."

"He's a thief and a liar."

"As I understand it, that's what he says you are."

"Garrett is an ass but it was never about him."

"What was it about, then? Why were you so upset?"

"An envelope. I couldn't open an envelope." I could see it in my mind's eye. The envelope I'd hidden in the glove box. The one I dreaded. The one that ate me up.

"An envelope?" Doc was suddenly very interested. "Why don't you tell me about it?"

"I couldn't get it out of my head." I knew I should shut up but I couldn't. "They kept going around and around in circles. They were driving me nuts."

"What was driving you nuts?"

"Words," I said but the dumb-fuck didn't understand so I tried again. "Words I was thinking over and over again. 'Open the envelope. Open the fucking envelope.' But I wasn't brave enough."

"Where are you right now?" Cutter demanded, sitting straight up in his chair. "And don't tell me you're here with me. Where are you when you think of the envelope?"

"Long Island. The lighthouse," I remembered and wished I hadn't.

"Where your wife found you the night before the wedding rehearsal?"

"The cops found me. Not my wife."

He smiled that dumb smile again but I didn't care. All I could see was the envelope.

"Tell me about the envelope, Mister Bloom. You're safe here. Tell me."

For reasons I'll never understand, I did.

2

Open the envelope. Open it. Open the Goddam thing.

The words. The bloody, fucking, horrible words I can't get out of my head. They keep coming. Relentless. Like armies of attacking tidal waves, fifty feet tall. Even sitting in a locked car parked in an abandoned parking lot there is no escape from the condemning words that want to kill me.

I know where the envelope is, of course. It is in my car's glove box locked tight so no one can find it. Including me.

My hands are shaking. When I look at them they seem strangely unfamiliar. Same knuckles. Same fingers. Same palms but covered with a patina of sweat. I cannot stop them shaking. It is like a horror show and they are someone else's hands. Not mine. Not David Bloom's. At this moment I want to be anyone other than David Bloom.

Open the envelope. Come on, do it. Be a man and do it.

I can't stop the words in my head. I didn't sleep more than a few hours all week because I am plagued by the thoughts of the unopened envelope. So I've driven here, to the very eastern tip of Long Island, hoping they'll disappear. But they don't.

I remember looking at the dashboard clock. It is past midnight. I know I should call Laura.

"Fuck Laura," I whisper to the clock.

I turn in my seat and look up at the Long Island lighthouse. It rises from the solid rock of a nearby bluff. I watch its beacon sweep the chaotic seas with revolving light. It reflects off the surf that is pushed in on the lee of a passing storm, foaming like deranged white dragons as it pummels the beach and solid rocks beneath. The wildness of the sea matches my horrifying, damning thoughts.

I always liked the lighthouse. Its steady beam sweeps far out to sea. Fishermen depend on it for survival. It gives them a true warning of dangerous shoals hidden beneath the illusion of an ocean's solid surface. It beats like the reliable warmth of a living heart or the neurons of a brain's relentless firing. If it wasn't for the lighthouse many would have foundered. I wish I was as solid and as true and as strong as the lighthouse.

When I have time, if work lets me, I come to the lighthouse. If it is night and good weather I stand on the beach, mesmerized by its steady display. If daytime, I take walks alone along an empty shore. I listen for the song of the American Coot and other seabirds that make this precarious place their home, and watch men fishing the tides along the point, and think how much it reminds me of home back in Ireland.

This night, sitting in the car, I think of Ireland. The thought leads helplessly to others. Careening across the Pinballed Wizard that is my mind. The directionless ball slams into fixed bumpers of neuron memory, setting them off like fireworks. Flashing bright. Blinding. Unwanted. Uncontrolled.

A far-off island. A house. Parents. The dog who was my friend. Glittering, fragmentary memories that want to kill me. I push them down but

she emerges anyway, bubbling out of the shadows toward the surface of my psyche; the image stabbing

My girl.

I track the bright beam of the lighthouse, looking east, wondering if over that inaccessible horizon…she still walks the island…what she is doing…if she is happy…if she waits or has forgotten me…if she gazes west…at this precise moment…thinking of me as I do her;

if she sits on the rocks beneath the Irish lighthouse where we once made love.

For a moment her memory is more solid than any reality. If I reach out I know I can touch her: the curling soft hair; the gentle smiling lips; the warm breasts.

But veracity strikes me as it has done for thirty years.

I lost her. I would have done anything for her. But I was forced to let go before she became swept up in accusation that would have destroyed us. Over the years I have tried to move on but the long-ago secrets I carry haunt and frighten me with occasional unwanted intensity. They ache and bristle as if my wounded soul was left festering for far too long. For years I have promised myself:

Stop thinking of the girl and the dog and my mother and father because they are gone.

They are part of a past I cannot change though I catch myself yearning it could be otherwise. For that reason, long ago I decided

I can never go home to Ireland.

In the car I shake my head like a steer fending off stinging flies. My brain buffets within the shuddering skull, fracturing the memories so they will retreat. Back into the past. Back into darkness. Back into forgetfulness so they cannot bite.

But not tonight. Especially not this night. I know why. The envelope and what it contains still waits. It is right there, behind the polished metal of a car's locked glove box.

Fuck the envelope. Fuck everything.

But my racing head will not stop. It has already been a week from hell. The words about the envelope become confused with other problems I face, both at home and at work.

Some of the problems at home are fixable. For instance, Rachel's wedding rehearsal is tomorrow, the wedding the day after that. I know I must buckle down. I haven't even written my speech. I'd done little enough to earn my daughter's love over the years though God knows how hard I'd tried. But the wedding is a no brainer. I will run through the motions at the rehearsal, then the following day give my daughter away with the rock-solid love that is easy to feel even if I don't have time to always show it. I am determined to make her wedding an event she'll remember the rest of her life.

I hope the surprise I have put together with her future father-in-law will help. Rachel is the easy part.

But then there is Laura and a twenty-year marriage gone to shite. The problems we face are harder to fix. Rachel put her finger on it when she found me in the living room a few months ago. I must have been brooding more than usual because she wrapped her arms tight around me.

"Dad, you and Mom just don't know how to listen anymore."

She didn't know what was going on, not all of it. I love my wife, maybe not as deeply or as truly as I had hoped or wanted, not with all the Irish baggage I carry. But I don't want to throw it away.

I remember smiling at my daughter. "There's a right way and a wrong way—" and Rachel finished it, "—and Mom's way. I know." Then she hugged me even tighter and the reality of her love made all the difference.

But Rachel is right. Laura and I don't know how to listen to each other and we haven't for a long time. Take the house for instance. A seven-bedroom, red-bricked executive monstrosity located in a stunningly beautiful Long Island gated community. It came with a clubhouse and indoor pool. A perfect place to rub shoulders with aspiring rich people if that's your idea of fun.

I remember when she found it. Rachel was about to start middle school. We still rented the apartment in Long Beach because the investment firm I'd set up with Garrett was a startup and we were broke. Not that our miniscule bank account stopped Laura. "It's just what I've always wanted," I remember her demanding. "It's private and looks out over a bay. It has great schools for Rachel. We'll get the money. David just go look at it. You'll love it."

I hated it.

We moved in two months later but only after I offered my left nut as collateral for the mortgage. Laura took to the new community and her upwardly mobile neighbors like she'd been born there. Not bad for a girl raised in rural Illinois to a poor alcoholic father and a neurotic mother. Not bad at all.

We've lived there for almost nine years. And though I hint at a compromise by moving somewhere a bit less Kardashian East, we are still there. I stopped trying to convince her a long time ago. I know the reasons for our problems aren't only hers. They're also mine because I don't have the balls to tell her what I want.

But the other problem in addition to Rachel and Laura, the one that competes so viciously in my head with the unopened envelope, is what I discovered at work.

It was a Monday, and just like every day of the fucking week the alarm hammered me awake before dawn. I struggled into one of the suits Laura bought at the exclusive tailors on West 42nd Street, which she hung up in a spare bathroom because I don't sleep in our bedroom anymore.

I hate those damned suits. I feel like a prisoner in them. But Laura insists.

Then I climbed in the car and fought my way into the City before the other masters of the universe. I'm responsible for finance and administration and though Garrett might go on and on about the importance of sales and client relationships, I know damned well what would happen if I made even one tiny screw up. Our company would be dead meat for the SEC and we'd end up in a federal penitentiary.

We're an investment firm and we agreed to start it the day Lehman Brothers went to the wall. Before that, Garrett and I worked at the same small brokerage firm for the same good old boy who'd given me my first real job in the States. That was almost twenty years after I emigrated from Ireland, following years of bad sus where I always teetered on the brink of financial ruin.

I met my future business partner on the first day of the new job.

God, he was larger than life. Garrett always drove the latest Caddy and dressed impeccably. He always wore three-piece tweed suits bought from fabulously expensive London importers, and always tucked a silk handkerchief into his breast pocket. He always wore red suspenders and matching red wool socks protruding from handmade loafers imported from Italy. He leased a mid-town apartment which cost a small fortune. Back then I knew he couldn't afford any of this, not on the salary we received from good old boy. But Garrett was driven to succeed. He covered his office walls with framed diplomas from Yale and Clemson and autographed portraits taken with gangsters like Carl Icahn and Donald Trump, and he exuded the perfumed stink of success.

When Garrett told me he was gay I wasn't surprised. Nor did I judge.

It was only later I learned the whole thing was fake. He'd financed his expensive lifestyle by stretching a bequest from his parents with personal loans and maxing out every credit card he could lay his hands on.

As to the degrees and signed portraits—complete phonies. By the time I figured it out it was too late.

When Lehman Brothers went bust good old boy let everyone go. I was out of a job again. But Garrett saw the crash as a rising tide of glittering opportunity.

Garrett found me where I shouldn't have been, in a local bar drowning my sorrows with a group of other suckers also ready to hang themselves.

"You know this is a turning point, don't you David?" Garrett had declared with persuasive insight. "The next action you take, your very next decision, could be the one to change your life."

Then he told me his plan. He wanted to form a new investment firm. I thought his brain was misfiring because he'd chosen me as his business partner. "David, we're going to make a killing when the market comes back. You've lost your job. What have you got to lose?"

He was out of his mind because neither of us had ever run a business. But it was better than telling Laura I was out of work. I could see her face: the smirk of disappointment almost hiding the unforgiving eyes that were the true give-away; the look that made me feel like a bum.

We set up Ledbetter & Bloom a week later. On Garrett's borrowed dime, I might add. No matter what he accuses me of, or what I think of him today, ten years ago Garrett saved my life.

Since opening the doors we've made a pot of money, more than I ever dreamed. But the race has been relentless.

My responsibilities include liaising with the stock exchanges and regulators like the SEC. All the financial reporting and audits are in my corner. And—here's the relevant one—I am also responsible for creating investment reports and analyses for our clients.

That Monday was the start of a financial car wreck that still hasn't been resolved.

I was preparing the quarterly report for a meeting with one of our important clients, Englewood LLC. We meet with selected clients every three months. This particular meeting was later that day. The report contained complete financials⊠the total amounts invested with us, quarterly stock and bond returns, cash payments made or received, fees paid to our firm, a full market analysis, and similar dreary details. One of the figures

I always report on is the client's cash balance we hold for them, and that's when I found the problem.

We were missing a hundred thousand bucks from the Englewood client cash account.

I blustered through the meeting but I don't think the Englewood execs believed a word I said, and neither did I. I made half of it up. And yes, I was lying. But I didn't know what else to do.

After the client left Garrett groused about the missing money but figured it was an accounting error. But that's not what bothered him the most. "What the hell were you thinking?" he fumed. "In the meeting you made us look like dicks. Don't you realize Englewood could pull the account? A half-million bucks in fees could go up in smoke."

I countered that I couldn't tell them the truth, not with a one hundred thousand dollar hole in their account. He told me to instruct our Financial Controller to find the cash which is when I talked to Peter. But now Garrett thinks the problem is much larger than a few missing bucks, and so do I. Which is why the Feds are on my tail. Or so I'm told.

"You want me to be honest, Doc?" I said still looking at the floor. "I really don't give a shite if they find the cash. I already have enough worries, you know?"

I felt like fuck: dizzy and with that disoriented out-of-control feeling I'd experienced since opening the envelope and Rachel's rehearsal. I hoped Doc wouldn't notice. I took a breath and tried to control the shakiness in my voice.

"Trish, my PA, brought the envelope into the office with a mess of other stuff. I was sweating over the Englewood issue and didn't notice. But then I guess I reached for something—"

"—and you saw it," the doctor finished.

"Trish usually opens everything. But this one wasn't opened. It was registered and had Private and Confidential stamped all over it. Then I saw the return address. It was from my father's solicitor."

"In Ireland?" the doctor asked. "Mister Bloom, how did you feel then? The moment you saw the envelope?"

"I can't describe it. Not in words that make sense. Part of me felt numb. Part of me wanted to scream. But I buried that part. As if I put my scream in a locked box inside me. But the voice kept screaming. It wanted out."

"It takes a lot of energy to keep a box like that closed, especially when it's inside you."

"I keep a lot stuffed in that box," I admitted and realized the bastard might actually feel some sympathy.

"Go back to the envelope. Why couldn't you open it?"

"Because I thought I knew what was inside," I said and couldn't stop the shaking in my voice.

"Keep going."

"So I locked it in the glove box of my car. I pretended to myself I'd never seen it. But I couldn't do it. I couldn't stop thinking about it. It became…" I searched for the word.

"Obsessive?" He frowned. "Go on."

"That's when I drove to the lighthouse. I knew if I could get some peace, some time by myself, I might find the courage. I finally got the guts to take it out of the glove box. But I wanted to rip it up. I didn't want to read what was inside."

"But you did."

My eyes teared up.

"When you read it, is that when you decided to come back to Ireland?" the doc asked. "I know you haven't been home in thirty years."

"I couldn't come back. Not after what he said. Not after what he accused me of doing."

"You mean your father." Cutter crouched in front of me, eye to eye. "You were a young man then. Your father was wrong to accuse you."

I looked at him. "You know?"

"Some of it."

Hot blood pulsed through my head like it wanted to sweep me out to sea.

"Then you opened the envelope and read what was inside. You learned your father was dead. You realized it was too late to tell him his accusation wasn't true. Mister Bloom," he pronounced, "you did not kill your mother."

I gasped when I heard Cutter's words. I wanted out. I wanted to be anywhere but beneath the pretend sympathetic gaze of a pretend boy psychiatrist.

"Did Dolores phone me?" I blurted, knowing my question was insanely incongruent.

Cutter's choirboy lips frowned. "Who?"

"Dolores Foley. Did she phone?"

"No, no one phoned you."

I started to cry. I didn't think I could ever stop. I needed to talk to Dolores because whatever the doctor had heard was wrong and Dolores knew it.

Dad had been right all those years ago.

I had killed my mother. I couldn't do a thing to change it.

3

"I don't trust him. I'll never trust him again."
Laura Bloom stood ramrod-straight in the Irish sunlight as she struggled with a difficult truth as if for the first time.

Near his patient's wife, Dr. Cutter sat on a bench in a secluded corner of the Unit's expansive private gardens. When the weather was good the psychiatrist brought the families of his patients here. He had discovered that warm light filtering through the tall oaks, and the gentle shadows they cast across the manicured lawns, were a source of comfort. The singsong of birds and whisper of the breeze mixed with the scent of early rose and lavender, providing a space of serenity to the tumultuous worry most felt. In the safety of the garden people were more likely to open up, telling Cutter what he wanted to know if he was to do his job.

He placed a small rectangular instrument on the bench.

"I'd like to record this."

"I don't care what you do."

He studied her for a moment. The facts about the woman were simple enough.

Name: Laura Bloom. Age: forty-four. Status: recently separated from David Bloom despite a twenty-three-year marriage. Notwithstanding the heat of the Irish spring sun she was dressed for winter, and impeccably. He assumed the elegant black woolen coat that shrouded her like a cloak was purchased from some high-end shop in America. The deep lavender dress it almost hid was form-fittingly tailored. A gold Tiffany pendant hung from her neck. The dark leather shoes and Prada hand bag looked too well made to be knock-offs. The outfit, together with the woman's demeanor, trumpeted conspicuous wealth and demanded respect.

Her long chestnut hair, almost black, was combed into a tight stylish bun but Cutter suspected she rarely wore it that way. Its severity set off a strong angular face and expressive dark brown eyes. She wore too much makeup. Cutter decided she could be beautiful if it weren't for the exhausted anger he sensed beneath the carefully crafted exterior, emotions that forced her lips into a tight pout.

Cutter wondered if he would have much success with this interview. He switched on the voice recorder.

"I understand your daughter can't be with us this morning."

"She's sleeping. Rachel is jetlagged and upset. Last night didn't help."

"I'm sorry. The admission process can be somewhat…challenging."

"It was hell." Laura pulled the thick coat tighter. "Can we make this quick, doctor? I'd really rather be doing something else."

Her desire to get the meeting over matched his own tight schedule. "As quick as we can," Cutter promised. "First, can you tell me about you and your husband? A background could prove useful."

"From the beginning?" she asked with a note of impatience.

"If you like."

"I don't." She paced further from him. "We met at a bar. At the time I thought he was the best thing that ever happened to me." She paused, thinking of the distant memory.

"Please go on," the doctor prompted. "But only if you remember."

"I remember all of it."

***

Laura Wilson had lived in the Bronx for a year before she met David. She had escaped from the no-nothing town of her birth in the mid-state county of Illinois just south of Peoria because she believed it offered no future. The rising Midwestern economy had bypassed her little town, and she was determined not to end up a farmer's wife or an assistant in the local hairdresser as had so many of her friends. She dreamed of places far beyond the rolling central Illinois cornfields, and set her sights on the impossible.

Laura knew she was no psychologist yet she recognized that a background of deprivation fueled her yearning. She was the only daughter of John and May Wilson, both born on farms near the town. They had married when May became pregnant. John rented a forty-year-old clapboard house, complete with peeling paint, in a low-income neighborhood on the wrong side of the tracks because it was the only house he could afford. John never did get around to repainting the house.

Though her Dad filled May's head with dreamy promises of something nicer, it was the only home their daughter ever knew.

Her father drank for a living. Until she turned eighteen Laura believed every kid in town came home from school to a father who was still sleeping it off, and a mother who said nothing because her stubbornness refused to acknowledge a truth she always denied.

Laura knew she received her penchant for dreaming beyond her means from John. She got her stubbornness from May. When she was old enough to recognize those God-given talents, Laura became determined to use them to confront an unfair world. Six months before she graduated from high school, she announced to her parents she was going to college. She would be the first in a line of rural ancestors to do so.

"We can't afford it," her mother had stated with no room for argument. "No one from this family goes to college."

"That's why I want to go," Laura pressed. But May was adamant: college was not an option. When Laura went to her father, she found him drunkenly supportive.

"My little girl going to college? That's wonderful news!" He had given her a sloppy kiss on the cheek and went to find another beer.

Laura's decision hardened. She applied to Illinois State University behind her mother's back. Her high school counselor promised to help with applications for financial aid. He had high hopes for Laura.

On the day Laura received her acceptance into the university her father, having spent most of the day at a local bar, rolled over the family's rusting Ford pickup truck. He lingered, comatose, in hospital for over a year.

"You're not abandoning your father," her mother had ordered on the day of the accident. "I'm depending on you." Laura deferred the acceptance and got a job as a waitress in a local restaurant. She told everyone she was going to college as soon as her father recovered. As she took orders for fries and cherry cokes Laura dreamed of future opportunities promised by further education. She was certain it was only a matter of time.

When her father finally had the good sense to die Laura thought her time had come. But May had other ideas. The stress of constant worry for John and a neurotic passion for silent suffering took its toll. A month following her husband's burial, May had a stroke.

When John died, Laura had reapplied to ISU. However, due to her mother's illness, she was once again forced to defer, this time to take care of May. Another year passed when her mother silently gave up the ghost.

Laura considered her options. She had just turned twenty and the thoughts of four years in college seemed pedestrian. She needed a fresh start in a place that offered excitement and opportunity preferably as far from central Illinois as possible. When probate was settled on her parent's estate, and to her immense surprise, Laura discovered she had over three-thousand dollars in the bank and with it the freedom to do as she chose.

She thought of moving to Chicago but even that seemed too close to the pain she had endured. Instead, she opted for New York. She moved to the Bronx because of its cheap rent, taking a job as a waitress, convinced it was all she knew how to do. In the busy café she served good looking men and handsome women, and when she wasn't working took the subway into the City to admire the fashion and stare at ornately dressed window displays of the high-end stores on 5th Avenue.

"I didn't think I'd ever be able to walk through the doors of such places," Laura declared, the woman's face transformed by strong determination. "When I was that age I remember thinking only that I wanted more. So much more." She confronted the psychiatrist. "I didn't need all that finery of course. All I wanted were simple things. A house to call a home. Some money in the bank for a rainy day. A child or two. An honest husband to share it with. That's not too much to ask, is it?"

Cutter smiled. "No, I don't think so."

Laura inhaled as if catching the breath of her memory. "I met David a year after I moved to New York. It was just one of those things."

"You fell in love."

"He was handsome. He made me laugh. He had dreams and I thought they matched mine. He had so much ambition. Did you know he put himself through college?"

"No."

"When he arrived in the States from Ireland, he was penniless. He had no real education. He set out to make up for lost time and ended up with a BA from one of the SUNY colleges—that's the State University of New York—and an MBA from Columbia. They're quite selective and very expensive. He did it all by himself. No one helped him."

"You're proud of him."

"I used to be. We married four months after meeting."

"So it was a whirlwind romance. How old were you?"

"Twenty-two. David was twenty-five. We were just kids. When I think about it I realize we didn't even know each other." Her face grew thoughtful. "He was always a hard worker. He always did his best to provide for Rachel and me. I admired him for that. It's just he was so…" Cutter waited as she sought to define her emotions. "…distant I guess is the word. It hurt."

"How would you describe 'distant'?" the psychiatrist asked.

"He didn't talk a lot, at least not about anything important. Oh, he was a great father and I like to think he enjoyed our company. But David preferred to keep to himself."

"Would you call him a loner?"

"No, not that. He always seemed to be thinking. It was as if he had no space in his head for us. He was…"

"Preoccupied."

"I was going to say 'unavailable'." Anger crossed her face. "It got even worse when he set up the business with Garrett."

"Let's talk about Garrett another time," Cutter suggested, deflecting the change in subject. "What do you know about David's life in Ireland?"

"Before he came to America? Not much. Next to nothing, in fact. When we first married I wanted to know all about it. You see, I love the fact he's Irish. I like his accent and the words he uses. I like his strong practical hands and foreign sense of humor. He was so different to anyone I'd met before. And…" she blushed. "I liked his eyes. In the movies, you hear about seeing into someone's soul. With David, that's what it was like. I'd look at his eyes and it was like seeing into his soul."

Cutter considered then asked, "Is this your first time in Ireland?"

She nodded. "Yes. I always wanted to visit but David refused. Now I get here but what a horrible reason to come to Ireland."

"He hasn't come home in thirty years?"

"He said he could never come home."

"Did he explain why?"

"He wouldn't talk about it. Eventually I stopped asking."

Cutter thought he knew why David would not let himself come back to Ireland but client confidentiality prevented him from sharing what he had learned. Instead Cutter asked, "Why do you think he wouldn't talk about his time living here, before he immigrated?"

"Something happened in Ireland when he was younger, something he wouldn't tell me. That's my guess, anyway. I thought he would but he never did."

"Don't you have any idea what happened?" the doctor pressed.

"He kept it a secret. One he couldn't even share with his wife."

"But you've been married for over twenty years. How do you feel about that?"

"How do you think? Dr. Cutter, are you married?" The young psychiatrist shook his head. "Then let me tell you how a marriage is supposed to work. Couples are supposed to share what's on their minds with each other. David couldn't. Or he wouldn't, which is even worse."

She laughed, thinking back. "My, but wasn't he always full of surprises. One minute he could be the life of the party. The next, as black and as silent as the Ace of Spades."

"Do you mean his mood would abruptly swing? He could become depressed?" Cutter asked, his curiosity piqued.

"I called them David's black holes. He could come home from work and not even say hello. I could see the worry in his shoulders when he walked up the stairs. At first I thought it was work that worried him. Then I thought it was me and Rachel. But I finally realized it was David. His sadness was as much a part of him as the color of his eyes. When he had these episodes it was like he was living in a place without any sun."

"How long did the episodes last?"

Laura thought back."A week. Sometimes more. When he was like that, he wouldn't talk. He could go days without sleeping or at weekends sleep around the clock. He wouldn't eat even though I'd beg him to. Then just as quick, he'd be back to his old self."

"Which was?"

"Responsible, of course," Laura explained."But he could get so… crazy. He'd work so hard and would never slow down. As if he thought his batteries would never run out."

"Did he ever seek medical advice?"

She shook her head."David hates doctors. He's like most men, I expect. I kept after him to go but he wouldn't. He said he wouldn't know what to say without embarrassing himself. Instead he just suffered. We all did."

"You still worry about him, don't you?"

"That's the easiest question of the bunch. I worry about him all the time."

"But you've separated."

"I told you. I don't trust him anymore. Marriage won't work without trust. But I still worry about him. I'll never stop no matter what he's done."

"You're talking about what happened at the wedding rehearsal, aren't you?"

"Not only that." Her voice trailed off.

Cutter studied her. She would not look him in the eye. The doctor rose from the bench, keeping his distance, sensing she did not want him to intrude."You mentioned a problem with alcohol."

"When I met him David seemed fine. We'd go out at weekends when we could afford it. Meet friends. Do what other couples our age did. Sometimes we'd both drink too much. But it wasn't a problem. Then he had a huge setback."

"Go on," Cutter encouraged.

"At that point David worked for a big rental car company in Long Island. It was the first good job he'd ever had. His employer liked David. He promised him the moon. We both thought life was turning a corner. But, well, it didn't turn out that way."

"He was made redundant?"

"If you mean, was he fired, yes he was. David and a lot of other people. For almost a year he couldn't get a job. It almost killed him. That's when he started drinking hard."

"You didn't like it."

"I hated it." Viciousness crept into her voice. "I told you my father was an alcoholic. I've seen the damage it causes. They say it's a progressive disease but Doctor Cutter, it destroys whole families. It kills their dreams. Rachel was almost ten when David hit the hard stuff. I didn't want her to see her father stagger into the house like I had to. David tried that a couple of times. A couple was more than enough."

"You confronted him."

She looked him in the eye. "I locked him out of the house. I told him if he didn't stop drinking I would divorce him. I'd take Rachel and move as far away from him as I could. He loves Rachel. He knew I'd do it."

"Did he stop?"

"For a long time. Oh, he slipped a couple of times. Right before he set up with Garrett, I suspect he had a drink though he denied it. He'd been fired from another job during the big two-thousand and eight recession, so I guess he had reason. Not that it's an excuse. Then he started the firm with Garrett. Since then and until recently I don't think he's taken a single drink. Not even a bottle of beer."

"Mrs. Bloom, do you have any idea why your husband started drinking again? I ask because many alcoholics drink to self-medicate. They bury emotional difficulties in a bottle."

"I can't be sure. As I say, he would never talk to me. If I had to guess, whatever happened in Ireland when he was younger ate him up. Whatever that was, combined with his determination to succeed, and the hours he worked at the office, and the frustration he felt when he failed…" Cutter could see tears in her eyes. "For years he was a good man. But he went too far this time."

"He started drinking again, as you've said. Mrs. Bloom, what would you say if I told you your husband swears he is not drinking?"

"David is a liar," Laura choked. "Alcohol makes him lie. But it isn't only the drinking. It's horrible what he's done to us."

"We're back to what happened at the rehearsal."

"It was his only daughter's wedding. You'd think he would have thought of her but he didn't," Laura said, angry words tumbling. "The night before the rehearsal he didn't come home. I thought he was dead. Did I tell you I had to phone the police to find him?"

"You said they found him at a lighthouse."

"David had passed out on a beach. You should have seen him. His suit was ruined. He looked like a crazy man."

"What happened at the rehearsal?"

Her shoulders rose as she breathed in, trying to find some balance. "First you should know that when I couldn't find him I phoned Garrett hoping David was with him. I've known Garrett for ten years. I've never heard him so angry. Garrett told me David wasn't there. He was ready to kill him because of the missing money."

"Money?"

"It started a month ago. David told Garrett one-hundred thousand dollars was missing from a client account. At that point Garrett thought it was only an error. David promised to get their accountant to trace the missing cash."

"But he couldn't find the money," Cutter guessed.

Laura laughed. "Garrett says David lied; he never even tried. A week or so passed and Garrett got impatient so he talked to the accountant himself. The accountant told him David had never mentioned it. That's when Garrett took matters into his own hands."

"What did he find?"

"The missing hundred-thousand? That was only a start." The woman's eyes narrowed. "Three million dollars. That's the total amount that was stolen. Three million! I met with Garrett just before the rehearsal started and he explained. At first I wouldn't believe it. David is not a thief. But Garrett told me he had proof."

She stepped closer. "The next morning, when David walked into the house after the police found him, I told him I didn't want him at the rehearsal, not if he had decided to drink again. After what Garrett told me, I was even happier David wouldn't be there because I knew we would argue about it. I couldn't do that, of course. Not at the rehearsal. We'd spent months preparing everything. We held the rehearsal at the local Presbyterian Church. Rachel's husband, Jacob, is Presbyterian and that's what they wanted. Twenty of our closest friends were there including Jacob's parents."

"It was important to you. You didn't want David to show up drunk and make a show of himself."

"Or me either. Doctor, our friends are some of the most influential people on Long Island. When David and Garrett set up Ledbetter & Bloom, I saw the potential it offered. I saw financial success as a way of protecting my family and giving us the safety I never had. I don't have an education. Not a good one, Doctor. And I certainly don't understand Wall Street or stocks and all that. But I'm good with people. People I understand. So I learned how to network. It took me years to learn how but I did. I made important friends. People that might be willing to do business with David's company. To be honest, I wasn't surprised when it paid off."

"What you did was your way of caring for your family, and you wanted to protect that," Cutter observed. "But David came to the rehearsal anyway."

"Rachel saw him first. She smelled alcohol on his breath. She knew he'd been drinking. Then I saw him. Garrett saw him at the same time. I tried to stop it but it was too late. They fought. I've never seen David so angry or so out-of-control."

"Your husband struck him."

"David went crazy. Jacob and the groom had to pull my husband off him. Everyone saw it. Even the Minister." She took a breath but the words kept coming. "I don't think I've ever been so humiliated. Not even when my father was drunk and made me feel like a fool in front of my friends. It was horrible. But David didn't stop there."

Cutter saw a look of bewildered shame in her face. "When they pulled David off all he wanted was a dog. Can you believe that? His business partner is flat on the ground but David is running down the aisle yelling for a damned dog. 'Here Prince. Here boy. Come over here!' Doctor, it was insane."

"But there wasn't any dog, was there?"

Laura's eyes locked on his. "What's wrong with him?"

Cutter thought for a moment. "From how you describe his history, Mister Bloom is experiencing Bi-polar disorder and has for a long time.

At the rehearsal he was hypo-manic. Delusional and psychotic too. Then add alcoholism."

Laura brushed lint from the thick coat. "David passed out after that. They had to carry him out of the church. We drove him to my GP. The doctor told him to stop drinking. He gave David a prescription for a sedative. I doubt he ever filled it."

"I've seen a copy of the doctor's report."

"Rachel was fuming. She didn't want her father at the wedding. Not after such violence."

"The wedding was the next day. He was prevented from attending his only daughter's wedding. He must have been incensed. Is that when David disappeared?"

"We couldn't let him attend the wedding. We were afraid he'd cause more trouble. When we left our GP, I wouldn't let him back in the house. I asked my son-in-law to drive him to a hotel and check him in. I was at my wits end but I had a wedding to get through and Rachel to protect. David phoned us begging to be allowed to walk his daughter down the aisle. After that we stopped answering. Rachel and I agreed he needed a time out. Doctor Cutter, he was drunk and behaving like a child. A time out seemed the best way to control his behavior." Laura's breath shuddered, remembering.

"The day after the wedding I went to see him at the hotel. They told me he had checked out. Do you know what he did before he left?" Cutter could feel her rage. "They handed me David's father of the bride speech, the one he was going to give at the reception. David had ripped it to shreds. He had scattered it all over the hotel grounds. I suppose he wanted to hurt us." She pulled out a white handkerchief, wiping her eyes.

"When I went back to the house I checked his room." Cutter heard embarrassment in her voice. "I guess I should tell you we don't sleep together anymore. David had his own room. He'd let himself into the house. Some clothes were gone. So was his passport and bag. It was obvious."

"You tracked him to Ireland."

She shrugged. "We were worried and it was simple. We rang the airlines. My doctor wrote a letter to the effect that David was a threat. The airlines were suddenly very cooperative. They told us where he went."

"As to the money. Do you honestly think David stole three million dollars?" Cutter asked incredulously.

"David and Garrett own a very successful company. The money was there. Now it's not."

Cutter considered. "He's never before been in trouble with the law? He's never been accused of robbery or fraud?"

"Not to my knowledge."

"So this theft. It's not normal behavior."

"Not for David, no. Neither is his drinking. At least it hasn't been for a long time. But then—" Laura's face set. "David is an alcoholic. It was only a matter of time before he started again. I should have known that."

A pair of robins sang in the sunlit garden as Cutter tried to piece together the broken puzzle of a troubled mind.

"One more question, Mrs. Bloom," Cutter asked. "Did David discuss an envelope with you?"

Her lips pursed. "What envelope?"

"It doesn't matter. Not now."

"Are we finished?" Laura asked. The anger had faded. All that was left was an exhausted woman who Cutter sensed to be at the end of her wits.

The psychiatrist turned off the voice recorder. "We are. Thank you, Mrs. Bloom." She turned to leave. Cutter thought of one more thing. "Mrs. Bloom?"

When she turned back all he could see was tired annoyance.

"Before you go I want to thank you. It takes a lot of courage to do what you've done."

"What do you mean?" she asked.

"Not everyone will sign an assisted admission order to protect their loved ones in a psychiatric unit."

"Why not?"

"Most find it too embarrassing. Few want to be associated with mental illness."

"You don't understand, doctor. David can't take care of himself anymore. We have to do it for him. Otherwise, he will hurt himself or someone else." Her eyes held his in an uncompromising gaze. "Now he's your responsibility."

4

I cannot stand because they force me to the ground. I cannot see or smell or taste or touch because they have robbed me of my senses. But I can hear: An angry mob, their howls born of hatred and blame; the final conviction shouted in a thick, familiar voice. "Here lies the liar. The thief. The traitor."

The condemnation rises to Heaven on words from Hell.

I am dragged across cold stone with no thought of mercy. When my unseen accusers drop me, I feel the bite of rough wood burrowing into my naked back. "See how he squirms, the coward!" someone shouts. Course hands grab wrists and ankles, pulling my limbs taught.

The mask covering my face is ripped away. I see my executioners.

Laura stands tall above me dressed in the red robe of mother of the bride. Rachel next to her, white bridal veil shrouding accusing eyes.

A Centurion clothed in an impeccable business suit strides from the mob. A clutch of spikes in one hand; in the other, an enormous hammer. He thrusts a sharp point into my sweating palm. His grin resembled the lying innocence of Satan. With a single blow, he drives through skin and bone, blood and water, into the thick wood of the cross.

As I writhe in agony, I know:

I will never experience resurrection. Only an endless, endless eternity of suffering. It is then I think to end my silence.

I scream.

***

First thing this morning, Doc made a point of telling me my scream woke the entire building. He asked if I knew what a persecution complex was. "Mister Bloom, do you feel blamed for things you might never have done? Do you consider yourself a victim? Do you," he said, pausing to clear the shite stuck in his throat, "think you are rather…paranoid?"

I didn't even laugh. Damned right I was paranoid. Wouldn't you be paranoid if the entire world was after you for no fucking good reason? The ticking in my head didn't help. It was ferocious and I could not understand why. I was certain my mother's grandfather clock was gone. Turned to ash along with the contents of my boyhood home. All burned up in a fire that was, I believe, an act of murderous vandalism because I cannot think of any other explanation. I assure you I did not start the fire. It was not me though no one has yet asked for the facts.

Despite the fire the ticking persists. Between that and the dizziness it is driving me mad.

The dizziness I experience is hard to fathom. It's like the entire world is slanted at forty-five degrees to true. When I walk it's as if I stagger across the deck of a sinking boat. It scares the shite out of me. To understand how I am now you need to understand the dizziness: everything I see is skewed to that crazy angle. I have no explanation nor do I tell anyone about it. Like the ticking, it's my secret and will remain that way.

As I say, I didn't laugh when Doc asked those stupid questions. I didn't laugh an hour earlier when they removed the restraints. In fairness, Nurse Bollocks had apologized. "You coulda hurt yerself," he taunted in a thick County Cork accent. He told me after I screamed, scaring the other prisoners shitless, I tried to break out of the Unit.

"By God, nothing would stop you. Do you remember?"

I had a vague recollection of terror, the aftermath of nightmare: stumbling from bed, running blindly through the ward. Falling hard on the tiled floor. Other patients waking in steel-framed single beds, staring at me with confused round eyes. Fleeing through the darkness to the interior courtyard. To the front door. Grasping it. Pulling. Finding it locked. Panicking, heart pounding, because it was the only way out.

I was trapped. Locked up in a psychiatric unit. Locked up because I was considered a violent animal which society deemed unfit. An animal who did not rate any human rights; who had been stripped of his freedom on a whim, an unfounded opinion, and a signature.

"Ah, but did a locked door stop you?" Bollocks continued, his dark eyes flashing with humor. "You ran back in here which is when I found you. Ya tried to get out the windows but they're locked too aren't they? And when I reached for ya, you gave me a box. Ya hit me good." He showed his head, a purple bruise blooming on the thick of his forehead. "That's when we had to restrain you. We shot you full of sedative too. How ya feeling now?"

He snapped his fingers in front of my eyes. I never blinked. Instead I spun in a world of thick cotton, at the edge of an unknown galaxy. But fuck if I would tell him.

"Don't worry. You'll come around. And don't mind the nightmares. It's because of the meds you're taking."

I couldn't remember any meds.

"The ones Doctor Cutter prescribed. One of the side effects is nightmares. Do you remember what you dreamed? Want to talk about it?"

I didn't utter a single word. I had talked too much yesterday.

"Suite yourself. We're here to help, Mister Bloom."

He had squeezed my shoulder with a huge paw then strode toward the next patient dispensing similar useless bedside psychiatry.

That was this morning. As I type it's now after six in the evening. The day has been anything but uneventful. Days in the Unit are supposed to be monotonously disciplined. Up at seven. Breakfast at seven-thirty. Meds. One-to-one psychiatry sessions. Dinner. More meds for those who need them. Then in the afternoon it's exercise or occupational therapy if the therapist bothers to show up. Or if you're very lucky, a pass into town (supervised or unsupervised, depending on your jailer's assessment of progress, not that I will ever qualify). A family visit in the indoor courtyard or outdoor garden might also be on the cards, if of course, those who love you want to look in on the crazies. Then evening tea followed by dessert of more meds. Finally some light reading (or counting the ceiling tiles if that's your preference). Lights out at 10PM. Such is the controlled, Petri dish life of a mental health patient.

This second full day in the Unit didn't quite live up to my clinicians' expectations of discipline. For one thing, and as I've written, I refused to talk. At the morning Psych session Cutter went ballistic.

"You were fine yesterday, Mister Bloom. You were willing to communicate. What happened?" I would not even fart. He called for a nurse.

This one was a pretty woman, late-thirties I suspect, with a good figure hidden behind a smart uniform. I'd met her before. First, when I was admitted. She had studied me with a long gaze as if I was a newly-minted species of unknown origin. I also met her at the physical exam she gave me each morning when she listened to my heart and checked my weight and blood pressure, and made sure I wasn't going to die. She always smiled, and was always kind, but I still wasn't certain of her true intent. In here, locked up against my will, I keep reminding myself to trust no one.

This time, just like always, the cute nurse smiled at me all the time she talked to Cutter. They chatted as if I wasn't in the room. Have you ever felt like an imbecile? You know, so stupid people think you don't understand simple English?

"Is he taking his meds?"

"Yes doctor."

"Did he eat this morning?"

"No."

"He didn't? Did he sleep last night?"

"Didn't you see the report?" She handed him a clipboard with the daily David Bloom Breaking News attached. He scanned it.

"I was told about the nightmare but not the subsequent outburst. Why wasn't I informed of this earlier? He was restrained?"

"I'm afraid so," Nurse Cutes answered and I was taken by her eyes; liquid blue eyes that seemed like quiet windows into a caring soul.

"Mister Bloom," Doc announced, finally addressing me, "I am increasing the dosage of your medication. Do you understand?"

Doc busied himself with a script, handing it to Cutes. "I'm seeing your daughter this evening, Mister Bloom. I'll inform Rachel you are being uncooperative. When you decide to talk again she might consider visiting. However, if you are not talking, a visit would seem out of the question."

My mouth fell open. I couldn't believe Cutter was using my only child as a bargaining chip. But he was wrong about his assumption. I was sure Rachel never wanted to see me again.

Oh God how I ached for my kid. It's like my right arm was amputated and the surgeon forgot the anesthetic. On purpose. Sitting in front of Cutter, I think of Rachel in the bridal dress I never saw, of her mother's curses, and suddenly understood my nightmare. Like Christ, my betrayal was complete. I would die for it.

Unless, of course, I could find a way to escape. Cutter says I'm not cooperating. No shit. I'm making a promise to myself here and now. I'm never going to cooperate again.

Not until they let me out of this madhouse.

***

Cutter was vexed as he drove to the Bantry hotel. Not only with his stubborn patient, but also with the daughter who refused to visit the Psychiatric Unit. Following that morning's disastrous attempt at one-on-one therapy with Bloom, he had phoned her. He had asked for Rachel but instead her mother picked up. Mrs. Bloom was much more difficult than she had been the day before.

"I've talked to Rachel," the woman growled. "She will see you but only at our hotel."

Usually, Cutter would have dismissed such a suggestion. He was far too busy for meetings outside the Unit. However, their hotel was located close to his apartment. He agreed to the inconvenience only because he needed more background information if he was to successfully treat his patient.

As he drove through the town's thick evening traffic Cutter had a sudden impulse to skip the meeting. He feared he would meet resistance from the girl. He could not understand why some people refused to cooperate, or were unwilling to be more helpful.

Cutter had been attracted to a profession in mental health for a number of reasons. First and foremost was his interest in what made people tick. In secondary school he had been considered a nerd due to his chubby physique and keen interest in the sciences. He had overcome bullying by attempting to reason with his enemies, a strategy which resulted in black eyes and assorted contusions. He became determined to understand why people could act so irrationally when logic suggested a different outcome. His interest continued as he considered university.

He was drawn to a science which delved into the unanswered questions of the human mind and the erratic behavior it sometimes caused.

At university, his curiosity resulted in early success. He had graduated medical school near the top of his class, receiving prestigious commendations. Throughout his psychiatric course work, he had been lauded by professors for his deep insight into the often-fuzzy intricacies of mental illness. His diagnostic capabilities, tested with written exercises and practical learning at *in situ* locums, often agreed with more experienced practitioners. Medical school was followed by two additional years of postgraduate study during which Cutter gained additional insight into clinical neuroscience and psychotropic therapies. He applied that knowledge for a year working as a junior staff member in the psychiatric unit of a prestigious English hospital. With hands-on experience under his belt, the young doctor yearned for more responsibility.

At the age of twenty-nine, Cutter's hard work paid off when he was appointed as the youngest psychiatric consultant ever hired by the Bantry mental health unit. Thus far, he had been on an upward trajectory which could see him achieve his primary ambition: a sterling reputation within a fiercely competitive professional field. He was determined not to fail.

But to achieve his ambition, Cutter knew he faced many challenges.

At university and throughout his locums he had worked tirelessly to learn the scientific skills needed to treat the puzzle of mental illness. Simultaneously, Cutter also became aware that mental healthcare services worldwide were dismally under-funded despite the fact that psychiatric hospitals were admitting more and more patients. Ireland was no exception.

Facing limited budgets, limited time, limited staff, but ever-increasing demand for patient services, mental healthcare employees like Cutter were expected to not only cope but succeed. The young doctor analyzed the situation with cold rationality. His conclusions were stark. To succeed in such a challenging environment, Cutter believed that every second spent with patients must be used efficiently. No time could be wasted. Patients who cooperated would make good progress. However, those who did not could prove much more difficult to treat.

David Bloom belonged to the latter category. He refused to cooperate. But Cutter also knew that the executives of Ireland's under-resourced mental healthcare system expected success anyway.

This added pressure weighed heavily on Cutter as he parked his BMW by the open square near the seaside hotel. He knew that any light Rachel could shine on her father's situation must help him get the intractable patient back in line.

5

"Mom told me you'd want to record this meeting."

The young woman who was his patient's daughter spun toward him. Paul Cutter saw stubborn resolve in her eyes. "You can't."

They stood together on the balcony. It was the only place that would give them privacy from the curious ears of her mother. Mrs. Bloom sat on a couch in the living room, separated from the private discussion by a sliding glass door. Cutter could feel the woman's intimidating eyes on the back of his neck.

Disappointed at Rachel's decision, feeling the prick of warning, the psychiatrist placed the voice recorder harmlessly on an outdoor table. He would have to rely on memory.

"What do you want to talk about?" she queried.

Cutter knew Rachel was in her early twenties. However, the woman's vulnerability made her seem much younger. She was dressed in dark jeans and a white blouse. She was barefoot. An expensive wedding band and engagement ring glittered on a slim, elegant finger so different from her mother's. Cutter wondered which side of the family she resembled. Her child-like appearance looked nothing like Mrs. Bloom. Nor did she take after Mr. Bloom. He noted the soft sweeping light brown hair which fell onto her shoulders almost covering the pretty face; the pert nose; the sensitive dark brown eyes. To the doctor, Rachel's demeanor broadcast the definition of forlorn.

"Let's start with your childhood—"

"I won't talk about that. It's not relevant."

Cutter drew back, reconsidering. The young woman knew her own mind.

"Perhaps we could talk about the wedding rehearsal," Cutter riposted. "Your mother and I touched on it but anything you might add could prove useful."

"Mom told me it would happen. I didn't believe her." Tears glittered in the young woman's eyes. "Dad got drunk."

"I'm sorry."

She sighed. "Okay, I'll tell you. It's embarrassing but everyone else seems to know. One more isn't going to make any difference."

***

I'm in trouble. Again. Which means my plan for assuming the role of uncooperative asshole must be working.

I was sitting here on my bed, minding my own business, writing nonsense. Then a few minutes ago Bollocks stormed into the ward. He told me it was time to take my meds. He noted I hadn't bothered showing up for tea. He pointed out I'd already missed breakfast and dinner. I told him I wasn't hungry, which was the truth. From his reaction, I know my decision to skip a few meals must not be in the rule book.

"You're going to eat, Mister Bloom." *Like, he's going to force it down my neck?* "You're going to take your meds." *Who says? You? Cutter? God?*

I ignored him and kept typing. That really pissed him off because he made a lunge for the laptop. I pulled it away before he got his dirty paws on it. He glared at me and looked at his watch. "You got exactly twenty minutes left with that thing, you hear me lad?" Then he stalked away.

I don't have anything against Bollocks. I'm sure on the outside he's a nice fellow. But in here? He can piss off. He doesn't know it yet but I've no intention of taking any more meds.

Cutter wants me to talk. Bollocks wants me to eat. They can both fuck off.

And as for the meds? It's called informed consent. If Cutter can't be bothered to tell me what I'm taking I'm not taking anything at all. Particularly not after what Cutes told me.

When Bollocks warned me the meds were causing nightmares, I tracked down the good nurse. She seemed approachable if not downright nice. I tried on my best smile and motioned her into the courtyard. By God but didn't she follow. The courtyard was deserted. I could blow my cover in confidence.

"I need your advice," I whispered. She managed a shocked look.

"Why Mister Bloom, I thought you couldn't talk."

"Don't tell anyone. Especially Cutter, okay?"

"I can't do that. I'll have to inform him."

"You don't want me to die in here, do you?" The statement got her attention. She crossed her arms and tried to look stern. On Cutes it never worked.

"What do you want?"

So I told her. I told her I didn't want to stand in the medication line like the other passengers on a journey to nowhere. I didn't want to be treated like an idiot out of *Cuckoo's Nest*. I didn't want—in fact I would not tolerate—taking a drug when no one had the courtesy to tell me what I was taking.

"I don't even know what it might do to me. The possible side-effects."

"No one told you? You should have been told." She thought it over for exactly three seconds. "Stay here."

I paced the courtyard trying to look normal. Through a window I could see fellow inmates sitting in the lounge. It's a sort of half-assed library: a few ancient leather chairs; some books on shelves; outdated magazines. The older fellow I saw when first admitted was reading a newspaper without much success. Damned if he wasn't still rocking. Another guy, a fellow as big as a whale, waved at me as if I was his long-lost best friend, an idiotic grin on his damp porky face. I was sure I could hear loose screws rattling around in his fat head, the poor fecker.

***

A quick side-bar to anyone reading this:

If, prior to my incarceration, someone had asked me to describe a mental ward and its patient inhabitants, in my mind's eye I would have thought of a scene straight out of a Hollywood horror film. I won't apologize. Like most of the general public I didn't know any better. Here's what I imagined:

A Victorian madhouse secluded in the dark basement of a five-storied dilapidated gabled mansion, buried in a forest somewhere out in the middle of nowhere. Underground: nothing but tiny barred cells. Underfed patients are chained to sweating cement walls, hair plastered in stink, eyes like pink rabbits, wrapped tight in straight-jackets. They all scream like zombies, struggling to get out. If they actually escaped, there'd be hell to pay because they'd attack the nice wardens with thick metal bars, beating our uniformed heroes to pulp.

But I was wrong. My Hollywood imagination didn't have a clue. Having some experience, I'll share the reality:

On the face of it, the psychiatric unit I'm held in looks decent. It's clean. It's bright and warm, sometimes uncomfortably so when an eejit dials up the heat. Except for a few residents who look like they've been run over by a truck, most of us patients look 'normal', if you want to use that word. We dress okay. We're usually clean. We look well-fed. You'd think nothing was wrong with us poor feckers. In some cases, you'd be right. But then, there are the others who really do need to be locked in here, despite the normal appearance, and despite the fact the treatment for their mental health problems often leads nowhere. Visit, and you'll leave thinking the place is great.

But if that's what you see and that's what you think, I suggest you think again. Stay for awhile and you'll know what I mean. Despite the nice looking interior, and the nice people-patients in it, and the even nicer people-doctors and people-nurses who mind us, a modern psychiatric unit is still a Victorian madhouse by another name. You won't see us chained to cement walls. You won't see us fighting to get out because we found out fighting doesn't work, so we struggle on in silence. You'll think, 'What a fine place to make people well.' But your thinking is dead wrong. The depression of being captured and kept like an animal in here cannot be described—unless you're too drugged-up to notice. To understand, you have to walk the walk of a mental health patient.

I guess it's one of the reasons I'm writing this. So you'll walk the walk and maybe understand.

End of the sidebar.

***

Anyway, after the whale-sized guy waved, Nurse Cutes hurried back. In her hand she held the thinnest slip of paper. She thrust it at me. "You can't keep this," she instructed. "Read it quick as you can."

The drug was Aripiprazole. It is an anti-psychotic used to treat, among other things, Schizophrenia, Bi-polar disorder, Depression, Autism, and Obsessive-compulsive disorder. I turned the paper over noting the side-effects:

Dizziness, drowsiness, nausea and vomiting, tiredness, anxiety, sleeplessness. These were the so-called insignificant side-effects. Then I saw the less common but more severe outcomes:

Involuntary repetitive movements, shaking, muscle spasms, fainting, seizures.

And at the bottom, in big bold print:

Suicidal thoughts may occur. Please tell your doctor if this ensues.

Suicide? I decided I was not going to have anything to do with Aripiprazole. Not until I could get a second opinion from a doctor who was somewhat older than a choirboy.

I handed back the slip of paper. "Nurse, can I ask you something? Cutter seems to think I'm manic depressive."

"You mean Bi-polar."

"Whatever it's called. How long does it usually take to reach such a diagnosis?"

"Typically, only after three to six months of observation."

"I've been here two days."

The words registered. She touched my arm. "I have to get back to work," Cutes explained and turned to go. She was almost out of the courtyard when she turned back. "Mister Bloom? Can I give you some advice? It might not seem like it but mental health patients have rights. Remember that."

As I said, Nurse Cutes is a nice person.

When she was gone I went back to the ward. I thought over what Cutter had said about Rachel's possible visit. Despite his attempt at blackmail I knew she would never see me. I'd lost that right along with everything else. My behavior at the rehearsal was monstrous. There's no other way to put it. Rachel thinks she knows why I got into the fight. She's sure of it. But she's wrong.

The night before the rehearsal, when the cops found me lying on the beach, they took me home. I was so fucked up I never went to bed. In the morning Laura and I argued. She accused me of being drunk and ordered me to stay away from the rehearsal. But I couldn't do that. Let down my little girl? Not a chance. So I went. I didn't even think to change my suit.

That's the problem: when you're in this dark pit you don't know what's going on. When I opened the envelope something in me broke. It was as if the locked box inside me exploded. All I could hear was Dad yelling at me. And the ticking. The fucking Goddam ticking. Part of me knew any sense of judgment was gone. Part of me knew the internal balancing apparatus I'd built during my years in the States had shattered. But though the rational part of David told me I'd busted like a cheap clock, the other part of me—the damaged part—took control. Changing my filthy suit was the last thing on my mind.

My father's loud accusation filled my head. I couldn't stop it. He was still yelling when I got to the Church.

"When Dad walked in I knew he was drunk as a skunk," Rachel told the psychiatrist. "Mom said he wasn't coming. She didn't say why. Only that she was glad of it, which really made me worry. Garrett was there, of course, because he was a close family friend. I saw him talking to Mom earlier. I knew something was wrong. You should have seen her face. But I couldn't figure out why Dad wasn't there. Mom warned me he was drinking again but I didn't believe her."

"Why do you believe he was drunk? Was he behaving drunkenly?"

Her face filled with disgust. "He was stumbling; he couldn't keep his balance. His suit was soaking wet and covered in filth. But when I first saw him, you know what? I didn't care. I was just happy to see my Dad. He's always been the best."

"What changed?"

She paused, reflecting. "I ran up to him. I was going to give him a hug. We've always had hugs together. But this time when I got close

I could smell it. Wine. If I had to guess I'd say he'd drunk at least two bottles of wine."

I remember the church grounds as being a terrific set-up. There was the church, of course. A Presbyterian statement located in the heart of Long Island. A rich church, too, because they must have owned twenty acres of land. They'd built a brand-new building next to it; a glass covered multi-purpose room. You know, a place to go after church services, get in out of the rain, and make nice with your fellow congregants. Laura had booked it for the wedding reception.

I parked the car in the parking lot. I'm late and in a rush to get inside. I'm confused and out of kilter because of last night, and Dad still yelling at me. But then this young man stops me. He's a polite lad, maybe mid-twenties. He doesn't even comment on my ruined suit. Then he asks me if I'm the father of the bride.

"You've got the right man," I said, and I remember the crazy pride I felt. I wanted to tell Dad to piss off. You think I'm a bastard, Dad? Take a look at the kid I raised.

The young man asked me if I have a minute. I explained I was late for the rehearsal but he promised he'd only take a minute so I followed him into the multi-purpose whatever it is. I was really impressed. It was massive and ornate; perfect for Rachel's launch into adulthood, and met Laura's high standards as well. The kid ran up to the bar. A half-dozen champagne bottles were lined up beside some upturned flutes.

"Mrs. Bloom has narrowed the wine selection for the wedding toast down to two vintages," the kid explained as he popped two bottles and poured a glass of each. "We were hoping to get your opinion."

I laughed. "It's nice of you to ask. But see, I don't drink so I wouldn't know."

He looked disappointed. "Then perhaps you could just take a sip. Your opinion matters. Besides," he said, pleading, "my boss told me to get your assessment. I'm depending on it."

So I thought, Oh what the hell. He seems a nice young man and I don't want to get him in trouble. I took a single sip from each glass.

"The one on the right. Now I'm out of here." He thanked me as I ran out the door to find my daughter, Dad's voice still screaming in my head.

I will be clear: it was two sips, not two bottles of the damned stuff as Laura thinks and as my daughter believes. I was not drunk. That's the truth.

"Have you ever seen him inebriated before that?"

"Once when I was a little girl. But nothing since then."

"Then there was the fight."

"When Garrett told Mom what Dad had done, Mom begged him to keep away from my father at least until after the rehearsal. But I guess it was asking too much.

"Doctor Cutter, I've known Garrett since I was twelve," Rachel continued. "He's a family friend. For years I called him Uncle Garrett, we were so close. He always liked Dad but I guess what he discovered was too much even for friendship."

"What happened?" Cutter asked.

"When I met Dad at the door and saw how drunk he was I got upset. I told him to go home. But he wouldn't. He marched down the center aisle of the church. I started yelling at him to get out. Then Jacob saw him. Then my Mom. Then the rest of our guests. Everyone was horrified at how he looked and the way he stumbled. When Garrett saw Dad, he must have seen red. He rushed my father, screaming like a madman." She stopped.

"What did Garrett say?" Cutter prodded.

"He said Dad had stolen three million dollars from the company's accounts."

I walk into the church. I see Garrett. He's charging up the center aisle like a raging bull. He's screaming at me. But I'm not seeing or hearing him. Instead I'm still hearing my father. He's screaming too. It was like a dam broke inside me. I could hear it break, as if a ship letting go its seams. That's when the room tilts like crazy. I know my breathing isn't right. I wonder if I'm having a heart attack. Then I see—really see—Garrett stampeding toward me, and this thing in my head tells me I'm being attacked.

"Then Garrett said something awful."

"What did he say?"

She found it hard to repeat the words directed at her father."He said:

"You little shit. You thieving bastard of a liar." Garrett's lying accusation fills the Church. You got the Minister and our friends looking at me wondering what the hell is going on. You got the groom and my daughter's future in-laws staring at me like I'm a roach. You got Laura studying the floor, shaking her head, thinking I'm a worthless nut job.

You got my kid, beautiful in her rehearsal dress, a face filling with disgust at her father. I knew right then she would never believe me no matter what I said.

So Garrett keeps coming. His face is blood red."You little shit. You opportunist. You lying fuck of a so-called friend. You stole three million dollars! I've told the directors. They'll cut you into a million pieces. You're fired, you asshole. Fired!"

I couldn't believe it. Garrett was calling me a thieving opportunist. Yet he was the one stealing my company.

"Dad was angry. I don't think I've ever seen him so angry. But he didn't do anything, not yet anyway. Then Garrett said something else."

For the first time I clearly hear the words of my father. Before that his voice was indistinct; as if he yelled from the bottom of a valley. Now each word is as clear as a bell. I know it's crazy. I know he's dead. I'd read the letter, hadn't I? And yet it's as if he's standing next to me. "You going to take that Davy?" Dad shouts. "What will your mother think?" I hear his disgust. "You're still a coward. Stand up for yourself, for Jaysus sake."

Then Garrett does what I hope he wouldn't. He bends down to look me in the eye. He says,"I called the SEC. You're going to jail, you fuck."

"Dad hit him. Garrett kept yelling so Dad hit him again. Then again and again. God it was awful. He broke his nose. He hit him until Jacob and some others pulled Dad off."

"Did Garrett call the police?"

"He wouldn't press charges. He knew Dad was in enough trouble," Rachel said and her voice hardened."Doctor, there's only one reason why Dad hit Garrett like that."

"Why?"

"Because Garrett was telling the truth."

There's only one reason I hit Garrett like that. He's a liar. I've never stolen a penny from anyone in my life. That's the truth.

When she started to cry Cutter cut short the interview. He'd heard enough anyway. He wanted to ask Rachel about the dog. Cutter knew he had to get to the bottom of Bloom's psychosis. But Rachel was too upset. Cutter would tackle that tomorrow. He'd also have to convince Bloom to take his medication and start eating. Then there was the matter of his silence. He'd have to take care of that too.

Cutter decided that Bloom was a stubborn pain in the ass. However, he was a patient. Cutter was confident he knew how to confront an uncooperative patient.

***

"Your daughter says you were drunk. You say you don't drink.

"Your business partner says you stole money. You say it's a lie.

"Your wife says you are delusional. You say you've seen nothing."

I see Cutter shift in his chair. "Mister Bloom, you are either a very clever liar with something to hide or you do not have a grasp of your own reality." Then the idiot asks, "Which is it?"

I do not utter one single word.

I hear his sigh. "Mister Bloom, I talked to the nurse. You still refuse to cooperate. Do you mind if I ask," Cutter says with lying patience, "when you will talk again? Or eat again? Or take your medication again? If you don't I will be forced to take action."

I realize my young doctor can't do a Goddam thing. I smile to myself. My plan is working.

6

It is the night of the second day. My ward is lit with intangible soft light from distant security lamps streaming through locked windows. I lay flat on my back on the uncomfortable bed, the stuffy room filled with the snores of fellow patients. It is like I am in a war zone field hospital. Those I sleep beside are the survivors of Platoon Misfit. The mistreated remnants of life's horrifying battles.
The lumpy island that is Whale Man rises on the next bed. He lays on his side, an institutional blanket half-covering his big naked ass. He's out for the count. Across the room, Ol' Fella cannot find sleep. He sits on the side of the bed, facing away from me, rocking, rocking, rocking—an ancient timepiece bent on self-destruction.

The other three lumps are patients I don't know at all, at least not yet, all asleep.

Earlier, the ward was visited by Cutes on her evening rounds. She carried a torch, tip-toeing through the darkened room checking on us. I'd rather have Cutes than Bollocks. His bed check on my first night was loud. I suspect he went out of his way to wake us. On the other hand, Cutes is always as quiet as a springtime breeze. She touched us with the glowing torch she held. Just enough to make certain we were there. That we were breathing. That we were alive. Even in the darkness I could feel her kindness in the torchlight.

When she got to me, I pretended to be asleep. I could feel her studying me. I wondered what she was thinking; if she viewed me as beyond help. If she was as by-the-book adamant as my assigned ass of a psychiatrist. I wondered what kind of woman she was and wanted to ask but when I opened my eyes all I could see was the shadow of her slim figure moving like a ghost to the front of the ward. Then she was gone.

I was comforted by her visit. But now, an hour later,

"I am afraid," I whisper to the night. But the night does not listen.

In the darkness my mind wanders to the wife and child who have not visited. I wonder if they are still in Ireland. I wonder if my daughter will see me before she leaves. The conviction that it will never happen twists in my gut like a knife.

I turn on my side. I think of my Irish girl. Maybe it's a sin to think of her because I'm still married even if I suspect Laura wants it over. Maybe the girl, who is now a grown woman, should never have found me. But she did and I wish I was young again. Back when I fell in love with her; back when my young life glowed like a lighthouse beacon with the bright promise of sunrise. Back before my unforgivable sin.

I think of her laughter and how we joked with each other. I think of the sun in her hair when we'd walk to the lighthouse and the secret moments we'd steal to love each other. I remember how we read books together in the barn behind the house where we also first made love on a sunny afternoon when my parents were away;

Of the urgent adolescent, still-in-training type of love we made because it was the first time, and how after, I stood naked looking down on her, hay in her hair, my jacket covering sweet naked breasts, and the shy smile on her face because we had both lost our innocence.

My thoughts tilt to when and why I left her; the poor eejit standing alone on an empty boat pier; of why I had to go though I never wanted to leave her. Of how it had all come apart because of the broken promise and of what I had failed to do, and how I worried the islanders would turn against my girl just as they would turn against me. The island is a small place and I feared Dad's accusation would spread like gorse fire, which it did.

Then images of the burning home pierce my mind, and with it the dread that having just found her, I've lost her again. I turn on my back and cover my face with the pillow so I can no longer think. In the darkness my body shudders.

When I was a child and through much of my adult life, I prayed just like any Irish Catholic. As I grew older I often forget to. This night I remember to pray the simple words my mother taught me as a kid.

Now I lay me down to sleep. I pray the Lord my soul to keep...

I forget the rest. It resides in another lifetime. But I will finish anyway.

Lord, even though it happened years ago, please forgive me for leaving Dolores because I promised not to. For fighting with her when she found me. God, how I wish I had never left her. God how I wish I had never hurt her. God how I wish I could take it all back.

Let her forgive me. It's a big ask. But please.

Let her come to me with the dawn.

When I finish I feel like a fool.

7

Day three and Dolores came to see me. She did not come with the dawn, but I was shocked the childhood prayer was answered because prayers are never answered, at least not for me. And yet my girl is here.

God knows how she got around Cutter. He was already pissed off by my silent treatment at this morning's one-to-one session. All vision and no sound is driving him nuts. Dolores is not a relative and I'm told does not have visitation rights. Whatever she did, it worked because when I skipped dinner I met her in the garden.

You can't see it from the barred windows of my ward cell but I'd heard fellow inmates talk about it. It's been over three days since I saw the open sky and its beauty was beyond expectation. The fresh air and bright sun enclosed me in a welcome fist of peace.

Sweet Jaysus but it was good to hold her again. We'd fought the last time we saw each other. I should not have worried because Dolores never carries anger for long. Her forgiveness comes as easily as a happy homecoming.

"I'm sorry. I was stupid."

"But Davy, you're always stupid. Forget about it."

I must have grinned like a madman.

"Close your mouth, Davy," she said, giggling like she always does when I hold her. "You'll be catching flies and they'll think you're a maniac."

I held her at arm's length to take in the curling auburn hair tinged with scattered grey; the secret smile that puckered her mouth; the elfin face with wide-open hazel eyes which always reminded me of a lush Irish forest. But it is her calm practicality that attracted me most; the way she considers the facts. It is as if I can hear her mind sorting through useless chaff in its hunt for truth. She's been like this since we were kids. "Davy," she'd say when still a woman-child, chiding me like she always did for some stupid remark, "stop dreaming and listen to the facts."

Why, dear God, did I ever leave this woman?

I buried my face in thick curls, smelling the deep earthy scent of her safety. I realized the ticking in my head had stopped. For me, Dolores was life. Since coming back to Ireland and finding her again, and despite what she said before the fire, I knew she had not changed. This time I would not let go. The only problem: I was trapped in a madhouse.

Taking my hand, she led me like a little boy to a bench. We sat close together. The sun was in her face. I reveled in her presence.

I noticed her hand. The ring was missing.

"I'm sorry you lost it."

"I should never have taken it off. It was my fault, Davy."

The fault was of course mine but I could hear forgiveness in the singsong notes of her Kerry voice. For a long moment we sat together rejoicing in the garden's fresh palette of colors, feeling the soft breeze in my face, watching it stir the curls that fell above her eyes. For a moment I felt blessed because I knew this could all have been taken from me.

"Did you phone the solicitor?"

"I tried but the line was poor. He couldn't hear me," Dolores explained. "Davy, are you sure you want him involved?"

"Sure I want him involved. Don't you want me to get out of here?"

You see, I had discovered an out.

During the admission process, when I was too angry to notice much of anything, someone or other—maybe it was Cutes— thrust a brochure into my hands. Its front cover announced:

RESIDENT INFORMATION BOOKLET: MENTAL HEALTH SERVICES AND PATIENT RIGHTS

I'd forgotten about it.

Last night, sitting on the bed before lights out, watching Bollocks lead Ol' Fella to the toilet to do his business and idly considering how the poor eejit would wipe his ass, I was still contemplating ways to escape. I knew getting out of the Unit wasn't simply a matter of walking through the front door. The door, after all, was locked.

It was then I remembered the brochure. I found it in the drawer of my bedside locker. Flicking through it I first thought the contents were useless:

What I Should Take with Me When I'm Admitted (*they never gave me a chance to take anything*); How to Cope with the Admission Process (*screaming didn't work*); Medication (*a sentence read*: 'If you feel your medication does not suit you, you can discuss this with your Doctor or associate nurse.' *Discuss it? The liars! What bullshit.*)

I almost threw the brochure in the bin. But then I found something else; the section on patient rights for those involuntarily admitted. I'd struck gold.

It turned out I had the right to appeal.

According to the brochure my involuntary admission was valid for twenty-one days. If during that time, and as a result of his psychiatric evaluation, Cutter decided I was nuts he could lock me up for a further three months.

However—and a big however—following my initial twenty-one-day admission my case would be automatically referred to a mental health tribunal. Apparently, the members of the tribunal, composed of psychiatrists, lawyers and lay people, would listen to my legal representative argue the reality of my sanity. As part of that process I would be examined by another consultant psychiatrist, one fully independent from Cutter, who would deliver a considered opinion. Having listened to both sides, the tribunal would decide if Cutter was right or wrong. If Cutter was wrong I would be released immediately.

The downside was precarious. If the tribunal found for Cutter, he could keep me locked up for another three months. Following that period, he could seek yet another renewal order. Once again my detention would be reviewed by a tribunal. If they agreed with Cutter, my involuntary stay could continue for an additional period. Unless I could prove my sanity, subsequent renewal orders—interspersed by what I feared would be unsuccessful tribunal hearings—could extend my detention indefinitely.

The brochure's words led to a terrifying conclusion: Cutter held my life in his hands. His power over me appeared absolute. If the nut job psychiatrist felt like it, and should my legal arguments prove ineffective, I could die in here.

I had no choice but to fight back. I read that as part of the tribunal, the Mental Health services would automatically assign me a solicitor. But feck if I would ever trust one of their lawyers. I wanted my own.

I had to sneak a phone call to Dolores. The goons had taken my cell phone and the only landline was kept in an enclosed reception cubicle which was usually locked. But when I sauntered out of my ward to scan the area, I realized some fool had left the reception door open. The place was unattended. Now all I needed was someone to watch my back. But Fortune smiled because that's when I saw Whale Man, the guy who grinned at me like a madman through the library window, steer his bulk down the hallway.

It turned out his name was Liam. He was as big as a house but I quickly learned he was a gentle giant. He sweated no matter what the weather; a rainfall of perspiration dripping from forehead and fat cheeks soaking the Thin Lizzy T-Shirt he always wore. He had a thing for robes. I never saw him dressed in anything other than that T-Shirt printed with the image of a fading band, a shoddy robe as big as a tent, and cheap Size 11 plastic sandals. He hummed *The Boys Are Back in Town* as if it were on eternal loop.

He'd been a resident at the Unit for months. Later I learned he'd been in and out of the place since he was a teenager, and always as an involuntary patient. Liam was convinced the world was nothing but one big conspiracy theory.

"The world's gone to shite," he confided, taking a time-out from Thin Lizzy when I introduced myself. "Did you hear Trump is planning to blow up Ireland? It was on RTE Radio One. It's a big fuckin' disaster waiting to happen but no one knows because it's a State Secret."

I'd listened to this morning's news on the funky radio set in the cafeteria which accompanied my non-existent breakfast, the one I refused before seeing Cutter, but couldn't remember that particular item. I wondered how, if such a monumental announcement regarding the planned incineration of The Republic was made on Ireland's public broadcasting network, it could be regarded as a State Secret. So I asked him.

Liam winked.

"Listen closer lad," he counselled. "The real news is always aired during the advertisements. It's hard to decipher because it's in code. Those in the know broadcast the true stuff in parallel bandwidths so to hide it from unwanted ears." He lowered his voice until it was barely audible. "Pay attention and you'll hear it. But you have to listen close; you have to understand her language."

"You're sure it's a her?"

"Sure I'm sure," he said, annoyed at my denseness. "Rose-Marie, that's her name. You listen close from now on. She's the source of truth and justice. Without her we're all fecked."

I understood why the big fellow was a patient. I also wondered what harm to self or others he had caused to rate his Involuntary status. Though he was beyond cracked, he seemed gentle enough to me.

Being locked in here with this nut case is supposed to help me?

I assured Liam that in future I would listen attentively to Rose-Marie. Then I got down to the business of seeking my own truth and justice. I told him of my urgent need to make a telephone call and asked for help. He agreed without hesitation. "Lad, if it's backup you need, it's backup you got," he wheezed. Liam positioned his bulk in front of the reception area, blocking my secret foray from the eyes of our common jailers. While Liam hummed, I found it simple to walk in and make the short call.

Dolores picked up instantly. We had not talked in four days, ever since our argument. She had watched as the fire brigade pulled me from the scorching blaze. Dolores was beyond relief when she found out I was safe. She listened patiently to my plea for help. She promised to make her way up to Bantry and somehow devise a pretext for a visit. She had done everything she had promised.

She even had the grace to forget that when we last met, she had decided to leave me.

Sitting on the garden bench in the sun I ran through my thin knowledge of the tribunal, emphasizing to Dolores why I required the lawyer. "They've locked me up because I'm supposed to be a threat to myself or others. Dammit Dolores I did not start the fire. I did not hurt anyone. You know I didn't."

"I know." Her usual sing-song voice was flat and unconvinced.

"You don't believe me? But Dolores, you were there. You saw it all."

"Davy it's not that," she objected and I could hear a lecture coming. She always lectured me when I started jousting at windmills. "Think about it for a minute. Think of what you've gone through. Now you want to fight? Don't you realize it's going to cause more stress? You don't need that right now."

She was, of course, talking about the reason I'd travelled back to Ireland after a thirty year absence. She was also referring to the fire which had almost killed me.

"You think I'm nuts too."

"No, I do not think you're mentally ill," she replied too quickly.

"So what are you suggesting? That I spend the rest of my life in this place? I'm not doing that. If a tribunal won't let me out I'll *make* them let me out."

"Of course you need to get out. I'm just asking you to be patient for a change. This tribunal won't happen for weeks. For now, take a breath."

"But it's so unfair. They're all idiots. Particularly doctor what's-his-fuck."

"Is what's-his-fuck your psychiatrist?" I nodded and she touched my cheek. "Let me guess. You're not helping, are you?"

"I'm not cooperating if that's what you mean. Fuck if I'm going to play by his rules," I said stubbornly. "So go on. What are you suggesting?"

"I'm suggesting you try on a bit of patience. I'm suggesting you get some rest. I'm suggesting you take a few minutes to relax. For now, for a few more days, you're in the right place."

"Then what?"

"Then," she said with more patience than I'll ever know, "we'll figure out where to go from there."

I looked hard at her. "So where are we going? What about what you said at the house?"

"When?"

"Before the fire. You said you never wanted to see me again." She did not answer immediately. It drove me crazy.

"I said that seeing me was hurting you. But I'm seeing you now, aren't I? Let's leave it at that for now."

She came into my arms and kissed me and for a moment all I could sense was Dolores and for the first time in days I was happy. I held onto her reassurance and didn't want to let go. Finally she made me. She promised to try the solicitor again. She implored me to control my temper and work with Doctor Fuck-Face. She said she would be back.

"You promise?"

"David, I'll be back," she repeated. But I worried at her lack of a reassuring promise. I watched as she left, floating through the door like an angel, consumed with the desire to follow her to freedom.

When Dolores left, her words haunted me. Maybe she was right. Maybe I was in the right place. Maybe, just maybe, my family and Cutter and even Ledbetter the Liar were correct and I am as mad as a brush. After all, if you're told often enough that you're a shite and a bad person and a lunatic, you begin to believe it. Maybe I'm a thief and a liar too. Maybe I'm all these things.

I knew that train of thought would lead me to no place good. So I lay on my bed and thought about Dolores and the dog and the lighthouse. I thought of how much I wished I could roll back time. How much I wished I had made different decisions and could get a do-over on my life.

Of how much I wished I could go home, back to the way most things used to be and the life I once had.

8

"You can't hide so don't even try! Prince, go find her!"

The lanky young man laughed as he searched for the girl, the black Labrador bounding in front of him. His voice rang true and steady above the whisper of rolling surf that snuck onto the rocks below the field where he ran. He could hear her taunting laughter hidden in the shadows of the summer's evening and the young man whose name was Davy Bloom scaled a small rise to look for her.

"Prince, where is she Prince? Go on, go find her."

The dog stood tall, nose to the wind, searching for her scent. He caught something because the dog, who was also a good hunting dog, leapt high across a stone wall and toward the sea.

"Dolores!" Davy called again and his voice echoed across the sheer cliffs above him. He stretched high looking for her, and his gaze turned to Ardnakinna Lighthouse which rose white and steady, as high as a striking blade, to dominate the western end of Bere Island. In the twilight its bright beacon swept the seas to the west and covered the entrance to Bantry Bay with pulsing light.

From where he stood Davy could make out the mountains of Mishkish where they rolled down to the sea, and the bulk of Dursey Island silhouetted against the horizon. The exposed limestone of the far island blushed the color of salmon eggs from the sunset's finale which held all of Beara Peninsula in its thrall.

He heard barking. He caught sight first of the dog as below him it scampered fast through the twilight across the beach on the sea. Then he saw her bounding between rocks, the white of the summer dress billowing like a ghost in her wake. He pelted after her, laughing the whole way down and caught up as she ran across a bare patch of sand. The dog rushed in circles around the young woman, yapping at having found her, and she laughed at its antics. She was still laughing when Davy tackled her, knowing the softness of the sand would break her fall.

They fell together in a laughing jumble, the dog dancing and barking, wanting to join in the play. Davy rolled her over and tickled.

"Stop it, for feck sake, will you stop?" she gasped as the dog licked her face.

"Prince, go on now," he ordered and the dog slunk to a bald place near the sea and sat, panting, waiting for them.

"Are you all right?" he asked, concerned he had hurt her. She grabbed him, pulling him down on her again. The struggle had pushed the bodice of her dress down and in the twilight he could see the top of her exposed breast and marveled at the mysterious change in color as it moved toward the areola.

He wanted her.

"Not here, silly."

"Why not?" He scanned the area. "No one's around. No one ever comes here."

"Prince is here."

"Prince doesn't give a feck."

She threw her arms tight around him and pulled him to her. Beneath the revolving light of Ardnakinna Lighthouse, with the dog keeping watch, they made love.

When they finished it was full night and darkness cloaked them but the onshore breeze was warm and they had the lamp of the lighthouse and the dog for company. It was not the first time the young couple had made love but they did so infrequently because she feared becoming pregnant. They used protection when they could find the hard-to-get rubber johnnys but had to bribe the mainland chemist because they were both underage. They feared pregnancy out of wedlock because like so many naturally occurring human conditions in 1980's Ireland, becoming pregnant *in absentia marriage* was a sin.

Davy Bloom knew this. He loved and respected Dolores. He tried his best to protect her. For those reasons their moments of intimacy were secret and occasional. But sometimes the madness of being human took hold and on those hot moments not even a society ruled by an iron fisted Church could stop nature's impulse to create. When they made love, it was both frightening and frustrating.

"It would be nice to make love in a bed," he said tightening his trousers belt. He stood up from the sand. Prince trotted over and he pushed the dog playfully when it presented its rump to be scratched. "See? Even Prince thinks so."

He reached down, grasping her hand, pulling her into his arms. He could see love in his girl's eyes.

"The island is our bed," Dolores replied.

"It doesn't have to be."

"We've talked about this. We're not getting married."

"Why not? It's a good idea."

"It's a bad idea. How old are you Davy Bloom?"

"Seventeen. But you know fucking well I'll be eighteen soon."

"Don't swear. And how old am I?"

"Sixteen."

"Sixteen. Too young by far. Besides, my parents would never give permission."

He knew she was right but ignored her practicality.

"Marry me," he pleaded. "Marry me and I'll pick you up and take you across the ocean." The dog whined as his master grasped the girl's hand, pointing to the dark line of the western horizon. "Look out there. I'll take you to New York. I'll buy you a big flat right in the middle of Central Park. We'll have a monster bed and make love as often as we want and the only company we'll have is pigeons."

"You're a crazy lad. Central Park doesn't have any flats."

"Then I'll carry you to California. I'll go mining for gold. I'll buy you one of those American skyscrapers and we'll live on top of the world. What about that?"

"You're as mad as a brush. Out of your mind," she giggled. "Davy, you know we can't do any of that." She sat on the rocks, dipping her toes into the falling sea. The dog sat at her side and she combed her fingers through its black pelt and marveled at the dog's intelligent eyes. "Don't you think he's mad, Prince? Don't you think he should stop dreaming and listen to the facts?"

"We'll take Prince with us," Davy decided and the panting dog licked its chops. "You'd like America, wouldn't you lad?"

But the girl who was almost a woman was done playing. "Prince thinks you're mad too. Davy, you know I still have so much to do. You know I'm going to college someday."

He sat next to her, the dog beside him. "Why do you want to do that? No one goes to college."

"Yes they do and so will I," she insisted. "I want to make something of my life."

"If you're going to college I will too," he said and she giggled again. "Are you making fun of me?"

"Oh Davy, no," she responded truthfully and took his hand. "Don't you see? You'll never leave the island. Even Prince knows that."

"I will too," he huffed, tightening his hand around hers. "I'm not letting you go."

"Stop dreaming. Think about what you said. Tell me how you would ever leave. You know you can't."

In his gut, Davy knew she was right. He loved the island. On the surface it didn't seem much of a place. Only a few hundred people lived there. It had only a scattering of roads and telephones were still few and far between. Only a handful of islanders chose to have a television.

Yet despite the apparent hardship there was something magical about Bere Island. It sat like a fortress at the mouth of Bantry Bay, its ruggedness guarding the coastal harbor of Castletownbere and southwest Ireland as if a courageous sentry. Its beauty was unique: tall craggy hills guarded square-cut fields of grazing land where sheep roamed freely. Gorse and fuchsia flowered in patchworks of bright yellows and painted reds throughout spring and summer. Whales, basking sharks, and dolphins plied the waters just off the rocky shoreline.

The only way onto the island was by ferry or boat because it possessed no bridge. Its people were fiercely protective of each other and considered it a privilege if one had the good sense to be born and reared on the island. Some had been forced to flee, seeking work in Ireland's cities or immigrating across the seas due to economic necessity. But always the travelers sought to come back to the island that was their home.

Davy had spent his life on the island. Over the years, and often with Prince, he had trod every hill, every trail, every field until the island's geography was part of him. He knew its coastline intimately and had swum like a dolphin in the seas near his home and played in the huge swells that came in on the lee of frequent storms. In summer he grew as brown as a nut though most Irish only burned in the sun.

He learned to farm from his father and with Prince set out to find lost sheep that wandered too far into the high fields where they sometimes grazed. He also learned to fish with his father, and became adept at steering the twenty-foot boat even in bad weather, and grew confident in his ability to navigate alone out past the lighthouse and beyond the mouth of the Bay where the waters gave way to the true Atlantic.

Though he was too young to realize it, and though his youthful ignorance of other countries gave him no means of comparison, to Davy the island was much more than home. It was a place of safety and wild freedom which few were lucky to experience.

But there were other reasons behind Dolores's statement; darker reasons for Davy's decision to stay on the island no matter what he might dream. It had been born of a promise he had given his father, one which had become a necessity following a storm of tragedy which had shattered their lives.

It came in the form of a telegram addressed to his mother Rose. Sparse, terrifying letters announced that Rose's only sibling—an older sister who had acted as mother, counsellor, and best friend after their parents had died too young—had committed suicide in America. Davy and his father Hector had watched helplessly as Rose's grief turned from despair to psychological chaos.

On dark days she would lock herself in the bathroom, howling like a wounded animal in a horrible scream of relentless pain that cut her son like a knife. When his father was away fishing or out in the fields, Davy would be forced to act as his Mam's guardian. Alone with a mother who had once been the best in the world, but who was now only a ghost of her former self, he tried to cope but it was a losing battle.

When she locked herself away in a prison of her own making, Rose would scream with words that pierced her son's heart. "I want Maud. I want Maud. I want Maud," she screamed, begging for her dead sister. Over and over again, as relentless as the revolving lamp of the lighthouse, the piercing voice filled the young man's soul with terror. He would stand at the locked door, helpless in the face of her madness. When he called for her, his cries filled with horrified concern, she ignored him. When he banged on the door, begging her to open it, she never answered. He yearned to do something, anything, to make the screaming stop and help his mother.

Davy discovered she had started drinking to numb the pain but the single short of Paddy's turned to much more. His father ordered the local publican not to serve her, so God alone knew where she found the whiskey. Every time Davy discovered an empty bottle she had drunkenly hidden, his heart turned to ice, a fist of anxious fear forming in his gut.

When Rose disappeared into drunken, screaming, desperate fugue states, she might wander unseeing out into the rain-swept fields or into the living room begging for Maud. Overcome with emotion, the heavy hand of mental illness reaching terrifying crescendo, she would pass out. Prince would find her. If he was outside, Davy would hear the frantic barking of his dog. He had lifted his mother from the floor more times than he could count. On those occasions he'd carry her upstairs with the dog padding silently beside him. He would put her to bed, ignoring the stink of drink, sponging the loving face which hid behind a mask of mental illness, combing tangled hair gone grey before its time, until she was as close to the image of his Mam as he could manage.

Finished, Davy would go to bed. In the night she would often wake and the relentless wailing would start all over. Davy would call Prince. His dog climbed up onto the bed whining with worry as his master hid beneath thick blankets, attempting to block out the desperate screams and ignore his pumping heart. Usually he would fail. He would have to ride the tide of his mother's horror until sunup when the screams subsided and he could know some peace.

When his father came home and his mother had sobered, with the house quiet, they found they could never discuss the problem because no one knew what to say or where to start. Instead, they trod on eggshells as the family tried to get on with their lives. They sensed Rose's embarrassment in the thin smile she wore and the careful words she used during the tense aftermath of those dark spells. Neither father nor son understood the problems Rose faced or how to manage them and Rose was not about to share the torment that rode her soul like a demon. Instead, they lived in desperate hope, thinking Rose would get better.

To protect her and guard against further humiliation they tried to keep Rose's problem a secret. Neighbors who had once been welcomed to the Bloom house suddenly found Rose to be unavailable. Weekly shopping excursions to the village or the mainland stopped. Rose rarely attended Mass. For a few weeks their tactics seemed to work because Rose stopped drinking and the loving smile she wore prior to tragedy grew like green shoots reaching for sunlight. Davy was sure his mother had come back from whatever dark place she had been forced to visit.

The respite lasted three weeks. When Davy found his mother passed out in the bathroom, an empty bottle of prescription tablets clutched in her hand, he ran to the fields with Prince to find his father.

She was taken by boat to the hospital in Bantry. The doctors pumped her stomach. There Rose appeared to recover. During the time there, Hector, hoping to find a solution, talked to a doctor. But what the doctor offered was even worse than the tragedy the family suffered. Hector knew he must share the grim news with his son.

"I know it's been hard lad," Hector sighed as the rough hand squeezed the boy's shoulder. "We got no choice but to keep looking after her. If we don't the doctor says they'll lock her up in an asylum. Davy, will you keep helping take care of your mother? Will you promise?"

Davy had promised because he loved his mother and father. He was fifteen years old. He did not know what it would cost him and even if he did, Davy could have done nothing less.

He made the promise because he had no choice. His beautiful mother, the tiny woman with the wide smile, the waterfall of light brown hair, the small elegant hands, and the many words of loving wisdom she conferred on her son; the woman who had been so careful about her appearance and whose voice sang with such lilting harmony in the local church choir; the woman who had been the center of his life and the anchor of their family; the woman who had always been more than a good neighbor;

That woman was gone, replaced by a stranger. Crushed by the twin gripping hands of mental illness and alcohol.

Davy began to notice a change among his friends. Some abandoned him. Some would not talk to him because they had heard their parents whisper about Rose and no longer knew what to say. Released from hospital, and denied medication because of the attempted suicide, Rose's dark spells accelerated. Davy did not know what to do.

He was too young to know it but Rose's demons were also becoming his own. Davy ate himself up with blame. He blamed himself for not being able to help his mother. He blamed himself for letting down his father every time he came home to find his wife passed out on the floor. Davy blamed himself for being a failure.

Blame soon turned to resentment. During Rose's dark times when the screaming went on for days Davy found himself wishing his mother was dead.

He hated himself for such unforgivable thoughts.

When his sense of failure became unendurable, he took Prince and walked to the lighthouse. He would shelter from rain and fog below the cliff and lose himself in the revolving beacon of hope. He prayed it would guide him to safety as it had so many others. Often his prayer was mixed with tears because he knew he was unworthy of rescue and beyond salvation.

But someone heard because eight weeks after Rose's attempted suicide God sent him a gift. On a morning following a night of vicious screaming which had kept the house awake, Davy had escaped to the island's small harbor. There, with Prince, he sat on the pier gazing at the water, trying to ignore the voices in his head that berated him with words of failure. He did not feel the light rain falling on his uncovered head or the call of seagulls circling above him, or notice the sweet smell of the sea mixed with rotting plant life exposed on a falling tide. He did not notice the ferry as it navigated toward the pier, reversing engines, losing way to bump lightly against the dock.

Beside him Prince stood up, tail wagging madly. Davy reached for him. "You're fine, boy. Sit still, will ya?" he ordered, stroking the dog. But Prince would not sit as he watched passengers walk off the Castletownbere ferry. His intelligent eyes opened wide when he saw the girl. She carried a bag in one hand and balanced an armload of stuff in another as she struggled to open an umbrella against the rain. When an object fell from her arms the dog bolted toward the pier.

"Prince! Prince you gobshite, come here!" Davy called but the dog was already by the girl's side and the boy was forced to follow.

When Dolores saw him coming she could not see the island lad clearly because of the rain. But as he walked closer, bending to retrieve the lost item, she noticed long thick brown hair curling with the damp and when he rose again she saw his eyes; dark brown liquid eyes that held a sadness her youth had never witnessed.

"You dropped this," he said, wiping the cover of rain, holding out a book. "Prince, come on boy," he called as she took it, and began walking away.

"Can you help me?" she asked and he was forced to turn back. In the rain he saw her eyes and the freckles sweeping like stardust over high cheeks, and the tawny auburn hair peeking from beneath the hat she wore, and though he knew he shouldn't because the girl appeared far too young for him, he could not help himself.

"What'cha want now?" he asked, the rough voice hiding embarrassment. She couldn't help but giggle.

"Are men here always so direct?" she asked and he heard intelligence in her accent.

"So they say about Bere Island men," he said with a swagger. Beside him Prince swung his tail.

"He's a beautiful dog. What's his name?"

"Prince."

"Prince. It suits him. He looks princely."

"He was Queen Medb of Connaght's dog but he got lost. A friend of mine fished him out of the Bay. He's a bit of royalty in him, don't ya know."

Her small smile grew round. "Are Bere Island men always such chancers?"

"Definitely. Every chance we get."

She laughed and he carried her bag to a shelter at the end of the pier. There, they stood out of the rain and he learned her name and that she was from Kerry. She had come to stay with an aunt who lived not far from Davy's home because her parents had traveled abroad to work. She was fourteen, and he would be sixteen in a month's time. He thought her far older because of the mature words she used and turn of phrase, and the way she carried herself, and something in him turned over. He realized it was because he had not felt as confident in another person's company, or with a girl his age, in a long time.

When her Aunt's car approached to pick her up, she turned to him.

"Thank you for finding my book," Dolores murmured.

"Don't thank me. Thank Prince. What's the book called?"

"*The Promise*. It's by Chaim Potok."

"Never heard of him. Where's he from?"

"He's Jewish. If you've never heard of him we'll read it together. You'll like it."

He smiled. "Do you always tell people what to think?"

She smiled back. "Always. I'm told it's my worst fault."

Then she was in the car, and the door shut, and Davy spent the rest of the day and far into the night thinking of the girl. They started reading the book together the following day. Since that time they were seldom apart. As they grew to know each other he realized she was becoming much more than a friend.

Without Dolores, Davy would not have coped with his mother's spiraling descent into madness. He worried how he would get by if Dolores ever left him.

It never occurred to him that he might be the one to leave.

Two years had passed since the reading of *The Promise*. Sitting together on the seaside rocks below the lighthouse, her question still echoed in his ears.

"You're right Dolores. I'll never leave the island," he admitted.

He reached into his jeans pocket. He wished he could have afforded a more expensive expression of his love. But the Irish Claddagh ring was made of gold and its two hands protected the single heart, just as he believed the girl's gentle hands protected his, and as he hoped his hands would always protect hers.

He gave it to her and she took it.

"Look inside."

The girl looked. Small engraving spelled *D+D forever*.

"Oh Davy. It's beautiful."

"If you go away to college you'll always come back. The island is your home now, too," he said with the earnestness of youth. "When you do, I promise I'll be here waiting for you. I love you Dolores. I'll always love you."

The ring fit perfectly. She came into his arms and for a long time they stood together with the dog and whisper of surf, beneath the light-house that pulsed as brightly as their hearts. Though he meant the words with all his soul, it would be one promise Davy would not be able to keep.

The fact he had no choice gave little comfort.

9

Paul Cutter could not find sleep. For a long time, he lay in the bed of his Bantry apartment and thought about Bloom. He thought back to what he had been taught about Bi-polar disorder and psychosis, and his experience with others suffering from these disorders.

He knew that progress with patients was made with medication and ongoing therapeutic counseling. Acutely ill patients—patients like Bloom—often required assertive intervention in the early stages. Assuming that even partial recovery was achieved, they could move onto less invasive therapies such as outpatient services, vocational rehabilitation, and continuing care management. While patients could experience recurring symptoms such as depression and anxiety, with the correct psychiatry, diagnosis, and drug therapy there was a good chance those suffering could successfully re-enter society.

That was Cutter's hope for David Bloom. However, despite current efforts the psychiatrist knew he was getting nowhere. Bloom's intransigence combined with the decision to cause further self-harm by starving himself to death was proving problematic. The doctor was losing sleep over the matter.

The young psychiatrist could not help but think that if he failed, Bloom could prove a disastrous blot on his budding career. He pushed the thought away knowing it was not compassionate and therefore not professional. Cutter realized that at all costs he must show compassion. It is what he had been taught and did his best to practice.

Cutter rolled over, unable to find a comfortable position, as he considered the dilemma. How could he show compassion if Bloom chose to kill himself? The law was clear: a patient was within his or her rights to stop eating.

He toyed with the idea of requesting Bloom's transfer to another Unit. By doing so he could off-load the problem onto another doctor, thereby avoiding the possibility of failure. But he remembered Bloom was only starting his fourth day in the Unit. He also reasoned that the patient would not be in any physical danger for a few days at the very least.

He rejected the idea of requesting a transfer. It was too early to think he would fail his patient. He had time to find a solution.

Sleepless, Cutter rose well before sunrise and booted up his laptop. He navigated his way to a series of legal websites. By 5:00AM he thought he had found an answer.

***

I want out.

I study the locked door, the barred windows, the concrete walls of my prison looking for escape.

I WANT OUT NOW!

I look around the ward. My fellow patients sleep in over-medicated peace. By day they shuffle between rooms; between treatment sessions; between meals and meds, handed off from nurse to nurse like circus animals. By night they snore, unconscious. I cannot sleep because my cough keeps me awake. I taste the steel-acid stench of smoke in my mouth. My cough turns to hacking—wracking spasms that force up a thick glue of dark particles. I wonder what else is lurking in my lungs.

Right before I was admitted to the Unit, the local hospital checked me for smoke inhalation. A medic put a stethoscope to my chest. He told me to breathe. He listened for a few seconds then patted my shoulder. "You're fine, Bloom. No harm done."

I didn't believe him then and I don't believe him now. I want a real examination by a real respiratory specialist. Not an incompetent who received his online medical degree from some quick-fix university chop shop.

The night of the fire I am asleep at home in my old bedroom. I dream I am a boy again.

Dad takes me to the summer fair and buys tickets to the Fun House. It is filled with mirrors and light. I scamper over angled wooden pathways, laughing at my distorted image reflected in crazy mirrors. I call for my father. He does not answer. The lights go out, the pathway splinters. I fall through darkness. Arms flailing, silent screams unanswered, terrified because I am alone.

I see blue flashing lights reflecting off suffocating twilight. I hear fists pound on a downstairs front door. A voice shouts, "Bloom! David Bloom!" Then the shattering of wood. Boot covered feet hammer up wooden stairs. I wake, gagging. The bedroom is filled with smoke, blue pulsing lights from fire tenders bouncing within it. Strong arms pull me from bed. I am dragged down smoke filled stairs where my family was standing moments ago. I scream for them but the fireman will not listen as I am pulled out the front door.

I remember Dolores. I am convinced she is still in the house. I push him off, running back inside. Dropping to my belly. Pulling myself through coiling smoke, howling for her.

I crawl to the front room. The fire is a living monster consuming my family's past with indifferent hot fingers. I push fast toward the raging blaze searching for her. The firefighter yells at me to stop. He grabs my legs, hauling me back outside. I fight but this time he will not let go. I keep screaming for my girl. For my parents. For my dog.

After he pulls me out, he leads me to an ambulance. As I stumble through night air, taking a breath, clearing my head, I realize: what I thought is impossible. Dolores went home when we fought. And as for my parents and dog? They are dead. All of them.

I am examined by the waiting EMT. He explains if I'd remained in the house for another two minutes I would have died. He advises me to go to hospital. I don't. I wish I had. If I'd done what the EMT suggested, I would never have been captured by Cutter and his henchmen.

I'm appalled by my lack of judgment and the stream of mistakes I make.

Rising from my Unit's bed, unable to sleep because of hellish memories, I stumble to the hall. I lean against the cold concrete wall, my body wracked by coughing spasms. I smell smoke and want to be sick. I search for fire. I want to run but unsteady legs will not carry me.

I do not understand I am having flashbacks.

I am too frightened to go back to bed. Instead I limp to the court-yard. It is almost dawn, the yard nothing but shadows. I find a chair and sit. I hear someone sobbing. I realize it is me.

"Ah lad let it go."

He is hidden in darkness. As he shuffles toward me, I think he is a corpse, so thin and vulnerable is he. Closer, I see the head with hollow, stubbled cheeks thrusting from a torn pajama top. Wisps of brittle hair crown passing manhood, as lost as yesterday. Loose bottoms, holed and stained, wrap the spindled legs. He leaves the stench of urine in his wake.

I recognize him when the bony hand clutches my shoulder.

"Do nightmares get to ye too?" Ol' Fella asks.

I see his eyes. They shine bright with medication but also with kindness and sorrow. He tightens his grip, not letting go until my sobs subside.

"Want to tell me what's wrong?"

"I want to go home," I whisper like a child.

"Lad don't you know we all want to go home?" He finds a chair and sits beside me. The rattle of his breathing is as comforting as a reliable old engine. He chuckles.

"What's funny?"

"Nothing. It's just my son is coming to see me today."

"Is he?" I ask between sniffles. No one is coming to see me today.

"He comes every week except when he's too busy. I know he has his own life. Mind you, it'd be nice if he came more often." In the shadows I see him rock. Back and forth, back and forth.

"Do you have sons?"

"Only a daughter."

"Does she visit?"

I can't answer. He stops rocking

"That's all right. It will be over soon."

"What will be over?"

"All of it." In the darkness his eyes grow bright. "We'll die in this place. And when we do we'll die alone."

He rocks again.

Later, Nurse Cutes tells me Ol' Fella's son hasn't visited in five years.

10

It is the morning of my fourth day and Christ I'm hungry.
I stand in the courtyard near the spot where I met Ol' Fella last night. I never did get back to bed. Now I don't want to.

A basketball net hangs from a drunken steel pole stuck in the middle of the yard. A ball sits on the concrete floor wanting to play. A simple pastime for simple people. A long time ago during an immigrant's previous life I learned to play basketball on the concrete playgrounds of Brooklyn. This is not Brooklyn. But I do it now to keep me from thinking about food or sleep; to quell the panic of locked doors; to forget the fire and an old man's words, and the girl I yearn for. Most of all I do it to hold onto something familiar that grounds me to a past that is much more real than any present.

I pick up the ball. I shoot. I can't sink a single shot. It drives me nuts. I dribble back and forth across the courtyard, the easy skill I had in my youth long gone. I try again; over and over again. The ball refuses to go into the net.

I sit, catching my breath. Coughing in deep spasms. Ignoring it because no one gives a damn so why should I? The cafeteria door is wide open to let in the air of spring. Patients from the Unit's six wards are finishing breakfast, about two-thirds men, the rest women (*men must go crazy more often than women,* I think) sitting in groups of six around fat tables. They shovel food into gaping mouths in what is a highlight of monstrously monotonous days. My mouth waters.

Nurse Bollocks walks past me on his way in. "Get in there," he growls. I ignore him, knowing he can't do a fucking thing.

I see my ward's table. Ol' Fella sits with two other patients. The old man has finished his meal. Most of it is left on his plate. He is dressed in a torn red cardigan. (*I wish I could buy him a new one. I wish I could make him feel human even if it is only a stranger's store-bought compassion.*) He rocks on his chair, staring into space, the remnants of boiled egg smeared on his chin. I see last night's sorrow in his eyes.

From where I sit I look past dining tables to the meds room. Bollocks has opened the top half of the security door. He stands behind it, dispensing morning medication. Patients stand in a queue waiting their turn. They are cowed, silent, obedient. I find it inhumanely striking. All the scene needs is Montovani's *Charmaine*, the soundtrack that underscored Medication Time in *Cuckoo's Nest,* and it would be perfect.

I notice Liam. Whale Man is next up to bat. Bollocks hands him two small paper cups. I assume one contains this morning's prescribed meds. The other water.

Nurse Cutes walks through the cafeteria blocking my view. She sees me. She slows and I sense she wants to talk. But Bollocks calls her over.

I get up, trying to shoot baskets as I watch. Liam still holds the now-empty cups in his pudgy hands, an innocent smile on a perspiring face. Bollocks looks suspicious. I sense an argument brewing.

Cutes strides up. Her mouth work as she asks Liam questions. The other patients shift in the queue. Whale Man shakes his head. Bollocks butts in. Liam is forced to open his mouth to prove he is not lying. He bends toward Cutes. She looks embarrassed as she examines Liam's mouth, looking under tongue and behind teeth. She smiles apologetically, satisfied he has swallowed his medication. Liam turns to Bollocks with a caustic grin. He drops the empty paper cups on the floor. He nods at Cutes and saunters away.

I go back to shooting hoops. I think how proud of the man I am.

***

The last thing the psychiatric nurse needed that morning was to make sure an overweight patient had taken his medication. Though necessary, she found the process humiliating to both parties. The tasteless chore over, she asked for a cup of black coffee from the Unit's cafeteria staff. She sat at a vacant table and drank.

Nurse Healy had not slept well the previous night which was due in part to over-tiredness and stress caused by working double shifts throughout the past fortnight. The Unit was under-staffed. Two nursing colleagues had resigned earlier in the year. Both left for better paying jobs in England. Both said they were tired of Irish working conditions, low salaries, and the belief patients were not receiving adequate care. The Health Board advertised for replacements but not a single applicant had stepped forward.

Under-staffing was endemic. Over two-thousand additional psychiatric nurses were required to meet government targets established for Ireland's mental health services. The psychiatric nurses' union had voted to strike a few years earlier, hoping to pressure the government into more funding. Despite their threat of industrial action, union members received only hollow promises which had never been implemented.

Nurse Healy had been employed as a psychiatric nurse for fifteen years; at the Unit for over ten. She had occasionally considered leaving but would not. Leaving would not resolve the problems at the Unit nor help her patients. She had chosen the field because she cared deeply for people but was appalled by the current situation. Inadequate staffing levels short-changed patient care. Most were supposed to receive occupational therapy three times a week. Often, therapists failed to turn up. Most required ongoing therapeutic counseling but sessions often led nowhere because no one had time to listen.

More critically, the experienced nurse believed the treatment of the mentally ill was undermined by the very training and methods of care adopted by many psychiatrists, a process she considered flawed.

Like most professionals in any healthcare service, psychiatrists began their studies with a firm foundation in the medical sciences—training, she believed, which could undermine effective psychiatric treatment.

In mainstream medicine, everyone from GPs to surgeons approached patient care using proven scientific methods. Patient treatment started with observation, approved diagnostic tests, and a verifiable diagnosis. This was followed by science-based treatments such as surgery, medication, or a combination of procedures which often had predictable outcomes. Medical science was therefore grounded in proven regimens of care.

Psychiatry, however, was a far more complex affair. The factors responsible for mental illness were often hidden deep within the opaque complexity of human minds, and therefore difficult to decipher or interpret.

Psychiatric diagnoses were often based as much on guesswork as verifiable facts though few psychiatrists would admit it. Subsequent therapies could be flawed and outcomes unpredictable. Some believed those suffering from mental illness could not be cured. Instead, their symptoms could only be managed. That viewpoint could condemn many patients to a lifetime of suffering.

Nurse Healy had often become discouraged by the reality of the profession within which she worked. But the nurse took heart in knowing she had become a contrarian. Unlike many mental healthcare professionals, she was convinced a holistic approach, which included factors often overlooked by many practitioners, must be adopted.

She believed that patients' relationships with family and friends, both past and present, must be considered. Their deep emotional character traits needed to be deciphered. Historic traumatic crises such as sexual abuse, death of loved ones, divorce, and exposure to dangerous or life-threatening situations must be explored.

Most of these fuzzy factors were difficult to interpret. Often, it was hard to prove what role these issues played in the mental illness of any single patient, if any. Certainly, those presenting behaviors consistent with mental illness could not be diagnosed or treated the way a medical doctor treated patients suffering a heart attack. It was never that easy.

And yet many psychiatrists relied on a strict by-the-book scientific approach. Their language was filled with words and phrases most lay people could never understand: neurobiology; psychosocial mechanisms; psychotherapy protocols; psychosocial intervention; psychotropic therapy; psychopathological frameworks. The obscure language, and the treatments they implied, created a culture of fear. Distrust between patient and doctor destroyed any chance of recovery.

The nurse believed if patients were to heal, they needed to talk about what they were experiencing. However, they could not if they did not trust those tasked to help them. Nor could they if staff did not have time to connect with them or think to listen.

In short, Nurse Healy had come to accept that kindness, connect-edness, compassion, and understanding were keys to effective treatment. Unfortunately, many mental health professionals paid these basic human attributes only lip service.

She knew Dr. Cutter was a good case in point. Like many psychiatrists he relied heavily on psychiatric scientific medicine to manage mentally ill patients. Though admiring the young psychiatrist's intelligence and zeal, Nurse Healy realized that due to his training, inexperience, and impatience, he was prone to misjudgments.

She saw it a few months ago as he worked with an older patient in the Unit. Cutter's latest diagnosis was schizophrenia. The prognosis poor. The therapy thus far ineffective. The fact the patient had been in and out of psychiatric care for years and had been subject to a wide variety of different diagnoses and treatments, all without substantive progress, did not seem to cross the young doctor's mind. That the patient had no support from family, and longed for them, was never considered.

She reasoned that patients deserved sound, all-encompassing psychiatry if they were to regain mental wellbeing. However, professionals like Cutter often rushed diagnoses. Therapeutic plans were based on incorrect or biased assumptions. In such cases, patient could be placed at greater risk.

She had come to believe this was true in the case of David Bloom.

Her concern was one of the reasons Nurse Healy had not slept well. She had spent three days observing him. While the first night and much of the following day had been filled with his outrage, the patient had settled. He always dressed neatly. He conducted his daily toilet promptly and remained well-groomed. Except for the outburst following the early morning nightmare, he was generally cooperative and caused no trouble.

She had noted how he interacted with her; his general comportment. He went out of his way to behave pleasantly to most people in the Unit, particularly fellow patients. She had noticed him with Liam. David's attitude to the large man was filled with expressions of immense concern. She had seen him with the older patient and witnessed David's compassion when they sat together in the courtyard or walked slowly down the hall, a hand at the old man's elbow.

When the nurse met David in passing, or when he entered the examination room for the morning physical, she had noticed the smile meant only for her. In those same eyes the nurse had also sensed intense hurt and suffering; the covert outrage; the plea for assistance which she associated with those who have been unjustly treated. She realized he could not cry out for help. He had already tried but those in authority refused to listen. Instead, he screamed his protest in silence.

Of course, there was also the ongoing feud with Cutter and the patient's rebellious refusal to talk; his stubborn rejection of food and medication which worried her deeply. But the nurse realized he acted much like any person would if trapped in similar circumstances. Though she did not agree with her patient's behavior, the nurse tried to put herself in his shoes.

If I was locked up in here against my will, what would I think? she asked herself. *How would I behave?* And most importantly: *What if I knew I was sane, yet no one would listen? How would I feel?*

"Enraged," the nurse whispered.

Nurse Healy glanced out the window. In the courtyard a middle-aged man played basketball. He was of normal height and weight. His balding head glistened with sweat, his face red with exertion as he ducked and weaved against himself. He looked just like anyone else who played alone with a basketball.

He could be my brother or my neighbor or the older man down the road who kicks at a football but knows he's too old for it. He could be an anyone or a nobody, a psychotic or a priest, a madman or...something else.

Sipping her coffee, Nurse Healy again considered the man who played against himself.

What if David Bloom is something else? What if David Bloom is: Normal?

Fully aware of the patient's original diagnosis, the nurse had searched for signs of Bi-polar disorder and alcoholism. Doubting her initial conclusion, one which differed completely from the Unit's consultant psychiatrist, she searched again. Yet every time she came to the same result, one she could not expunge because it was so unsettling.

Finished with her coffee, she again studied the ordinary-looking man who still played basketball. He was dressed in a loaned black track suit. His eyes were clear. His focus upon the game as intense and as frustrated as any victim caught in a similar situation.

"How would I behave if I was David Bloom?" the nurse puzzled. Other than the single patient the yard was empty. Nurse Healy realized the time for observation was over.

She must act.

I still shoot hoops but not one damn ball will go in. I dribble toward the basket determined to make a layup. Instead, the ball bounces off my foot and skitters across the concrete floor. A woman's hands deftly catch it. It is Nurse Cutes. She walks to the far end of the yard. She turns back and I know she wants to talk. We find a secluded corner.

She hands over the basketball. Her face is serious. I wonder what I've done wrong this time.

"Mister Bloom, I've observed you for three full days," Cutes states, her voice professionally matter-of-fact. "Here's what I've concluded." The words which follow grab my gut. "You demonstrate no signs of alcoholism. I have not seen any DT's except perspiring and occasional tremors, nor any signs of addictive behavior. You do not seem to be obsessed by alcohol or thoughts of where you can find the next drink."

Her searching blue eyes fix on mine. "Mister Bloom, I do not think you are an alcoholic."

I clutch the ball tighter. "No shite. No I am not an alcoholic."

She nods at the confirmation.

"Good. Next there is the matter of Doctor Cutter's Bi-polar diagnosis. As I previously mentioned, it can take months to make such an assessment. I believe the doctor has been—" and she searches for an appropriate word, "—pre-mature. Symptoms can sometimes be confusing. Doctor Cutter has made a mistake."

Her eyes do not leave mine.

"I have not detected any depression in you. I have not witnessed any mania except for the other night which, of course, could be construed as manic behavior. But that could be explained by your nightmares."

"What nightmares?" I say embarrassed, thinking little kids have nightmares.

"Oh come on. You tried to get out of the Unit and had to be restrained. You had to be sedated."

"You think I'm crazy, don't you?"

"I do not. The other nurse thinks your agitation was the result of nightmares brought on by earlier medication. I agree with him." She does not take her eyes off me. "I suspect you have been misdiagnosed. You present a variety of symptoms. All of them are consistent with Post Traumatic Stress Disorder. Do you know what that is?"

I nod and want to throw the ball high. "Are you sure?"

"That is my professional opinion. For instance, nightmares also occur as a result of PTSD. Or take the matter of your trembling. That is a symptom of PTSD, too."

"What trembling?"

"David, your hands are shaking."

I look down. My hands grip the ball and do not shake. But the ball shakes.

"I get the shakes," I admit. "Alcoholics get the shakes."

"Have you ever seen an alcoholic in Detox? It's much worse." She places a hand on my arm. "I know you were in a fire. I give you a routine examination every morning, remember? I've heard the congestion in your lungs. There is also the matter of your weight loss. You've lost six pounds since you were admitted."

"Is that a lot?"

"In three days? Of course it is. If you continue losing weight it gives your doctor an excuse to keep you here. Won't you please eat something?"

My head swings like a stubborn mule. "I'm not eating until Cutter tells me when I can get out of here."

"I understand."

We stand for a moment's silence in the warm sunshine. I feel real sympathy for the first time since I was admitted.

"Mister Bloom," she says, "as an authorized officer, I also act as the Unit's patient rights spokesman. Call me an ombudsman if you want."

"Ombudsman? What's that?"

"It is my duty to look after the interests of our patients, including those who have been involuntarily admitted." Then she makes her most powerful statement yet. "David, if I was told to appear before a mental health tribunal and asked to testify, I would state I do not think you are a danger to yourself or others."

I don't know what to say. Here is a professional medical practitioner disagreeing with the very basis for my involuntary admission.

"Then I can leave?"

"It's not as simple as that. Doctor Cutter has to agree."

"Cutter won't agree to shite. I want another opinion. I want to see another doctor."

"It doesn't work that way. Patients held in the Unit are not free to get another opinion."

"You're feckin' kidding me."

"No, I'm not."

"Then I want to be transferred to another Unit. I don't want to be here. Not with Cutter."

"It won't happen. Your Irish residence is Bere Island. Bere Island falls within the catchment area for the Bantry mental health unit. You can't go anywhere unless the consultant psychiatrist orders a transfer."

"Cutter has that much power?"

"David, almost everywhere in the world, psychiatrists in charge of mental health units have that much power."

"So I really am a prisoner. I don't have any human rights."

"Calm down. You know you do. Legally, you can be held for twenty-one days. At the end of that period a mental health tribunal will hear your arguments for release."

"That's over two weeks from now," I snap. "You said I'm okay. You know I'm not a threat. There's no reason to keep me here."

"David, that's the law. You have to wait."

I study the cafeteria. I see Ol' Fella. I wonder how long he's been held here. I do not want to become another Ol' Fella.

"Isn't there any way for me to get out earlier? Don't I have any other options?"

"Yes, you do," she explains. "Do you have a solicitor?"

"I'm not allowed to use the phone. How can I contact him?"

"I'll see about that. Your solicitor can file a writ of habeas corpus. He or she can argue to a judge that you are being held illegally. If the judge agrees he'll order your release."

"And if my solicitor fails?" Her silence speaks volumes. "Isn't there any other option?"

"Yes, but it's even more challenging." The nurse takes a breath. "If the consultant psychiatrist believes the reasons for your detention are unfounded or flawed, if he accepts you are not a threat to yourself or others, then he has the power to release you."

I eye her. "Cutter can release me?"

"Yes."

"How? He'd never do that."

"He might, if he can be convinced." I see decision in her face. "I'll talk to Doctor Cutter. I'll lay out a case for you. He'll interview you again. You'll have to convince him."

"How soon? Today?"

She gives my arm a gentle squeeze. "Be patient. And please," she says, "eat something. Your body needs it. And Cutter could use it against you."

She turns to leave.

"Nurse, before you go can I ask something?"

"What's that?" Her smile rises like a summer sun.

"What's your name?"

"Mary."

"Thank you, Mary." She smiles again. I can't take my eyes off this messenger of hope as she walks out of the courtyard.

I'm still holding the ball. My hands are no longer shaking. I measure the distance to the net. I shoot.

The ball goes straight in. Swoosh!

11

Cutter paced his office, too agitated to sit down. He recognized that Nurse Healy had responsibility to protect the interests and legal rights of the patients she served. But that was not the point.

To Cutter the point was simple: the nurse was wrong. In this case dangerously so.

In Cutter's mind, her arguments were weak and ineffectual. Yes, perhaps Bloom did suffer from PTSD. But she was not taking into account the interviews with his wife and daughter. What about the violence? What about the psychosis? What about the lies and theft? This behavior took place prior to the fire on Bere Island. The underlying conditions that had caused the uncharacteristic behavior were still evident and must therefore be treated.

And as to the alcoholism? Cutter recognized the only way to prove if Bloom was an alcoholic was to live with him. But that was not possible. Cutter knew most alcoholics lied about their intake. Many denied the presence of the disease. Most were good actors. The doctor suspected Bloom to be a *very* good actor and a good liar as well.

Cutter based his opinion about Bloom's alcohol dependency on what he had learned from Mrs. Bloom and Rachel. He had no reason to think they were lying. They had no logical rationale for fabricating a story about something so serious. Bloom was an alcoholic no matter what his nurse thought. As to his Bi-polar condition? Cutter had to admit he may have rushed his diagnosis. But caution prescribed he should assume the worst-case scenario in order to protect his patient. For now, Cutter would stand firm on his diagnosis.

Cutter grabbed Bloom's patient file from his desk. He reviewed recent notes on even more serious matters at hand. These concerned Bloom's continuing rebellious streak, as well as its consequences. He re-read the morning patient report which highlighted Bloom's weight loss. It was much more than he had anticipated. He feared Bloom was walking into dangerous territory. And yes, while Bloom might not cause himself serious harm for weeks without eating, he could turn to other harmful behaviors. For instance, what if Bloom refused to ingest fluids? It would kill him in days.

The nurse didn't think of that one, did she?

Yet the nurse was adamant. Despite Bloom's self-harming behavior, she had concluded he was not a threat to himself or others. She believed the involuntary admission was unwarranted and responsible for unnecessary emotional harm. She suggested Cutter consider an immediate release. Even more shocking, the nurse had informed the doctor that should the patient remain at the Unit throughout the initial detention period, she would make her opinion clear to any tribunal.

Piqued, he threw the report back on his desk.

Cutter knew that as part of the tribunal process, an independent psychiatrist would be appointed to determine Bloom's mental fitness.

Cutter believed that any psychiatrist, having learned the facts and observed the patient, would agree with him. Certainly, such a conclusion would undermine Nurse Healy's ill-considered opinion. However, he had other worries.

Due to his patient's refusal to eat, and the possibility he would cause himself further harm, the young psychiatrist knew he had to act to protect Mr. Bloom from his own hand.

His early morning research had provided such a strategy.

He was determined to prove that his diagnoses were correct. He was certain Bloom was Bi-polar. He knew he suffered from psychosis. All he had to do was execute his plan to prove it. In the meantime, he had no intention of approving the nurse's request for release.

He strode to his office door, ordering a male nurse to bring in the troublesome patient.

***

When Bollocks tows me in to Cutter's office, I am expecting to find Cutes but Mary is nowhere to be seen. Cutter asks me to take a seat. I refuse. I stand.

He shrugs. I can tell he has talked to Cutes. His boy lips are set in an angry, defensive pout. I gather he's already having a bad day. Good. He sits behind his desk. His ratty eyes refuse to look at me.

"Nurse will join us shortly," he whines. He props elbows on the desk, joining hands. I want to laugh like a fool because I've seen the Promised Land. But I know I have some work to do to earn my freedom. I remember I'm a businessman. I stand tall, smoothing the wrinkled tracksuit, trying my best to look professional. Serious. Focused.

Sane.

"Mister Bloom, while we're waiting on the nurse can I ask you something?" the rat asks. "I know you won't respond but even a nod would be helpful." I have the satisfaction of hearing a loser's disappointment in his voice. "Have you always been such an effective liar?"

His question sounds as reasonable as a priest's, catching me off-guard. "Don't you understand your protest has consequences? Don't you realize your refusal to eat constitutes a hunger strike?"

His words are as solid as cold steel. He shrugs.

"The law is clear. Anyone including you Mister Bloom, who is competent to make their own decisions, can refuse to eat. If I force you to eat it can be considered assault. I emphasize the word competent, Mister Bloom. *Competent.* It all comes down to that single word." His voice trails off. He stands, strolling to the far corner of the office. The ass seems to be contemplating the wall's peeling paintwork because he won't look at me.

I pray the silly words are his last gasp before releasing me. But my belly rumbles. I hear distant ticking. The room starts to spin and I have to sit down.

I take a breath, remembering what Mary told me. *He has no way out. He's lying. You're going home.*

But Cutter isn't done. "Mister Bloom? Might I point out that even as you seek your freedom you have a major problem?" He spins, facing me. "As the Unit's Psychiatric Consultant, I believe you lack mental capacity. I believe you to be _incompetent_."

I back deeper into the chair.

"The law makes that situation clear too. Because you are not competent, I have a legal obligation to protect you if I believe you are in peril. You are in peril, Mister Bloom. I have no other choice but to protect you."

I notice that Cutter has a red mole below his left eye. I find it fascinating.

"Do you know what I will do to protect you, Mister Bloom?" He walks closer. The mole is huge. "I will force you to eat." He points at my stomach. "I will order a gastro-intestinal tube inserted right there. Do you know what a gastro tube is? I will pump you full of the food and medication you refuse to take."

His ratty eyes are vicious. My heart races. I want to go home.

"You will eat, Mister Bloom. You will take your medication. You will talk to me. Do you understand?" The room spirals. A smile plays on his mouth. "But there's yet another consequence for your incompetence. Do you know what that is?"

I can't move.

"Your stay with us could become protracted. Perhaps even—" and I swear I hear a steel door clang shut, "—indefinite."

Light sweeps over me, blinding. I close my eyes tight. *God help me. I don't know what to do. Please, please God let someone rescue me.*

I open my eyes. I see Prince. He stands at the closed door. He squirms and dances like he always does when greeting me. I stand. God knows how I keep my balance. My eyes fix on Prince as I step toward him.

"Mister Bloom—" Cutter states and follows my gaze to the spot where Prince waits. I see Doc's pupils dilate, the fucker.

He thinks I'm insane.

"What are you seeing Mister Bloom? You are seeing something, aren't you?" He asks the question as if unraveling a big fat fucking secret.

The door opens. It's Cutes.

"Mister Bloom, I'm so sorry I'm late."

She notices my open mouth. The sweating face. The fixated eyes focused on a spot inches from her nurse's shoes. She looks to Cutter.

"He's having a psychotic episode. Don't you understand?"

I call for Prince. The last thing I see as I escape past Cutes and out the open door is Mary's concerned, compassionate, upturned face.

I sprint down the hall. Prince scampers ahead of me.

I want out. I HAVE TO GET OUT.

I hear the Goddam ticking. Louder now. So loud I cover my ears with both hands. I race past Whale Man. His perspiring face turns to alarm. I hear Cutter yell for Bollocks.

I look back. Doc is running furiously. Bollocks trundling behind but catching up. "Grab him!" Bollocks reaches. He misses. I run into the courtyard breathing hard. In-out, in-out. Cutter and Bollocks are through the door. They close and lock it.

I try the cafeteria. The door is locked.

Prince barks. He senses my distress. Cutter watches as I stroke the thick black pelt. "Calm down, Prince. Calm down boy."

"Mister Bloom, I promise we'll take good care of you. Forget about the gastro tube. I was exaggerating. We won't hurt you."

The yard fills with cutting revelation. I realize what Cutter said back in the office is all a set-up. "You fucker. You lying fucker!" I shout. "Prince! Prince! Get them!"

The dog runs. I charge the two of them. Bollocks wraps his arms around me. He leverages me to the ground.

"I want to go home. I want to go home. Please, please let me go home."

"Keep his head up." I hear Cutes as distant as a far-off rain shower. "Don't let him fall."

I'm dragged down a hallway. I struggle hard within Bollocks' arm lock. I see Whale Man crying. Ol' Fella's ancient face trembles like melted pudding. I know someone is in trouble but can't figure out who.

I'm thrown on a hard table. A vice squeezes my arm. Cutes is taking blood pressure. Light sweeps across my face. *Odd. What's the lighthouse doing here?*

I wonder where Prince is.

Cutter is shouting at me. "Mister Bloom, don't go to sleep. Keep your eyes open."

My body trembles. I don't give a fuck.

"David, David, relax, okay? But don't go to sleep." What a great idea. I think I'll take it easy. I'll let the current sweep me away.

I open my eyes. I see Prince. He licks my face; his ears prick in recognition. I look toward the door.

"Davy," my mother asks, "when are you coming home?"

"Mam," I ramble. "I already came home, remember?" My eyelids are heavy. "I can't come home again. They won't let me, Mam."

Cutes stroke my face with a damp cloth. It feels good. I wonder where Dolores is. The light on my face grows stronger. I close my eyes. I see the lighthouse. Its shines bright on our home. I'm surprised. The fire didn't do much damage after all. I smile.

I sleep.

SECTION TWO

PSYCHOSIS OF DAVID BLOOM CLINICAL NOTES

Lecture Extract 'The Trap of Misdiagnosis' Dr. Anne Tenbrooke, Consultant Psychiatrist St. James Clinic, Dublin

"Recently, I read a report written by a prominent American psychiatrist. A forty-two year old male spent almost half his life—let me repeat that: *half his life*—detained in residential psychiatric care due to psychotic and catatonic episodes. Family feared he would harm himself though no self-harm was ever observed or proven. Over the course of his treatment, ever-changing medical diagnoses ranged from catatonic schizophrenia, undifferentiated schizophrenia, unspecified psychosis, and a host of other disorders.

"Treatment for this alternating range of diagnoses relied on an array of anti-psychotic medication. Yet the prescribed course of action failed to resolve either psychotic or catatonic episodes and did not advance the patient's mental health.

"This patient's case troubles me. As it turned out, the patient had been misdiagnosed. When the patient was properly diagnosed, and subsequently received appropriate one-to-one counseling and correct medication, he recovered quickly and was released.

"Unfortunately, he found freedom only after suffering twenty years of unnecessary confinement.

"This is an example of the confusing nature of mental illness, the momentous power of psychiatrists, and how harmful misdiagnoses made by well-intentioned professionals can ensnare human lives. The American psychiatrist's report emphasizes a stark warning:

"Patients are at the mercy of mental health professionals. Their trust in us must be earned. We cannot fall into the trap of careless misdiagnosis or use of unsuitable medication. In short: we must tread carefully."

12

I fall.

Shuddering within a storm of distorted words, disassociated from any sense of time.

"Clusters"

"Stupor"

Within the boiling ether I hear questions.

"David? David, answer me."

My tongue will not move.

"Mutism"

I force open my eyes. The ceiling is curiously blank. Someone-is it Cutes?-raises my arm. I see outstretched fingers. Rigid. Index finger pointing toward the center of the universe. The rest splayed. Frozen.

"Immobility"

Lights on the flat horizon of a living sea. They twinkle as distant as Orion. The ceiling cartwheels with surging waves.

"Cataleptic"

The sea parts. It rushes to me as I fall toward its center. I know I will die. I want to scream but cannot. Someone takes my hand. I feel the suppleness of familiar fingers. I clutch tight, holding on as our speed reaches infinity.

"Schizophrenic"

Contentious words live in a distant parallel universe. My sky fills with puffy clouds of sometime memories. As we fall through them, they glow with surreal iridescence.

"David, come back!" Dolores kisses my cheek.

"Davy," she says. Her lips do not move but I sense her love."Come home." I can only think: which one?

13

Rachel sat down on a hard bench in the departures area of Dublin Airport's busy Terminal Two. The flight to New York would board in forty minutes but they had not yet cleared the gauntlet of security. Laura, who did not like to fly, fretted at her side, urging her daughter to join the long line of passengers.

"Are you sick?" Laura demanded. "Rachel, get up. We have to go."

"Don't you feel it?"

"Stop talking in riddles."

"You don't understand." Rachel's stomach was in knots. She wanted to be sick. "We made a mistake. We have to talk to him."

"Talking to him will make things worse. It's called 'enabling', remember Rachel? Let the doctor do his job."

"I don't trust the doctor. Dad's in trouble. He needs us. He shouldn't be in there."

Her mother's face resolved into a stubborn mask. "Your father is exactly where he should be. I told you. He's an alcoholic. Now come on or we'll miss the flight."

"I'm going back."

"Where?"

"Back to the Unit." David Bloom's daughter stood, picking up her carry-on.

"What could you possibly achieve? Your father is sick. Let the professionals handle it." Laura sensed her daughter's indecision, placing a hand on her arm. "Don't you want to go home to Jacob? He's expecting you." The young woman had no response to her mother's manipulation.

As the aircraft took off Rachel was nagged by the thought she had swallowed her mother's opinion without thinking; that she had made a mistake. The thought grew louder as she crossed the Atlantic. It filled her heart as she was met by Jacob and the bear hug he had for his new wife.

"Why are you crying?" he asked when he felt her shudder in his strong arms.

Within the safety of his understanding she told him. "I don't care what Mom says. I'm going to help Dad."

The only issue was how.

***

I am high over mid-Atlantic, hovering between homes, lost at sea. Westerly, I make out the steady lighthouse perched tall on the tip of an American long island. I spent over half a lifetime there. A daughter. A wife. A life.

To the east another bright island beacon beckons. A mother. A father. A girl. A dog. The ghosts of distant past.

I am torn asunder.

I feel the squeeze of her hand. *"You can stay here if you like," she whispers. "Right here in the middle of the sea where no one can hurt you."*

Her words tear at my heart. I think back on what has gone before and what has brought me to this horror. Of the where and the when and the how, knowing I will never understand the why. But perhaps by knowing, I can find myself again.

I squeeze her hand once more and let go. I am in freefall.

I blow westward toward the continental coastline. I must remember why I came back to Ireland after so many years in America and my promise to never come home. If I can, then perhaps I can find the will to forgive. Not only my family. I know I must forgive myself.

The storm clouds beneath me grow dark. Lightning forks as I plunge through.

I see Long Island. Time has collapsed. It is now only a few minutes and a few miles after I am bundled from the wedding rehearsal. I am in the distant unfamiliarity of a doctor's office; a doctor I do not know, the one who is not mine.

Laura stands at the door, arms crossed and hard-eyed. The doctor peers at me from across a cluttered desk, a deep disapproving frown on his pockmarked face.

"David, if you drink again it will kill you. You must take responsibility for your actions. Aren't you listening? Please, say something."

I can't because I *know* I'm responsible. In my mind I see a business partner's surprised face, a broken nose and blood all over a carpet. I remember wanting to die in front of the Presbyterian masses. I'm humiliated by actions I do not understand, those that belong to a man I do not know. Those of a stranger.

"I don't drink."

He sighs. I hear their distant words. Something about locking someone into a treatment center for a week or a month or a lifetime to dry out.

He gives Laura a prescription for sedatives which I need to take every four hours. She says she doesn't care what I do. She drops the script at my feet saying I must get them myself. I dumbly pick it up. Later I throw it away.

"It will take a few days until we can organize the treatment center," the doctor says and asks, "Where will he stay in the meantime?"

I know she will not let me into the house even if it is also mine. Then the door opens. The man who tomorrow will become my son-in-law walks in. He helps me from the chair.

"Come on Dad," he consoles. "We're going for a drive."

I'm glad. I like Jacob. He already calls me Dad. I wonder where we are going.

***

When Bloom remained unresponsive the psychiatrist knew that while he had confirmed his diagnosis of psychosis, he had made a serious mistake. His intentional confrontation with the patient was a misjudgment which required immediate action. He ordered Nurse Healy to contact the hospital's A&E department. His patient was transferred. Knowing the healthcare risk, Cutter accompanied him. The nurse insisted on attending.

At the hospital, Cutter was relieved when learning Bloom's vital signs were near normal. The attending medical physician ordered a precautionary ECG and CT scan. The first would monitor Bloom's heart rate and electrical activity. The second would focus on the patient's brain to detect strokes or other anomalies that might give reason for Bloom's inexplicable physical condition.

With Bloom stable, the medical doctor drew Cutter aside.

"Doctor Cutter, is there anything else you can add?" he asked.

Cutter glanced at his patient. He lay on the table staring at the ceiling with fixed eyes. "He hasn't been ingesting foods."

"For how long?"

Cutter looked to his nurse. Mary stood beside her patient. She took David's hand, raising his arm to near vertical. She let it go. It did not move from the uncomfortable position. When she began to lower the arm the psychiatrist objected.

"Leave him," Cutter insisted and joined her at bedside with the medical doctor. They studied the patient's rigid, raised arm.

"Catatonia," the medical doctor agreed.

"If you're finished may I make him more comfortable?" Mary demanded. Not waiting for an answer, she lowered David's arm.

"Nurse, when did the patient last eat?" the psychiatrist asked.

"Three days ago."

The medical doctor made a note to order a liquid diet to be administered intravenously.

"Medication?" the doctor queried.

Cutter told him then added, "Ignore that. I want to change his script."

"Why?" Mary challenged but Cutter addressed his male colleague instead.

"The diagnosis has changed. Another medication will prove more effective." When the psychiatrist named the drug Mary said nothing.

"Dosage?" the medical doctor asked. As Cutter prescribed it Mary struggled to maintain her professional silence.

As Cutter moved to the door, the medical doctor asked, "Doctor Cutter, what's your new diagnosis?"

"Schizophrenia. It's the underlying cause of his current catatonic state as well as previous psychotic episodes."

When they left Mary excused herself. She found a woman's toilet. There she let down the mask of professionalism. She leaned against the wall, breathing heavily. The nurse had already informed the psychiatrist of her opinion regarding their patient. He had not agreed. When he refused to order an immediate release, the nurse realized she must wait until the tribunal took its course. But the patient's descent into catatonia had changed everything.

The nurse knew that any tribunal would find David Bloom incompetent. They would never consider a release, not until the underlying causes were identified and treated. What galled Mary was her firm belief that Bloom's involuntary detention, together with the psychiatrist's attempted intervention, had contributed to her patient's decline. She believed Cutter's latest diagnosis of schizophrenia was absolutely incorrect; the new drug inappropriate; the dosage excessive. As importantly, she worried the psychiatrist's future actions might place her patient in even greater jeopardy.

Nurse Healy had a duty of care to her patient. She was tasked to raise concerns if she believed patient safety was being compromised by the practice of a colleague. Established procedures were in place for such a situation. If she followed protocol, the nurse would approach the Unit manager. Failing that, she could direct a complaint to the Mental Health Commission. However, she suspected that these actions would result in failure. After all, it was the consultant psychiatrist's professional opinion against hers. In a 'he-said, she-said' confrontation, the nurse would in all likelihood lose. Mary realized if she lost so would David Bloom.

To succeed she needed to approach a professional with knowledge and experience of such situations; someone with a greater understanding of the complexities who could act as her patient's advocate.

The question was: who.

***

We drive down a busy freeway. I don't know where we're going. I see an exit sign: JFK International Airport.

I ask Jacob why we're going to the airport.

"Dad, you're going to love it. We got you a big room at the Hilton all to yourself."

I don't get it right off. I chatter stupidly about not having my tux with me. I need it for the wedding. The wedding is tomorrow.

Jacob can't look at me.

It is his silence that makes me get it. I get it and I want to throw up.

My daughter does not want me at her wedding. I am an embarrassment to her. I am a failure.

I break down and cry. I cry all the way to the hotel. My future son-in-law is too distressed to look at me.

***

When they arrived home from the airport, Rachel had sat up with Jacob until dawn, explaining everything. At first kicking herself for not objecting when she had the chance, and now questioning the very basis for her father's psychiatric admission, she knew that doing nothing was no longer an option. However, she was not certain what action to take.

One of the reasons she had married Jacob was his cool logic and ability to get to the root of most problems. He was decisive under fire. His practical intelligence was why a top New York law firm had hired him right out of Princeton Law School. Though Jacob's father was the firm's senior partner, nepotism had nothing to do with the appointment. Like his son, the elder Ryan was interested only in results and therefore highly selective.

"If you're confused then let's start by reviewing the basics," her husband suggested. "Explain to me what problems your father is facing."

"Jacob, you know what they are."

"Explain them again."

Rachel ticked them off but he challenged every one. "Alcoholism."

"Are you certain? When was the last time you saw him drunk? Are you certain he was drunk at the rehearsal? Would you swear to it in a court of law?"

"Mom swears he's an alcoholic. Jacob, you saw him."

"On what grounds should I believe your mother? And yes, I saw Dad. But I could not swear he was drunk. Did you see him drink anything? I didn't. I'll ask again: could you swear he was drunk?"

Rachel realized she could not be sure despite what she had witnessed or what her mother might think, or even what she had told her father's psychiatrist in Ireland. She admitted she had not seen her father take a drink since she was a girl.

"Next," Jacob said.

"His violence, stealing, and lies."

"What about them? Explain."

Rachel was forced to recount what Garrett had yelled in the Church. "You heard what he said. Dad stole a shit-load of money. How can you forget that? Dad's a liar and a thief, Jacob."

"Are you certain?"

"Garrett told Mom he had proof."

Her husband considered. "Yes, but until you see that proof Garrett's statement is only hearsay. What else."

"What about the violence?"

"Okay, he got into a fight. And yes, if Garrett had chosen to press charges Dad would probably have ended up in jail. But when was the last time you saw him in a fight? Is he predisposed to violence?" Jacob shook his head. "I don't think so. Based on what I've seen, violence is not in your father's vocabulary. He fought when he became upset, and then only because he was pushed. It was a one-off. Next."

"What about the SEC? You heard Garrett. Dad is being investigated."

"Are you certain? Again, it's hearsay. It's only Garrett's word. What else do you find troubling?"

"The psychiatric ward. I don't think he belongs there. I know he needs help but the treatment he's receiving is shit."

"Can you prove that or is your statement an emotional judgment?"

"I never visited Dad, if that's what you mean. I never asked anyone about the treatment they were giving him."

"Then you have no way of justifying your suspicions."

"Jacob, sometimes you annoy the crap out of me."

Jacob laughed. "I love you too but any good lawyer would ask the same questions. Rachel, you still haven't told me what you want to do for your father." He took her chin in his strong hands, pulling her face toward him. "What do you want, Rachel?"

"I want to get him out of there. I want to protect him," she said with tears in her eyes. "Jacob, maybe Dad really is an alcoholic. I don't care if he is or isn't because it doesn't matter. I know he is not a thief. He is definitely not a crazy man. We both know he isn't. I want him home."

She looked sadly at her husband. "I wish Dad had been at our wedding."

"I do too," Jacob replied. "But that's in the past. If you want him home then that's what we'll do."

They talked for an hour longer. Rachel was scheduled to return to Hofstra University that next week. She was finishing her senior year as a communications major and faced a tough roster of late spring exams. But exams could wait. If worse came to worse she would defer for a year or even two. "I can always go back to school. Dad is far more important." Her husband concurred.

Rachel then turned to possible actions she might take. One of them included Garrett. She was determined to get to the bottom of the as-yet-to-be-proven accusation.

"That's sensible," Jacob said. "But you can't do anything today. You're too tired. Let's go to bed and we'll figure it out tomorrow. I'll see you upstairs." He kissed her on the cheek.

"Jacob?"

"What?"

"Do you think Dad is a good man?"

He smiled at the concern in her voice. "All you have to do is look around. Your father is as good as they come." He again kissed his wife. "Come to bed soon, okay?"

When Jacob left, Rachel sat on the sofa and ran a hand over the silken fabric. She glanced around the living room. It was all brand new. She took in the new curtains and the new furniture and the wedding gifts stacked against the wall, many still unopened because there had been no time.

The house and furnishings were a wedding gift from both sets of parents. She had learned it was all her Dad's idea. Such a loving idea is not born from the mind of a bad man, she told herself. She had learned that Dad had approached Jacob's father with the suggestion that their kids needed a leg up. They had plotted in secrecy for months. Not even their mothers knew about it.

She found out the night of the wedding, a wedding her father had not attended because she had forbidden him. On that evening, she was standing with Jacob in the fashionable multi-purpose building her mother had rented for the wedding reception. They were greeting guests. Rachel was embarrassed due to the previous day's events and her Dad's insane behavior. She could not seem to embrace the joyful wedding congratulations friends showered on her.

When Jacob's father walked over, she did not know what to say. He broke the ice.

"I need to talk to you kids," he said comfortably. They found a corner away from prying eyes. He slipped them a set of door keys. He explained the gift and what her father had instigated, and how he had wanted to give them a home.

"Not even your mothers know about it," he explained. "In fact, unless you tell them they still won't know."

"I don't want it," Rachel exploded, and tried to give back the keys.

"Give me a chance to explain."

"I told you I don't want it. I don't want any part of Dad."

"Honey, let him talk, okay?" Jacob objected.

She got control and made herself listen.

"Rachel, I don't know what happened to David," her father-in-law said. "I don't know him well but he impresses me as being level headed and a good guy. It was his idea to give you the house. I never would have thought of it."

"I don't believe you," Rachel shot back.

"Well he did," her father-in-law corrected. "Now listen, Rachel. And please take this on board. A few years ago my life was pretty grim. I had a lot on my plate. A lot of stress at work. I damned well near went crazy. Jacob's mother was ready to leave me." He looked to his son. "Ask him if you don't believe me. Rachel, I was at the breaking point. I think that's what happened to your father."

"I know you mean well," Rachel insisted, "but Dad wasn't just crazy. Not unless being crazy means beating the shit out of someone. Not unless it means being a repulsive liar and criminal."

Her father-in-law was a tall man just like his son with the same thick hair only gone grey at the sides and the same confident smile, and the same honest eyes that drilled right into you. She could not look away from him though she tried.

"You have to forgive your father, Rachel," he suggested.

"Why? He made a fool of me."

"Your Dad broke, don't you understand? It's not about you or your mom or Jacob or me. It's about your Dad." He placed a hand on her arm. "Rachel, everyone has his or her own breaking point. Your Dad found his, that's all. Let it go. Don't you realize he needs your help?"

On the day of the wedding Rachel had ignored her father-in-law's advice because she was not yet willing to give her father anything, much less help or forgiveness.

But just back from Ireland, sitting in the living room of the new home her father had given to her, she reached for the phone with a sudden need to check on him. But the night nurse who answered would not provide any information. "It's against policy. Besides, do you know what time it is?"

"Is Dad okay?"

"As I said I'm not allowed to discuss him with you. You'll have to ask Doctor Cutter in the morning."

"I'll phone back. Would you tell the doctor I rang?"

"I'll leave a message. I can't guarantee he'll return the call."

When she hung up Rachel began to formulate a plan. First, she would talk to Garrett, just as she had promised Jacob. Then she would talk to her father's psychiatrist in Ireland. Finally, she would talk to her mother.

In Rachel's mind, only one thing was certain. She would move heaven and earth to bring her father home.

***

I am thrown by violent gusts between angry black clouds. Thunder and lightning rip through me, my world ablaze. I lose sight of my steady lighthouse beacons within torn skies, praying for the first time in years.

The clouds part. I hover over a dangerously familiar structure: the Hilton Hotel.

A man I remember stands alone on a balcony. He pleads into a cell phone for permission to come to a wedding. When they hang up, he knows they will never listen again.

He sobs. In his other hand he holds a father-of-the-bride speech he had at last spent so much time preparing. He knows he will never give it because he will never have another chance. He rips the pages into countless ribbons, tossing loose shards to the skies. They flutter like forgotten love, descending across a distant world many floors below.

His eyes focus on the solid steel balcony rail. I remember he wonders what it would be like to follow the drifting paper and fly. He decides, placing a foot on the rail. He knows those he loves are right. He is a bad man. Bad men deserve bad endings. He measures the distance to the ground. It is a long way down. Enough to do the job.

Barking distracts him. I follow his gaze. It is our dog. We saw the dog at the rehearsal, my wayward friend and I. We thought it was a mirage born of one too many false accusations or two sips of wine. Yet here again is our loyal friend.

Prince bounds toward us. We know the dog can't be real. But when Prince comes into our arms, when we feel its prancing warmth, we know he is as solid as any reality. We crouch, holding the dog hard to us.

"Oh God, you're here." We look into the dog's intelligent bright eyes. "What should I do, Prince? Tell me what to do." The dog licks our face. It scampers to the front door and we realize he has come to lead us home.

Then he disappears. Poof! Just like that. We call for him. We search every room. Our Prince will not be found.

We sit on the couch, taking deep breaths, trying to figure things out. We think of the dog who is not there anymore and our mad behavior at the rehearsal, and of the disturbing voice of a now dead father screaming false accusations. We think of the girl and how we abandoned her, whose guilty memory has always shipped in on haunted sails. We think too of the ticking in our heads from a grandfather clock displaced by thirty years and three-thousand impossible miles. We know something within us has broken, and has been for a long time. We think we know why.

For too long, ghosts from our past have torn us like sharp knives. Their accusations control us. Their words make us think we are bad. Those whom we love also think we are bad.

It is a terrible realization. Within a strange hotel room, we pace, hands slapping our head until our ears ring, too anxious to sit; trying to quash the critic's voice within, the one yelling that we are a terrible man, beating us up. Part of us knows we are not bad. All we need to do is prove we are not.

We know we can no longer go back to the Long Island home we have made in this immigrant nation. The woman we have spent half a lifetime with will never let us in again.

We walk back onto the balcony. We look easterly to light pulsing across a darkening sky. We remember that beyond the lighthouse of our present there is the lighthouse of our past. It stands like a sentry atop a small island off an Irish coast. If we are lucky its light continues to shine.

We remember the instructions contained in the envelope. It is safe in our coat pocket. We pull it out, rereading. As we do, we consider the ghosts of our past and weigh those against our desperate hopes for a future, and make a choice. We will follow the Irish solicitor's typed instructions to the letter.

After all this time we will struggle to put our ghosts to rest. We will prove our innocence if only to ourselves. We will apologize for the broken promises we have made. If she is still there, we will find the girl who once was ours, but now lost, to make amends. We will forget about death and instead choose life so we may move on.

To achieve all of this, all of these impossible tasks, we finally know what we must do.

We must go home.

14

To: Garrett Ledbetter   URGENT
From: Rachel Bloom-Ryan
Subject: Dad

Dear Garrett,

First may I apologize for not emailing sooner. I'm just back from Ireland and finally have time to reach out.

Garrett, I'm so sorry about what happened at the rehearsal. I'm sure Dad feels the same way. I tried phoning the office a number of times. I talked to Trish (she says she's now your PA?) who told me you weren't available. Could I see you? It's urgent.

Trish tells me you received treatment for the injury. I hope you recover soon.

I'm sorry you couldn't be at the wedding. Please take care of yourself. Could you kindly make room in your diary to see me as soon as possible?

Fondly, Rachel

To: Doctor Paul Cutter   URGENT

From: Rachel Bloom-Ryan
Subject: Status of my father David Bloom

Dear Dr. Cutter,

I've tried phoning you many times—5 to be exact—but am always told you are unavailable. I have been informed I must talk to you to learn about my father's current condition. Having been unable to reach you, I have been in touch with Nurse Mary Healy who also has a keen interest in my father's situation. Though she was unable to go into detail for legal reason (?), Ms. Healy informs me that my father is quite unwell though stable. I would very much appreciate it if you could urgently respond. I need to discuss further actions we can take to help my father. I expect to hear from you within the next 24 hours.

I have also contacted the U.S. Embassy in Dublin regarding my father's involuntary admission.

Sincerely, Mrs. Rachel Bloom-Ryan

cc: Mr. Jason Ryan, Attorney at Law

To: Mr. Frank Harrington,
Harrington & Sons Solicitors, Castletownbere, County Cork, IrelandURGENT
From: Rachel Bloom-Ryan
Subject: My father Mr. David Bloom

Dear Mr. Harrington,

I am the daughter of the above-named person who is being held involuntarily at the Psychiatric Unit, Bantry, County Cork. I am very concerned for his safety.

Though I understand my father is unwell, I am not certain his treatment is appropriate. More importantly, and having talked to Nurse Mary Healy who is assisting in my father's care and who gave me your contact information, it is my belief his involuntary confinement is not warranted. As a U.S. citizen I am unclear regarding Irish law or actions I should take to release my father and bring him home. Though I have a U.S. attorney working on my father's situation, we believe that local representation could prove more effective.

I tried phoning a number of times but have been unable to get through. I would be grateful if you could respond to this email as soon possible.

Sincerely, Rachel Bloom-Ryan

cc: Mr. Jason Ryan, Attorney at Law

***

Once he was Davy: a son, a friend, a student of island life. Then he was David: a father, husband, struggling miner of wealth in a strange new world.

Today he did not know who he was.

He stood at the periphery of a small crowd of island people gathered for ceremony on a field overlooking the sea. Within a sundered mind, he could not help but notice it was an even smaller gathering than the last service he attended thirty years before. Within his confusion he wondered if the island was dying.

The words of the old priest were lost on the wind. He could not understand them nor did he care. He had made it in time and that was all that counted.

He studied the people, and though born on this rocky fortress felt an outsider. While some seemed familiar, they appeared faded and bent, like old sepia photos left too long in the sun. He remembered the tall owner of the island's pub, wearing a soft cap over curling grey hair, a long mac against the spring rain, and how in the distant past he had tried to help his family. He saw a group of church women who had sung at a funeral Mass thirty years ago. He remembered how their fresh young voices had soared with harmonies of grief. They did not sing now.

He observed the dogged shapes of three old fishermen who had once been neighbors. Bent with age and rheumatism, they paid tribute to a fallen friend who could never come home.

He saw a heavyset woman he knew to be the daughter of the shop keep whom he thought must have died because he was not present. It was unlike him because he was the village gossip. The grown woman, now carrying the heavy waist of a fat trawler's beam, had been only a slip of a girl when last he saw her.

He noticed the ferry master, thin as a spindle but still possessing a sailor's iron forearms, who had worked his trade for over forty years and had ferried him to the island that morning on the final leg of this long trip from America. The skipper had not recognized him because a lifetime had passed since he gave a lad who was now a man passage on a reciprocal heading.

Yet nowhere within the small crowd attending his father's funeral could David find the woman who mattered. He knew she was gone. Everyone that mattered to him was gone.

He looked to the west and an overcast horizon. He could see the spring tide break, foaming onto a rocky shore. He took a breath, trying to steady trembling legs. He inhaled the sea-scent mixed with the earthy odor of animal dung which had been a heady companion in his boy-hood. Though nothing else made sense it smelled of home.

Despite his hurt he still had reason to be grateful. His father's accus-ing voice which had followed him throughout the flight to Ireland was silent. He worried it would come again, ruining the thin balance he had achieved on the slippery slope of his mind.

His eyes roved along the shoreline. He could not see the lighthouse because it was hidden by a tall hill upon which he grazed sheep in his youth. He knew soon it would begin its revolving beacon of warning.

He heard the priest's words of final benediction. The oak coffin which contained the mortal remains of his father lay in the rain, droplets scattered across its surface like keening mourners. A pair of fishermen worked the ropes, inching the box into cold earth. An old woman, a neighbor his mother's age, bent double, sobbing, to mark an end.

When the crowd dispersed, they shuffled by the man dressed in the blue serge suit wearing no hat to protect his balding head from the rain. They said nothing because they thought him a stranger. When the old priest passed he smiled in wan forgetfulness. The baptism forty-eight years ago was too distant to remember.

With the field empty, David Bloom stepped across thick tufts of grass growing wild between rows of family plots. Grey cement borders protected lichen covered headstones chiseled with names and dates of those who had fallen.

He paused at his mother's marker. He could not look. He turned to the freshly dug grave next to it. A hill of damp clay stood near. Soon the dirt would be used as fill by local men who also volunteered as gravediggers.

He looked into the deep hole. Bright carnations and roses glistened with rain, covering the wet surface of the wooden coffin. A fake brass crucifix attached to the top reflected the bent shadow of his face.

He read the brass plaque screwed near the foot of the coffin: HECTOR BLOOM.

David began to cry. He could be certain the solicitor's letter was true. His father was dead. But he could not be certain the voice of accusation was also dead until he visited the house. He was not yet ready to go. Instead, he stood in the rain, alone.

"David Bloom?"

The rough voice startled him. A tall, solid man wearing a dark overcoat stood at his shoulder, a full gray mustache damp with rain. He extended a huge mitt of a hand. "I don't think you'll remember me. Frank Harrington, your father's solicitor. I'm sorry for your loss but I'm glad you came home. Could I have a word?"

***

Rachel woke early. She had spent all day yesterday attempting to contact people on her list. She had tried Garrett a number of times. He had not returned her calls. She had phoned Ireland every hour until she thought it pointless. Finally, she was put through to a psychiatric nurse.

Rachel asked about her father's status. Three thousand miles and five time zones away, Mary Healy worked hard to choose her words.

"Your father is safe."

"Safe? I don't understand. What does 'safe' mean?"

Though hamstrung by client confidentiality, on this occasion Nurse Healy knew the emotional state of a patient's daughter depended on her answer. Due to his condition, the nurse decided to throw confidentiality to the winds.

Standing in the Unit's enclosed reception area she glanced down the empty hallway. It was late afternoon. Everyone was at tea. Mary took a breath and lowered her voice. She briefly described David's condition.

"I'll come back on the next flight," Rachel said, voice edged with panic.

"Rachel—can I call you Rachel?" Mary asked. "Rachel, I want you to take a breath. Your father is stable. He's receiving excellent care, I promise you."

"I should have stayed."

"But you didn't and that's okay," Mary replied. "Yes, do come back. If he saw you it could help. But please, take your time. I won't let anything happen to him."

They discussed the situation a moment longer. Rachel admitted she had urgent business to attend to that could help her Dad. She promised to fly out as soon as she finished.

"Nurse, is there anything else you can tell me, any other information that would help me to help Dad?"

On the other side of the Atlantic, Mary asked Rachel to hang on. When she came back to the phone she said, "Rachel I want to read you something."

Nurse Healy read the brief letter she had found in David's bedside locker: news that the grandfather whom Rachel had never met was dead. A request that her father attend the funeral. The name and contact details of an Irish solicitor. At least Rachel knew why her father had returned to his island home after a thirty-year absence. As importantly, she had the name of a lawyer who might prove useful.

Rachel thanked the nurse. She promised to let her know as soon as she booked the flight. When she hung up, she phoned the Irish solicitor. Nobody answered.

When no one on her list called back, Rachel went to bed fuming. Still upset, she woke early and fired off three straight emails before sunrise. She made sure the correspondence to the psychiatrist was particularly tough. She forgave herself for lying. No, she had not contacted the U.S. Embassy. Not yet anyway. Rachel hoped the threat would get the doctor off his ass.

When Jacob woke, they discussed the frustrating situation over a pot of coffee. He agreed with her: she could not take silence for an answer. He also agreed she should tackle the geographically closest target first. Together, they talked through the plan she had devised.

"Do you think it will work, Jacob?"

"I don't know. All you can do is try to force Garrett's hand." He took her in his arms. "I'm sure glad you didn't go into law."

"Why?"

"Because I'd lose every time."

She kissed him, got dressed, and left their Long Island home.

She fought the morning traffic into the City and arrived early at the office. When she explained to the security guard on duty, he let her in. She waited in reception, sitting on a low leather couch with an easy view of the revolving front doors and the ranks of elevators. As she waited, she wondered if her father had ever sat in this same seat. The thought of him made her more determined to get answers.

The windows looked out on a morning sidewalk crowded with people forced to rush through their lives, always on the move. She realized her father had spent his career doing the very same thing, a thought that had never before struck her. She had a sudden desire to thank him. To hold him. To tell him how much she loved him. She wished other people felt the same way.

The thought of her father led her to think about Garrett Ledbetter. She wondered again why he had not returned her calls. She knew, of course, that he might be as busy as her father's Personal Assistant, who now seemed to work for Garrett, had told her. Rachel knew that people employed in the firm were always busy. But the discussion with Jacob caused her to think deeply about her father's business partner.

Rachel remembered the Christmas when she was twelve, the year the firm was founded. Her dad had invited Garrett to dinner. When the doorbell rang, she ran to the front door. An immense impeccably dressed man filled the doorframe, jovial face hidden by a mountain of presents he carried and had bought just for her.

She remembered how excited she was as she opened the fabulously wrapped gifts and how impressed her mother and father had been with the extravagance. Finished, surrounded by hundreds of dollars of sweaters, computer games, and cell phones, she had planted a kiss on his cheek. She allowed herself to be wrapped in a huge bear hug.

She remembered not liking the pretentious aftershave he wore.

"Oh thank you, Mister Ledbetter," she remembered her twelve-year-old self squealing.

"Call me Uncle Garrett," he chortled. She called him that for years afterwards. Yet she also remembered the discomfort of that first embrace; the sense of distrust; the whispered feeling she was being manipulated.

Even at that young age, Rachel knew his gifts were a bribe. Yet she could think of no reason why he would bother because she had nothing to offer. She never mentioned the suspicion to her father and certainly not to her mother. But Rachel had wondered about Garrett's true intentions ever since.

Now, sitting on an uncomfortable leather reception seat within an antiseptic City office building, she thought again about the talk she had with Jacob and the advice he had given her. Garrett's accusations against her dad were as yet unproven. The unreturned phone calls made her even more suspicious. Yes, if Garrett could prove his odious statements, she knew she would have to accept those findings. But until then she had to focus on rock-solid beliefs: her father was not a thief nor a liar.

A half hour passed. Office workers scurried in holding blue and white cardboard coffee cups in one hand balanced by heavy briefcases in the other. She watched a woman rush to the ranks of elevators, hammering the call button, as if hoping her frantic will alone would master computerized electronics.

When an hour passed, Rachel wondered if her planned ambush would prove fruitless. She knew if he did not show up she would return the next day and the next and the next, for as long as it took.

A tall man wearing a grey coat strode toward the elevators, his face obscured by the wide brim of a stylish hat. For a moment she thought it was Ledbetter. She was disappointed when he turned to blow his nose with a clean white handkerchief and realized she did not recognize him.

Thirty more minutes passed. Still on duty, the security guard stood behind a wide desk. He glanced her way. She felt pressured to either leave or have him phone upstairs. She was fairly certain if she talked to Trish, she could convince the PA to let her wait in the firm's offices. But that would defeat Rachel's strategy.

When Rachel spotted the tall elegantly dressed man walk through the front entrance, she turned her back hoping he would not recognize her. She counted to ten then looked toward the elevators. Her father's business partner waited at the rank of closed doors, absorbed in the morning's *Wall Street Journal*. From where she sat, Rachel could see the elevator floor indicator lights. A car was descending. When an elevator door opened she followed him, marching across the marble reception floor, entering just as the door slid closed. No one joined them.

Alone with him in the closed confines of the car, he stood with his back to her still concentrating on the newspaper. She waited until the elevator began its ascent.

"Good morning Garrett."

He startled, turning to her. She noted ruddy embarrassment rise into boyish cheeks, his nose still covered with medical tape.

"My, don't we look spiffy today," Rachel bubbled, admiring the tailored three-piece suit. She stepped closer, unruffled by the imposing stature which towered above her.

Then she asked, "Garrett, what are you hiding?"

Garrett Ledbetter did not even blink.

15

I sit at a table shoved against the back wall of the small island pub watching the crowd. We always came here after any major event: weddings, baptisms, confirmations, funerals. I would sit over there, on a high stool at the end of the polished bar with Mam and Dad, surrounded by friends who sought my father's opinion.
"Should I take the boat out to scrape her hull this week or next?" a fisherman friend would ask.

"This week," my father advised. "The weather is getting up next week."

"Should I make the first cut of silage now or wait for more growth?"

"Now. This good spell won't last forever."

If it was a funeral, then in between they would talk about the dearly departed, remembering the good times as well as the sad, celebrating a life. I was proud of my Dad, back before the darkness. I was proud to be the son who neighbors said looked so much like him: a man of average height but of immense strength, confidence and ability; a man of value and kindness. A man of good fortune. "His luck came in on the tide the day he was born," friends always said of him. No one ever thought it would leave him.

That was before Mam got sick in the days when I was happy. While Dad talked to his friends, I'd sit in short pants beside my Mam, drinking orange squash because it was cheap but tasted good. She'd stroke my back with warm fingers as she listened to female friends discuss the bereaved family and what foods to bring them over the coming weeks. She always took on the baking because it was known throughout the island that Mam made the best tarts and tastiest scones, and her baking always gave comfort. For that reason I always looked forward to funerals. It filled our home with the warm scent of love.

With their duty done the women turned to other things. I listened to Mam's soft voice talk of the next shopping trip to Castletownbere or the next choir rehearsal at the church, and as she talked her hand smoothed my hair as if I was the most precious thing in the world.

Now I sit at a cold table remembering the happiness, and long for her touch again.

I study the crowd. Some of the islanders glance my way, curious at the presence of a stranger. No one recognizes me.

I see Harrington. He holds a pint of Guinness. He shakes the hand of a solid-looking farmer I should remember but don't, then makes his way over. He sits across the table from me.

"You sure you don't mind here? We could go out to the car."

I shake my head. Anywhere will do. I'm sure this won't take long. He sips his pint.

"I can't buy you one?"

When I again shake my head, he rummages around in a beat-up briefcase and pulls out a fat cardboard folder. I see the word Bloom scrawled on its front cover in thick black marker.

"David before I go through this I want you to know how sorry I am. Not only for the loss of your father but for the trouble when Rose died."

I stare at him.

"I know how your mother's death shook him. I know it shook you as well."

Nice words. But I don't remember meeting this man so his sympathies mean little.

He opens the folder and extracts a thin document. The page is crowded with type. "The last will and testament of Hector Bloom. I'm going to read it to you."

***

They sat across an immense desk from each other. Garrett chatted about nothing for half an hour. He talked first about a mutual friend he had sailed with weeks ago and belittled himself with a story of his awkward inexperience at sea. He wanted to know about her new house but did not wait for an answer. He moved on to the weather and how the humid city heat forced him to spend a fortune on dry cleaning.

Garrett Ledbetter apologized for the cluttered office, half-filled with boxed books and files, explaining he was relocating to another office with better views of the City. He did not mention where.

When Rachel asked a question, he held a silk handkerchief to his broken nose, looking for sympathy. She decided to change tactics by giving him what he wanted.

"Garrett, does it hurt?" Rachel asked.

"It's not much, not really." Which meant she was to think it a very big deal. He glanced at his watch, folded his hands, and sat back. "I've been rattling on like a fool. I have a client meeting in fifteen minutes. Now what can I do for you?"

In all the time he had been talking, not once had he mentioned the forceful comment she made in the elevator. Rachel marveled at his control. She sat as tall in the low chair as she could. She had dressed for the occasion: dark suit, black pumps, a floral silk scarf completing the ensemble. If she was going to confront Garrett in his own lair she wanted to look as impressive as she could. It was the one thing her mother had taught that proved of real value.

She leaned forward. "I want to talk about what you said."

"Rachel, I say a lot of things," he replied with a chuckle.

"About what you said to Dad. About your accusation at the rehearsal."

"Oh Christ!" Garrett interrupted. He slid open a desk drawer and withdrew a large envelope. "I almost forgot. I was going to give this to you at the wedding. Of course I never had a chance." He leaned across the desk, handing it to her. She was forced to take it. "Come on, Rachel, open it."

"Garrett, I came here to talk."

"Open it and then we'll talk. I promise."

Rachel opened the envelope. Inside was a wedding card. In the card was a check payable to Rachel Bloom-Ryan. The amount was for fifty thousand dollars. Her Dad's partner beamed at his overly-generous gift. He wasn't beaming when she laid the check back on the desk.

"Garrett, you have accused my father of fraud. You told him he was being investigated by the SEC. I want one thing. Proof."

"You don't believe me?"

"Why should I?"

"What happened to the little girl I used to know? How could you possibly think I'd make up something this serious?"

She sensed vacillation, certain the entire thing had been a ruse.

"You don't have proof, do you?" she demanded. "Do you realize my father could sue you for slander?"

Garrett pushed the intercom button on his phone. "Trish, please bring in the file." The office door opened. The PA placed a thick file on the desk in front of Garrett. Though they had known each other for almost ten years, as she left Trish did not once look at Rachel.

Garrett tapped it. "Are you sure you want to see this?"

Rachel was stunned by the thickness of the file. He picked it up, standing. He walked around the desk. With exaggerated gentleness he placed the heavy file in her lap.

"Three million dollars, Rachel. That's what your father stole. It's all right here." Garrett frowned. "Sweetie, your Daddy is going to jail."

***

The lawyer speaks in a low rumble. I strain to hear as he runs through the banal legal language. "… hereby revoke all former wills and testamentary dispositions heretofore made by me. I appoint my only son David Bloom originally of Bere Island but now of America as sole Executor of this my Will and I direct that he pays all my just debts, funeral, and testamentary expenses."

It is the final twist of a vengeful knife. Dad has encumbered me with his debts even from the grave. The lawyer glances up with a sympathetic smile. He keeps reading.

"I Hector Bloom having no other living relatives hereby give, devise, and bequeath all remaining assets to my son David Bloom. In witness hereof I have hereunto signed my name."

He holds up the paperwork. I see my father's signature.

"David, your father has left you everything." He leans into me. "Don't you understand?"

He means the house and land. I shudder. Of all the gifts my father could leave me, the house is one gift I do not want.

16

CLINICAL REPORT REVISED DIAGNOSIS

__NAME__: Bloom, David __CONSULTANT__: Cutter

When first admitted, the patient displayed extreme irritability, elevated mood, grandiosity, making unwise decisions, mania, and increased alcohol intake. His family was concerned by recent changes of behavior including delusions (psychotic episodes), increased energy, reduced sleep, and uncharacteristic theft /violence directed at his business partner. Following the fire at his house in Bere Island, first responders reported possible self-harm / harm to others. Cause of fire not yet known; currently under investigation. *Suspected suicide attempt.*

__PROGRESS WHILE IN HOSPITAL__: Patient lacks insight into his condition and is uncooperative: refusal to ingest foods; refusal to take prescribed medications; refusal to interact with consultant during one-to-one sessions. Patient deemed at extreme risk.

__CURRENT STATUS__: Catatonic

__REVISED DIAGNOSIS:__ Schizophrenia / Alcoholism⊠continuing periodic episodes of extreme mania and psychosis.

__REVISED TREATMENT__: Medication⊠Clozapine (550mg). Admission to acute hospital care. Continual monitoring.

__FURTHER ACTION__: due to ongoing patient risk, and following the initial period of evaluation and assessment, consultant will execute Three Month Renewal Order.

When the young psychiatrist finished the report, he scanned it, confident of the revised diagnosis, subsequent treatment, and further call to action. For now there was little else he could do. His patient remained in acute care, monitored by a team of medical practitioners. So far there had been no change in his condition: vital signs were stable but the patient remained unresponsive. Cutter knew catatonia often ran its course quickly. Bloom would wake. When he did Cutter would move to treat the schizophrenia. The psychiatrist remained confident.

Satisfied, the doctor printed the report, inserting the paperwork into Bloom's ever-growing file.

Despite his patient's setback the doctor took comfort in a simple fact: Nurse Healy's request for immediate release would never happen. Cutter had been right all along. The patient was a threat to himself. He required continuing treatment. When the Mental Health Tribunal considered Bloom's case, they would agree with his findings and recommendations. They would allow the psychiatrist to continue effective treatment. A renewal order for an additional three-month admission period would see to that.

Satisfied with his decision, Cutter's mind turned to the communications from the patient's daughter still sitting unanswered in his email inbox. He remembered the insistent demand for information and the threat regarding the U.S. Embassy. He had considered a variety of ways to respond but believed any words he used would raise more questions. On reflection, he thought it better to wait until Mr. Bloom recovered and was released back to the Unit. At that point, the doctor would be able to deliver a much more constructive appraisal of her father's health.

Certain that inaction was the best course of action, Cutter decided that a reply to Rachel's demands should wait. He instead turned his attention to other patients. After all, Cutter had a great deal of work to do that day.

***

The house was built by my father in the year I was born, constructed on the foundations of the home built by my grandfather, who in turn built on the foundations of my great-grandfather. I cannot prove it but I've been told the Bloom family has lived on the island for over seven generations. Oral history tells me here I have roots.

It is still a pretty house, I think, as I sit in the rental car on the island road overlooking our land. Years ago, Dad told me Mam directed its design and construction. To some it looks like an unadorned box. To my eyes, even after a thirty year absence, it is a treasure.

Two stories tall, its pebble-dashed walls are painted robin's egg blue in honor of Our Lady, in whom my mother was devoted. Large front windows let in light to rooms at the front of the house. Twin chimneys rid our home of smoke from a cast iron stove located in the living room which burns both coal and wood, as well as three other stoves scattered throughout the house. In the great room at the back, a twenty foot long plate glass window looks out on Bantry Bay and the true ocean beyond. Mam pleaded with my father for that window. I remember Dad steaming about it. "She wants views of the sea but you would think she'd want warmth instead," he complained to his mates. "Heat goes right out the window. She can get sea views just by walking outside."

Then he'd laugh, remembering how she'd won. He never said it but I think he enjoyed the views from the back window as much as she did.

The house sits on a bluff fifty feet above sea level, just below the main road, and well below the island's high point of Knockallig. Peaking at 267 meters, the hilltop crowns the western end in a glorious pile of sedimentary rock. We have twenty-seven acres of land, enough for the sheep and occasional beef cattle Dad keeps. The animals also graze on the island's commonage. A stone walled barn erected by my grandfather still stands though Dad replaced the slate roof a few years before I left. He's built a few other outbuildings during our time living there.

From my bedroom window I could see everything.

My room was on the top floor and north facing. Throughout my life on the island, I would kneel on the bed which was pushed against the back window and look out to sea. The hills protected us to the south but we'd get hit by weather from all other points on the compass. I would watch the squalls roll in from the southwest or west, north or east. The black sheets of rain and wind swept toward us until the Bay boiled whitewater and the island was caught up in them. Sometimes the rain was mixed with hail and my ears filled with drumming like gunshot as ice plundered the roof above my head and hundred kilometer an hour gusts shook the window.

On days when mist and fog didn't roll in, I could see across the finger of Bantry Bay which was the straight running between the island and the mainland, and into the harbor mouth at Castletownbere. I'd watch the trawlers head in with holds full of fish, or steaming toward the Atlantic to start new expeditions, as well as tugs and other vessels that sheltered from storms in the town's safe harbor.

From the window I could see Dad driving the old red Massey Ferguson tractor we owned on the days he cut grass in our fields for silage, and when he saw me he'd wave until I waved back. I could watch Mam work in the vegetable garden she'd dug herself, rich soil where spuds, rhubarb, carrots, onions, broad beans and other vegetables grew thick during summer months, or walk out to feed the beasts on those occasions when she went without me because I was sick or she thought me too tired from long days at school.

I could see Prince running like a madman through the tall grass of our fields no matter the weather, surprising the lunatic seagulls that sought the stale bread Mam threw into the back garden. I'd laugh at his antics as he leapt high trying to catch them but I knew him to be a good dog because he always missed as the birds took awkward flight. He'd come into the house after his chase and, panting, pad up the stairs to my room. We'd sit on the bed together, his heavy square head on my lap, until it grew dark and we could see the lights of the town glitter across the water, and the ghosty white, red, and green navigation lights of the trawlers as they steamed down the straight.

From my window Prince and I could see the lighthouse rise from its rocky base at the gap between the island and mainland, and together we'd watch until the light show started. I always wondered how far the beam stretched and imagined it could bend over the horizon all the way to Labrador which my father had shown me on the framed world map he kept in the great room. When I was a lad I thought our home was the center of the universe. For years it was the root of my being. But a frantic life has darkened my memories as if shrouded by storms years in the making.

Sitting in my rental car, studying the fields and buildings, the rain stops and the scud clears. My scalp tingles when the setting sun breaks through. It washes the house in a light of lustrous gold, clearing away the darkness. What I see is beyond real.

It is morning again. Brighter than that. Our fields shimmer in swirling sunshine. An echo of a tractor engine. A woman bent to work in a vegetable patch. As a dog barks, I smell the scent of cut grass and a loving past.

Within the depths of surreal remembering, I am struck by a thought:

Here I was happy.

Then the magical image tilts crazily. The house and lands are again covered in grey misting rainfall. I realize: I have imagined the vision of golden happiness.

I put the car in gear. Hot fear knots my stomach as I steer onto the gravel drive that will lead me home.

I do not know if I will find the courage to open the front door.

***

Nurse Healy studied the rigid arms and legs; the open eyes staring at nothing; the forehead soaked in sweat. David Bloom lay in bed, still catatonic. For the past two days she had looked in on him every four hours though it was not in her remit to do so. The acute care staff managed him and some were growing impatient at her presence.

Earlier that day she had checked his patient file with the revised diagnosis and confirmation of new medication. Every few hours it dripped through an intravenous tube and she resisted the urge to rip the needle from his arm.

Mary Healy was familiar with Clozapine. For years the drug had been used to treat schizophrenia but it was the subject of hot debate. Many psychiatrists relied on it as the drug of first choice because some research proved the drug to be effective at controlling hallucinations brought on by psychosis. However, others disagreed, calling it the drug of last resort because of its many adverse side effects. In some patients, the use of this new generation anti-psychotic could lead to significant falls in blood pressure, sudden fever, rapid heart rate and breathing, and skin abscesses. Clozapine could also cause *agranulocytoisis,* a condition which destroys white blood cells leading to a variety of infections including sepsis.

Nurse Healy had watched people die from sepsis.

Standing next to her patient, the nurse feared for him. She believed he should not have been held at the Unit in the first place. She believed he was neither Bi-polar nor schizophrenic nor alcoholic. She believed his sometimes-erratic behavior was brought on by a fire, family breakdown, and overwhelming trauma with which most people could not have coped. She believed when first admitted, he had been improperly diagnosed and improperly treated. Now the situation was growing out of control.

She had read Cutter's notes. He would issue a three-month renewal order. When her patient did not respond to revised treatment, and she believed he would not, the doctor would in all likelihood revise his diagnosis yet again. He would prescribe either an increased dosage of Clozapine, or move to another drug. When that didn't work, he would authorize another renewal order. It could become an inept merry-go-round of misjudgments that would destroy her patient's life.

The nurse again checked his pulse. It beat at a rate slightly above normal but was within acceptable limits. She checked his respiration. He breathed normally. She noted his temperature and blood pressure. Both were slightly elevated but stable.

Satisfied her patient was for now safe, Mary left the building determined to engage the woman she hoped would save David Bloom's life. To do so, she would have to skirt usual Health Board protocol. She feared she would fail. And even if she succeeded Nurse Healy realized the course of action could place her career at risk.

Her position as a psychiatric nurse could be terminated.

***

I walk up three wooden steps at the front of the house. My legs bend like putty, as if I wade through thick mud. I stand on the porch and stare at the front door, the entrance to past failures. I take the key the solicitor gave me out of a pocket. I fumble, dropping it. I breathe deep then bend to pick it up and insert it into the lock.

I open the front door of my boyhood home and step inside. As I close it, the hinges squeal just as they always squealed. I remember Mam telling my father to fix it. He never did.

I stand in the darkened entryway, listening. I hear nothing, not a single sound. The house is as dead as my father's grave.

I must make certain.

I peer into the front room, the one Mam used when she invited friends to tea. The cast iron stove is cold and dark. The walnut coffee table covered in a grey shroud of dust. A lampshade sits at an angle, drunk. The floral-print curtains Mam took so much pride in still hang from the windows, sun-bleached and stinking of dank mildew. The room lies in shadows, barren of everything, even memories.

I step into the shadowed hallway, past the stairs rising to the first floor, and into the kitchen. The old Belfast sink is full of used teacups; the pine kitchen table cluttered with plates. Remnants of cut sandwiches rest on them, covered in mold. I wonder who sat there last and why they left in such a hurry.

A small pot which once contained my mother's blooming flowers stands on the windowsill, its colorful display withered and dead.

I pass the downstairs toilet. No one used it much and I ignore it. I pass the dining room without going in. The room was only used when my mother had the priest to Sunday lunch.

I enter the rear great room and its expansive window. Here it is almost like it was when I was a kid: Dad's map of the world; his old stained easy chair; the battered leather couch; the oak table where we sometimes took tea or played cards; the place at the window where the Christmas tree was always erected, colored lights twinkling out on the Bay like merry trawlers. I scan the horizon. I cannot see much of anything through the thickening mist.

The room smells of damp abandonment.

It is growing dark. I flick the switch to the overhead light but it does not work. I try a lamp. No luck either. I suspect the electricity has been turned off at the mains. If I decide to stay here I will have to do something about light.

I know I must go upstairs.

The wooden steps creak as they always creaked, for as long as I can remember. I come to the deep return of the stairway. The platform ten-foot square; enough room for a table or a chair or even my mother's grandfather clock, where it still lives.

I stand in front of it. Neither of us move.

The clock was over one-hundred years old when I was born. It is older now by the measure of a son's lifetime. I force myself to look at it. It has not changed. I guess it to be eight foot high. Its dark walnut case is carved in a nineteenth century Irish relief: roses, bees, fuchsia, deer, heather, butterflies. A carved sphere and two lions of Ireland adorn its pinnacle. I know if I open the case I will find twin brass pendulums. I am certain they do not move because the clock is not ticking.

It is only in my head I have heard its ticking. But in the abandoned house even that is silenced.

My eyes gaze up at the clock face. I remember Mam telling me it is carved of ivory; the numbers marking time made of obsidian.

The hands of the clock point to a single hour. Ten o'clock. Which could be construed as either morning or evening but which I know is the latter. I can hear my mother instruct me as she did so many years ago at this exact spot in front of her grandfather clock. "If the big hand is on the twelve and the little hand is on the ten, what time is it Davy?"

"It is ten o'clock at night," I whisper. "It has been ten o'clock in this house since the day she died."

I am certain then. Despite the passage of time, my father never forgave me. He has left the silent clock to remind me, as if I ever needed reminding. The knot in my belly grows taut.

I ascend the rest of the stairs two at a time. I look into my parents' bedroom. The double bed is unmade; the drawers to Dad's bureau pulled open. A pile of clothing is dumped on the carpet-covered floor as if someone packed for an unexpected journey. My eyes rest on Mam's tall wardrobe. Inside, I will find my mother's clothing. Dad would not have given them away.

I walk down the hall past the family bathroom. I have to pee but can't go in. I eye the closed door that was often locked against me. The white paint has dulled with time. I listen for her mad cries but I hear only silence.

I decide to use the downstairs toilet when I am forced to go.

My bedroom is on the north side, under the eaves, at the very end of the hall. The door has been left open. When I enter, I find a surprise.

The bed is made with the gingham quilt Mam bought years ago, pulled over fat feather pillows. The room is free of dust. My fishing rod stands in the corner next to its tackle box, waiting for me. Posters of Van Morrison, The Who, Sinead O'Connor, and U2, who were popular in my youth, hang from walls. I open my chest of drawers. They are full of clean socks, underwear and T-Shirts neatly pressed.

I am gobsmacked. I had expected the room to be washed clean of me. Why has my father bothered when I have been dead to him all these years?

The curtains are closed. When I open them I see our lighthouse. It stands solid before a darkening horizon, shining with brilliance. I place a hand on my bed. I expect to feel Prince's silky head sharing the view with me. But the bedspread is cold to the touch; after thirty years, my dog long dead.

I am certain then. The house is empty. The three-thousand-mile trip to confront a past of guilt, a useless undertaking. The voices and images I experienced in America were the trick of a bewildered mind.

My father's voice is dead. It is as dead as his grave and as dead as I feel.

17

At sunrise, the kitchen filled with golden light. It rose steadily through open venetian blinds, finding a marble floor, glinting from hard appliances, at last illuminating the woman.

Laura Bloom sat alone at the island wearing a beige silk dressing gown David had bought her the previous Christmas. She had not slept that night. Since arriving home she had not ventured outside except for yesterday's aborted trip to the bank. She had not answered the landline or cell phone when they rang. Rachel had already left three messages on voice mail. She had not phoned back though she knew she must.

She had not eaten nor drunk anything except glasses of water. Thirst consumed her. She had missed two meetings with the neighborhood social committee for which she was co-chairperson. She did not think to notify the other members of her absence.

She sipped water from a crystal glass, ignoring the pain in her chest, the one radiating into her heart; the one reminding her that the world had shattered, falling apart while she was not looking. She had tried to glue it back together like a favorite coffee cup, but had failed because it would not stick. She did not have the energy to try again.

Her eyes wandered across the large sun-filled kitchen, taking an inventory.

The Amish-influenced cabinetry was painted deep mystic blue. Immense twin double-door refrigerator/freezers stood beside two stainless steel ovens with matching extractor fans. The stainless-steel sink with its instant hot water gadget was nestled within fine Calacatta marble countertops. The solid oak island with its built-in wine cooler offered comfortable seating for six. The kitchen cost a small fortune, reflecting the enormous price of the house.

It dawned on her: *From now on I'll be the only one to enjoy it. Her chest tightened. Maybe I deserve this. Maybe I tried too hard. Maybe I didn't try hard enough. Maybe I didn't take care of my family. Maybe I didn't take care of myself.*

She remembered the conversation she had with the psychiatrist in Ireland. *Maybe the doctor was wrong. Maybe I wanted too much.*

When it started, Laura Bloom could not stop the sobbing She shook with loss because she had tried so hard to make a happy life for her family. She cried because she loved them. She cried because she missed them.

She cried because perhaps she was wrong and Rachel was right: perhaps the husband whom she still loved was in the wrong place after all. However, Laura knew her stubbornness would not let her admit any of this to anyone.

"I know I'm not God," she sobbed, unable to stop the tumbling words. "We did what was best. David couldn't take care of himself. What other option did I have?"

Then she remembered what she had learned when visiting the bank, and forgot about David. His monthly salary had not been deposited into their account. Her hands pressed hard on her thighs, pushing down the fear she would lose everything she had spent the last ten years building.

Laura wiped her eyes. She breathed in, sitting up straight in the chair, pulling herself together. She knew there was only one thing to do.

She reached for her cell phone and dialed. Despite the hour Garrett answered immediately. When they finished the brief conversation, she went upstairs and showered. Having carefully applied makeup, she entered the cavernous walk-in closet-cum-dressing room. She chose deliberately, selecting a dark cashmere and wool ensemble which had protected her even on the stormiest days.

She studied her reflection in the full-length mirror, adjusting a stray piece of dark brown hair where it fell unwanted across her cheek. Then she smiled. Laura Bloom knew she always felt better when she dressed well.

"Are you sure Trish can't get you a cup of coffee?"

They sat at an intimate meeting table in the corner office which used to be her husband's. Through the window Laura watched a ferry push its way up the Hudson River. Late morning sunlight glinted off choppy water. She realized she had not heard the question.

"I'm sorry Garrett," she apologized. "What did you say?"

He studied her, seeing tired, silent anxiety. "Trish, can you bring in a thermos of coffee?"

The PA had greeted Laura with only a few words when she arrived. Usually the women talked about everything: shopping and food, the newest restaurants, the latest fashion, and the state of play of their children. But today Trish had little to say. Now the attractive assistant silently left to complete the errand. When the door closed, Garrett leaned back to consider his partner's wife.

"I'm glad you called," he said when they were alone. "I wanted to talk to you."

"I need to talk to you too."

"Ladies first."

Words came in a rush. "Garrett, why hasn't David's salary been deposited to our account? Yesterday I stopped at the bank to get some cash. I thought the ATM was out of order. Then I realized we were overdrawn. What's going on, Garrett? Did they really fire David?"

"Of course not," the executive insisted. He stood up, striding to the window. "I was angry. I shouldn't have said that. Ledbetter & Bloom is a private company, not a public one. David is still an equal partner. No one can fire him, not even our board of directors."

"Then why isn't he being paid?"

"Have you talked to Rachel?" he asked, turning to her.

"No, not yet."

"I saw her yesterday. I gave Rachel a full financial analysis of our internal findings. You should read it too."

He sat again at the table, face earnest despite the bandaged nose. "David violated a number of SEC regulations. It's a deeply troubling situation. The partnership is facing difficulties. Word got out. Some of our clients heard. We're not only being audited but now the company is bleeding cash. We've already lost some important accounts. I expect to lose more."

"Do you mean the partnership could go out of business?"

Garrett didn't respond to the question. Experience had taught him that silence often did a much better job. When she stared hard at the table, he continued.

"Laura, we can't pay David until the SEC is done with its investigation. We need to be seen to cooperate. Paying David could be construed as tacitly agreeing with his actions."

"I don't understand."

"If we pay David the SEC might think we're condoning fraud. We could be charged as accessory to a possible crime. When the SEC is finished we might be able to reinstate some sort of salary. In the meantime, he'll still get dividends assuming we make a profit this quarter."

"How long will the investigation take?"

"Christ knows. Months I'd imagine." He leaned forward, meeting her anxious gaze. "If you're stuck I can lend you some money."

The woman's chin quivered. "Thank you. We have plenty in savings."

"Are you sure about that?" he questioned.

"What do you mean?"

"Maybe you should check with your bank. Laura, we both know David hasn't been in his right mind. All I mean is, well, if he took money from the partnership, just maybe…"

Terror flashed beneath the carefully applied facial makeup. Laura snatched her bag from the floor, rising from the table.

"Don't go yet. I've got plenty of time. Trish is bringing in coffee."

"I need to see Rachel. She wants to talk to me about her father." Laura stepped toward the door.

"How is David? What's the prognosis?" he asked, rising.

"I've no idea. All I know is Rachel wants to bring him home."

"Oh," Garrett replied, following her to the door. "Laura, I think you should leave David exactly where he is."

She stopped. "Why do you say that?"

"David is locked up in a mental ward, right? The SEC can't get to him. If he came back to the States I'd bet my last dollar they'd instruct the FBI to arrest him."

"The FBI?"

"David could be subject to both criminal and civil prosecution. If that happens, the repercussions to you of a personal financial nature would be severe." He saw that his words made no sense to the woman. "Laura, David could not only end up in jail but any judgment and fines could cost your family millions. Do you understand?"

The color drained from her face.

"If I were you, I'd tell that to Rachel, too," Garrett stressed. "Mind you it's only a suggestion."

His words finally registered. Again she turned toward the door. He had one more nail to drive home, just to make certain.

"Oh, and Laura. Before you go. Can an old family friend offer one final piece of advice?"

"What's that?"

The man in the three-piece suit took her hand. "It's time you learned to protect yourself."

"I don't understand."

"It's going to be a rough ride, Laura. At all costs you have to put yourself first. You've worked too hard to lose it all. Not at this point. Be careful, okay?"

Her knees buckled. For a moment he thought she might faint. He gripped her arm, steadying her. But she seemed made of steel. As he watched he could see her visibly gather new strength. It was one of the reasons why, on some levels, he admired this woman.

She pulled her arm away. "Thank you Garrett. I'll be just fine." Laura turned and marched from the room.

When she left he called his PA. "Trish, ask Peter to come up."

It was such a pity, Garrett thought as he waited for the firm's financial controller. Things could have turned out so differently.

Having seen to his partner's wife—his ex-partner's wife, he reminded himself—Garrett readied the next part of his plan. He knew he would relish it.

On her way home Laura stopped at the bank. The bank manager was free. She explained what she wanted to do. She was relieved when he did not ask questions. When she left she held a new checkbook. A new ATM card and PIN number would be mailed in the next few days.

Laura had stripped almost everything from the joint savings accounts she owned with David. Just over two hundred thousand dollars in cash had been deposited to her new bank account. She was the sole signatory.

As she climbed into the car, she rationalized her action, knowing it was the only choice. Garrett was right. She must do everything she could to protect herself. She knew she must also do something about their joint investments. However, she realized she would have to talk to Peter about those. In addition to his job as the firm's Financial Controller, Peter had long helped the couple with their family finances. Laura had always found him to be a kind, understanding man. She knew he would understand this time, too.

Arriving home, she made one more call. Two hours later a locksmith came by and changed all the locks in the house. When he handed her the new set of keys, she clutched them hard, the cut edges biting into her palm. Even if Rachel brought her father home, he could no longer walk into the house unannounced. The fact that Laura's action was illegal did not dawn on her.

With her day's chores finished, she knew she should phone Rachel. However, Laura was exhausted. She decided she would talk to her daughter after she rested.

Laura locked all the doors, went upstairs, and fell asleep alone in her bedroom's immense, luxuriously covered bed. It was the best sleep she'd had in over a week.

***

"It can't be true," Rachel blurted.

She stared hard at the dining room table. The massive oak surface was strewn with paperwork from the file Garrett had given to her. A yellow legal pad was covered with extensive handwritten notes and figures. A calculator and two laptops rested near. An Excel spreadsheet, open on Jacob's computer, was filled with neat rows and columns of numbers they had constructed as part of their analysis.

"Look again. That's what it says." Jacob sat back in his chair, rubbing both hands over tired eyes. "Three million dollars. Just as Garrett said."

"I still don't believe it," Rachel retorted, sitting in the chair beside him.

The couple had worked into the early hours tearing apart the various financial reports. They had risen at dawn to continue analyzing the profit and loss accounts and balance sheets; the statement of sources and uses of cash; the bank statements; the stock purchases and client account balances. None of it made for happy reading. Hoping to prove Garrett wrong, they had instead uncovered an uncomfortable truth: based on the analysis, Rachel's father was a thief and a liar. The documents proved it.

Jacob shoved the laptop toward her and pointed to the Excel cash flow analysis.

"It all adds up. Every month for the past eighteen months, client trades were ordered but never executed. The cash allocated for the trades was pulled from the correct client account but was never used to pay for stock purchases. Instead, whoever had their finger in the cookie jar did this." Jacob reached for a piece of paper and a list of typed numbers. Beside each number a cash balance appeared."The cash ended up in these off-shore accounts. Add together all the cash in these accounts and it exactly matches what was moved from the client accounts for the purported stock trades."

Rachel studied the list."But these are numbered accounts, not named accounts. There's no proof they were my father's."

"On the surface I agree. But then there's this. Read it again." He pulled over another accusing piece of paper. This one was a four-paragraph letter typed on Security and Exchange Commission letterhead.

In terse language it disclosed that the SEC had embarked on a full audit of Mr. David Bloom. Initial discovery had led the federal agency to a number of off-shore bank accounts and cash balances, information which it was now providing to Ledbetter & Bloom stakeholders. Furthermore, the agency had proof that the accounts had been opened, and were owned by, the person in question. Finally, the letter stated that full findings would be provided only when the audits of Ledbetter & Bloom and Mr. David Bloom were completed. A separate page demanded an exhaustive list of additional financial information from the firm.

Rachel took her husband's hand."What do we do?"

"Well, it seems to me we have two options." Jacob took a sip of coffee from a large mug, but finding it cold, put it down. "We could, of course, just give up. We could assume this information is true and correct, and that Garrett's accusations are completely valid."

"And if we do, what happens to Dad?"

Jacob shrugged. "I don't know the law in this area very well. I assume Dad will be offered some sort of plea bargain and fined, or face trial. Sweetie, if he's convicted, I suspect he could go away for a long time."

"Is there any other option?"

"There's also a completely different way of looking at this."

"Which is?"

He studied her. "We assume it's all a lie."

"What do you mean?" Rachel said, sitting back.

Jacob laid his hand flat on the SEC letter. "What would happen if we viewed everything in here as phony. All the balance sheets. The profit and loss statements. The bank statements. The foreign accounts. The SEC letter. All of it. It's only a smokescreen that's covering up something else."

"But what would it cover?"

"Damned if I know."

Rachel thought for a minute. "Why don't we just phone the SEC and ask them about the audits? If they could give us more information we might discover what's at the bottom of this."

"They're not going to tell us anything, Legally, we're not an interested party."

"Then how do we prove it's all fake? Assuming it is?"

"That is the three-million-dollar question." Jacob considered the ceiling, thinking it over. "My law firm uses a forensic accountant. She's pretty good. If it's okay with you I think I'll have a word with her. I wouldn't mind handing her a copy of this entire mountain of financial rubble and see what she thinks."

"It's okay with me. What else?"

He pulled a Ledbetter & Bloom internal memorandum from the pile of paperwork. "I also think we should talk to the Financial Controller. This guy here. Peter Lawrence." Jacob pointed to the signature. "Do you know him?"

"I've met him once. He wouldn't remember me. Mom knows him, of course."

"Maybe you could ask her for an introduction. But we'll have to approach him carefully. I doubt Garrett would appreciate it if he knew we wanted to interview the firm's financial officer."

"Anything else?"

He grinned. "How about some sack-time with my new wife?"

She grinned back. "Only when I see some results, Counselor. In the meantime…"

"In the meantime I know you're going to be busy."

"What do you mean?"

"First," he replied, standing up and walking behind her, "you're driving over to see your mother later today." He began rubbing her shoulders.

"Why do you say that?" she asked, surprised because she planned on driving over that afternoon.

"Because you haven't heard from her in days and you're worried about her."

Rachel stretched, feeling his strong fingers work cramped shoulder muscles. "It seems you know me too well. What else, Counselor?"

"Second, you're going back to see your Dad."

"Now how did you know that? I haven't told you yet."

"Because I heard you talking with his nurse last night. I also noticed the Aer Lingus webpage you left open on your laptop. And, you happened to leave a note of the confirmed booking and flight numbers right here." He slid a scrap of paper in front of her.

"And here I thought you were a mental giant and read my mind." She kissed him. "You know what?"

"What?"

"That idea you had about sack-time? Maybe you've earned it."

"Man, and here I was thinking I'd already offended my wife."

She stretched high and kissed him again. "You'll never offend me, Counselor. I love you too much." They took the stairs together, two at a time, giggling like children all the way to the bedroom.

An hour later they sat down at the living room table, back at work.

***

When on the previous evening Rachel had phoned for the latest on her father's condition, Mary Healy had nothing new to say. David Bloom remained in Acute Care. He was still catatonic. Clozapine and assorted nutrients still dripped into his veins. Though he remained stable the nurse reiterated that Rachel's presence could be of enormous value.

"I fly into Dublin in three days. I'll let you know when I arrive in Bantry," Rachel had confirmed.

"By that time I hope to have some better news," Mary replied.

They promised to keep in touch.

Mary's reference to 'better news' meant much more than an improvement in her patient's physical condition, though that would be a wonderful outcome. The nurse had not yet shared with Rachel the additional measures she was taking for her father. Ethically, Mary believed she had an obligation to confide her lack of confidence in David's psychiatrist, as well as her skepticism about the present treatment plan, to Rachel. However, she decided to wait until the young woman arrived. She knew her explanation would prove far more comforting if conducted face-to-face.

With her patient still catatonic, Mary became even more determined to intervene in his care. As she finished the call with Rachel, and though she had not said a word, the nurse felt she was making progress. It was far too early to be certain that her efforts would bear fruit, however, and Mary knew she still had many more hurdles to climb.

At the end of her shift, Mary left the Unit but rather than waiting for the bus to take her home, decided to once again look in on her patient. On the way to David's hospital room, she had run into the Acute Care Charge Nurse who had given Mary a nasty look. Not that it made much difference to Mary.

Her patient remained just as she had left him four hours earlier: unmoving but with all vital signs stable. Tired, she sat for a moment in a chair next to him. It had been a long day. She took heart in knowing she had made something of a breakthrough.

She had at last made contact with Anne Tenbrooke.

That morning, when Tenbrooke returned her call, Mary had to take it in the Psychiatric Unit's Reception area. She listened rather than talked, afraid her nursing colleagues might guess the contents of a conversation she decided to keep quite secret. She then made excuses to Cutter, stating she had to run out to visit an aging aunt. Cutter only remarked that he hoped she would keep the visit brief.

But rather than go to her aunt's suburban home, Mary took the bus to a small medical clinic on the north side of Bantry. Tenbrooke had come down from Dublin for private consultations with locally-based patients. She had managed to squeeze Mary into a busy day.

Though Mary had never met the psychiatrist, she had attended a number of lectures the formidable woman had given. The psychiatrist's energy, compassion, and intelligence had left a lasting impression.

Mary had learned that Anne Tenbrooke had practiced psychiatry for almost thirty years. She still maintained a practice in Dublin. However, her interests had branched out over the course of her career. At the age of forty-one, Tenbrooke had received a master's degree in Legal Medicine from Ireland's Royal College of Surgeons. Her time was now split between treating mental health patients and protecting their rights. She had already assessed thousands of victims of institutional abuse, worked countless hours on Mental Health Tribunals, and was frequently called into court to provide expert testimony. If anyone could help David Bloom, Mary believed Anne Tenbrooke could.

When the women sat down in the clinic's small meeting room, Mary was again impressed by the professionalism of the woman combined with a sense of moral justice that was beyond reproach. Tenbrooke's closely cropped blond hair and steel grey eyes, combined with the light grey suit she wore, spoke of confidence, great ability, and determination to protect those she served. But the smile she wore also demonstrated an innate compassion.

When Dr. Tenbrooke asked Mary to describe the situation, the nurse did so without reservation because she knew the doctor could be trusted. Tenbrooke did not use a device to record their conversation. She did not take notes. Instead, Mary knew the doctor would remember everything because she listened without interruption.

At the end of the hour they both sat back. For a full five minutes the doctor studied the ceiling in silent thought.

"Do you think you can help him?" Mary asked.

"Perhaps, but I can't promise anything." Tenbrooke leaned across the table. "However, if I can prove what you say is true, I'll turn the wolves on Cutter. I'll do my best to get your patient out of there and into appropriate care."

"What can I do to help?"

"For now, nothing. But please remember—and you know this: if I was punter I wouldn't make a bet on winning because it has long odds." The advocate sat back, considering. "During the tribunal, it will be a Catch Twenty-Two situation. Everyone will defer to Cutter because he's the consulting psychiatrist. He'll say 'I alone have professional insight into this patient's condition. I alone know how to assess and treat him.' In my view it's an abuse of power.

"As you know more than most, psychiatrists have huge power and authority," Tenbrooke continued. "Everyone defers to them because they are the so-called experts. But while most professionals would agree that psychiatry is undoubtedly the weakest of the medical sciences, psychiatrists hold more power than any other type of medical practitioner. As far as I'm concerned, it's folly, often unethical, and more to the point, we simply don't deserve it."

"But there's still a chance to help him?"

"There's always a chance. But for now, and as far as we're both concerned, this conversation never took place. Isn't that correct?" Tenbrooke concluded.

"Of course it's correct," Mary replied, caught in the warmth of the doctor's smile.

Now, almost a working day later, sitting with David in the Acute Care unit, Mary reviewed the conversation. She knew for the first time her patient would be given the voice of a determined advocate: a professional voice; an insistent one; a voice that would seek to give meaning to his silence.

The nurse noticed the flutter of eye movement beneath her patient's closed eyelids. She knew David was experiencing Rapid Eye Movement. REM was often present in catatonia, which was a condition known for its roller-coaster psychiatric effects on patients. During periods when a patient was gripped by full-blown catatonia, the entire body was often rigid and unmoving. During other periods, so-called latent periods, patients could appear more relaxed, almost quiescent. Studies had revealed that REM increased at the end of these latent periods, during which it was thought patients dreamed.

REM could also be present during the latter stages of the illness, when symptoms were improving. Mary knew REM could therefore be an indicator that a catatonic patient was about to wake.

She studied her patient. He breathed evenly. His face had been freshly scrubbed by the Acute Care team. For all intents and purposes he looked healthy. But the nurse knew he was not. She glanced at the monitor. His vitals were still normal. His temperature was elevated by a half degree but was no cause for alarm. She felt his face and hands. They were clammy but not hot. If his vitals were still normal in an hour's time she would go home.

Nurse Healy took David's hand. She said a silent prayer that he would soon gain consciousness. She also prayed about his dream. Whatever he dreamed she hoped it made him happy.

In the chair, the nurse made herself comfortable and waited.

18

The day dawns cold with showers and low overcast. I look out my bedroom window. The fields lie below me, lifeless and fallow, stretching to a steel-grey sea. Water stagnates in the choked drainage ditches my father and I dug when I was a boy. My mother's vegetable garden is overgrown, yellowed with withered weeds.

In the morning light I am even more certain. No one is home.

I slept in the house last night. I was too tired to drive into the village to seek refuge at the hotel or a local B&B. Or perhaps I had no desire to meet anyone who might ask questions. Instead I found a box of candles in the kitchen drawer where Mam always kept them. The box was unopened. When I picked it up I wondered if she had held it; if my hand touched the same places hers had touched. I opened it anyway.

Last night the house came alive with the golden glow of candlelight. I slept in my boyhood bed, hugged by the warmth of gingham blankets, candlelight bathing my room because I fell asleep before I thought to extinguish it.

I did not dream.

Now it is morning. The candle has melted, cold wax covering the brass candleholder like brittle bones, running down onto the windowsill where it makes a hard, white pool. I open the curtains and stand at the rain-spattered window contemplating the day ahead. I realize I do not want the house because I cannot stay long. It holds too much suffering. Today I will contact the solicitor, Harrington. I will instruct him to put it on the market. I will find a place to live in the mainland town until the house sells. Then I will leave and go… I will go—

My dull brain grasps the brutality: I have no idea where I will go because there is nowhere left.

I gaze at my hand. It shakes again because I am alone. I think back on what has happened over the course of only days. I know I am lucky to be alive.

I dress and walk down the hall past the upstairs bathroom that will forever remain silent. The stairs creak as I make my way downstairs. I hurry by the clock and its accusing 10PM memory. I pee and brush my teeth in the downstairs toilet. I do not shower but rub a washcloth soaked with cold water over my face, arms, and torso. It will do. When I walk into the kitchen I realize there is nothing to eat because no one lives here. Despite my reluctance I drive to the harbor.

The small square is deserted when I arrive, the parking lot unoccupied. It still rains as I get out of the car. I glance toward the deserted pier. I remember how in another life a young man met a young girl on a day much like today. But she is not there and I push the memory away.

The bell of the shop door jingles when I push it open, just as it jingled when I was a lad. A woman stands behind the counter, heavyset and dowdy, the same woman I saw at the cemetery. As I enter I feel her assessing look, the one Islanders give any stranger. Our eyes meet and in her face I see the curious possibility of recognition. I hurry to the shelves. Because there is no electricity at the house I keep my purchases simple: a loaf of bread; a box of cereal; milk; butter; a packet of sliced ham; a small bag of apples.

When I finish I approach the counter. The woman smiles but I see no welcome in her eyes. She tots up what is owed. I do not have much cash so I give her a credit card. Because it is an American card the PIN will not work and I must sign my name.

When she sees the signature she is certain. Her suspicious gaze turns to one of cruel remembering. I grab an empty cardboard box from a pile near the door and pack my purchases. As I turn to leave I hear the Tsk-Tsk of accusation.

"Davy Bloom," she says as if my name is a criminal discovery. "I didn't think you'd have it in you to come back. Sure, isn't it a blot on your mother's memory?"

I am certain she fills her departed father's shoes as the village gossip. Soon every person on the island will know of my arrival.

I jog to the car, throwing the box of provisions into the passenger seat. My heart races; my face burns with humiliation. My world tilts at a violent new angle. I glance to the pier.

The ferry has returned and is tied fast to the pilings. A young man stands in the rain, alone on the cement dock, carrying a single busted suitcase. I remember he is doing his best not to cry. We search for our girl but she has not come. We suspect her aunt will not let her be seen with us. Or worse, Dolores rejects us because of the false accusation, our forced exile, and gutless inability to stand up to our father.

We need to talk to her. But she is not there. Alone we board the ferry. As it departs we look back at our village. Our hearts break.

I know the vision cannot be real because it is thirty years old.

In the car I stamp on the accelerator, tires throwing wet pebbles, running from the memory that is much more than a waking dream. I manage to steer out of the village and onto the high road. My eyes blur with tears. I do not see the hairpin curve. I turn at the last minute. Skidding, I bring the car to a stop in the middle of the road.

Oh God, I hear myself whisper between frightened breaths. *Please, please let the visions stop. Goddammit, give me peace! I beat up the steering* wheel in angry frustration as if I beat up myself.

I must have fallen asleep. When I wake the car is still in the middle of the road. The sun is out. Its golden light has swept away the rain. I open the car door and step out. I hear a tractor's engine in the distance. I stand taking in the view below the road. I am awed by what I see.

Our house glitters in sunshine. Many of the fields are newly mowed. A red Massey Ferguson is cutting the last section of the nearest field as Dad makes silage.

A dog barks. A black Lab bounds from tall grass which has escaped the threshing. He scampers toward a flock of seagulls who busy themselves near neat vegetable planters rich with blooming growth. The birds scatter, flying toward freedom.

At the door the porch light has been left on. It beckons with electric brightness.

I am stunned. I get back into the car telling myself I am still sleeping. But I am not. I know the visions have come again but this time with a vengeful realism that is impossible. I steel myself. I know if I am to ever take my life back I must silence the ghosts of my past.

But as I start the car a lopsided grin furrows my face. I know what I see is crazy; what I must do madness. Yet I feel the sudden titillation of homecoming.

The nurse must have fallen asleep. She did not know what woke her. She looked around the room. No one else was there. She checked the monitor. His temperature was still a half-degree above normal but stable. She checked his blood pressure. It was slightly low. She knew both readings could be due to the Clozapine in his system.

Mary Healy leaned over her patient. His forehead was beaded with sweat. His eyelids still shifted. They fluttered in synchronicity with his dreams.

When I open the front door the house is full of the rich smell of Mam's baking. I can hear her singing. It is a tune from *Finian's Rainbow*. My father always told her it was a stupid film and an embarrassment to the Irish.

"Sure, did you ever see a Leprechaun?" he would tease her. "Or a pot of gold for that matter?" I could remember her laughter.

"Hector, can you not at least give me my dreams?"

I remembered after her sister died, on the days she was well, Mam took refuge in the magic of the film's story and its song of impossible love.

Standing in the front hallway to our home I can hear her singing the song, though I know it is madness.

"How are things in Glocca Morra? Is that little brook still leaping there?" she sings in a pretty baritone voice. Her song leads me to the kitchen.

She stands at the counter wearing the soft yellow dress I remember, the one scattered with floral prints, and a pink apron covers it, spattered with the snow of flour. Mam has both hands in a mixing bowl. Sunlight from the window burnishes her fawn-brown hair in a halo of brilliance. Beyond her, a pot of colorful flowers blooms in the warm sun.

I watch as she washes her delicate hands at the sink then checks the oven. She removes a full tray of baked scones and their aroma overpowers me. She piles them on a wire rack set in the middle of the table and opens the kitchen window wide.

"Davy! Davy! Come in now. They're ready!" she cries. "Bring your father!"

Tears prick my eyes at the familiar call.

"Mam?" I ask in awe but she does not hear me. She closes the window and busies herself making a pot of tea. I walk closer. "Mam? Mam, it's me." But she still does not hear.

I cannot believe I am again seeing my mother. My heart races. I am light-headed and unsteady.

The front door squeals as it opens. My seventeen-year-old-self bounds into the kitchen. He wears a faded pair of jeans, a thick red Cork jersey, and a pair of green Wellingtons. I well remember the jersey. Dad brought it home following Cork County's All-Ireland Hurling championship win. I took it with me to America. I wore it until it was beyond repair then threw it away.

"Mam, they smell a swank!" Davy proclaims, washing his hands at the sink.

"Sit down and eat," she replies and plucks a long blade of grass from his sweat-filled hair. He sits at the table as Mam pours us a cup of tea. I remember this. I know what will happen next. He will reach for a scone. And then

"Fuck it!" He bends, retrieving the dropped scone.

"And since when did you swear? Don't eat that one. Give it to Prince. Get another."

The front door bangs open, squealing again. The dog bounds into the room, already begging. My Dad follows. His hands are covered with dirt and grease, hair filled with cut grass. He also washes his hands at the sink.

I must sit. I am seeing my father. I am witnessing my family's love. I am mad as a brush.

"Smells good in here, Rose."

"Hector, when will you fix that door?"

Dad grins, drying his hands on the blue overall that is his favorite, and sits at the table.

"When you stop giving out to me."

He picks up a warm scone and butters it. He turns to his son. "Your Mam's beautiful when she's giving out, isn't she Davy?"

I see Mam blush. I know she is happy and so am I. Dad adds strawberry jam. He takes a huge bite. "Who's the best cook on the island?" he asks and leans over to kiss Mam on the cheek.

"Mam!" I say needing to share their joy but no one hears.

"Mam!" Davy beams. He feeds Prince the wayward scone then studies our mother. "You're having a good day today, aren't you Mam?"

Her eyes sparkle like bright jewels.

"When I'm with you two it's always a good day," she says. Her face holds too much joy. Her eyes glitter with too much happiness.

We both know our Mam is lying though my father does not see it. I hear foreboding in the pit of my growling stomach. We sit at the table nursing our doubt. They do not see me and I know they are not real. They are only a figment of my shipwrecked mind.

Then I remember why I am here. I have been swept away by remembrances but I know I must get down to business. I must drag myself back to reality by extinguishing my past.

"Go away," I order. They do not hear. They must hear. "I told you to go away!" My voice fills the room but it makes no difference. I get up, storming from the table to stand rigidly at the sink. I close my eyes willing the visions to be gone.

"Do you want another scone Davy?"

"You are not real. You cannot be real," I hiss through clenched teeth.

"Sure."

I cannot help but open my eyes. Mam pushes the rack toward my younger self. The smell is so powerful I cannot help myself. I step closer, reaching toward the mountain of baked goods. My shaking hand feels their heat.

"Oh Christ; Oh Jesus bloody Christ, help me," I whisper because I know for certain I am cracked.

Prince looks up from the floor where he finishes the destroyed scone. He grins and his tail thumps the floor.

"Davy, have another."

Davy gets up, kissing our Mam on the cheek. "I'd better get back to work."

"Work?" our Mam teases. "Would work perhaps be a young woman named Dolores?"

His cheeks redden. "Ah Mam."

Dad winks at us. "You owe me half a day, you hear me Davy?"

"Deal!" Davy says and bolts from the room.

I follow him. As we both run upstairs I rant:

"You are imaginary. You are killing me. This is not real. It is impossible!" The steps creak as he runs. I realize my feet do not make a sound on the old wooden stairs.

I stop when I hear the ticking. Mam's grandfather clock is alive. Its hands, moving in easy synchronicity, say it is almost noon. I shudder because I know it is only an illusion, a trick of a deranged mind.

We walk into our bedroom. I watch as he pulls open a drawer, taking out a clean T-Shirt. He looks in the mirror and frowns as he combs the curling brown hair. I remember we want to make an impression on the girl who is now much more than a friend.

"Forget about her," I order. "You leave her. She does nothing but haunt you."

The thought of Dolores makes him smile. "I remember what you're thinking," I carp. "You're thinking of the ring you gave her yesterday. You wonder if she wore it to bed last night." The young face in the mirror turns more serious. "Now you're thinking you want to tell Mam and Dad we gave her the ring. I told you. Forget about her. You lose her!"

Prince runs in. He jumps on the bed, panting, looking first at his young master then toward me. I swear he huffs in greeting.

"Oh God. Oh God!" I shout. "Just go away. Go away, all of you! You don't exist!"

I fall to the bed, hands over eyes, pressing tight. They will be gone, I tell myself. I will turn and find nothing but an empty room. I will banish them from my soul. I will know peace.

I hear a distant rumble.

"What the feck?" he wonders. Davy peers through the window, his strong young body as solid and as alive as I am. "Fuckin' hell," he says and

I look too. Dark cumulus taller than we've ever seen fills the northwestern horizon in a dense line of squalls.

I lurch from the vision which at last confirms what day it is.

Dad rushes into the room. He wears a raincoat. "Davy, I need to get to the boat. The wind will be getting up and I want to check the ropes. Stay here and mind your Mam."

"What about Dolores?" he objects. "Mam's having a good day. She'll be fine on her own."

Our father's hooded gaze tells us our mother will never be fine on her own. "You can see your girl another time. Promise me. Stay with your mother. I won't be long."

Davy's nod is as thick as a mule's. Dad leaves knowing his son will obey. But I know on this occasion my father is wrong.

Davy sits on the bed. I shiver because I know what will happen next.

Mam walks in with a cheerful smile. My younger self looks at the ground. He does not see the secret plan hatching in her eyes nor hears the loving manipulation in her voice.

"What's this your father is saying? He wants you to stay here?"

"Don't worry, Mam. I'll see Dolores later."

"Don't be ridiculous. You can't disappoint your girl." Her voice is solid and unwavering. I marvel at how well she masks the storm beneath. "I'm not a child, Davy. I'm perfectly capable of taking care of myself. That's why your father makes you stay, isn't it. Because you don't trust me."

"Mam…" She stops him with a firm hand on his wrist.

"All that happened an age ago. I'm fine now. Don't you know how foolish it makes me feel to have you all watching?"

"Don't listen to her," I warn.

"I promised Dad I'd stay."

Mam pouts with a look of cloying hurt that always destroys us. "Not even my own son will trust me."

"Yes, I do." He measures her and I see his promise break in two. "Are you sure you'll be all right?"

Her smile is warm and convincing. "Of course I will. Please stop fussing."

My stomach knots. The naïve fool is falling for it. "Davy, don't do it. Don't believe her."

"Dad won't be long," Davy crows and I remember why we are so comfortable with our decision to leave. With Dad, we'd swept each room two days ago. We found all her old hiding places. We are certain not an ounce of drink remains in the house.

He kisses her on the cheek.

"I told you to stop fussing. Now go see your girl."

"Don't go!" I shout.

"I'll be home soon."

"Take your time." He is out the door.

"You fool! You fucking idiot! She's lying!"

When the front door slams shut, Mam's sneaking smile of madness, the one she conceals so well, crawls across her face.

"Oh God Mam. Don't do it," I plead.

The dog whines. I see worry in his loyal eyes as his tail beats the floor.

My fragile, loving, broken mother strokes Prince's head. "You won't tell anyone, will you boy? They'll never understand."

She hums the refrain to the old American film musical but this time there is only haunting sadness. Then she is gone to the kitchen on a well-charted course.

I should do something. *How?* I leer to myself. *They are ghosts. What can I do to change anything?*

"This is the past, dammit!" I roar. "They can't see me!" I sit on the bed, futile tears coursing down my cheeks. I know I am caught in the vice of madness.

I feel the warm wetness of a dog's tongue licking my hands. When I open my eyes I find Prince standing at my knees.

"Prince?" His tail beats the floor. "Prince can you see me?" I hear his acknowledging huff.

Yes, I convince myself. *He is real.*

I remember seeing him at the Hilton hotel days before. I remember his warmth as I held him. I remember thinking he had found me and would take me home, rescuing me from the pain I suffered. But I also remember my conclusion regarding that visit: that I was ill. That the visions were only an assault by a sick mind.

Prince huffs again. He waits for me. His body quivers with excitement.

I reach out in disbelieving wonder. As I run my hands through his soft thick coat I am certain. My dog, dead for years, has come back.

The room flashes in the light of lightning. Thunder cracks close at hand. Hail hits the window like gunshot. My mind plays with the possibilities.

If Prince is real, is Mam real too? And if Mam truly is real,

Maybe this time, maybe this one time, I can save her.

Nurse Healy was alarmed by the sudden rise in temperature. It was now 37.7ºC. While still within the envelope considered normal, it was high nonetheless. She felt his hands and face. Both were still clammy but now cold as ice.

***

I wake. I cannot remember falling asleep or where I am. In the distance I hear the rumble of thunder. Hail hits the car windows hard, like gunshot. But I am wrong because it is not hail. I roll down the window. A woman stands near the car holding an umbrella, a hat covering a nest of greying auburn hair. She is the one who has knocked on the window. She stares at me, wondering, with clear hazel eyes.

"I heard you'd come back but I wouldn't believe it," Dolores whispers.

For a moment I think I am still dreaming. Then I realize what I see is true. My girl stands in the rain inches from me.

I climb out of the car. I think she will run because of my abandonment so many years before. Then she is in my arms. This time I will not let go.

When his temperature rose to 38ºC, the nurse went to find help. She returned less than a minute later with an Acute Care specialist in tow. She watched as the doctor examined their patient. When he was done he assured her David's vitals were within acceptable limits.

Yes, his temperature was elevated. Yes, his blood pressure had fallen slightly. Both were due to the anti-psychotic drug. When he growled that he had to leave to attend other patients, the nurse objected. She wanted constant observation. Exasperated by the nurse, the doctor told her it wasn't possible due to staffing shortages. He reminded her that other team members would look in on him as part of their usual rounds. When the doctor left, the nurse believed it would not be enough.

Mary Healy knew that if she went home her patient would be alone. No relative or friend would sit with him. Not even an acquaintance.

The nurse pulled the chair closer to her patient. This time she would not sleep.

19

Peter Lawrence hurried to the corner office in answer to the unwanted summons, caught in a vice at least in part of his own making. As he strode through the busy offices of Ledbetter & Bloom, the financial controller could not help but think what had led him to this disturbing situation. Like many, in 2008 he had faced financial ruin when the Great Recession had swept across the United States, then the rest of the world. A day prior to disaster he believed he was poised for redemption. Unfortunately, fate had not smiled on him then nor, he thought, would it ever.

Peter's previous life had been fraught with indecision and difficulties. Twenty years earlier, he had married late in life. A bitter divorce followed eight years later which had halved his meager assets. Ongoing alimony payments for his ex-wife's maintenance and only son's upbringing⊠a son who remained forever estranged since the dissolution of his marriage⊠caused ongoing headaches and heartache. But he had found refuge in a small New York investment firm and there worked hard to rebuild a future. Though initially unfamiliar with the world of financial trading, Peter had become a trusted member of the accounting staff due to his tireless efforts, and astute attention to numbers and corporate structures. He husbanded his monthly salary, and upon advice of traders with whom he worked, invested wisely. Or so he thought.

Ten years ago, on the day before the great crash, he had looked forward to early retirement and a period of well-deserved peace. Then the market imploded and the small firm went to the wall. His investments evaporated. He was unable to make court-ordered alimony payments much less pay for the rudiments of living. Peter thought himself in a hopeless situation.

When the two younger work colleagues approached him with an offer for a position in the startup financial services firm of Ledbetter & Bloom, he did not think twice. He vaguely knew both men. While somewhat skeptical of Ledbetter's flamboyance he had always trusted Bloom's disciplined work ethic. Peter told the partners he was in.

For ten years Peter had reported directly to Bloom. They had learned to rely on and trust each other. He was proud to say he had become a confidante of such a well-meaning man. However, it had not lasted.

What Ledbetter had confided to him earlier in the year, the complaint about Mr. Bloom's performance, accusing his partner of administrative and client errors, Peter did not pay much notice, thinking it was only hubris and hot air. He had no cause to believe the accusations because he never detected a mistake on Bloom's part. But Ledbetter's comment had planted a seed. Whenever he met with Mr. Bloom he studied him closely, listening to the subtext of his comments and actions. Peter detected exhaustion in the younger man's voice. He suspected lapses of judgment. He began to worry that what Ledbetter said was true.

It was only later that he realized he was being groomed as an accomplice in an amoral act of corporate piracy and betrayal.

When Ledbetter approached him with the unlikely proposal, Peter balked. What the firm's partner intimated was unethical and illegal. But Ledbetter had him over a barrel and both knew it because he understood Peter's financial struggles. If the financial controller did not cooperate, Ledbetter would find someone else. Peter was long enough in the tooth to realize that if the partner's cutthroat plan came to fruition, if he ejected Bloom from the company, the financial controller would be next up for extermination.

Peter was sixty-seven years old. Even with the investments he had made during his tenure at Ledbetter & Bloom, and if he included monthly Social Security income, the money would not last him through retirement. Every time he ran a pro forma the figures always pointed to a stark financial future: he would die destitute. For that reason, he had agreed to Garrett's demands but only because he had no choice. If he resigned from the firm, and at his age, he knew he would be unemployable.

Since then he had followed Garrett's instructions to the letter. However, it had come at a cost. As Peter hurried down a hallway leading to Mr. Bloom's old corner office, he knew he had come to hate his new overseer, as well as himself, for the profound cowards he believed both to be.

As he knocked on the office door Peter glanced at the PA. Sitting at her desk, Trish's greeting was filled with remorseful longing for the old days when both worked for a foolishly trusting but honest man. When he entered the office, Peter found an elegantly dressed imposter sitting behind his former employer's desk.

"Peter. Have a seat," Ledbetter ordered with impatient bonhomie. Peter waited while his new boss scanned a report containing a pro forma analysis of anticipated future Assets Under Management and subsequent client fee income which the financial controller had prepared earlier.

"This is good, Peter. Very good. Much better than planned. Do you think the rest of our clients will fall in line?"

Peter shrugged. "Most of them. The market is strong and the firm's investment performance positive. It's human nature. Most clients won't risk the success of a proven financial track record."

He watched as Ledbetter rose from the desk, striding to the window and its expansive views which his former partner had once enjoyed. "Your analysis means NewCo can count on over a billion under management and ten million in fee income for our first year," Ledbetter cheered. "Well done, Peter. You should be proud."

But Peter was not proud. The ruse had been easy. The original gambit had, of course, been Ledbetter's idea. His instinct to hit Bloom with the lie of stolen client funds when at his lowest emotional ebb had achieved results even beyond Ledbetter's expectations. Re-creating the various fictional financial spreadsheets which had been presented to Mr. Bloom's daughter had been child's play. Peter had balked at creating the fake SEC paperwork and fictitious numbered offshore accounts, but when Ledbetter reminded him of his precarious personal financial position, he had complied.

Bloom's subsequent psychological meltdown, as well as his family's confusion, proved fortuitous to the traitorous business partner. Ledbetter had leveraged the welcome situation into a ruthless business plan which was presented to the firm's clients.

PRIVATE & CONFIDENTIAL

To: [client name]
From: Garrett Ledbetter, Senior Partner, Ledbetter & Bloom
Dear Valued Client:
As your investment partner, it is our duty to inform you of a recent, unfortunate series of events, resulting in swift but necessary actions required to protect this firm, our clients' interests, and your historically high returns on investment:

David Bloom, partner and administrative officer of Ledbetter & Bloom, has experienced a severe psychiatric breakdown.

1. Mr. Bloom is being held in an Irish psychiatric unit three-thousand miles distant. He is therefore no longer in a position to carry out his duties and responsibilities as a partner and officer of this firm. Due to this unforeseen situation, Mr. Bloom has been released from his position with immediate effect.

2. It has come to light that Mr. Bloom had removed large sums of money from the firm without authorization. Fortunately, due to our stalwart mission to always protect client interests, the staff of Ledbetter & Bloom has already recovered 100 percent of stolen assets. Additional extensive security measures have been expedited to ensure an issue of this type will never again occur.

3. To protect the high historic returns this firm's clients are enjoying, and following extensive consultation with internal and external business and legal advisors, we are immediately restructuring our company while simultaneously launching an effective new business and investment strategy.

4. The senior partner of Ledbetter & Bloom, Mr. Garrett Ledbetter, with the support and encouragement of the firm's Board of Directors, has established a NewCo:

5. Ledbetter & Associates Financial Services

6. As a valued client, we encourage you to transfer your investment and asset management activities to this new entity. All current contracts, methods of investment, and staff who have worked diligently for your success will transition to the new firm. Existing investment portfolios and client cash balances managed by Ledbetter & Bloom will move to Ledbetter & Associates Financial Services upon receipt of your written authorization. Following this transition, Ledbetter & Bloom LLC will be wound up.

7. For all intents and purposes, this is a simple re-branding exercise. Note that our larger clients have already agreed to the above measures.

8. Finally, may we point out that Mr. David Bloom has for the past ten years worked exhaustively to serve the interests of our clients. We send him our continuing thoughts and prayers, as well as to his family. We pray that through ongoing professional medical treatment he will soon regain his health. We wish him a speedy recovery and a brighter future.

9. Sincerely, Garrett Ledbetter
Senior Partner, Ledbetter & Bloom LLC

The letter had been hand delivered to wealthy clients operating throughout the country. The action had been followed with a video conference, helmed by the self-appointed 'senior partner' of Ledbetter and Bloom, which covered finer points of the transition. Smaller clients received the letter and a phone call from senior account managers. So far, the results had been impressive.

Standing at the enormous office window overlooking the Hudson River, Garrett Ledbetter realized his ambitious financial dreams had at last come to fruition. He rationalized the betrayal of his ex-partner with brutal logic.

First, while in the early years Bloom had proven to be an effective partner, Garrett had long suspected deep emotional weakness within the man's character. He had come to believe the Irishman would not have the longer-term resilience or fortitude to succeed in the ferociously competitive world of financial trading. Bloom's recent inept performance at the Englewood meeting cemented Garrett's hypothesis.

Second, Garrett's suspicions had been proven correct due to the man's mental and emotional meltdown at his daughter's wedding rehearsal. Had Bloom survived the test match Garrett had decided to play against his old partner, he believed he would have reconsidered subsequent actions. Despite the ten-year relationship, business was, after all, business and weakness would not be tolerated. To Garrett, his findings were worth much more than a broken nose.

Third, Garrett knew that nothing would ever stand in his way of the wealth he had so long craved. He well remembered the days long ago when his financial wellbeing hung precariously. To succeed Garrett had risked everything. He had personally financed the formation of Ledbetter & Bloom. Bloom had risked nothing. Garrett's own hard sales efforts had realized significant growth and profits. His partner provided mere administrative support. Garrett was, therefore, entitled to the fruits of that risk and labor, no matter the so-called ethical or moral considerations he might tread upon.

Due to all of those facts, Garrett reasoned that the actions against his flawed ex-partner were justified. He knew that nothing could now stop his inexorable climb to heady success.

Ledbetter turned to study his financial controller. He had never liked Peter and had balked when years ago, Bloom had suggested him. The man was too old for the position; his thin graying hair too unkempt; his physique too fragile. Yet the timid but intelligent employee still had his uses because he was easily manipulated.

"Now we're ready for the next stage," Garrett beamed.

"I'm sorry?"

"What's the status of NewCo?"

"Ledbetter & Associates Financial Services LLC is registered and licensed for trading. All banking requirements are in hand," Peter replied and hated what he said next. "As the sole shareholder and Chief

Executive Officer of the new entity, I need only your authorization to begin operations."

Garrett's eyes sparked like a lion ready to gorge on fresh meet."-Good. You know what to do?"

Peter glanced at the list he held."One. Gut Ledbetter & Bloom. Fire all staff. Notify the SEC, our accountants, and legal advisors that we are ceasing trading with immediate effect.

"Two: for those clients who have already agreed to our measures, credit note all outstanding client fees owed to Ledbetter & Bloom. Immediately re-invoice those fees from Ledbetter & Associates Financial Services.

"Three: begin the immediate transfer of all Ledbetter & Bloom client cash balances, various client-related trading assets, and all other client-associated materials to the NewCo." Peter looked up."You realize the new Ledbetter & Associates may incur additional taxation because of those transfers?"

"Keep going, Peter. What else?"

"Four," Peter started then coughed to wet his dry mouth before trying again."Four. Re-hire all former Ledbetter & Bloom employees into the new firm. And five: begin trading."

"When it's finished how much cash will Ledbetter & Bloom hold, belonging solely to our old firm, net of the client accounts?"

Peter glanced at his notes."Four million, five hundred thousand, two hundred and ten dollars. That includes unrealized write-offs we may have to incur, but does not include the accrual for yesterday's cash transfer for the—ah—Canadian venture."

"And what are the outstanding contractually-binding bonuses, loans and expenses due to existing Ledbetter & Bloom partners?"

"Just over three million dollars," Peter noted.

"Which will, of course, be paid to the beneficial party," Ledbetter stated, knowing that as the sole remaining partner he would personally receive the subsequent funds transfer."After that, how much cash will remain in the old firm?"

"Approximately one-million, two-hundred thousand dollars. Mister Ledbetter, don't forget this final cash balance can't be transferred to NewCo because the remaining assets legally belong to the old entity."

Garrett smiled. "And God forbid we do anything illegal. What about current trading creditors?"

Peter did not have to look at his notes this time. "Current trading creditors will not, of course, be transferred to NewCo. They will remain on the Ledbetter & Bloom balance sheet."

"And how much are they?" Garrett asked.

"Just over one-million, three-hundred thousand dollars, which again includes unrealized creditor write-offs but does not include the one-million accrual for the Canadian venture," Peter answered from memory. "When it's done, Ledbetter & Bloom will be insolvent. It will be forced to liquidate. NewCo will have approximately eight million in cash deposited to various client accounts with no trading creditors."

"As well as ten million dollars per annum in recurring client income. Don't forget that."

"Yes. That as well." Peter stated. He loathed the smile creeping over Ledbetter's insatiable lips. For a brief moment Peter remembered that once, long ago, he had possessed a spine. "We'll need a dissolution order. According to Ledbetter and Bloom's corporate rules, a majority of share-holders must vote for liquidation. Because you and Mister Bloom are equal shareholders, you both need to sign it."

The partner reached to his desk and handed a single piece of paper to his financial controller. "I think you'll find it all in order. Note the date. David and I discussed restructuring months ago. We both recognized the stress he was under. He wanted out."

Peter scanned the document. The corporate resolution called for the immediate liquidation of the firm. It was dated a month ago and signed by both shareholders. If was, of course, a complete fake.

"Just file it and forget it," Ledbetter stated impatiently. "If anyone asks questions, my former partner is no longer in a position to answer them. Now what else?"

Peter felt his throat constrict. He decided to throw down a final challenge. "To establish the new company we had to register with the state."

"What about it?"

"The state of New York requires us to take out a series of advertisements in major papers to announce the formation of the new company. The ads started yesterday."

"So?"

"Mrs. Bloom will find out. So will her daughter."

Ledbetter laughed. "They'll both find out anyway." He thought for a moment. "Better yet, I think I'll phone Laura. She has every right to know the old firm is being liquidated. She'll of course tell Rachel. Honesty is, after all, the best policy, isn't it?"

"But what if Mister Bloom's daughter starts asking questions? I understand you've given her the various reports."

"Trust me, Peter. It won't make any difference. I doubt she'll prove troublesome. And even if she does, she'll find nothing. What's there to find after all?" Garrett queried. "Even if she does a deep dive it only backs up what we've already reported."

Ledbetter inched closer to the financial controller. "Three million dollars was fraudulently transferred to offshore accounts by her father. She can never access those accounts because they don't exist, and even if they did exist she couldn't because the accounts are private and therefore secure. As part of our investigation, three million dollars was found by staff and returned to the firm. All of it is transparent. All of it right there in black and white and part of our banking and financial records.

"And as for the SEC investigation?" Ledbetter growled. "As part of our discovery we learned of a dissatisfied employee. One of your accounting staff members with access to our investigation wanted to cause trouble and was fired for his efforts. The SEC investigation was fake, the documents forgeries. We have already reported it to the appropriate authorities and apologize to any affected parties."

"But we haven't reported anything to the authorities," Peter faltered.

"Peter, you worry too much," Ledbetter laughed, then thought for a moment. "Okay, how about this? Destroy everything you have. Everything. The false financial statements, records of cash transfers, and anything else you find. Double-check the computer hard drive and backup systems and delete any copies. If anyone wants to dig deeper they'll come up against a wall of nothing. Even if another party insists on a complete audit of our finances, there's nothing to hide." Ledbetter's eyes narrowed. "Peter, that's an urgent request, by the way. Destroy the documents today."

The financial controller nodded, too shocked to respond.

Satisfied, Ledbetter gave the final order. "Mister Lawrence, push the button. Ledbetter & Associates Financial Services LLC begins trading tomorrow morning."

As the financial controller turned to the office door he heard Ledbetter chime, "Oh and Peter? When you hire yourself into the new firm, give yourself a raise. You've earned it."

Peter wanted to throw up at the man's callous uncaring naïveté.

20

We sit in the car. I hold her hand and will not let go as I prattle on like a frightened schoolboy. I worry she will have second thoughts and disappear.

Why shouldn't she leave? I think between rushed sentences. *When I left I never even said goodbye.*

I fill the car with blurted apologies for my long absence and for having never contacted her. I tell her how much I regret leaving and what a miracle it is that she has found me. But my words end in curtained silence that descends like lies.

Dolores does not respond. She stares out the window at lifeless skies and falling rain.

I take a long look at her. She has changed little. A scattered aurora of grey dusts her rich curling auburn hair. Furrows have begun to etch the smooth skin of a freckled forehead and apple cheeks. But her hazel eyes remain as clear and as present as the day I left.

I notice the color of her face.

"You're pale," I say and she is. "Are you cold?" Dolores is soaking despite the umbrella. I reach for my coat.

"No," she states, pushing my arm away, and I know the awkward words have cut. I start the arduous process of trying to explain why I had to leave; of my father's accusation; of my cowardice.

"Don't," Dolores implores, withdrawing her hand from mine. "You made your choice. Explaining doesn't change anything." Her eyes find mine. "I thought I wanted to see you again. I thought I needed to remember what we were like…before. It was a mistake. It hurts too much." She reaches for the door.

"I didn't *have a choice*," I complain. It is then I notice her left hand. She wears the Claddagh ring. On her finger the polished gold glints in the shadowed car, two hands forever clasping a single heart.

"You still wear it," I whisper but my discovery does not stop her. She is out the door, slamming it shut, opening her umbrella. "Dolores, please," I plead but she is gone. I follow her into the rain. "I should never have left. My life was here."

"Don't you mean *our* lives were here?" she snaps, marching toward the village. "That's what you promised. You told me you'd always be here."

"He told me to leave."

"Don't blame your father. He was mad with grief. He didn't know his own mind."

"What was I supposed to do? Don't you know what he said?"

"You could have explained it to him. You could have stood up for us."

"I tried but Dad wouldn't listen. Don't you understand how much I wish I could do it over? How many times I wish I had told him to feck off and stayed with you?"

"But you didn't. You forgot about me." The depths of her bitterness register for the first time.

"No. I never did. I came back because of you."

"That's a lie. You came because your father died. You got married, David. You have a daughter. How old is she now? Ten? Eleven?"

"How did you find out?"

"Bere Island people travel, remember? Some went to New York like you did. They hear things. Didn't you think I would too?" Her lovely face crumbles. "Go home and leave me alone."

"My home is here." I reach for her but she is done with me. She walks faster, down the island's wild high road. "Yes, I got married but it's over. Yes, I have a daughter. Her name is Rachel. She just got married."

"Congratulations. Time certainly has moved on."

"Didn't you ever get married?"

"What do you think?" Her voice is acid; her steps quicken.

"Dammit, Dolores. Stop! I need you."

"You don't need me, David. You need your wife." Her footsteps never falter as the tiny figure recedes down the road. When she turns at the hair-pin corner she is gone.

"Dolores. I'm sick. I'm so sick," I stutter but the words are hidden by the voice of falling rain and I know she will not listen.

Somehow, I make it back to the car. I lean against the door. I tell myself that this time I will be the man my father always wanted. Instead, breath shudders. Hands shake. I lower myself to the ground, resting in the muddy tracks of the road.

I cry though I have promised myself not to.

I feel a hand on my shoulder. When I look up she is studying me, the anger forgotten, concern in her eyes.

"You're sick?" She helps me to my feet. "If you're sick you need to see the doctor."

I'm tired of feeling helpless. I'm tired of keeping the secret to myself. But now I do not know if I can tell anyone, not even her.

"What's wrong, David?"

"You won't believe me."

"Tell me."

My words stumble with shame. "I see things."

"What did you say? Davy, look at me."

I raise my eyes, prepared to be dismissed as a lunatic. "I see things. Things that shouldn't be there."

Dolores does not know how to respond. "David, I'm not sure I'm the one who can help."

"Yes you are. You're the only one."

She looks away and I know she is on uncertain ground. Then she looks back. "What do you want me to do?"

"I want you to come back to the house with me."

"Your house?" she asks and her face screws into a tight question. "-Davy, what's at the house?"

I look her in the eye.

"My parents."

***

Rachel struggled with the front door lock but her key would not fit. She rang the doorbell a dozen times before it opened. Though it was well past noon, her mother still wore a bathrobe. Laura stood unmoving, blocking the entrance, not seeming to register her daughter's presence.

"Aren't you going to let me in? What's wrong with the door?" her daughter questioned.

"I changed the locks."

"Say that again?"

Laura turned, slipping back into the house.

"Will you tell me what's wrong?"

The young woman followed her to the kitchen. She found Laura standing statue-straight at the sink. Whatever she had planned to ask during this visit was replaced by the sudden concern she felt for her mother.

"Mom, what's wrong?" she asked again and when Rachel reached for her mother's shoulder Laura looked at her daughter as if for the first time.

"Garrett just called."

"Garrett called?"

"He's closing your father's company."

It took Rachel a moment for the words to register. "That's impossible."

"Why is it impossible, Rachel?" Laura sat heavily at the island. "Garrett said he had no choice. Your father insisted on it. Oh, don't look so shocked. David signed the papers a month ago. He wanted out of it, just like everything else. Of course that was before Garrett discovered your father's deceit."

Rachel stared unspeaking at her mother.

"Don't you understand?" her mother scolded. "David thought he could get away with his theft by burying the evidence. If the company closes no one would think to ask questions, would they?"

"Dad wanted to close the company? Garrett never said a word to me."

"Why should he? It's not your company. It was *our* company. *Ours.*" She clenched the edge of the island so tight Rachel thought her mother would break it. "Garrett said he was trying to avoid it. But after all that's happened, he thinks closing it is the only way out." Laura banged the marble countertop. "That bastard. The lying bastard. Your father is trying to take everything from me."

"Garrett is lying."

Laura swung on her. "How can you say that? Your father is a raving drunk. He's a lying lunatic. He's destroyed everything I have. Everything I worked so hard for."

"I won't believe it."

"Why not? Garrett told me he gave you proof. Isn't that what you found? Proof of your father's horrible behavior?"

"Mom, everything Garrett gave us, all the paperwork. It could all be… inaccurate. That's what Jacob thinks."

"Is that so?"

"We want to talk to Peter Lawrence about it, the financial controller." She glanced at her mother's silent, angry face. "I was hoping you could introduce us. We have some…questions."

"You want an introduction?" Laura snarled. "Oh and why not. Can't you just hear the phone call? 'Peter, this is Laura Bloom. I'm sorry for interrupting your busy day but I was hoping you might talk to my daughter Rachel. She accuses Garrett of being'—how did you put it Rachel?— '*inaccurate*. She wants to ask some questions. Oh, and Peter: don't let Garrett know anything about this. God knows we don't want Mister Ledbetter to believe we think he's *lying*.'" Laura glared at her daughter. "Don't you go near Peter," she commanded. "You'll only cause more trouble."

"Dad did not do this," Rachel countered.

"Well then, I know what you should do. Go back to Ireland and ask him. Your father will deny everything. He'll blame Garrett or me or anyone else he can think of. Anyone other than himself." Laura folded her arms. "He's a lying alcoholic. He'll tell you anything but the truth. But by all means, go back and talk to him if that's what you want."

"I am going back. I'm going back because he's ill. He needs help."

"Your father doesn't need any more help."

"I talked to a nurse. Something's happened. Dad has become worse. He's really sick."

Laura's eyes fell. "I didn't know."

"Of course you didn't. You don't want to know. I leave in three days. As soon as he's better I'm bringing him home."

Laura's eyes narrowed. "Don't. Don't bring him back."

"Of course I will," Rachel insisted. "It's his home. I can look after him here."

"Rachel, I want you to listen to me. If David is brought back here, he'll be arrested. He'll be sued. He'll go to court and then probably jail."

"We'll fight it."

"You don't understand do you? He'll lose and when he does I'll lose too."

"Why would you?"

"I'm his wife," Laura raged. "If David loses everything, I lose everything. Rachel, on no condition will you bring your father back here. There's no place for him."

The information stung. She met her mother's eyes. "I didn't realize. Mom, I'd never hurt you."

"I'm already hurt." She placed a hand on her daughter's cheek, just as she had done when Rachel was a little girl. "Sweetie, don't you understand how much I need you right now? If your father comes back I'll lose everything I have. You don't want that, do you?"

"No."

"Promise me. Leave your father in Ireland, at least for now. It's the best thing for everyone."

Rachel said nothing as she left the house except for a promise to visit her mother again the next day. When she arrived home, Rachel sat at the dining room table with Jacob and in a broken voice recounted every word she had spoken with her mother. When she finished, Rachel was surprised when he laughed.

"What's funny?" Rachel demanded. "It's all a mess. I can't bring Dad home or he'll end up in jail and I could hurt Mom. She told me not to talk to Peter so we'll never know the truth. Dad's in some hospital three thousand miles away and he's sick. How can you think anything is funny?"

Jacob handed her the daily Long Island newspaper. It was opened to the business section. "This. Look at the notice. Bottom of the page. This is what's so funny."

Rachel found it and read. It was a legal notification for the establishment of a new company: Ledbetter & Associates Financial Services LLC.

"Dad is setting up a new company? How could he?"

"It's not your father. Read it again. It's Garrett."

"But why?"

"Why do you think?"

"Garrett thinks he can get away with this?" she fumed. "This isn't funny, Jacob."

"Oh it's funny, all right. It's funny because he really *does* thinks he can get away with it. And, honey, that's not all. Your husband has been busy while you were out. I contacted that legal auditor I mentioned. I sent her the file. She started with the offshore accounts."

"She's already started?"

"Yep. And she's already found something. That list of numbered accounts? They're fake. Every last one."

"Fake?"

"The auditor contacted an old boyfriend, a guy who works in global banking. He told her he couldn't do anything but she reminded him of the old days when he was managing assorted offshore tax scams. He agreed to take a look. He told her he couldn't find anything. He's sure the accounts never existed."

Rachel sat back. "So what do we do now?"

Jacob strode around the table to his wife. "First we're going to eat something. It's almost six and I'm starved. Second, I have to go to the office. I missed an entire day and need to get caught up at work. Then I'm coming home and we're going to bed. Tomorrow morning I'll start phoning Peter Lawrence until I bug him so much he'll take a call. I don't give a damn what your mother says. I'm not her daughter and we have to talk to him."

"And what am I going to do in the meantime?"

"You're going to get packed."

"Why? Jacob, I'm not leaving for days."

He took her hand. "Honey, we got a call from Dad's nurse. She tried your cell phone but you forgot it when you went to see your mother."

"What did she want?"

"She wants you out there as soon as possible. I called the airline. I rebooked your flight for tomorrow."

"Why? Is Dad worse?"

"Yes," he said and Jacob was no longer laughing. "Honey, I'm afraid he's very ill."

***

By his reckoning, Paul Cutter had slept three hours. Now he was facing into a trying day for which he had not planned. Striding toward the Cork City hospital in response to yesterday's unexpected message, Cutter felt both peeved and perplexed: peeved because the meeting would eat into a day already booked tight; perplexed because the assistant who had phoned him did not have the simple decency to explain why the young doctor was being summoned.

He glanced at his watch. The drive from Bantry to Cork City had taken almost two hours. He was already ten minutes late due to heavy traffic and the difficulty he had finding parking. Good, he thought to himself. The man whom he would meet was inevitably a highly-paid suit. A few minutes cooling his heels served him right.

The young doctor knew his foul demeanor was also due to the other phone call which had disturbed much needed rest. When Nurse Healy phoned him just after four that morning about the apparent, sudden turn of patient David Bloom, Cutter had been fast asleep. He was forced to climb out of bed and spent the next half-hour on the phone talking to medical staff, finding out what was going on.

The doctor on duty had reassured him: Bloom's vitals were pushing the outside of the envelope but he believed Cutter's nurse had over-re-acted. When the medical doctor suggested discontinuing the patient's anti-psychotic medication, Cutter had pushed back.

Bloom's sudden onset of mild arrhythmia was in all probability caused by the patient's medication but the young psychiatrist had antic-ipated such a reaction. In any event, the high pulse rate had already nor-malized. When Cutter was reassured that the sudden problem was not serious, both doctors agreed that at least for now medicinal treatment should continue.

Following the discussion, Cutter had not been able to again find sleep. Despite his busy schedule, he was certain of one action he would take. He would order his nurse to confine herself to official Unit duties and stay away from Bloom. But that would have to wait until he was finished with this inconvenient, unanticipated meeting.

Entering the City hospital, Cutter pushed down his annoyance long enough to ask the receptionist for Patrick Towney. While he was at it he asked for the official title of the man he was about to see. He waited while she consulted a computer database.

"All it says is that Mister Towney is a member of the Mental Health Commission."

Cutter went cold. The Commission was responsible for the various codes of practice for Ireland's mental health services. It also appointed professionals and lay people to mental health tribunals when tribunals were scheduled.

"I've never heard of Patrick Towney," Cutter prodded. "Does it say anything else?"

"Sorry. Want to look?" she invited, motioning to the monitor. Cutter declined. "Mister Towney is in room 313," the receptionist continued. "The elevator is just down the hall."

"I know where the elevator is."

Wondering what the hell was going on, Cutter skipped the elevator and jogged up the stairs to the third floor. There, he made his way past a series of doors. He found the right office and knocked.

"Come," a voice answered. When Cutter walked in, he found a man in his early sixties sitting behind a small desk. He rose as the young doctor walked up. The executive was dressed in a pair of pressed jeans and matching blue shirt. The older man's relaxed attire contrasted markedly with the young psychiatrist's own expensive business suit. The Health Commissioner offered a firm handshake.

"I'm Patrick Towney, doctor. Thank you for coming. Please take a seat."

"I think I'll stand. I've quite a full day on, Mister Towney. Can I ask why I'm here? Your assistant never mentioned it."

The man smiled and Cutter found he did not trust the laugh lines framing the full lips. "That's because I thought it best we meet first."

Cutter was suspicious of Towney's apparent affability. "Now we've met. Do you mind if we get down to it? I have to get back to the Unit as soon as I can."

The sparkle in Towney's eyes died. "I'm afraid this will take a bit of time. You see, doctor, we've had a complaint."

"Have you?" Cutter responded. "I take it this is about David Bloom? Mister Towney, the man is intent on causing himself personal harm. He refuses to cooperate. As a result he is now quite ill. Currently, he's being strictly monitored. I'm not sure there's anything to discuss until he shows an improvement. So unless this meeting can be kept to a few minutes, I'd like to reschedule. I really must get back."

A woman's voice shot out from the back of the room. "Doctor Cutter, I'm afraid what we have to say is quite urgent."

Cutter turned to find an attractive middle-aged woman studying him with acute steel-grey eyes. She sat in a chair, hidden from the psychiatrist's view when he walked through the door. He had never before met her.

The woman rose and advanced. She never extended a hand. "I'm Doctor Anne Tenbrooke. Sit down, Doctor Cutter. I assure you, what I have to say will take much longer than a few minutes."

***

In Bantry Hospital, Mary Healy continued to monitor her patient. She was still unhappy with Bloom's condition. His temperature remained at the upper edge of acceptable limits. His blood pressure was still depressed. But the sudden early-morning presentation of arrhythmia, which disappeared just as quickly as it started, had spurred her to additional action. She had again called for a doctor. While he examined Bloom, she had made the brief call to Cutter despite the early hour. She hoped the change to his patient's vitals would force the psychiatrist to reconsider his present course of treatment. However, Cutter's characteristic response, made even more impatient due to being woken, precluded such hope.

The young psychiatrist had hung up on his nurse and phoned the medical doctor. Following the terse call, the Acute Care doctor had lectured Nurse Healy. Annoyed by what he interpreted as continuing interference, the medical doctor treated the experienced woman like an uninformed first year nursing student.

"Clozapine can cause occurrences of rapid heart rate. While arrhythmia is not desired it is also not life threatening. You're supposed to know that."

"Which I do know and which is an undesired side-effect as you just stated, doctor," the nurse had bristled.

"The tachycardia has passed. His heart rate is normal."

"His heart rate was always normal prior to the administration of Clozapine."

"So what do you suggest?"

"Discontinue the treatment."

"Really? Then might I suggest you advise Doctor Cutter of your opinion? The patient is his responsibility. Or have you forgotten that, nurse?" He folded his arms. "Doctor Cutter has ordered an increase to the target dosage."

"Which is?" Nurse Healy demanded.

"Four hundred-fifty milligrams daily. If you have a problem I suggest you talk to your boss."

Stung by his rebuke, the nurse demurred when the doctor suggested she leave the premises. At a stalemate, he had made a quick exit and left her to it. Now late in the day, Mary Healy had sat with David ever since. Yet despite the setbacks the nurse still held onto new optimism.

Just before noon she had heard from Anne Tenbrooke about the meeting with Cutter. Mary was assured that her opinion regarding David Bloom's involuntary detention had been brought to the attention of the Mental Health Commission. While the Commission did not have the power to release the patient, it had provided a forum for Tenbrooke to share critical views with the consulting psychiatrist. Those views were now a matter of record.

Tenbrooke had also been reassured by a member of the Commission that she would be considered for the role of impartial, independent psychiatric specialist at the patient's forthcoming tribunal. If appointed, Tenbrooke would act to independently evaluate Bloom's mental health and make recommendations for his release—or not.

Tenbrooke also assured the nurse that if appointed to the tribunal, and as part of her evaluation, she would review the patient's treatment plan, including all medications.

Mary realized that David Bloom now had hope. But she also knew that Cutter's professional ego had received a bashing. "Mary, if I were you I'd stay as far away from the man as possible," Tenbrooke had warned. "He did not appreciate the criticism I leveled at him. By the end of the meeting, our young doctor was ready to explode. He's a by-the-book hothead and bound to take it out on someone. Don't let that someone be you."

Mary promised she'd do her best. "Good," Tenbrooke replied. "You might want to phone Bloom's daughter. Ask if she's been able to get in touch with the patient's solicitor. You'll need him."

Nurse Healy had waited until after teatime to phone Rachel knowing it would be only noon in America. With Bloom's daughter unavailable, she had instead informed Rachel's husband of the change in David's condition. She had explained the variation in vital signs. She had disclosed the onset of mild arrhythmia which, while the doctor thought it inconsequential, gave Mary cause for concern. She strongly suggested that it would be prudent for Rachel to visit her father as soon as possible, thinking his daughter's presence might prove both comforting and healing. She asked if Rachel had managed to get in touch with her father's solicitor. Jacob stated he was unsure, but had promised he would pass on the urgent message as soon as she returned.

Now, it was getting on to evening. Nurse Healy had not eaten since breakfast. She would not leave the hospital because the nurse did not care for her patient's coloring. She continued to worry for him despite the doctor's insistence that his vital signs were within acceptable limits.

What bothered her most, however, was David's lack of movement. He had not moved his extremities at all for at least five hours.

As she examined him, Mary realized his eyes once again fluttered with REM. He was dreaming. She was surprised when his right arm twitched. Slowly it rose toward the ceiling. Fixed. Rigid. His hand opened as if in his dream he reached for silent reassurance.

"I'm here, David," Mary whispered, moving closer. "See? I'm here."

She placed her fingers in his palm. Within his dream, David Bloom gripped her hand with all his will.

21

Kitchen

I grip her hand. I worry this is all a horrible dream.

She squeezes back with reassuring reality.

We have been in the house for over an hour. Nothing is as it was. I correct myself. Everything is as it was. The kitchen table littered with unwashed plates. Cups piled in the sink. The potted flowers dead on a windowsill.

I searched downstairs and upstairs a dozen times. Room to room. Again and again. They are empty of my family.

I try the kitchen light switch. Punching it. On, off. On, off. No light. Nothing.

"They're not here, David," she says just as she has said countless times. "Listen."

I hear her voice. Nothing else. Dead silence.

"But they were. I swear."

I cannot breathe. The room tilts. My body shudders.

"Sit down." Her voice is kind but words are cautious.

"Dolores, I'm not lying."

"David, please sit down."

"My name is not David. My name is Davy."

I storm from the kitchen.

Hallway

The grandfather clock stands tall on the stairway return. Obstinate hands point to 10PM. She has followed me.

"The clock is stopped, David."

"But it wasn't. It was working. They were here. All of them."

"I'm sorry."

I swing on her. "Why are you sorry? You don't have anything to be sorry about."

"Yes I do." Her eyes fill with sadness. "I shouldn't have come."

I see regretful decision in her face. She slips the Claddagh ring from her finger. She studies it, longing. She holds it to me. I will not take it. She cannot face my horrified look and walks away.

Living room

The room leans.

"I can't see you again."

I will not believe her words. She studies my face. "You're not Davy anymore. You're David. All I see is sadness. Don't you understand? I was wrong to find you. What we had has passed. We've lost each other."

"I can change it."

She smiles. "No you can't."

"I love you."

"Long ago you loved me. You have another life. Go back to it. Your love for me is killing you."

The golden ring glitters in the palm of her hand. She places it on the dusty coffee table. She hurries to the front door.

I follow, grasping her wrist. Hard too hard.

"David, stop." She shakes me off, rubbing. I have hurt her. I see fear in her eyes. She has never been afraid. Not of me.

"Listen to me. Please listen. Dolores, I need you. Don't go."

She is angry. "You haven't needed me in thirty years. Why should you care now?"

"Don't be stupid."

"I am not stupid! You won't listen." She pulls at the front door. It squeals on hinges. "Goodbye David."

"Don't!"

But she is gone.

In the kitchen I hear my mother singing.

***

Mary Healy bent over him. Tight closed eyes rolled in his sweating head. She again checked the monitor. Heart rate was 89 beats per minute. Respiration rate had increased to 21 breaths per minute. Blood pressure was falling. His temperature had increased to 39ºC.

She ran to find the doctor. This time she would make certain he listened.

***

Living room

It grows dark and hot in the house. I open the window. My mother's curtains billow like ghosts in the wind.

I light a candle. I place it on the windowsill. Its flame flickers in the breeze, casting shadows on the twisting curtains. From it I light another. Carrying it with me to find her.

"How are things in Glocca Morra? Is that little brook still leaping there?"

Kitchen

I shudder. In candlelit shadows the vision repeats itself. Why isn't Dolores here to see this?

Mam pulls fresh scones from the oven. She calls out the window. "-Davy! Come in now. They're ready!"

My younger self runs in. Dog and Dad follow.

Ticking. On the stairs it is no longer 10PM. Instead, the grandfather clock keeps the time of yester-year.

Davy runs to change his shirt. I rush to follow. My feet do not squeal on the wooden steps. I know I am not here. I am but a ghost; an unacknowledged visitor. I run on because I must.

Bedroom

In our room, Prince enters. Dad follows. He worries about the boat and the storm. I hear Davy promise he will not leave.

"Stay this time. Please, stay!" I beg.

Mam walks in. Convincing my younger self to break his promise. Thunder booms. He escapes toward the door.

This time I will stop him. I lunge for him. My hands clutch thin air.

***

The doctor was convinced. Mary Healy watched as he halted the flow of Clozapine. He drew blood from the patient. He called for an assistant who hurried away with red vials filled for analysis. David Bloom's temperature had soared to 41ºC. His blood pressure continued to fall.

"Do you want to phone Doctor Cutter?" Mary encouraged.

"You call him. What will you tell him?"

"Sepsis."

"So would I." He glanced at the nurse. "Set up a bolus of saline."

Her inclusion in the patient's treatment was the only apology Mary Healy would ever receive.

***

Entryway

I pound down the stairs after Davy.

"Don't leave!" But he does not respond.

He grabs a coat against the rain. He turns to Prince. "You stay here, lad," he says and strokes the dog's head. Our dog whines.

"Don't go!" I am in his face as he pulls on his coat. He does not see me and walks out the front door. "You'll kill her!"

My dog gazes at me. His tail pounds. I touch his warmth. He is real.

I look at the grandfather clock. Time has accelerated. It was 6PM a moment ago. Now it is almost seven.

I hear singing in the kitchen.

"How are things in Glocca Mora?" Her words are already slurred. "Is that willow tree still weeping there? Does that lassie with the twinklin' eye, come smilin' by and does she walk away."

She sits at the kitchen table. Drinking whiskey from a tumbler. The bottle almost empty. Eyes filled with bright tears of doomed insanity.

She finishes the glass. It falls to the floor, shattering.

"I wonder where everyone is?" she pants. Her drunken voice is filled with lilting madness. "Maud? Maud are you there? Is that you I hear?"

It is only the ticking of the clock. Already it is past eight.

"Maud isn't here, Mam. She's gone. Please, Mam. Wait for Davy to come home."

"Maud?" she asks again. The dog stands at attention next to me. He gazes at his mistress with woeful eyes. She says, as if of no consequence:

"I think it's time to go see Maud, don't you Prince? Yes, that's what I think I'll do. I'll go see Maud.

"How are things in Glocca Mora?" Her song is as thin as a ghost.

She stumbles up the stairs. Past the clock that counts down the relentless minutes. Into the bathroom.

"Mam, wait for me. Please wait!" But the door closes. It locks. I beat on hollow wood but make no sound.

On the stairs below the clock strikes: 9PM.

***

Following the nurse's phone call, Cutter had broken speed limits to get to the hospital. When he entered the room he ignored the nurse which was fine by Mary Healy. If she'd been given half a chance she would have sliced the young psychiatrist in two. Instead, he consulted with his male medical colleague. They discussed the diagnosis of sepsis and the actions the doctor had ordered. Cutter did not argue. Following the psychiatrist's abrupt departure, Mary thought she had never witnessed such silent fear in a medical professional.

With Cutter gone, the Acute Care doctor ordered a broad spectrum anti-biotic. As they waited for the medication, the nurse worried her patient would slip into septic shock.

Mary Healy was fully aware that more than fifty percent of catatonic patients died if consumed by septic shock.

***

Bathroom

I bellow at the locked door. "Mam, Mam, don't. Please don't!" Beside me Prince barks like a madman.

Downstairs.

The door bangs open. Davy is home. Looking into the kitchen. Seeing the empty bottle and shattered glass. Smelling the stink of whiskey.

Knowing.

Pounding up the stairs, screaming our mother's name. "*Get her out of there!*" I yell but it makes no difference.

He bangs on the locked bathroom door. Bangs again.

From inside we hear the insanity of Mam's drunken, terrifying fugue state: "Maud! Maud! I want Maud!" Then she screams. It fills the house.

"Mam hang on!" Davy hits the door with his shoulder. It does not move. He hits it again. The frame splinters.

Inside, the wailing stops. Her silence drives our panic.

"Mam!" He hits the door again with all his young strength. It gives way.

He finds our mother on the floor. Hair mixed with blood. Blood, blood everywhere. Spattered on sink and mirror. On walls, toilet, and bath. Pooling on the floor. She is covered in it. We stand, helpless. It is too much too much too much for anyone.

Prince wails, barking wildly.

The front door opens. My father is come home.

He hears barking and knows. "Rose!" he yells, rushing upstairs led on by Prince's wild voice. He sees his wife. He sees the blood. He turns to his son. Seeing the drenched coat. The soaking hair. The horrified guilt in the young man's eyes.

He knows we have broken our promise. He knows we were not home.

I can no longer watch. I stagger away knowing what will happen next.

Dad will say nothing as he frantically checks for his wife's pulse.

His hands covered in her blood.

Removing the razor blade he finds in her unmoving palm.

Reverently wrapping slit wrists with clean towels to hide the shame. Blood, blood everywhere,

Silence breaking to wailing wailing, course manhood of wailing, picking up her blood-soaked corpse in strong arms and wailing while holding her to him;

as if he hoped to stop time and with his strength move back the clock so he could save her but he had left that task to another, a son he knew he could trust to watch over her but he was wrong dead wrong and here is the proof in his arms.

His son stands at the door, witnessing a father's grief at his mother's death.

His father lowers his love to the bloody tiled floor. Ignoring younger me as I stand there like an eejit, like a fool, like a murderer caught out, unable to do a thing. Not asked to do a thing. Knowing he blames me fully for her death.

We know he is right.

Bedroom

I lurch into our room. I crawl into bed. Covering myself tight with the blanket she gave me. Wrapping myself in her love. In the darkness I remember what happens next.

Davy follows Dad down the stairs. Hector will not listen to indefensible explanations so we plead for forgiveness. Stopping only when our father is distracted as the clock chimes the mad hour.

The farmer's hands open the case. The fishermen's fingers halt the pendulum, stopping time; the hands of the clock forever pointing in silent accusation:

10PM.

He swings to his son, eyes filled with crazed grief, voice rising like death.

"Get the fuck out, Davy. Get out of our home and don't come back. Get out now! The sight of you sickens me."

His son gasping, tears pricking, retreating beneath the harsh accusing words.

"Dad, please."

"Shut the fuck up!" His dead eyes fill with hatred. "You killed her Davy. You feckin, feckin murderer."

"Dad, I didn't."

The slap to the face is sudden and hard, the strength of ten bringing Davy to his knees.

"Get out!" he hisses. Then turning his back because we are dead to him. Leaving us alone within our guilt. Knowing then:

We can never come home.

In the bedroom, beneath the blanket, I clutch my shaking body, knowing I cannot endure anymore. I close my eyes. I sleep the sleep of a dead man. I dream of happier times; of a tilting funhouse of long ago and a father who loved me.

Held by my dreams, I do not smell the smoke.

***

When the anti-biotic arrived, the doctor ordered Nurse Healy to administer the drug. She pumped the maximum allowed dosage into her patient.

She hoped it would be enough.

***

"Bloom! Bloom! David Bloom!"

I dream of lights. They are blue. I dream of laughter. It calls my name. Within the dream of a funhouse the nightmare repeats yet again. I am powerless to change the outcome. Ever. But I see it again:

"How are things in Glocca Morra? Is that little brook still leaping there?"

"Bloom!"

Davy walking out the door to see our girl.

"Bloom!"

Mam at the kitchen table drunk as a skunk:"Maud!"

"Bloom!"

My dog wagging his tail because he knows I'm home.

"Bloom!"

I know it is all pointless. Useless. I cannot change the outcome no matter how many times I must endure this damning memory.

"Bloom!"

"How are things in Glocca Morra?"

"Mam. Mam!" The grandfather clock strikes. 10PM.

I cough. I gag. Choking wakes me. I swim upward out of swirling darkness. The room is thick with smoke.

"Bloom! David Bloom!"

From my bed, I hear the front door shatter. The determined clump of boots on wooden staircase. A fireman's strong hands grasp me. As he pulls me from the room I see

Davy my mother my father
standing on the landing next to the stopped clock
drifting in and out of curling dense smoke
ghosts of my past haunting my present
They reach toward me.
I know they reach for help

I scream. I struggle. But the fireman's hands are vice-like. He drags me down the stairs.

I look into the living room. It is alive with bright fingers of fire.

As he drags me to the door I see: the coffee table surrounded by flame. Our ring resting on the table top, glistening bright within golden fire.

Dolores.

God let me change things. Please, God. Please. Let me do it over again.

*****

Mary knew there was nothing more to be done. Despite the drug, his temperature climbed to 42ºC. Respiration was up to 24 breaths per minute. He was receiving oxygen. The blood test was back. His white blood cell count confirmed the sepsis. If they could not halt it, David Bloom would suffer catastrophic organ failure. After that, the prognosis was simple:

He would die.

*****

On the porch, I kick at my rescuer. Screaming there are others in the house. The fire will kill them. Through the smoke I hear my girl. *"- Davy, it's here."*

I push him off, escaping, running back into the house.

I am on hands and knees, inching beneath thick murderous curling smoke, crawling into the living room. It is alive with flame. Burning curtains billowing, lethal, with flaming fingers reaching out to kill me.

I see

Dolores.

She stands in the burning room. Pointing to our ring. Resting on the flaming coffee table.

"It's here, Davy. It's here when you need me."

"Dolores," I breathe. The smoke is as thick as a storm.

Strong hands grab my ankles. They haul me away.

Entryway

Davy stands on the shadowed stairway landing beneath the clock.

I scream. "Davy!" I beat the floor with my fists as the fireman drags me.

Our dog hears. He runs to me, whining. I know what to do.

"Prince, get him Prince. Show him!" The dog does not know what I want. "Show him, Prince. Show him now!" His intelligent face turns from me to the younger master who stands on the stairs.

Our dog understands.

He bolts to our younger self. Barking, barking, barking in his face.

The room spins. The brightness of the constant lighthouse enters the house. It streams through smoking windows lighting the stairway in endless golden wonder.

It settles on the young man's face in the brightness of infinite possibility.

I scream again. "Davy! Look at me. Look!"

Our loyal dog keeps barking.

Davy peers through smoke, looking down the stairs. Toward the door. Where I am. Dragged like baggage through the smoke.

"Davy! Davy!"

Within the lighthouse light I see his face. He looks at me.

"Davy" I shout again. His eyes narrow at my voice. I am sure his eyes register my presence.

I am sure. As I am carried from our burning home, I am as sure of it as I am the constancy of our lighthouse. I am certain that...

***

Nurse Healy leaned over him. David Bloom's face streamed in rivers of perspiration. Vital signs showed promise. His respiration had dropped to near normal. They had discontinued the O2 treatment and removed the mask. His temperature, which had fallen three degrees to 38ºC, continued its descent.

His body remained torpid. He had not moved at all since the beginning of this emergency, when he had raised his arm and she held his hand. And yet, despite his continuing catatonia, and within the depths of illness, Mary sensed a profound change.

The REM was sudden and severe. His eyes vibrated as if they would explode.

David Bloom opened his eyes. She bent close to him.

"David? David, I'm here," the nurse whispered.

In the soft light of the room, his dilated pupils searched for her.

"I'm sure he did."

She did not understand.

"What are you sure of, David? Who did?"

When he spoke, she had never before heard three words filled with so much hope.

"He heard me."

SECTION THREE

IRELAND MENTAL HEALTH COMMISSION MENTAL HEALTH TRIBUNAL

INDEPENDENT PSYCHIATRICASSESS-MENT ASSESSOR: DR. A. TENBROOKE PATIENT: DAVID BLOOM

RTE Radio 1   Program: Morning Ireland

Guest: Dr Anne Tenbrooke, Psychiatrist   Interviewed by: Dominique Geary

<u>Partial Transcript</u>: [From 01:08—To 03:59]

Dominique: Doctor Tenbrooke, last year over two thousand people were involuntarily detained by Ireland's mental health services. Some of our callers ask a simple question: why so many? As a nation are we that mentally ill?

Anne: Dominique, records show we're not the only ones. As far back as 1999, over 300,000 people were admitted against their will across Europe. That number does not include Russia, Asia, North America… You can more than triple it for a global total. What if I told you the number of detentions is rising precipitously not only in Ireland but internationally?

Dominique: I'd be absolutely flummoxed. Why so many?

Anne: Do you know how Ireland's involuntary admission process works?

Dominique: Go on. Tell me.

Anne: Let's assume I'm your sister and believe you are mentally ill. I think you are a threat to yourself or others. My opinion is based only on an unsubstantiated report I've received about an accident you were purportedly involved in that put yourself and / or others at risk. I become concerned because I suspect you intentionally caused the accident. I take my opinion to a doctor or the police.

Dominique: But they'll conduct an investigation before they act, won't they?

Anne: Investigate? No. If they think my opinion is competent, they will recommend an involuntary admission. If an approved mental health unit agrees, they will issue an Admission Order. You will be picked up and detained for a 21-day assessment period.

Dominique: Against my will? But what if there's no proof? What happened to due process? It sounds to me like a person can be detained on a whim.

Anne: It's a balancing act. On one hand, psychiatrists are tasked to protect the mentally ill from harming self or others. On the other, they must consider the primacy of human rights. Often, these concerns clash. Too often, human rights are repressed.

Dominique: But Anne, that means anyone can be locked away for no proven reason at all. My own mother could lock me up if she felt like it. It's crazy.

Anne: That is the law. Similar laws exist in most countries all around the world. And yes. If your mother thought you had a mental disorder and was a threat to yourself or others, she could request your immediate involuntary admission.

Dominique: But what if my mother is wrong? What if I know I'm mentally competent but am simply going through a hard time? What if my mother's opinion, even if made with the best of intentions, is all fake news? How do I get out if I'm admitted?

Anne: After the 21-day evaluation period, you have an automatic right of appeal to a Mental Health Tribunal. If the Tribunal agrees with your argument that you are not a threat to yourself or others, they'll release you.

Dominique: And they usually agree, right?

Anne: No. Tribunals often agree with the consulting psychiatrist because he is reputed to have sole patient insight. In that case, you might experience additional hardship.

Dominique: Hardship? Of what nature?

Anne: You could be detained against your will for a further 3 months, then 6 months—perhaps years. Most of your civil liberties evaporate. All at the stroke of a pen. If you are an involuntary patient, there is little you can do about it.

—END PARTIAL TRANSCRIPT—

22

Dark.

"Dad?"

Not even stars. Or moons. Or the bright beam of a lighthouse.

"Dad? Can you hear me?"

Dark. Unfathomable darkness.

"Daddy? Please wake up."

Words echo. Receding into night. I have become a black tomb of hurt.

"David. It's time to wake up."

I never want to wake up again.

"Come on David. Sit up."

"Daddy, sit up."

Daddy. I know that word. Someone once called me Daddy.

"Sit up, David."

Strong hands grip both shoulders. Insistent hands grasp both arms. Pulling. It hurts everything hurts. Why won't people listen and leave me alone?

"Dad, Daddy? I'm here."

Sweet breath on my cheek. Whispered love in my ear.

"Daddy, please look at me. Won't you look at me?"

Eyes glued shut; damp cloth stroking eyes forehead ears eyes cheeks eyes nose mouth chin neck eyes.

"David, don't you want to see your daughter?" I know that voice too. "David, open your eyes. Look. Rachel is here."

Light. Sudden. Blinding. Twisting through my head like thrusting knives. I blink. I know I blink. Fuzzy pictures of a face I once loved. Coming clean like bright diamonds. I blink again.

"Rachel?" a man whispers.

"I'm here now."

She is in my arms.

23

Cutes wraps me tight in a clean white robe smelling of fresh washing. She helps me with my slippers. Then stands me up and searches my face.
"How do you feel?"

I don't know. What happened? Where was I? I want to remember. I think I remember. I had a hell of a dream.

"The confusion will pass. Tell me what you remember."

Not much of anything—not yet. You sat with me. You didn't leave me.

She smiles. "No I didn't."

But there's more. Something in the dream. Smoking dream. Flashing glimpses of importance. In my head I see… The fire.

"You remember the fire? Yes, David. You had nightmares. But the fire was weeks ago."

Was it? I must remember. It's something else. Something vital. A truth just beyond memory. Where's Dolores? I see things and reach for them but they're gone.

"You'll remember. How do you feel?"

Like shit. Everything hurts. Look at my legs. *Odd how they shake.*

"Let's sit you down again."

She balances me on the edge of the hospital bed. I will ignore the pain shooting through legs and feet, arms and hands.

"The pain will pass. I promise."

I doubt it just as I've doubted everything else these people have put me through. Except for Cutes, of course. Except for my loving nurse. You're nice.

"Why?"

You listen.

"You're easy to listen to. You make me listen."

Am I? Do I make people listen?

Then I remember. Like a soundless thunderclap. In the dream. Someone listened. Who? I stare hard at the floor trying to remember. All I see is smoke. I smell it. I taste it. Curling, clawing, killing smoke.

"David, look at me."

I don't see her. Instead I see faces. Smoke-filled faces. Flashing between tongues of fire. People I know. Loving people.

"Are you still thinking of the dream?"

She will never believe me. Instead: How long have I been here?

"Fourteen days."

You mean since they brought me to the Unit?

"No, fourteen days since you were brought to hospital."

Fourteen days? I've lost fourteen days? I grasp to calculate time. It's been over two weeks since the fire. Over two weeks of imprisonment. Where did all the time go except into a dark murderous hole?

What happened?

I sense she does not want to tell me. I remind her I have a right to know. She explains. When she tries to gloss over the cause of sepsis I press her. She names the drug. She makes me understand no one can be certain it is the primary cause. She promises the medication will never be used on me again. I don't have to ask who prescribed it. I already know.

Cutter. He could have killed me.

Cutes understands my dawning rage. She places hands on trembling thighs.

"David, try to breathe."

Breathe? Bullshit. Rage does not require breath.

Cutes leans closer. Her face full of no-nonsense concern.

"You're going to have to forget about it. Let it go."

Let it go? How can I let it go? Where do I put it, this rage I feel? Who do I give it to?

"David, listen to me."

The rage breaks like torn clouds. Within the light I see Davy's face. The image washes over me and through me. Like a mirror of fractured self-recognition. A dog barks. A young man on a fire-lit stairway. Me being dragged through dense smoke shouting like a madman. And I saw… I'm sure I saw…

"Remember how important today is. Remember who you're meeting. They're here to help you. You have to stay calm."

I don't want to stay calm. I want to hold onto the memory of his face. To know. To make certain. I'm sure he heard me. But I am addled by rage. I am frightened by it because beneath the rage there is fear. And beneath the fear, only endless mirrors of a fractured mind and a face I no longer recognize. It goes by many names: Mental. Cracked. Psychotic. Worthless. I am forever fractured. A billion pieces of humanity. Of the David I once was. And never will be again.

Oh God. *Cutes holds me.* I need to throw up.

I was cracked at the wedding reception. But I have become worse. I was cracked to the power of two when Dolores found me. But now? After the consequentially inappropriate care I have received? I am cracked to a power of ten. Beyond recognition.

Cutes deposits a plastic bucket on the floor in front of me. Puke projects from my mouth in a pink bomb that spatters my face with stink.

What did I see? When did I see it? Was it only in the nightmare? Or did I truly see them all on the night of the fire? I realize: I no longer know the difference between reality and dreams.

I puke again. She wipes my face with a cool cloth. As she does I clutch at the possibility.

The young man heard me. I am sure of it. In the dream. He heard my voice.

"You said that when you woke up. But you never said who. Would it make you feel better to talk about it?"

No. I can tell no one. They'll think me madder than I am. But what I experienced; what I saw: it is something more solidly practical than any dream. I still don't understand. Understanding rests beyond a far, dark horizon waiting to be discovered. What does it mean?

She takes my face in her hands. "It was only a dream. Look at me. Do you want to cancel the appointment?"

Rachel will be waiting. So will the lawyer. No, I need to go.

"Then let's get you ready. Davy, are you sure you know what today is about?"

You've never called me Davy before.

She smiles. "It's only a first meeting. It's only a start. But if it all ends well…"

If what ends well?

"If the tribunal ends well you'll be through with all of this. You can rest. You can go home."

Home? I see it in my mind's eye. A house in burning gold. Voices. Dog. Davy. Dolores. The ring. My mother's singing. My father's curse.

I can go home? When?

"Soon. In a few days. If it works out."

How? Tell me how?

My good nurse smiles again. "You have to talk to your solicitor first."

Will he tell me how?

The nurse takes my hand.

***

Rachel sat with her injured father at a table placed in the sun. She gazed out upon the front lawn of the hospital perched on a hill overlooking the southwesterly town of Bantry and the Bay beyond. While they waited, she held his hand and tried to make small talk. But she realized there was nothing small to talk about because everything was huge.

Rachel explained she had managed to contact the solicitor, Harrington. To do so she had driven her rental car from Bantry down the coast of the Peninsula. She had found Castletownbere without effort because she had been there once before. Having asked directions, she discovered the lawyer's small office located along the single main street. She was disappointed to find the door locked and a note in the window saying the office was closed. When she approached a local shop-keep she was told the solicitor was away on holidays but would return later that day. With a few hours to kill, compelled by curiosity, she had decided to take the ferry back to Bere Island. Rachel avoided the small local bed and breakfast like a plague because she would not be reminded of the complicity in her father's detention. Instead, she drove along the high coastal road, finding the old family home without trouble.

Though she would not go inside, Rachel had walked around the house, inspecting the fire damage. Then she hiked across the farmland she only recently learned was her grandparents'. She thought she had never been anywhere that held so much remote, staggering beauty. She admired the deep square-cut fields and old stone outbuildings, and the white ghosts of sheep grazing in the serenity of the hills. She gazed with awe at the sea cascading along a distant shore, wondered at the lighthouse thrusting high from its promontory, and felt the soft hand of sea breeze come alive in her hair.

In a pasture near the house, Rachel waded through tall grass like a ship lost on high seas. She stumbled across an old tractor engulfed in overgrowth, its red paint eaten by rust. Clambering up onto the old machine, she sat on the cold metal seat, grasping the round black steering wheel, her hands resting in the same places as her father's and grandfather's many years before.

Rachel looked out over the sloping sun-bleached hood to the damaged house and the rugged sunlit cliffs rising beyond. "What would it be like to live here?" she thought. "What kind of life did Dad have when he was a boy? It's so peaceful." She found herself wanting to know more.

As the sun moved toward mid-day, she drove to the pier and took the ferry back to the town on the mainland. When she returned to the office, she found the solicitor behind his desk.

Harrington was full of concerned apologies. He explained that because his practice was so small he had never employed an assistant. Moreover, when he went on holidays he was determined to remove himself as far away from civilization as possible. That included leaving behind his cell phone and access to voice and email messaging. Rachel almost laughed. To her urban eyes, Castletownbere already seemed far removed from civilization.

It took an hour to discuss her father's predicament. During that time, she came to realize the solicitor had not heard about the fire. He was also staggered by her father's involuntary detention.

As they talked, Rachel discovered Harrington to be solidly competent. As importantly, he had a knowing grasp of Ireland's mental health laws. When he asked her what she hoped to do for her father, Rachel promised: "I'm bringing Dad back to the States. I don't care if I have to smuggle him out."

Harrington agreed to do everything in his power to achieve her uncompromising objective. But he also informed Rachel of the nature of the Mental Health Tribunal her father now faced and its many challenges. He made certain she understood its importance and the binding nature of the decisions it made. They agreed to work together to prepare her father for a process that could yield his release. But as she drove back to Bantry, she worried, knowing her father's fate would hang upon the outcome of legal mechanics she did not fully understand and people she did not know and therefore could not trust.

That was yesterday. Now she waited with her father to begin that risky process. Again she squeezed his hand. "What are you thinking Dad?"

He roused himself. He had been thinking about a vision he could not share with anyone, much less his daughter. Instead he smiled at her. "I'm glad you went to the house. I wish you had met your grandparents."

"I wish you had been with me. I wish you had told me about it before. Maybe, someday, we could visit together."

"Maybe. If someday comes, I'd like that."

Rachel studied his face. She remembered how strong he once looked when she was a child. He did not look strong now. His face was pale in the spring sun; his hands clammy to her touch. She squeezed his hand tight.

"Dad I'm so sorry about everything."

"It's all right. You did what you thought best. It wasn't your fault."

"Yes it was. I let you down. You've always been there for me. I wasn't." Her voice choked. "I'll never leave you again. I promise."

He reached out, touching her cheek. "I'm glad," her father said. But as he said it he knew he could never return the promise his daughter gave to him; he could never promise he would never leave her.

David knew that on many levels he had already left and could never come back.

They sat together until in the sunlight, a solid looking Irish solicitor dressed in a brown woolen suite tromped across the lawn toward them.

***

We sit together in the sun: me, my daughter, my lawyer. I try to listen because I understand the import of the conversation but it is impossible. Davy's puzzled face intrudes into the rough singsong of the solicitor's West Cork voice.

Harrington talks about the Tribunal. It will take place in three days' time. We must prepare. "A number of people will attend, David. Your admission will be reviewed by a three-person panel which includes a tribunal lawyer who will chair the meeting, as well as a consultant psychiatrist and a lay person."

I pretend to hear with focused attention. But my mind conspires on higher hills. I see young eyes squinting at me through curling smoke. *What if Davy did hear me? What do I do about it?*

"Who is the lay person?" my daughter asks.

"It can be a teacher. A builder. A homemaker. It can be anyone but another lawyer or doctor."

I look past Harrington to a Bay sparkling in the late morning sun. *If I could leave, I would fly down the Bay's sunny waters. Past Glengarriff and Adrigole. Down the spine of Beara. All the way to Bere Island. I could sail home.*

"If you didn't have a solicitor, the Health Commission would assign one to you. But you have me. I have informed the Commission I will act for you."

I would take my bearings from the steady beam of the lighthouse. I would find the house again. It rises on wings of gold. I would walk through the front door. I would fix things. All I must do is discover how.

"I have already met the independent psychiatrist. Anne Tenbrooke has an excellent reputation. We're lucky to have her."

"What does she do?"

"She will interview your father. It is her responsibility to develop an honest, independent evaluation regarding David's mental state and make recommendations to the tribunal. Her opinion is important. The tribunal will listen."

Listen. "Listen."

"Dad, did you say something?"

I shake my head. I cover my shock. I must keep this discovery to myself.

Of course! If Davy can hear me. If he can listen! Then maybe I can make him understand… maybe we could take it all back… if we can change things then maybe…

"The tribunal panel will take evidence from the independent psychiatrist and listen to our arguments for release."

If he will listen, I can stop him. I can make sure he never leaves the house.

"I've talked to the insurance company. They are conducting an investigation into the causes of the fire. Their conclusions will also be crucial."

I will convince him to stay to protect our mother.

"Why?"

"If the report concludes the fire was accidental, that your father did not start it with intent, the psychiatric services will have no basis for continued detention. They must conclude that he was never a threat to himself or others. But even in the event of such findings, the other side will fight back."

We'll fight back by doing what is right, what we should have done.

"The panel will take evidence from the treating psychiatrist."

"Do you mean Doctor Cutter?"

But how do I stop a thirty year old memory?

"Cutter will argue to uphold the admission order."

How do I stop a specter of my past?

"And what if the admission order is upheld?"

How do I make a ghost obey?

"A renewal order will detain your father for a further period. Additional tribunals will be initiated every three months as part of subsequent renewal orders. If at any time they find for your father, he will be immediately released. Otherwise, the detention will continue."

How do I make certain we do not sin again? Is any of this possible? But if he heard me... if I can warn him....if I can make him listen...

"Dad? Dad are you listening to this?"

I rouse. I nod but their words have no meaning. My impossible goal overpowers my mind. *I do not know how to make him obey. Not yet. But I will. When I go home I will make him listen. We will work together. We will change things.*

"Mr. Harrington, can I ask one more question? Where will Dad go now?"

All I have to do is escape from my jailers. Then I will go home. I will find Dolores. Dolores will help me. With her, there is always hope. There must be. When I go home...

"Now that he's recovered, your father will be returned to the Unit."

The Unit?

"The Unit?" a man trembles.

I hear a gull cry. I watch it soar overhead. A thick bile of rage displaces fractured plans. I stand unsteadily in the sun.

"Dad, sit down."

My daughter places a protective hand on my shoulder. I shrug her off.

"I can't. I won't."

"David, calm down."

"I'll never go back. They can't make me."

"You have to go back to the Unit. I'm sorry David."

The gull above me cries with raucous sorrow. The whole world is sorry. But the world doesn't give a shit. Not if they think you are mentally ill. If they think you are mentally ill, there's not a Goddam thing you can do about it.

My rage screams high across the lawn.

"Fuck the Unit. Fuck Cutter. Fuck all of you!"

24

"Welcome home!"

Whale Man captures me in a long bear hug. I am assaulted by his presence: by his bulk and thick body odor; the smell of foul breath; the crust of a dirty robe. His perspiration coats my cheek in a fetid storm. Yet I am steadied by the honest welcome of my inescapable homecoming. At least someone has missed me. The big man holds me at arm's length, sleepy drugged-filled eyes making a careful examination.

"You look like shite, David."

"Thank you, Liam. You look shite too." I gaze out onto the sunlit courtyard. It tilts at forty-five degrees in familiar unfamiliarity. Its bright countenance a noxious poison. My legs tremble; I will them to stillness. I grasp his robe. I hope he does not guess I cling to him out of desperation. "What's the news? What's Rose-Marie broadcasting? Any breaking headlines?"

"Ah, nothing's changed. Everyone's still here, no one's left. The food is still crap; the nurses worse looking; Cutter still a pain in the arse."

I startle at the name, terrified by the pounding in my head; the distant toll of familiar ticking.

"Hey brother. You okay?"

"I'm fine." Someone is using my brain as a percussion drum. "You hear anything?"

He listens, unperturbed at the odd request made by a fellow psychiatric patient. "Naw. It's all quiet. Maybe Rose-Marie is trying to reach you."

I doubt it. I push down a vision of Cutter's grasping eyes. My hope he has been jailed for attempted murder is shattered. I force myself to ignore the drumming, drumming, persistent drumming in my head.

"What else is Rose-Marie saying?"

He smiles broadly. "Rose-Marie has been talking about you."

"About what?"

"She's saying you're getting out of here." I realize news of my pending tribunal is making the rounds among fellow prisoners, rousing hope. The big fella punches my shoulder. "Rose-Marie is working hard to sway the bureaucrats."

"And how is that?"

He leans in, his tone conspiratorial. "Cutter's gonna get his throat cut when you win. It's gonna make national headlines."

I study him. "Let's keep Rose-Marie's news to ourselves." I sense something more troubling under the man's podgy smile than a psychotically-induced radio news announcement. "Liam, has Rose-Marie mentioned when you're getting out of here?"

He shakes his head. "Nope. I had a hearing while you were in hospital."

"What was the verdict?"

"Renewal. It'll be two years this June. The old man and I have a bet on to see who's gonna break out first."

"The old man? You mean Ol' Fella? How?"

"Our own *Great Escape*. I'm gonna get a motorbike just like Steve McQueen. I'll break down the door with it. Wanna come?"

"I think I'll pass. I'll take my chances with the tribunal."

"I wouldn't count on the bastards." He leans in again. "When I saw 'em, I told 'em I was an upstanding citizen of Ireland. I told 'em I have it all figured out in here." He points to his addled head. "What with Rose-Marie and her code, I promised they can count on me to warn about impending foreign invasions. It's their patriotic duty to release me."

"What did they say to that?"

His big face breaks into a pout. "They didn't believe me."

"Better luck next time, right?"

"Feckin' right." I see the struggle in his face. I know what it is. When hope is quashed it takes immense strength to find it again. In the

Unit, hope is necessary for survival. But it is never a given, always elusive, and easily shattered.

When his sweating cheeks pucker into the facsimile of a smile, I know he has again won the battle if only for a moment. He punches my shoulder again. "Not to worry. It's only a matter of time. I'll get out. You'll see." He pushes in closer, his grin warm and familiar. "We're just glad you're home. We missed ya."

"I'll bet," and I'm sure they did. When you're in a Psych Unit you grow a reluctant attachment to your fellow detainees. Solidarity in the face of adversity may be a cliché. In a mental health unit the need to lean on each other, however lightly, is much more credible than any cliché.

I watch the big fella negotiate his way across the courtyard's sunlit concrete. I take a deep breath. Not for the air. No not that. I breathe to quell the terror I feel at Liam's words. To still the shaking that is the horrible result of continued incarceration. To stop the panic of an uncertain future that makes me want to run; a future held in the hands of a faceless professional jury, and a psychiatric enemy who wants me dead. Two years of involuntary detainment? I wonder at the length of my own sentence and how I will survive.

The drumming, the ticking, grows louder.

They must let me out. They must. Without freedom I have no life.

I take another breath, steadying myself. I force back the mad ringing until I hear only pulsing blood course through my head. I force myself to think of what is necessary for survival. When it's my turn to stand before the tribunal I must keep the new realization of my island home and its waiting occupants to myself. I must not divulge my true plans or intentions to anyone. I must act normal. In my present condition, still weak from illness, still fighting the voices and visions I remember, I know it's a big ask. But I must get through it; I must. I know if I confide my thoughts to anyone, particularly the professionals, then just like Whale Man and Ol' Fella my stay could last indefinitely. Just as Cutter threatened. Just as Cutter promised.

I wish Dolores was here. I yearn for her to hold me. To tell me it will all work out. She would help me to maintain hope long enough to fight these bastards and go home. I wonder where she is. Does she not feel my desperation?

I lean against the wall. The hope I willed for myself vanishes. That's when I see Cutes. She stands at the cafeteria door, across the courtyard from me. Her face is filled with concern. I force a smile and nod to her. She thinks I'm okay because she buys the lie I transmit to her at so much cost.

Her neat nursing uniform and reassuring smile calm me. I remember what she said before we left hospital: of a life I would soon reclaim; of the promise I made to her before she walked me back through the Unit's locked doors. I remember why I made the promise. Too much was at stake not to make it.

"This time do what they ask, David."

"Okay."

"The tribunal is in just a few days. Be patient."

"I will."

"Actions speak louder than words."

"I promise."

Across the courtyard, she winks at me and hope finds reluctant renewal. No big deal. I will keep it together. I remind myself that few prison sentences last forever and even the most hardened criminals get time off for good behavior. So it will be for me when I present myself to the esteemed members of the tribunal. I must remember: I am David Bloom. Once I was a whole human being. I will be again. If they let me out. Which they will because they will think me as sane as they are and will believe the lies I will tell them.

I take another breath. Steadier, I am determined to head back into the fray. No matter how dizzy I feel. No matter how familiarly unfamiliar this place is.

The cafeteria. Breakfast. My compatriots sit at tables like they do every morning, food dribbling from drugged mouths. I nod hello. Some nod and smile back. Some wish me luck though the tribunal isn't for another three days. Others stare with profound concentration at nothing.

Bollocks stands close by. It's medication time and I see the sneer on his red face. He can't take his eyes off me. Still suspicious of my motives, I'm sure. Unwilling to believe what he's heard. I saunter to the food counter in a wake of luminous normality. A nice woman, with graying hair tucked beneath black hair net, stands behind it smiling.

"It's good to see you, Mister Bloom. Can I get you something this morning?"

"Whatever's going, thank you. I could eat a mountain." I surprise myself. I sound normal. I sound healthy.

Her old eyes glitter. "It's good to see you finally with an appetite."

I raise my voice for Bollock's benefit. "Pile it on if you don't mind, missus," I ask and sneak a look behind me. His suspicious eyes gawk as I accept a trayed mountain of food from the old cook: a steaming hill of scrambled eggs, sausages, black and white pudding, back rasher, and fried potatoes. A liquid mass of baked beans runs like a river through it. My benefactress adds a plate of toast, a glass of orange juice, a cup of tea.

I have the sudden urge to throw up.

Instead I sit at a table beside Ol' Fella. He looks far worse for wear since my hospitalization. A shaking hand shoves a fork full of mashed egg into his mouth. His rocking is more pronounced. He is the husk of a broken metronome waiting for a final coda. But he smiles and I am aware he takes genuine pleasure at my return.

"It's good to have you home, David."

"I can't say the same but I appreciate the sentiment."

He smiles with broken teeth.

"Did you hear my son is coming to see me? Sometime this week." He shovels food into his mouth. "We hear your daughter is come over."

"She is. She's staying in town."

"That's grand. I'm happy for you." He eats more, his face thoughtful. "It will be good to see my son again."

"What's his name? I never asked."

"Sean. He's a good boy."

"I'm sure he is." But I know he is not. Based on what Cutes told me, the prodigal son will never come home. Ol' Fella's chin is covered in egg. I take up a napkin and he lets me wipe it. I notice tears in his rheumy eyes. He grasps my hand tight.

"When you get out, will you contact my son?"

"I don't have to. You're seeing him in a few days, remember?"

"When you get out, find him for me. Tell him I miss him. Tell him I'm sorry."

"Honest, you'll be able to tell him yourself."

He smiles with knowing resignation. "Don't coddle me. I'm not mad all the time, ya know. Not like they think."

"I don't understand. But you said…"

"Don't you think I know? Don't you think I have to con myself too, sometimes, and play the lying bastard to survive? I know he's never coming." His sigh is full of pain. "Someday, I'll find him myself."

"Sure you will."

"There's only one problem."

"What's that?"

"I'll be dead then."

I do not know how to reply.

He wipes his eyes and picks up a fork. We get back to eating. I worry about him and the years of silent suffering he has endured. I am outraged at my powerlessness to help him. I can barely help myself.

I clean my plate. When I'm finished I make a point to hold it up so Bollocks can see my new commitment to cooperative détente.

"Meds time," I say to Ol' Fella. But when I place a hand on his bony shoulder he cannot respond. I squeeze his arm. His struggle gives me new strength. I will not fail. I will win not only for my sake but for the comrades caught in the grip of unrelenting suffering.

I will win because I must go home.

I get up. Bollocks now stands behind the open dispensary door. Contrary to past personal promises, I make myself queue with other patients. When it's my turn I stand before my jailer. He hands me two paper cups.

The memory of our last meeting washes through me as I consider the white tablets rolling at the bottom of the paper container. I meet his gaze.

"Let me guess. Lexipro."

"Who told you that?"

"A lucky fairy." I throw the tablets down with a chaser of water. "Hmmm, my favorite anti-depressant. Yum! Wanna see?" I open my mouth for inspection.

"Don't be cute."

"I promise you, Nurse. I'm a changed man."

"I'm glad of it."

"I bet you are."

"I told you don't be cute."

"And I told you I'm a changed man." I hold out my hand. "It's true. Shake on it." He eyes my outstretched hand then takes it. My skin crawls at his touch. His grin is scathing.

"Cutter wants to see you."

"I gotta pee first."

"He wants to see you now."

I forget my promise to Cutes. Instead I bend close to him. "Want to know a secret?"

"What's that?"

"I don't give a shite what Cutter wants. In a couple of days I'm outta here. Go fuck yourself." I smile. The nurse smiles back.

"Wanna bet?"

***

"I wanted to see you before you met with the independent psychiatrist."

Paul Cutter sat behind his desk. His patient stood near the door. "Please sit down."

He was surprised when Bloom complied with the simple instruction. He looked well, all things considered. Good coloring. Neatly dressed in blue jeans and maroon jumper. Earlier, Cutter had glanced at the Nurse's morning report. The patient had gained three pounds. His vital signs were normal.

"Are you still experiencing any weakness?"

"Physical or mental?" Cutter was surprised by the patient's quick riposte.

"Physical."

"I feel good. In fact I feel better than I have in months. Mentally? I guess you'll have to be the judge of that. At least for the next few days."

Cutter shifted in his chair at the implied threat of the tribunal. In the days since Bloom's hospitalization, the young psychiatrist had reviewed his course of action when treating this patient. He believed he had acted as any mental health professional would have if facing simi-lar circumstances. However, the members of the tribunal would scrutinize his prescribed treatments as part of their proceedings. While he was still confident, Cutter worried in silence. However, Bloom was still his patient. His patient's well-being must come first. But Doctor Paul Cutter was also aware his own self-interests must also be considered.

For that reason, he had thought at length about this meeting. Now, confronted by the patient he had placed at risk, the doctor was not certain how to proceed.

He clasped his hands tight, finding shelter behind the compassion that was at the core of his professional training.

"Mister Bloom, first I should apologize. I did not realize the previous medication would prove harmful. Most patients benefit from it. I believed you would too."

"No problem Doctor."

"Every patient can react differently. In your case the reaction was… unexpected."

David Bloom grinned. "You mean you didn't want to kill me?"

"I said I apologized."

"And I said I understood."

The doctor glanced at the patient notes. "You know you're now taking Lexipro."

"Nurse Healy told me."

"You are aware of its side effects?"

"She told me that too. I'm grateful someone has finally decided to advise me of my therapy. Being advised of your medication is a patient right, isn't it Doctor? It's enshrined in Irish healthcare legislation, isn't that true?"

"Yes."

"Then why wasn't I advised my previous medication might kill me?" Bloom waited for an answer. When he received none, he grinned again. "Gotcha, Doctor."

Though the young psychiatrist's face reddened, he wasn't about to take the bait. He could have pointed out that Bloom was hampered by psychosis and therefore had been unable to process such information. But such a comment could lead to an escalating discussion of finger-pointing. Instead: "So you'll take the new medication?"

"I already have as you know." Bloom crossed his legs. "I'm now the model of cooperation. You tell me to jump and all I'll ask is 'how high?'"

Cutter studied his patient, unsure of his intent. "You still believe you don't need help, don't you Mister Bloom?"

His patient leaned in. "Doctor Cutter, I need all the help I can get. I was a sick, sick puppy."

"But you're not now? You aren't seeing or hearing things?"

"I guess the drugs you gave me worked after all." David Bloom's face was remarkably composed. "I don't see a thing in this room, except you. As I said, I feel well. In fact, when I get out of here I'm going to write you a glowing testimonial." The patient glanced at his watch. "Can I go now? It's almost time for my next appointment."

David Bloom didn't wait for permission. He rose and strode toward the door.

"Mister Bloom, one last thing." His patient turned back. "You realize I must do everything in my power to keep you here."

"Why?"

"Because I know you are lying."

Cutter thought he saw fear cross his patient's face.

"Then it's going to be your word against mine, Doc," David Bloom stated. "When anyone asks, you know what I'm going to tell them?"

"What?"

"I'm going to tell them the psychiatrist who is charged to heal me tried to kill me. I'd keep that in mind."

David Bloom walked out the door. As he did, Paul Cutter realized that at the tribunal he would not only have to argue for his patient's continued detention, he would also be arguing for his reputation.

***

fuck cutter fuck cutter fuck cutter fuck cutter fuck cutter fuck

I stand in the hall. Outside a door. Beyond, a private meeting room and redemption.

The door is steel grey. I place a hand on its cold surface. Steadying myself. Breathing, breathing, breathing. Why did Doc want to see me now? He knew it would upset me. Is that what he intended? To put me off balance? To make certain I would fall apart at this next meeting?

I kept my cool. But at what cost?

The pounding in my head has started again. The hallway lists. I must regain my composure. I remember what Harrington told me and how Rachel pleaded with me. "Just tell her the truth, Dad." "Keep your head, David. Keep your answers short and to the point." I breathe deep. I must follow their advice and not let them down. If I do …I do not want to think of what will happen if I do.

I knock. The door opens. She greets me with a cool, appraising handshake. Anne Tenbrooke is good looking in a professionally-intense kind of way. We sit in a small room. Two Unit folding chairs face each other. She smiles at me. I know she is trying to reassure me. But within the depths of honest eyes, I know her evaluation will determine my fate. Finally she starts:

"Mister Bloom, first I must ask you a standard but important question. I need you to answer truthfully."

"Go ahead." *I can do this.*

"Mister Bloom, do you think you are a threat to yourself or others?"

Thank God it's easy. "That must be the most popular question in here."

"Why do you say that?"

"Because I'm asked it all the time. No. I am not a threat to myself or others and never have been." *Good answer. Keep it up.*

She leans back, her look one of careful appraisal. *I feel like a bug under a microscope. What does this lady want?* "You're not on my side, are you?"

"Mister Bloom I must be completely independent. It's not a matter of taking one side or the other. All I'm after is the truth."

"About my mental health?"

"Yes."

Listen to her. Be careful. "Do you know why I was detained here in the first place?"

"There were a number of factors." I could see her choosing careful words. "The situation in New York. Your trip here. Chiefly, because some people believe you burned down your parent's home with the intention of harming yourself. You claimed at the time there were others in the house with you. Hence, you were considered a threat to yourself and others."

"I never tried to burn down the house."

"Unfortunately, Mister Bloom, you don't have proof of that."

Bullshit! "But I will. Soon. When the fire report is complete." *Keep it together. Sound reasonable.* "Okay, right now I can't prove that I didn't try to burn down the house. But Cutter can't prove that I did. As far as I see it, we're at a stalemate. The basis for my involuntary admission is invalid." *Take it easy. Sound intelligent.* "Miss Tenbrooke, can I ask a question?

"Go on."

"What happened to the presumption of innocence until proven guilty?"

"Mister Bloom, this isn't a prison."

"Isn't it?" *Damn. She smiled at that one. Tell her what you want.* "Look. All I want is to get out of here. You tell me how to do it and I'll do what you say."

"All I want is for you to be honest with me." *See? Just be honest; as honest as I can. I can sway her.* "I've met with Doctor Cutter and Nurse Healy. I've reviewed all of your patient notes. Why don't we start with your visions."

"Visions?" *Oh Jaysus. Here we go.*

"When did you start experiencing them?"

Is she setting me up? "You know when."

"At the wedding reception." I nod. "That was the first time?" I nod. "And then again at the Unit, before you were hospitalized?" I nod one more time. "Mister Bloom, have you experienced visions more recently?" I shake my head. No. "Are you certain?" I shake again. No. "Do you want to tell me about your dog? What was his name? Prince? Tell me about him."

"I don't see him anymore."

"Are you sure?"

Be firm because it's the truth. "Positive."

She sits back further. "Doctor Cutter informs me you thought you saw your mother."

Is that sweat on my face? "That's a lie. I miss my Mam. I miss my father, too. If your parents were dead you'd miss them wouldn't you? But we can't see them because we know they've passed on. I told you. It's a lie."

"How are you feeling right now?" *Christ, she doesn't believe me.*

"How do I feel?"

Oh fuck. Just don't don't don't rant, don't do it.

"Miss Tenbrooke, how would you feel if you were in a fire that almost killed you?

You're doing it

"How would you feel if a group of goons locked you into a psychiatric unit for reasons that were never explained to you?

Ranting

"What would you think if your whole family betrayed you, and you couldn't get out?

Spinning out of control

"Do you know how I'm feeling, Miss Tenbrooke? I feel like I am nothing. I feel like I'm a useless piece of shit that's better off dead."

Dead? Why am I standing above her with my fists clenched?

"Don't ask me how I feel.

She must think I'm going to hit her.

"You'd never believe me.

Get it together, Goddammit!

"Never!"

"Mister Bloom…"

"I'm sorry. I'm upset." *Sit down, for fuck sake.*

"You don't have to apologize." *Is that kindness in her voice?*

"I promise you. I didn't do anything. I'm not crazy. Ask my daughter."

"Mister Bloom, your daughter was the one who signed your admission request."

"You know damned well her mother put her up to it. Rachel's changed her mind."

"I know. I've talked to Rachel."

"If you don't believe her, then ask someone else. Talk to my lawyer. Talk to Dolores. She'll tell you."

"Dolores?"

"She's a good friend. She knows what happened."

"She was there?"

"She'll tell you. I am not crazy." *Why am I shaking? The room…it's so damned dark.*"Let me out of here." *Oh Christ. Stop!*"This is illegal. If the tribunal won't release me, I'm suing the health service. I'm suing Cutter. I'm suing you. I'll make you all suffer just the way you've made me suffer. Don't you see what you've done to me?" *Why am I breathing so hard? What the hell is wrong with me?*

"David…"

"I'm sorry. I'm so sorry. I didn't mean to."

"Perhaps we should meet another time." *I hear compassion. I don't care.*

"Don't touch me. Leave me alone. I am not lying!"

The door opens. Bollocks puts his head in.

"What the hell is going on?"

"You. You're the first one I'm going to sue. When I'm done, I'll level this building and everyone in it right to the ground."

I storm past Bollocks and out of the room. As I stumble down the hall I feel hot tears on my face. And I know:

God save me. I've hung myself. I've threatened the one person who can help me.

***

MENTAL HEALTH TRIBUNAL
INDEPENDENT PSYCHIATRIC ASSESSMENT

Name: David Bloom**Independent Psychiatrist**: Dr. A. Tenbrooke
Meeting Number: Preliminary**Location**: Bantry Psychiatric Unit

PRELIMINARY INTERVIEW & OBSERVATIONS

During our first meeting, David Bloom was distracted and unfocused. He strongly denied having thoughts of self-harm. He also denied any continuation of the reported psychosis. During our few minutes together, he experienced rapid emotional changes: anger, sadness, hope, fear, regret, and extreme betrayal. Due to his upset, we were forced to end the meeting.

His lack of trust in this interviewing psychiatrist (which translates, I suspect, to the general psychiatric community) means he may be unable to cooperate in any future discussions. This understandable lack of trust is due to the ongoing trauma he has experienced: complexities of family separation and parental alienation, followed immediately by a life-threatening fire, all compounded by the appalling manner of his detention, and ongoing treatment while at the Unit. I fear he will not be able to demonstrate to me a reasonable level of mental competency. Should this happen, I will have little positive to say to the Tribunal panel.

I fear Mister Bloom's stay at the Unit could become protracted through no fault of his own.

25

Her objectives seemed impossible to achieve in the time. Her To-Do list improbable. Yet within the few days remaining until the tribunal began its work, Rachel stuck doggedly to the tasks required to save her father. Scanning the handwritten action-items she had scrawled within a compact, dog-eared notebook, Rachel focused on two points she believed were critical to her father's release. First: she must obtain the fire report. Assuming what her father said was true, it would prove he was not responsible for the blaze and therefore not a threat to himself or others.

Second: Jacob must find and pin down Peter Lawrence to neutralize Garrett's accusations. She must cast doubt on her father's alcoholism and establish beyond question he was neither a thief nor a liar. By achieving those aims, Rachel would undermine the very basis of her father's involuntary admission.

So far she had accomplished neither objective. She was running out of time. As importantly, Rachel worried at what she might ultimately discover.

Still battling jetlag due to the long trip from New York to the remote Irish seaside town, she slept little at the hotel. The few hours she managed were interrupted by nightmares. In one, Harrington announced he had succeeded in retrieving the fire report from the insurance company. Yet when she opened it with trembling fingers the conclusion was always the same. Bald accusing letters shouted: CAUSE OF FIRE—DAVID BLOOM.

In the other she stood at Jacob's shoulder as they interrogated the financial controller. He would not answer their questions. Frustrated, she demanded, "Tell the truth, Mister Lawrence. Did my father steal three million dollars or not?" In the dream, Peter shrugged his shoulders, an uncommitted smile on thin lips. It always ended with her Dad, screaming like a crazy man, being cuffed and dragged away by the FBI.

The nightmares reinforced her dilemma: by trying to prove her father's sanity, she might hand Cutter the fodder he needed to convince the tribunal that further detention was justified.

Sitting at a table within the crowded hotel restaurant, Rachel glanced at her watch. It was already past five. She had not bothered with lunch and knew dinner was out too. She had juggled the day with morning visits to her father, telephone calls with Harrington, and endless calls to the insurance company regarding the elusive fire report in hopes of prodding them to action—calls they would neither take nor return. She had held discreet discussions with Nurse Healy about her father's current emotional state, and urgent video talks with Jacob about his pursuit of Peter Lawrence. Her day had already been frantic. It had not yet ended.

Rachel remembered her father had been scheduled to see Dr. Tenbrooke earlier that morning. She had forgotten. Her tired mind mulled over possible outcomes. Had her father kept his cool? Had he convinced the independent psychiatrist of his sanity, thereby increasing the odds of release? Or had he roared like an injured animal just as he had roared his fearful anger in the hospital garden that morning?

Her ringing cell phone broke a troubled mind. It was Harrington. She listened hopefully before interrupting: "What do you mean it isn't ready? Haven't they finished it?" Rachel's angry voice disturbed nearby diners who looked up with startled curiosity.

Sixty kilometers west, the solid solicitor sat in his small office. "They say they haven't. They describe it as being in progress."

"It's criminal. Can't you make them finish?"

"Rachel, calm down and listen." Harrington leaned back in a deep leather chair, picturing the petite young woman, her pretty face fired with anger. "Insurance companies are notoriously difficult. The adjuster I talked to smells a claim, possibly a large one. My suspicion is they've finished it. But they're not going to release it. Particularly if it shows the cause of the fire was anything but your father's negligence."

Rachel was stunned. "But aren't they obliged to release the report, no matter what the cause?"

She heard Harrington's short laugh."Of course they are. But only when they're damned well ready. Assuming they're facing a valid claim, they'll do anything they can to bury it." The solicitor paused."Rachel, they're aware your father is in psychiatric care."

"What about it."

Anger edged the deep voice."What they're hoping is your father will spend years in the Unit, then die."

"Say that again?"

"If your father passes away, any claim will die with him. That's how most insurance companies work. Put everything on the long-finger. Stall until people get tired of fighting or literally pass on. With any luck, claimants will just go away."

"That's absurd." Her thoughts turned desperately."Mister Harrington, it's not about the money. We need that report."

"And we'll get it."

"How?"

"We'll sue them."

The enormity of his strategy staggered her.

"But that could take years!" The couple behind her looked up again. Rachel lowered her voice."How is suing going to help?"

"It's called discovery, Rachel. I can force them to give us the report, assuming it's ready." In his office, Harrington thought quickly."You told me your husband worked at a large New York law firm."

"That's correct."

"Perhaps they would be willing to work with me. A well-known American firm might shake things up. If an initial letter to them were composed correctly; if we threatened effectively; if we pointed out the urgent reason for the request, and offered to drop any further action if the report's release was expedited…"

"They might give it to us."

"They might."

She considered possible actions."I'll phone Jacob and tell him you'll be in touch. I'll text you his number."

"Don't take too long."

"That's a promise. Mister Harrington, can I ask one more thing?"

"Go on."

"If we don't receive the report in time," Rachel hesitated, "if Jacob can't prove my father innocent of theft, do we still have a chance to get Dad released?"

"As I've said, in that case it's up to Doctor Tenbrooke."

"And if she thinks he must be detained?"

The solicitor's pause was far too long. "Then we keep fighting. Rachel, I promise you. We'll use every means at our disposal to have your father released, including a writ of Habeas Corpus."

As she hung up, Rachel knew Harrington's words offered only the thinnest strand of hope. She picked up the phone again, first texting Jacob's number to the solicitor. Then she left the table and found a secluded corner in the reception area. There, she messaged her husband, hoping his news would deliver renewed confidence. By the end of the call, she was again disappointed.

***

It was just past one in the City as the young lawyer finished the conversation with his new wife. As he gazed out the law firm's tenth floor conference room window with its impressive sunlit views of New York's Financial District, Jacob imagined he looked down the barrel of a loaded gun. He still had no good news to share with Rachel. With her father's tribunal less than forty-eight hours away, he was running out of options.

In the days since his wife's departure, Jacob's confidence of catching up to Peter Lawrence had ebbed and flowed like a strong spring tide. When his initial calls, texts, and emails went unreturned, two days ago Jacob had decided he had nothing to lose and took a cab to his father-in-law's former mid-town offices. If he could find and confront Peter, he would convince the accountant of his ethical obligation to come clean.

He had never met Lawrence. He did not know the man other than the thin background Rachel had shared with him. When he arrived at the impressive building, he realized he could not take the elevator up to the company's exclusive offices. If he did, there was a chance he would run into Ledbetter. Jacob had of course met Garrett at the wedding reception. He feared repercussions if he was recognized by the man Jacob firmly suspected of fraud.

217

Instead, he walked into the building's vaulting foyer, checked in at the security desk and asked to use the phone. He talked to the reconstituted investment firm's receptionist, identifying himself as a privately-engaged financial analyst, stating he needed to talk urgently with Mr. Peter Lawrence. He very much hoped the financial controller of the new company would see him. He was certain the visit would prove of mutual interest. He informed the uncommitted voice he would wait in the lobby.

Jacob took a seat. Lingering in the busy waiting area, his eyes ran over the impressive digital building directory and its list of office occupants. He picked out Ledbetter and Associates Financial Services LLC. Bile rose in his throat because he knew the neutral lettering hid a grotesque lie. All he needed was proof.

At the end of an hour, still with no sign of Peter, Jacob realized he had been on a fool's errand and kicked himself because he had wasted valuable time. If Lawrence had not answered his calls and emails, he would not meet him unannounced in a crowded public lobby. Frustrated by his own naiveté, he rose to leave. As Jacob walked toward the revolving doors, he noticed a petite middle-aged woman standing at security, talking with a guard. The uniformed old man pointed in Jacob's direction.

As the attractive woman marched toward him, Jacob sensed a no-nonsense demeanor clad like armor behind an expensive dark-blue business suit; a mane of black hair cascaded down a straight back; strong adept hands protruded from the tailored jacket. Nearing him, he noted the perceptive eyes: green and as sharp as crystals, the only empathetic feature of an otherwise clearly cool customer.

Her handshake was formal. Prim. Disconnected from the warmth he saw hidden in her eyes.

"I'm Trish Sullivan," she offered.

"Jacob Ryan. Thanks for coming down."

"Mister Lawrence sends his apologies. I'm afraid he's unavailable today."

"That's unfortunate. Perhaps he could see me tomorrow?"

"He's unavailable tomorrow. In fact, I'm afraid he's unavailable to see you at anytime."

Jacob frowned. "I suspect he misunderstands the reason I need to see him; the gravity of the situation."

"He understands completely."

"He does?"

"Mister Lawrence knows who you are, Mister Ryan. He was expecting you." Jacob fought back his instinct to squirm as she studied him. Though he was much taller than the personal assistant, and while she was forced to look up at him, Ms. Sullivan exuded colossal confidence. "Peter has a considered opinion of why you want to see him."

Jacob reached into his suit's breast pocket, withdrawing a business card.

"Would you give this to him?"

"I'll consider it." She smiled, taking it. When she smiled her face lit up, the professional chill vanishing beneath the soul of a warm human being. "I need to go back up. I'm sorry your visit was a waste of time. Now if you'll forgive me," and she turned on her heel.

"Miss Sullivan. Trish…" She hesitated. "Would you please tell Peter that David sends warm regards from Ireland, as does his daughter?" Jacob noted the look of veiled empathy. "I understand that Mister Lawrence and Mister Bloom have been friends for many years."

She did not reply but he saw sequestered compassion in her eyes.

"Would you tell Peter: as a friend, David needs his help?"

She continued walking toward the elevator. Then turned back as she reconsidered his plea. "Mister Ryan, may I ask you a favor?"

"By all means."

"Don't come back. Mister Ledbetter might see you. If he did, it could make things very uncomfortable for Peter." She smiled again. This time Jacob thought he saw a glint of sorrow. "If you talk to David, tell him Trish says hello. Tell him I worry about him." Her smile turned to one of reminiscence. "It's been a long time since I was in Ireland."

"You've been there, Miss Sullivan?"

"Isn't Sullivan a give-away, Mister Ryan?" Her eyes twinkled. "Even if we're only descendants of the Celts, we Irish have to stick together, don't we? I'll give your card to Mister Lawrence. I understand its urgency."

Then she was gone.

It had been forty-eight hours since Jacob had made his reckless foray to the mid-town office building. He had yet to hear from Peter Lawrence or the woman with Irish blood flowing through her veins just as it flowed through his own. But now, just off the phone with Rachel, he knew he could take other actions.

Rachel had given him Harrington's number. He decided not to wait for the expected call and instead beat the Irish solicitor to it by phoning first. It took only five minutes to discuss the situation and the desperate favor the Irishman required. When they finished, David turned to his laptop, quickly drafting the letter. Then he sought an urgent meeting with his father. When he knocked at the door to the expansive office of the firm's senior partner, he was ushered inside by a grim-faced male assistant.

Sitting at his desk, Matthew Ryan pushed aside a mountain of paperwork to listen to his son. Then he scanned the letter. "David Bloom is now a client of this firm?"

"Well, almost a client," his son admitted. "We'll be retained soon. Rachel is seeing him tomorrow."

"And this Harrington. He knows what he's doing?"

"I've never met him but he's experienced enough to know he needs help. Particularly with the timescale involved. That's why he came to us."

The senior Ryan considered the situation. The firm of Ryan, Willowby & Latham were well known litigators. Over the years they had represented young and old, famous and infamous, and rich and poor against injustice. The firm had made its name in successful healthcare and pharmaceutical case work. Since then, it had branched out into a variety of specialties including intellectual property, corporate law, and M&A. The senior Ryan took particular pride in the amount of pro bono work they provided, last year delivering more than one hundred thousand hours of professional services free of charge to hundreds of people and causes across the United States.

Jacob's father grinned as he studied the letter. "I see you want me to sign it."

His son grinned back. "I thought the signature of the senior partner would carry more weight."

His father re-read his son's skillfully crafted words, an apparently simple proposition to an Irish insurance company with which the senior Ryan was unfamiliar. Legally, the letter carried little weight. The company could choose to ignore the veiled threat of litigation. Ryan had employed such strategies in the past. Often, the illusion of threat failed. However, it was also possible the insurance company could comply with the request and release the report.

Ryan liked David Bloom. He was also very fond of the young woman who was now his daughter-in-law.

The senior partner picked up a silver fountain pen given to him a decade ago by an African-American president who had also sought justice in the face of obstinacy. They had met when they chose to aid some of the same national causes. While Bloom's situation was not of national import, Ryan could not bear the man's suffering.

Ryan signed and handed the single page to his son.

"Just don't get us into trouble, Jacob."

"Dad, I promise."

Three minutes later Jacob faxed the letter to the rural Irish legal offices where Harrington still waited.

In Castletownbere, the solicitor added his own cover letter which he had prepared following the brief talk with Jacob. He signed the letter, scanned the paperwork, and emailed the digital package to the insurance company's claims adjustor.

Finished, the solicitor looked at his watch. It was almost seven in the evening. He shut down his computer and walked out of the office. As he locked the door, Harrington grimaced. He knew his action was a last-ditch effort in a game of chicken they had every chance of losing. But the solicitor very much hoped that when the insurance company's management team read the letter the next morning it would set off a large administrative bomb, with collateral damage to match.

But Harrington, who was an avowed pragmatist, also recognized: if he was thwarted by insurance company obstinance, the failure would be his alone. Unfortunately, it was his client who would continue to suffer.

Over three thousand miles west Jacob also looked at his watch. He had time to take one more action. He loathed his plan but firmly believed it was necessary because, in light of Peter Lawrence's continuing silence, he had little choice. He returned to his office, there opening the files Garrett had given to Rachel. He extracted a single page at the very top of the pile, glancing at the neat column of numbers.

He hoped the new financial analysis he had completed earlier in the day would be persuasive. All he had to do was convince Laura Bloom of the theft she had in all likelihood also suffered.

As Jacob left the office, he doubted his mother-in-law would give him the time of day much less an audience.

26

I sit, shivering, in the shadows of the dimly-lit courtyard. I no longer own my emotions, my mind, my heart, my soul. I know from Cutes that for a few days until my anatomy grows used to this new invasion, they are owned by Lexipro, the anti-depressant coursing through my veins and arteries.
I curse psychiatric medications. While I suspect they may help some, they do not help me. I vow that when I am released I will never again take drugs of any kind.

I curse the pharmaceutical companies who make them, the ones whose profits are engorged by stinking patents and enormous cash mountains made off the backs of those who suffer. I curse the witch doctors who prescribe them; the lazy ones who believe a drug on its own will deliver a fix. Though I am no psychiatrist, my instinct tells me fixing the mess that is my mind with scripts of ceaseless drugs will never work. Particularly when the patient believes he is not afflicted by depression but from something inexplicable to define.

I tremble on a cold plastic courtyard chair, reviewing a day of disaster: of my anger in the morning with Rachel. Of my rage in the afternoon with Tenbrooke. But held in the grip of the drug, I no longer care because I cannot think or feel.

Tomorrow I must muster the strength to find new rationality when I again see Tenbrooke. But right now? I don't give a shit. Cutes told me it would be this way, in the first days of Lexipro.

Lethargy. Dizziness but much different from what I'd experienced before. Drug induced shaky anxiousness that contrasts with a dull mind that does not cares.

I shake too because I know I've traded one kind of hell for another.

I stir myself. I think of Rachel. I worry because she has not phoned or visited since I lost my head. I consider the plan she and Harrington have hatched. Of an insurance report they desire to unearth. Of a strategy which they only hint at. I suspect they are clutching at straws, or they have given up and are telling lies.

I think of Dolores. I have not seen or heard from her since the garden visit and of course in my dreams. I have not mentioned her name to anyone in days. Except for Tenbrooke, I remember. I told her to talk to Dolores. Maybe she did. And if she did, wouldn't Dolores visit? I suspect my girl has decided to cut her losses. To let me float away on the drugged sea that is modern psychiatry, as she should have done all along.

I wish someone I care about is with me.

I am cold. I wrap my arms tight around my robe-covered torso. A self-prescribed hug that is as comfortless as masturbation.

I hear subdued sobbing in the shadows. I strain to look behind me. I see the dark silhouette of the human mountain that is Whale Man, and the spindled figure of Ol' Fella, comforting him. A pat on the shoulder. A whispered goodnight. Casting off like a perspiring sea mammal as the big fellow makes way for an early bed and sleep.

It is only 7PM, or so says the clock on the wall.

In the psychiatric unit, sleep is a welcome friend if you can find it. An elixir of darkness in which all you hope is that the nightmares won't come and the next hours of confinement will drift away. I wish I could sleep. I know that tonight, the Lexipro will not help.

Ol' Fella sees me; shuffles over. He places a thin hand on my shoulder. For a time he stands in silence. I see sadness in the old face; worry eating him up.

"David if something happens to me keep an eye on him, will you?"

I do not have to ask why. I know what has happened. Whale Man has lost the battle. The false hope he had gathered when greeting me earlier is lost in the night. As he sleeps he will dream, and when he does will see only a lifetime of confinement: shouting mouths of tribunal monsters agreeing with the views of a malevolent, ignorant psychiatrist. For all I know, the big man could be right. He could be locked in here forever.

In the Unit, it is hopelessness that can kill a human being, even one as large and as indestructible as Whale Man.

In the darkness, Ol' Fella sighs. "When did ya say your tribunal is scheduled?"

"Two days' time. Day after tomorrow."

"Win and go home. You'll give the big lad some hope. You'll help him make it."

"Make it? Make it how?"

"Make it. From one day to the next to the next and the next. Make it so you can face the shite meals and the endless drugs and a tomorrow's sunrise and sunset you will never see, and the ceaseless days after that, and you don't give a shite. Not when you lose hope. Especially when you lose hope."

I understand because I fight the same feelings. But I wonder at the hollow resignation in the old man's shaking voice. "What about you?" I ask. "You gonna make it?"

I see the thin smile. "Lad, don't you worry about me. I don't need to make it."

"Why?"

"Cause I already don't give a shite."

I smile back. "Maybe we both don't."

I hear anger in the shadows. "Oh, don't you say that. Don't you ever say that. You got to give a shite. Promise me you'll always give a shite."

He makes me promise and when he leaves, I wonder if I lied to him or if I truly do? Do I really give a shite, I ask myself? Having lost it all, do I still have the courage to find it again? This night, in the grip of new medication, I am visited by the fear I will give up. I close my eyes to forget the drugged aloneness.

Sitting in the cold plastic chair I get back to the business of shivering.

27

As she drove from the bank to the home she now considered a private though lonely fortress, Laura Bloom felt safe for the first time since David's wedding reception meltdown.
The bank manager had been at first suspicious of the large deposit. Hiding her annoyance, she had explained it was a loan from a friend, an answer that was almost the truth. Apparently satisfied, the manager had changed course. But Laura rejected his complicated investment advice because she had decided on the spot to leave the windfall in cash.

Upon receiving the check from the unexpected source, Laura had calculated quickly. She had added the considerable sum to the balance already held in her new checking account. She divided that sum by anticipated monthly expenses. While not certain what the IRS would take, Laura suspected she now had enough cash on hand to last four years. And that was even without her husband's old salary or touching the couple's joint investments. Though Laura had considered talking to Peter about the Bloom stocks and bonds, she realized they were no longer critical. Accessing the investments could wait for the divorce settlement, and the division of assets which would follow.

Driving through the sunny tree-lined streets of the exclusive neighborhood, Laura contemplated her most recent decision. She had decided to divorce David. Hanging on to a man she could no longer trust was a ridiculous waste of time. She had decided to start a new life. And though Rachel would object, Laura was certain the decision was the only one she could live with; one that would allow her to move on from the hurt and embarrassment David had caused. More to the point: she now had the financial means to do so.

Laura reviewed the actions she must take. First, there was the matter of finding fresh legal representation. While David had retained lawyers over the years to sort out family business, she was determined to start from a strong, clean slate. Laura knew female friends who had experienced divorce. She had heard all about the bloody strategies both sides employed to wrestle a fair distribution of assets from an angry spouse. Though she doubted David would engage in a fight, she recognized it was best to be prudent.

She would find a skilled, tough, energetic lawyer, preferably a woman, who would represent the sole interests of Laura Bloom. She did, after all, have the right to a respectable future, particularly after years of loyalty to a husband who was no longer capable of caring. If David objected to the terms she had in mind, Laura would go to war.

As she pulled into her home's wide driveway, still considering the legal tactics a future lawyer might suggest and the battle plan they would jointly devise, she was surprised to see Jacob's sleek Lexus parked in front of the garage. She spotted her son-in-law standing soberly on the covered front porch.

Pulling to a stop, Laura opened the car door. "Jacob, what's wrong? Is Rachel all right?"

"She's fine," he affirmed. "Nothing to worry about."

She liked Jacob. She appreciated the fact her daughter had attracted such a handsome, successful young man to her marriage bed. Laura also recognized that her dreams for financial security would finally take full form with her daughter's union to a family of wealth and reputation. Laura would occasionally catch herself wishing she had been so lucky; that she had also married into a family of substance rather than a man with a background not much better than her own. And though he had possessed great energy, David had proven himself emotionally very weak. Laura realized that had she made better choices life would have been much easier.

Usually, Laura took delight in Jacob's rare visits. But on this occasion, studying the strong shoulders stooped with worry; noting the humorous eyes that this time held so much seriousness; seeing the thin leather briefcase he carried; Laura grew wary of this unexpected visit.

She glanced at the gold Cartier wristwatch David had presented to her eight years ago when his fledgling company first turned a profit.

"It's still early," Laura said, striding up the graceful front brick steps. "Why aren't you at the office?"

"I need to talk to you."

His clipped sentence cemented her concern. "I'm not talking on the porch, Jacob. You'd better come in."

When they entered, she led him to the kitchen. "How's Rachel?"

"She sends her love."

Laura's look was ice. "She hasn't phoned since she left for Ireland."

"She's been busy. She promises to call you tomorrow."

"Don't apologize for her. She should make time to phone her mother."

Jacob placed the briefcase onto the marble-surfaced island. He withdrew an office folder, opening it. Laura saw a stark-white page covered with uniform columns of black numbers.

"This is what you want to talk about?"

His nod was grim. Laura folded her arms, seeing Jacob's uncharacteristic embarrassment.

"I know Rachel asked you to help us contact Peter Lawrence but…"

"Is that what you want?" Laura interrupted. "I thought I made myself clear. On no condition are you to approach Peter Lawrence." Sudden guilt flushed her son-in-law's young face. "But you have, haven't you? Even when I forbade it."

"No I haven't. He won't return my calls. He won't see me."

"Good for Peter. At least someone knows when to mind their own business."

"You don't understand…"

"Oh yes I do. Rachel is doing everything she can think of to protect her father. She won't believe he's a lying bastard. She forgets who suffered from his theft."

"You did," Jacob admitted. "But you have it wrong. David wasn't the thief."

"Oh, I see. Let me guess. Now it's back to Garrett. You're telling me he was the one who stole three million dollars?" Her angry laugh echoed within the cavernous kitchen. "Jacob, I didn't think you were such a fool."

Jacob's intelligent eyes narrowed. "Will you please give me a chance to explain? You're correct about Garrett. He didn't steal three million dollars."

"So you finally found proof. David did steal it."

"No, he didn't. Mrs. Bloom, Garrett stole much more than three million dollars."

Laura felt the first intimations of alarm. "That's a lie."

Jacob pushed the page of analysis closer.

"Look at this," he said, index finger pointing. "Last year, Ledbetter and Bloom had total assets under management of just over one thousand million dollars." His mother-in-law's face filled with confusion. "In other words, Mrs. Bloom, the firm's clients entrusted your husband's company with one billion dollars of their own money to invest."

"A billion? Are you sure?" she said, looking at the page. "David never said."

"David was never one to brag. By City standards, your husband's firm was small potatoes. But it had been growing exponentially ever since he set it up with Garrett; growth that would have continued."

Jacob's voice took on a serious new layer. "Mrs. Bloom, do you have any idea how much your husband's company would have been worth if he had sold it?" He saw a tiny shake of the woman's head. "Let me explain this simply. If the partners of Ledbetter and Bloom had sold the company at fair market value to another investment firm, they would have received about two percent of total assets under management. Do you want to do the math?"

Her look was helpless in the face of such huge numbers.

"A billion dollars times two percent. That's twenty million dollars, Mrs. Bloom. Which means if David and Garrett had sold the company, your family would have walked away with half of that, or approximately ten million, pre-tax."

"Ten million dollars?" Laura gasped.

"But consider this." His finger moved to the bottom of the page. "If the firm doubled in size over the next few years—and based on past performance I suspect it would have—assets under management would double. Which means the sales price would also double."

"Twenty-million," she whispered, her astonished gaze meeting his eyes. "We would have made twenty million dollars?"

"But now you can't sell it, can you Mrs. Bloom? You can't because Garrett has liquidated the partnership. My guess is he's transferred all assets into his new entity, Ledbetter Financial Associates LLC. A company, I remind you, owned solely by him."

Jacob stepped closer. "Garrett Ledbetter stole a minimum of ten million dollars from you and your husband. That of course does not include the future salary and bonuses David will no longer receive from his old firm. But Garrett did more than that. He also stole the possibility of additional financial gains derived from anticipated growth. Growth which your husband, as an equal partner, also helped create and to which he was legally entitled. As you were, because you are his wife."

"But that's impossible," Laura objected, hands covering her mouth. "Garrett came to see me last night. He explained."

"Did he. And what did the fine Mister Ledbetter explain?"

She found a stool, sitting. "He…said he was worried about my future. He told me about the new company he was setting up. He explained it was all for the best. It was the only way he could protect me from possible legal action against David and the old company. He told me what the IRS would do."

"And what did Mister Ledbetter do then?" Jacob pressed.

"He gave me a check. He called it an *ex gratia* payment to make up for all the trouble. He hoped it would help secure my future."

"How much was the check for?"

She could not look at him. "One hundred and seventy-five thousand dollars."

"Which isn't ten or twenty million is it. Did he ask you to sign anything?"

She nodded. "Some sort of document. I don't know, I didn't read it. Garrett said it was all above board. He needed my signature before he gave me the money. He explained it protected me from anything the IRS might find."

"It was probably some sort of forfeiture of rights," Jacob grumbled. "If that's what you signed it means you have no right to seek additional compensation."

The words were too much for Laura Bloom. She stood up, finding her way to the sink. "Garrett would never do that. We've been friends for years."

"Friendship and business don't always mix."

"We trusted each other."

"Greed often overrides trust."

"Garrett couldn't do that. Not to me." Then she demanded, "Jacob, I want proof."

"I don't have proof. Not yet."

"See?" she pounced. "You don't know! You're guessing."

"I know enough to suspect Garrett of fraud. I know enough to realize he's been conning David for over a month, maybe longer. I know that if David were taken to court, they would not convict him because no one could prove beyond reasonable doubt that he ever stole a penny from the company. Don't you want to know the truth?" Jacob appealed. "Don't you want to prove that David wasn't responsible? That it was all a lie and a cover up? Call Peter. Convince him to talk to me."

"You think Peter has proof?"

"I'm sure he does. I need his help. Not for me, but for you. For David and Rachel too. Mrs. Bloom, won't you please call him?"

Laura remained silent, her face stark white beneath heavy makeup.

"I'll let you think about it," Jacob offered, picking up the briefcase. He left the one-page analysis lying on the elegant kitchen island. "I'll leave this with you. If you have any questions, call me. I'll be at the office."

As he started toward the door, the young man turned back to his mother-in-law.

"Mrs. Bloom, can I ask you this? Why would Garrett Ledbetter pay you one-hundred and seventy-five thousand dollars when he didn't have to pay you a cent? Let me answer my own question. He paid you because he worried you'd find out what really happened. In that case, he'd have to pay you a whole lot more. Either that, or go to jail. Instead, he manipulated you into signing a piece of paper that strips you of your legal rights and future wealth. You have to believe me. David wasn't the cheat. It was Garrett all along. Please, Mrs. Bloom. Call Peter."

Then he was gone.

In the sudden silence of her elegant kitchen, Laura Bloom walked unsteadily to the island. She picked up the analysis and studied the numbers. Her confused mind would not allow her to understand. She knew she did not have a head for numbers. She was not a business person. She did not understand why she had been thrust into such a tangle of accusations.

She studied the page, eyes moving to the bottom. Seeing the last line item:

$20,000,000

Twenty-million dollars! Was it possible Garrett had stolen it from her?

She wished she could talk to David. He would know what to do. But he was not there. He was in a psychiatric unit three thousand miles distant. A place she had committed him to because she believed he could no longer take care of himself.

She had a sudden urge to kick herself.

Her cell phone rested on the island countertop. She picked it up. Peter Lawrence's contact details were in the phone's directory. She opened it, hunting for the financial controller's number. She would talk to Peter. He would work with Jacob to break through the curtain of lies and protect her.

But with fingers on the phone she had a sudden thought.

If she was to believe her son-in-law: if Garrett really is lying, if David had lied to her in the past, why couldn't Jacob be lying now? Could Rachel also be lying? And if Jacob and Rachel were so intent on getting to Peter; if they wanted her to call him no matter what…what if Peter was a liar too? Perhaps it was all a trick.

Suddenly, Laura did not know who to trust.

She thought over the discussion with her son-in-law. She remembered what Garrett had told her the previous day, and the unexpected check he had written to her, an amount safely in her bank account.

She again picked up the analysis, studying the cold hard numbers, realizing with sudden clarity that Jacob's visit wasn't a complete waste of time. His numbers held a key if she was brave enough to use it.

A billion dollars under management. Ten million dollars, and perhaps as much as twenty, if they had sold. But it was all gone now. Even if Garrett had lied to her, the old company was bust. She had signed the paperwork. What was left had been pillaged and transferred to a new company, one owned only by Garrett and beyond her reach.

Or was it?

Laura knew if she couldn't trust anyone else, then the only person she could trust was herself. She had taken care of herself for many years before she had met David. She knew she could do so again.

Accessing the ex-partner's phone number was a simple matter of re-dialing because she had talked to him yesterday. When he came on the line she did her best to put a sunny smile in her voice, masking the suspicious anger within.

"Garrett, it's Laura. Thank you so, so much for your visit yesterday. I was hoping you could see me again. Jacob just left and he gave me some figures about our partnership." She smiled, knowing she had stressed the '*our*' perfectly. "But you see, I don't understand it at all. He suggested I phone Peter Lawrence for an explanation, but I thought…" She listened for a moment, detecting wariness in the man's voice. Or was it fear? "No, I haven't talked to Peter. Not yet, anyway."

She heard relief though he worked so hard to hide it, then the quick recovery and an offer to meet. "Yes, the sooner the better. I'll come to you. Tomorrow morning? Eleven? That's wonderful. And Garrett? Thank you so much again. I'm sure you can explain it all in a way I'll understand."

As Laura hung up, she felt the return of old confidence. She thought about tomorrow. It would be exactly like dealing with her parents back in the old days. But unlike that situation, things would turn out different. No one would cheat her of the life she deserved. Not ever again. All she had to do was make clear what she wanted and why she wanted it.

From Garrett, she knew she wanted a lot.

28

I breathe.

In.

Deeper.

Hold.

I am told to push trembling feet hard against soft-dew-covered-grass-of-earth. Right first. Left next. Soft ground yields to human effort.

Exhale.

Repeat. In. Hold. Push. Exhale.

Living breath expands my lungs. Drifts to arms and legs. Lifting torso and head. Grounding me to the light.

I sit with Cutes in the late spring of the Unit's garden. Warm sunshine washes my face. I slept little last night. Awash with medication, I have proven through dark insomnolence that drugs alone cannot stem the tide of anxiousness entombed within; of the fear of what this day and the next will bring. Fear which lit my tired head in warring starbursts, lighting the battlefields where I have fallen, bloody from conflict's aftermath. This morning, nurse suggested respite. After breakfast she leads me to the garden where I have not been since last seeing my girl. Cutes' sensitive eyes drift to fitful hands.

"Adrenalin is your enemy, David," she says like whispered birdsong, sitting next to me on the sun-warmed bench. "When you encounter stress, your body releases adrenalin and it causes panic. Fight or flight. I'm sure you're familiar with the term. Today will be stressful. The medication can't overcome all of it." She closes her eyes, the pretty face relaxed in sunshine. "Breathe deep and stop a racing mind. Cool a troubled heart."

I mimic her but I am not convinced. Too many colliding thoughts to consider.

Dolores still has not called. I crave her company but feel knotted worry in a growling belly, facing the reality of her abandonment. Rachel's absence is also troubling, though Cutes told me my daughter phoned earlier to leave a message. She apologized for not visiting last night. She left word she will see me later in the day with Harrington. She passed along a promise of hope but I fear progress will come too late. It is ludicrous that I must battle my fears only with breath.

"Rachel is a good daughter," Cutes comforts as if tuned in to my psychic combat frequency. "Trust her."

But though I will myself to do so, I cannot be certain. Too much has happened.

"Now again, David. This time close your eyes. Breathe."

Yesterday morning when I met Rachel with the solicitor, I remember her mentioning Jacob and Peter Lawrence. At the time I thought little because my angry mind could not assimilate. But now my head floods with warring possibilities. If the financial controller is involved it means one of two things: Laura and our investments, or Garrett and the company. I think back. Recalling my partner's empty threat to have me fired. I remember now he can't do it. He does not have legal authority. And Laura would not touch our assets without talking to me first. Would she?

Deep within I know: adrenalin is not my sole enemy. Wife and partner are also enemies. Confined to my psychiatric prison, I cannot stop the possibility of more betrayal. My mind illuminates the actions they could take, filling the bright morning with dark permutations. One consequence leaps to mind: I could be made destitute.

Breathe. Breathe. I tell myself to breathe.

When I see my daughter, I must share my suspicions. I must trust her to protect me though I am appalled to rely on anyone, must less Rachel. I have no choice. For weeks, I've had little reason to trust. But I realize if I do not trust I lose, and in losing will have led a life of vain worthlessness.

I open my eyes. Blue and white Nike trainers make solid impressions into damp sods below me. I force myself to acknowledge: I own those shoes. I bought them last November when Laura and I went shopping at Roosevelt Field. I know I am alive because they survived the fire with me. One of the few possessions that did. They prove my existence and the chance to fight on.

I wonder: what is it I want to fight for? The old life back in the craziness of a City of old reality, a life spent years building; or a life of renewal which will come when I am released and go to the fire-damaged house I am convinced I can again call home? If Davy listens to me, of course. Only if he listens.

No matter which course I choose, I remind myself it is all dependent on recapturing my freedom. Which leads to tomorrow. I cannot stop my mind tripping over the hot crucible of tribunal and what will happen if I fail.

Cutes sees sudden deep anxiety.

"Whatever it is you're thinking about, let it go on the breath, David," she instructs and we breathe in again. "Remember. You can choose not to think about things that might harm you. They may never happen."

I exhale but thoughts remain, racing racing eternally racing. Choose? How? *What the fuck are Garrett and Laura up to?*

We exhale. "Remember, let it go on the breath. Push the thoughts away." *Where are Dolores and Rachel? What are they doing?*

"Breathe out, now. Breathe out and find the calm." *Calm? Where?*

We finish. She instructs me to stretch. I do. It feels good despite the screaming tantrums in my head. Cutes smiles like sunshine. "Are you ready?"

"For what?" I ask and force myself to smile back.

"Doctor Tenbrooke," Nurse Cutes reminds me. "She's waiting for you."

Tenbrooke. Balled-up apprehension uncoils in my stomach. "I'll do fine," I say trying to convince myself.

She takes my arm. "I know you will."

***

Jacob was late to bed, the plan to get needed rest interrupted when his cell phone chirped just before 5AM. He picked it up from the bedside table worrying why Rachel had texted so early. But when he scanned the message, he saw it was from his mother-in-law.

Jacob I won't call Peter Lawrence. I've decided to talk to Garrett. I'm sorry.

The few words grated. He did not know why she was up so early. What he did know was he would not be able to get back to sleep.

Jacob went to the kitchen and made a pot of coffee. As he sat at the kitchen table, he pondered Laura's few texted words. He was not certain why she would talk to Ledbetter, though he had some idea and wouldn't put it past her. Though he would never tell Rachel, Jacob believed her mother to be a mash-up of humanity's best and worst traits: courage, greed, caring love, persistence, compassion, manipulation, fear and vindictiveness. It was a dangerous combination.

As he sipped the first cup of the day, Jason glanced again at the simple message. Whatever was behind the reason for Laura's text, he realized he now had little hope of gaining help from Peter Lawrence.

He closed the text and opened the phone's video messaging application. He did not look forward to the call he would make to his wife.

***

Following the disappointing conversation with Jacob, Rachel stood on the balcony of the second-floor hotel room gazing, unseeing, at the stunning views of Bantry Bay. Her arms broke into goosebumps at the thought of failure. The financial controller's cooperation was vital.

The previous day, Jacob had informed his wife of how he hoped to force her mother's hand. Rachel thought it was a long shot and said so. Her mother was rarely forced to do anything she did not believe was in her family's interests. Moreover, she was never forced to do anything that was not in her own best interests.

Moving back into the living room, Rachel considered phoning Laura to plead her case. She rejected the idea. Her mother believed her father was where he belonged, and had made her views of contacting Peter Lawrence clear. Rachel knew if she phoned, they would argue. She didn't have the time or energy to argue.

The tribunal was tomorrow, in less than twenty-four hours. Her sharp mind moved to the single action she had left to take. She had already talked to Harrington who had confirmed the transmission of the email file to the insurance company. The solicitor had agreed with her simple plan. A personal appearance might be enough to set off the threatening legal bomb he had, with Jacob's help, lobbed at them. Rachel knew this plan was also a long shot. The insurance company might well be telling the truth: the fire report may not be finished. Or they could see the threat for what it was—mere bluster— and ignore it. But out of options, Rachel had to try.

Thirty minutes later, dressed in a no-nonsense corporate uniform of black power suit and matching pumps, Rachel drove her rental car out of the remote town. In the light mid-morning traffic, she found the road for Cork City. As she turned onto the coastal road, she glanced back toward the high hill overlooking Bantry, to the spot where the Unit lay hidden.

Rachel prayed she would be in time to help her father.

***

As Laura Bloom stood up from the low office chair, she hid the dawning sense of self-achievement behind an innocent mask of gratitude.

Thank you for your time, Garrett, she said to him. You've explained it all simply so I could understand! she lied dumbly. *Of course I'll give you a few days to consider things. After all, what are friends for?* she hedged nicely.

And then the ball-breaker: *When do you think I will be hearing from you with an offer, Garrett?* she pressed, leaving the threat of legal action unstated because she did not have to.

What she had said during their edgy fifteen-minute meeting had been enough. As she ran through Jacob's typed analysis, it was apparent her son-in-law had done his homework. Garrett's face had drained of color. When she asked with just the right note of joking disbelief, *Garrett I can't believe Jacob is right. Were you truly thinking to steal from me?* he blushed. It was then she knew her son-in-law's logically-drawn assumption was the truth.

Laura Bloom gave him the two options she had decided upon just before the sun rose; the breathtaking choices which forced her awake so early.

The first was a straightforward cash buyout at a fair market price to be determined by a third-party representative, based purely on Jacob's damning numerical analysis. When Garrett asked what she thought a 'fair market price' might entail, she pointed to the figure at the bottom of the page, then smiled her threatening 'let's see what happens' smile she had always used in life's past disputes. When he asked about the other option her coy smile broadened.

"I was thinking a shareholding in your new company would be appropriate, don't you Garrett?" she had suggested. "Fifty percent would seem fair. It would replace what has been…lost…wouldn't it?" They both knew what 'lost' meant.

She took pleasure in watching her husband's ex-partner choke on his coffee. He was not used to negotiating with women who knew what they wanted. When he whined, she scolded him like a child. When he dismissed Jacob's analysis as a fabrication, she reminded him it was based on the financial spreadsheets he had supplied to Rachel. When he threatened that she had already signed an agreement and accepted a fair, final financial settlement she returned the threat, fully knowing he had nothing to fall back on except more lies.

When he sought to rebuke her as a fool, she tapped the white paper and its column of numbers, assuring him that if he was not interested she would find someone in authority who thought otherwise.

Laura noted the sudden perspiration covering the square-set forehead, and wondered how she had ever respected this man whom she now believed to be nothing but a coward.

The meeting ended in abrupt silence. It was obvious Garrett needed time to process the new information.

When Trish opened the door, the personal assistant's smile was unreadable. *Traitor*, Laura's thought as she saw her. *Why didn't you tell me I was being robbed blind?*

Laura took her time leaving. She could see Garrett's discomfort—or was that fear?—as she glanced at the desk. Jacob's analysis lay exactly where she had left it, the damning numbers broadcasting the ex-partner's tricks. She shook his hand, delighting in its limp dampness.

"Thank you again, Garrett. I expect to hear from you soon. Have a wonderful day." Then she was past Trish and out the door.

When she left, Garrett Ledbetter ordered his personal assistant to bring in Peter Lawrence. When Trish responded he was out on a day's leave, her boss steamed toward her. For a moment Trish thought he would hit her. She noted his face, mottled in a fascinating veined pattern of ruddy red.

"Trish, I don't care where the fuck he is. Find him and get him in here!" But as she stepped toward the open door he ordered, "Wait."

He held the offending analysis in a large hand. She was surprised to see it shake. "Put that where no one can find it."

She took the paper, never glancing at it.

"I'm going out. Tell Lawrence he'd better be here when I'm back or he can look for another job." Then he stormed out the door.

When she returned to her desk, Trish busied herself with paperwork until she was certain he had left the building. Then she read the financial analysis Garrett had given to her, which only confirmed her suspicions. Finished, she unlocked her desk's side-file, withdrawing two identical thumb-drive memory sticks from where she had concealed them. Next, she picked up the phone.

"Peter," she said when he came on the line. "Mrs. Bloom has left. So has Garrett. You know the option we discussed? It's time." She listened to the accountant's faltering objections. "We already discussed this. I understand it's hard, Peter, but we need to do it." Hearing worried hesitation, she made the decision for him. "You promised we'd meet. I'll see you at two. I expect you to be there."

When she hung up on the frightened financial director, Trish inserted one of the thumb drives into her computer system. She found the critical files and saved them to her personal, securely encrypted cloud storage. She repeated the process for the second thumb drive. Then she spent fifteen minutes printing out a hard copy of everything. When she was finished, she placed the paperwork into two well-used file folders. Together, the files were over three inches thick.

Next, she printed out the letter of resignation she had drafted weeks ago, following David's abrupt replacement by the thieving imposter. Even then, she knew it was only a matter of time before she used it. The wait was over because she had had enough. When she saw Laura, she sensed what the woman was after. The analysis she had read confirmed it. She would not hang around to watch years of hard teamwork turn into a train wreck as greedy people fought over stolen spoils. Besides, she had never liked Garrett Ledbetter and could not stand working for the man.

Trish walked back into David's old office, now usurped by treachery, and placed her resignation together with the analysis, which she had decided not to hide, onto the oversized executive desk. She rarely used obscene language but Trish had satisfaction in hearing herself curse like an Irishman. "Garrett, go fuck yourself. Hide your own lies."

She laughed at herself, thinking what she had told Jacob during their first uncomfortable meeting was true: like it or not, the Irish really did stick together.

For one last time, the personal assistant's warm eyes turned to the view through the expansive windows, and the mighty Hudson River flowing below towering office blocks. Trish Sullivan thought herself to be a loyal employee. Certainly, she had been steadfastly loyal to David Bloom throughout the almost ten years she had worked for him. Except for Peter Lawrence, she was the firm's most senior employee. She knew she would be loyal to David, no matter what he did. Before now, she had not believed she was in a position to help him. But today, armed with what she had found about the actions Ledbetter would soon take, Trish could again prove that loyalty. Her honesty would cost a good paying job but there were other jobs, after all. Even for a forty-eight-year-old personal assistant like Trish Sullivan, there would always be opportunities for those who did the right thing.

Ruminations complete, she hurried back to her desk. She placed the bulging folders together with the thumb drives into the large executive Gucci briefcase David had given to her a few Christmas's ago, which she always carried. Then she put on her coat and took a cab to the Financial District.

In a busy café, Trish sipped a cold glass of Acqua Panna and waited for Peter Lawrence. When he arrived, ashen-faced, he immediately ordered an uncharacteristic afternoon glass of wine. As Peter gulped his drink, Trish knew she would again have to convince the financial director of the actions they had discussed which he was so reluctant to take. She knew she would twist his arm even if it meant betraying him to the authorities. She hoped it would not come to that. She liked Peter.

But with him or without him, Trish O'Sullivan knew that by the end of the day she would execute the plan to save her former employer whom she also considered a friend.

***

Following the second interview with patient Bloom, Anne Tenbrooke sat alone in a seaside café, stirring milk and sugar into a cup of tea. As she looked out at anchored sailboats and trawlers bobbing in a tranquil harbor, the psychiatrist noted how the delft teacup shook in her hand. She hadn't realized the extent of her exhaustion. Exhaustion was part of the job.

Doctor Tenbrooke could not recall how many Mental Health Tribunals had asked her for service or the number of people she had tried to help. Nor did she care to ruminate on the specifics of the few times justice had been served to a psychiatric patient who suffered. Despite the many setbacks, she chose to fight the challenging battles on behalf of these patients for two reasons.

First, because they were often unable to defend themselves against inscrutable bureaucratic authority, and complex medical and legal processes, most could not understand. Second, she fought on because so many professional psychiatrists had a chokehold over those they sought to treat; power that was often unearned, undeserved and many times misdirected. Power that could cause more harm and hardship than good for the patients they were supposed to serve. Anne Tenbrooke had spent much of her career fighting an uphill battle as she attempted to change an outdated, suspect, and autocratic system of care with arguments driven by justice and compassion. She would not stop now.

Though victories were rare, she could not afford to wallow in the pity that followed the many defeats. Instead, she remained persistent in her belief that with enough energy and opportunity, mental health patients not only in Ireland but globally stood a real chance of being healed. Not by a system that pigeonholed them into various diagnostic black holes, there to be managed with often inappropriate psychiatric drug therapies and treatments. But rather with new, insightful compassion that treated whole human beings as just that: complex people who had the inalienable right to get sick, and if they did, to seek successful treatment and again become mentally well.

Her stubborn advocacy, rarely under-estimated by those she chose to fight, was the cloak of hope she used to keep going. Like anyone, she needed hope to keep fighting the good fight. Which was why, earlier that morning, she had not looked forward to meeting again with David Bloom. With this patient, and what she had experienced at their first interview, she believed she could not advocate as she would like for one simple reason: she feared that David Bloom was mentally unfit.

However, by the time the second meeting finished, Anne Tenbrooke had changed her opinion.

The interview had lasted over an hour. She could see his nervousness the moment he entered the small room they had again been assigned in the Unit. She noted the attention he had given to his dress: the neatly pressed jeans; the carefully washed, newly shaven face; the wary smile he did his best to keep relaxed and open.

She could also detect terror hidden just beneath the dark maroon jumper he wore, the emotion he controlled with furtive rhythmic breathing.

Despite this, his language was fluent. His attention span adequate. The answers to her questions purpose-filled, direct, logical, competent. He was rational, his anger gone. Or at least controlled by a man who had known only grave injustice and had every right to be angry. She recognized that such control was an amazing mental feat in and of itself.

When the interview concluded, he offered her a hand of gratitude. "I'm sorry about yesterday. I was angry. I also wanted to say how much I appreciate your time, Doctor," Bloom had emphasized. "I know your opinion must be independent but I also hope I've convinced you. I'm not a threat. I'm sane. Let me go home."

Now two hours following the meeting, Anne sat alone at the window of the café, sipping her tea, considering the patient's situation. She knew his continued confinement was cruel and unjust. She was convinced David Bloom had been as normal as anyone else prior to experiencing such profound trauma. She also knew that if he had received correct treatment, he should be well along the road to recovery. Justice demanded he be set free.

However, there were complications. She could, of course, keep the facts she had unearthed an hour ago a secret. She could recommend his release into an often-threatening world and allow him to go back to an old life. But she also recognized the possible consequences of that decision.

First, the patient had no old life to go back to. Past routines and relationships were severed by family separation, business disasters, and legal squabbles. Based on her discussions with him, the patient had not yet grasped the enormity of what he faced in America.

The second series of consequences were even more difficult to ignore. While it was possible he no longer experienced psychosis—he continued to claim he had not seen or heard anything unusual since returning to the Unit from hospital—she was certain that if he curtailed the use of current medications, he would relapse. In that event, he could become a risk to himself or others. She had suggested he hire home nursing help to manage the proper use of medication. And she had recommended continuing therapeutic counseling should he leave the Unit. He had agreed to both recommendations. However, if the Tribunal gave David Bloom his freedom, and should he go back to America, she realized there was no method to monitor his progress from Ireland, or ensure he complied with their agreement.

Anne Tenbrooke finished her tea and paid the bill. She decided to mull things over during the trip back to Dublin, a long journey she would make to meet another patient late that evening. As she left the café, Anne had a good idea what she would recommend when tomorrow, she returned to speak to the Tribunal.

In the meantime, she cursed Paul Cutter and similar psychiatrists for their incompetence. She prayed that somehow, someday, they would listen.

Until then, she knew there would always be more David Blooms.

29

I grip the plastic chair, fingers strangely deformed by the intense pressure I apply. Emotions are at war with chemicals in my body. Lexipro pours through me, attempting to induce calm by distorting natural Serotonin released by my brain. But rabid thoughts conflict with medicinally-attempted peace. Cutes was right. The drug can't control the tsunami of my emotions.

The courtyard clock reads 9:45PM. Tomorrow is Tribunal. The evening's medication time was an hour ago. Now, Bollocks growls it's almost lights out and orders us to bed. A group of patients follow instructions and shuffle out the door. Across the way on a cheap wooden bench, Ol' Fella rocks as he gets in a last word with Whale Man. I know he still worries for the big man. They will leave soon because those are the rules.

But fuck if I will.

The Tribunal is scheduled for 3PM. Rachel left an hour ago with solicitor Harrington in tow. My optimism following the meeting with Tenbrooke, the belief I had enlisted aid in the battle for release, has broken on solid rocks of hate.

I want to kill.

Bollocks saunters toward me as I fume.

"Time for lullabies, Bloom" the smart ass says. "What's wrong wit' you? You gonna change for bed aren't ya? It's your day tomorrow," his dumb voice sneers.

I am attired in a fashionable Magee three-piece pinstripe; white linen button-down shirt with burgundy-paisley silk tie; black Oxfords fresh out of the box. Rachel bought them and before leaving insisted I try it all on. She said it was an early Father's Day gift.

"You can't walk into the Tribunal dressed like a bum," she warned. "You must look like the winner you are."

But as I consider her hour-old words, my raging mind realizes it was a peace offering for gifts she could not yet bring as well as for the unwelcome surprise I had uncovered before her arrival. I can't help but wonder if she had prior knowledge of the discovery and is lying for my benefit. Now, I cannot find a reason or the energy to change my smart new clothes.

I flick a black sleeve of the expensive suit coat. "You want it cause I don't give a fuck anymore."

His fat face scowls as he examines the suit. "Not my style. Give it to the Simon Community if you don't want it. What's the matter, Bloom? Get some bad news?"

He knows damned well I got some bad news. The entire community knows though only Bollocks would have the gall to say anything. "Do me a favor and piss off."

"Get to bed."

"I'll go when I'm ready. Leave me alone."

"You got ten minutes. I'll be back."

He saunters toward Ol' Fella and Whale Man undoubtedly to give them similar cheery directives.

I hate Bollocks the most. When the time is right, I'll kill him first. Dismissing my murderous thoughts for another occasion, I instead review the glorious news I received earlier. My day fell apart right after the meeting with Tenbrooke and a few hours before Rachel's visit.

***

I sit on the bed warming in sunshine sailing through the bars, congratulating myself for keeping my head in the face of Tenbrooke's intense questioning. My happy new confidence is interrupted when the Unit's finance guy pays me a visit. I've never met him before and marvel that such a nervous, dour looking creature had managed to get a job at all.

"Are you Mister Bloom?" he whines as he takes off a cheap suit coat. When I nod, he drops the coat on the bed next to mine, making himself at home. He squeezes together pallid sweating hands. I notice he bites his nails to the quick.."I'm sorry to bother you. I tried to get in touch with your daughter but she seems unavailable."

When he mentions Rachel I round on him like a hunting dog."What's wrong with Rachel?"

His wan smile is apologetic."Oh it's not about her, not at all. Something else entirely. I'm Joseph Cronin, Mister Bloom, the Unit's accountant. It's embarrassing and I shouldn't be asking but I have a report to get out tomorrow morning, and, well...."

His voice trails off to nothing.

I look at Joe and the petty too-thin face; the flaxen hair framing liquid eyes."Joe whatever you got to say go on and say it because I've got all the time in the world."

"It's Joseph, please, Mister Bloom," he snivels. Then he sits beside me, like a guy trying on a best-buddy act. He squirms and takes a deep breath.

"The current bill is due," he breathes."Because you are no longer resident in Ireland you will, of course, be charged foreign residency rates. Unfortunately the balance due is rather large."

"Like how large?" I ask Joe, and I do not know where this is going.

He tells me just north of six grand which is easy money, I think, compared to what healthcare costs are in the States, particularly if you don't have medical insurance. But I have insurance in spades and tell him so.

He glances at me with apologetic eyes wide as a fawn's."We contacted your insurance company but they point out your policy does not cover psychiatric care conducted outside the United States." I can tell he wants to bite the nail of his left middle finger right off.

Oh fuck, I think, like I need this right now because I have much much bigger fish to fry and tell him so.

"Medical bills, Joe? Who gives a shit? I have a tribunal tomorrow." My thoughts darken."Look. I didn't ask to come here. I don't want to be here. Why in hell should I pay anything?"

"But the bill is due," he squeals.

I look around. A fellow patient, a young guy named Sweeney who's been here a few weeks longer than me but looks far worse for wear, sits on a bed and pretends not to listen. His long blond hair is a tangled dirty mop and he wears pajamas though it's only late afternoon. I know he's memorizing every word he hears. The entire Unit will know about my visit before the dinner bell is rung.

I ignore Sweeney and instead consider Joe and this new source of administrative frustration. I want to tell him to go away, but realize he's only doing his job and a few grand isn't going to break the bank. I tell him I'll authorize an electronic transfer from my Long Island account if he submits the request.

Joe won't look at me. "We tried that, Mister Bloom. I phoned your bank manager but you see, well…" The pause is way too long. "I'm afraid there isn't enough money in your account to cover it. The request was returned as insufficient funds."

My stomach rolls over. "What do you mean insufficient funds? There's plenty of cash in the account."

"Just for your interest," Joe continues, and out of the corner of my eye I see Sweeney straining to hear, "your bank manager suggests you ring him. I explained that might take some time due to your current, ah, circumstances. He swore he tried to contact you to discuss, um, an exceptional withdrawal your wife made from your joint accounts."

Perspiration pops across my forehead.

"My wife?"

Joe keeps squirming. "The bank manager says she was perfectly within her legal rights, of course, but he heard you were unwell and as a long-term customer thought you should be notified. When I called, he asked me to pass on the message. Confidentially, of course." Joe coughs into his hand and goes on. "He also asked me to say he honestly tried contacting you. He phoned you at your City office but was told you no longer work there."

"I don't? Who told you that?"

Joe shrugs. "That's what your office said to the bank manager." He squirms again. "I'm sorry Mister Bloom but there is still the matter of the outstanding balance and I'm wondering how you intend to pay it." He pulls a clean white tissue from a pocket and gives his running nose a swipe.

I stare at the mousy little man sitting beside me. My head swims with the new information. Then it's all too funny.

"I don't see what's so humorous, Mister Bloom," Joe croaks as I begin to giggle.

"Oh Christ. Oh Jaysus!" My giggles turn to guffaws and I can't stop laughing. "You don't see what's funny? Jesus, Joe. Where's your fucking sense of humor?"

I drape an arm around him, pulling my new best-buddy close. "Joe do you know what I'm worth?"

His thin face is stark white. "I've not a clue."

"Millions! But not anymore, Joe. Not now. Now, I'm worth half-nothing. All I got left is this!" I raise my arms, embracing my prison universe.

My laughter becomes helpless convulsions. I collapse onto the bed, hands to my gut. "Nothing in the account! Oh God in heaven she took it all!"

"Please Mister Bloom. Calm yourself." He looks around for help. All he sees is Sweeney who only shrugs. "Perhaps I should call a nurse?"

The laughter stops.

"Joe, do me a favor."

"What's that Mister Bloom?"

I grab his coat, thrusting it at him. "Go fuck yourself."

"I beg your pardon?"

"Why don't you evict me for failure to pay. Throw me out. What do ya say Joe? Is it a deal?" I pick up my pillow.

I tower over the poor slacker and shake the pillow at him. He rises quick at the mad attack and back-peddles toward the door. "We'll talk later, Mister Bloom. I'm sure your credit is good. I'm so sorry to have bothered you."

"Get out!" I throw the pillow at him. He leaves, terrified. I see Sweeney. His jaw hangs slack, staring at my antics.

"You, too," I yell. "Go on, get the fuck out!"

Sweeney flees after the accountant. Good thing Bollocks isn't around. He's the type who would love to witness a first-class killing, unless of course I kill Bollocks first. Maybe then they'd all leave me alone.

After Joe vacates, I try to process the new information and can't get my head around it. When Cutes calls me for dinner I tell her I'm not feeling well which is the truth. She lets me avoid the stares of fellow patients whom I'm certain now know the dreary details of Bloom's most recent folly. I lay flat on the bed, exhausted.

Only later did Cutes confess to me that the mouse accountant broke every rule in the book by talking to me about financial affairs while confined to a psychiatric unit.

Later, I steam into the courtyard to meet Rachel when she arrives with Harrington. Nothing is funny anymore as I reveal what the accountant told me.

"I don't have a company anymore?" I yell. "Why didn't you tell me? Didn't you think it was important?"

"Dad, calm down. I didn't want to upset you."

"Your mother has cleaned out our accounts? I can't believe it! The bitch!"

Rachel's face turns red. "She didn't tell me. She wouldn't do that."

"David, if it's true we'll take appropriate action," the lawyer promises, but Harrington's face tells me no action is possible.

"What the fuck is going on! Christ, let me out of here." I rush from our table, storming in circles around the empty courtyard. I stalk to the locked door, striking it in hollow frustration. "Let me out!" I yell and Cutes rushes in. Rachel waves her away but the nurse stands close, ready to intervene.

"Dad, sit down. Please. Let me explain." I reluctantly sit.

That's when she tells me everything. Of Garrett's betrayal. Of the financial information she was given, the lies it contains, and what Jacob discovered about foreign bank accounts. Of the plan to enlist Peter's help to prove Garrett's thievery and deception, and the other plan to get their hands on the fire report to prove my innocence. My daughter is adamant she does not know anything about her mother's decision to rob me blind.

Rachel also admits that to date, she has been unable to achieve any of these essential objectives.

When she finishes I glance to Cutes. She has heard everything. I see dis-believing sadness as she leaves, letting us talk on alone.

I turn to my daughter. I see how tired she looks and for once ignore my own rage. "You're working your arse off for me, aren't you?"

She reaches across the table and takes my hand. "You're worth it."

"Tell me why you're so tired."

So she does. She explains she has been sitting all day in the Cork City offices of an elusive insurance company, badgering them to give her the fire report. So far, it hasn't paid off. "But it will. I'm going back in the morning," she promises. "I'm calling Jacob when we're finished here. I'm certain he'll have good news about Peter."

"I hope so."

I shudder. I realize that without Rachel's proof my chances of release grow ever dimmer despite this morning's winning performance with Tenbrooke.

We distract ourselves with a bit of business. Rachel has me sign the retainer Jacob had emailed to her. I worry about payment to Ryan, Willowby & Latham, knowing I don't have enough cash to pay current medical bills much less legal fees. But Rachel says the law firm's clock isn't ticking, and won't ever.

"Good thing cause I'm broke," I say.

"Dad, you still have your investments."

"Do I?" My daughter can't look at me. "Thank Jacob and Matthew for me, will you? I owe them one."

"They're glad to help, Dad."

I study the writing of the retainer and am impressed at being represented by such a renowned group of lawyers. I want to talk about next steps—of what I can do to help—which prompts Harrington to turn to tomorrow: of what he will say and when he will say it; of what I must say and when I must say it; and of critical import, he reminds me again of the role each member of the tribunal plays in formulating an opinion regarding my mental state and possible release.

"Be careful of Cutter. Don't react to him no matter what he says."

"Even if he says I'm a complete maniac and should never see the light of day?"

"Even then."

Harrington asks how it went with Tenbrooke. I try to forget recent troubles. "I think you'd be proud of me. I think I convinced her."

"Let's keep it that way, okay, David?" the solicitor responds and I understand his intent.

Then Rachel makes a big deal of giving me the gifts and insists I try them on. After I change she asks me to turn full circle.

"I was guessing on sizes but it's perfect. There's my Dad," she says with pride, seeing me in a business suit for the first time in weeks. When we finish, she kisses me on the cheek and I escort the pair to the locked door.

"See you tomorrow, David. We'll beat this," Harrington states.

"You better," I respond and my eyes cannot leave my daughter's. "I'm counting on you."

"I know you are Dad. We're doing our best. I promise."

"I know. I love you." It's all I can say.

Then the door unlocks and opens; closes and locks and I am alone.

I glance at the courtyard clock. They left just over an hour ago. For a few minutes I force myself to bask in the light of hope that always comes in my daughter's presence. But as minutes pass, what I have learned earlier from the accountant gnaws at me. What Rachel has revealed infuriates me. With no more need to conceal rage, I sit at the table, hands grasping the plastic chair tight, unmoving—emotions surfacing like sea monsters.

I want to kill.

***

Two hours later, and at the hotel a mile away, Rachel was woken from fitful sleep by the ringing of her cell phone's video messaging. She had talked to Jacob earlier right after she had returned, despondent, from the visit with her father. At that time her husband still had no good news to share with her. But now the phone was ringing again.

She found the bleeping phone in the darkness and answered. Jacob's face filled the screen. For the first time in days she was greeted by a deep, confident smile.

"What?"

"Bingo."

"Bingo?" Rachel sat up in bed and turned on the light. She glanced at her phone's clock. "Jacob, do you know what time it is?"

"Just past midnight your time."

"So what's bingo got to do with anything? I was asleep."

"Hang on." The phone's image wobbled across the organized chaos of a lawyer's office. It settled on a large cluttered desk. Two tiny black rectangular bits of computer hardware filled the screen.

"What are those?" she asked.

"I'll give you three guesses."

"Jacob, it's too late for riddles. If you're not going to tell me I'm going back to sleep."

"Okay, I'll stop teasing. It's proof."

"Proof?"

His grin grew wider. "Peter Lawrence and Trish Sullivan decided to pay a visit."

She sat up higher in bed. "Peter and Trish were with you?"

"They're still here. They're in the boardroom."

She considered the news. "Will they help?"

"Why do you think they're here?" Jacob held up the hardware. "These are thumb drives, Rachel. Storage for miscellaneous data. Stuff like old To Do lists, or recipes, or backups of ancient Christmas photos. Or even," he explained, "information that could lead to jail time. It all depends on what's on them."

"You mean you haven't opened them?"

"Of course I've opened them. I'm a lawyer, Rachel. I open everything."

"Stop screwing around, Jacob. What's on them?"

"What's on them?"

"If you don't tell me what's on them right now, it's no sex for the rest of your life."

"Okay, okay." He grinned again. "We've got everything we need."

"Everything?"

"We got Garrett, honey. He did everything we suspected and more. We still have work to do but we're going to nail him." His smile filled the screen. "Go to sleep. I'll go through it all with you tomorrow. But it's great news for Dad."

"Thank you," she whispered. "I know Dad would say thank you too if he was here."

"Don't thank me. Thank Peter and Trish."

After he wished her love and hung up, Rachel thought of contacting her father to reassure him that after weeks of work, they were making progress. However, she knew he was sleeping. The good news would have to wait until morning. Now, at least she had what she needed to prove her father was never a thief or a liar. One down and one to go.

Rachel settled back in bed knowing she had to be up at six for the drive to Cork City. She had one more piece of the puzzle to weasel out of an obstructionist insurance company. Her efforts at their offices earlier in the day had been a write-off. Tomorrow would be different. She planned to be the first person to walk through the front door and this time there would be hell to pay. As she pulled the thick duvet tight around her, Rachel's tired brain turned to her father and the hope she now held for him.

She fell asleep certain that tomorrow would see him freed.

SECTION FOUR

IRELAND MENTAL HEALTH COMMISSION

PATIENT: DAVID BLOOM

<u>TRIBUNAL</u>

EVALUATION AND OUTCOME

People can easily be held against their will in psychiatric facilities

Mon, Sep 10, 2018, 21:00 by Conor Gallagher, The Irish Times

One of the best insights into the experience of involuntary psychiatric care is offered by Emma Bainbridge who, as part of her doctoral studies at NUIG [National University of Ireland, Galway], surveyed patient experiences shortly after their detention and again three months after discharge.

More than a quarter of the patients who spoke to Bainbridge experienced"at least one coercive measure" while detained. Of these, 81 per cent experienced physical restraint, half experienced seclusion and 70 per cent received forced injections of medication. One person was physically restrained 12 times while another was put in seclusion on 16 occasions.

More than 57 per cent of interviewees said they felt threatened into taking medication, a figure which only dropped slightly to 51 per cent at follow-up.

"Many patients do not believe that the whole tribunal-based governance around involuntary care is truly independent. Importantly, these perspectives persist in many patients even when their symptoms (usually of psychosis) settle," says Prof David Meagher, a psychiatrist who has worked at most stages of the involuntary admission process.

Bainbridge's study illustrates the stark reality of involuntary admission. The State, through the health service, has the power to take away many of the basic rights everyone takes for granted. The check on this power comes from the Mental Health Commission (MHC) and its mental health tribunals: cold, formalistic processes run by sympathetic people who do their best by the patient while trying to minimise risk.

(Partial extract,"People can easily be held against their will in psychiatric facilities", Gallagher, Conor, The Irish Times, 2018.)

30

When he finished talking to Rachel, Jacob jogged back to the board-room. Trish and Peter sat at the boardroom table as they had for the past three hours. The polished oak surface was covered with spreadsheets and correspondence. Empty coffee cups littered a side table. Though tired from an evening of unexpected work, he still couldn't believe his luck.

The visit had come as a complete surprise to the young lawyer. That morning, he had come to work full of dark hopelessness. Due to Laura's recalcitrance, he had written off Peter's cooperation. Instead, he spent a frustrating day considering other methods to obtain proof of his father-in-law's innocence. Nothing he thought of would work.

He had tried to distract himself with client appointments but knew his performance suffered. More than once he had to ask a client to repeat a point, a lack of concentration very unlike the young professional. Jacob's mind was elsewhere. He knew he had failed his father-in-law. In doing so, he had also failed his wife.

Disappointed with himself, he decided to escape the office early. As Jacob slipped on his coat, he received a phone call from reception. Two people wanted to see him. Jacob glanced at his watch. It was past 4PM. He could forget about beating evening rush hour.

"Who are they? Do they have an appointment?"

"No. But they say you're expecting them," the receptionist replied. "Mister Ryan, where do you want me to put them?"

"The boardroom. Tell them I'll be ten minutes."

Jacob went to the men's room. As he combed his hair, he groused to himself about the frustrating practice of law and fatheaded clients who showed up without an appointment. When the full ten minutes had elapsed, he let himself into the boardroom.

Trish O'Sullivan, dressed in a tailored grey business suit, stood at the window gazing out on the impressive City views. Nearby, at the long boardroom table, sat a thin, nervous-looking man Jacob had never met before.

"I hope you don't mind the imposition so late in the afternoon," Trish said, misunderstanding Jacob's surprised face. She motioned to the man seated at the table. "Jacob Ryan, may I introduce Peter Lawrence."

Jacob approached the financial director thinking he was more unassuming than Rachel had described. His stark white face looked scared to death. Perspiration covered a narrow intelligent forehead.

The three shook hands. They all sat down. Without a word, Trish placed a thick file and two thumb drives on the table between them. Jacob's heartrate jumped.

"What's that?"

Trish smiled. "Justice."

The pair spent the next few hours taking Jason through the mountain of material. Peter explained how easy it had been to create false trading accounts for the partnership; how Bloom's purported theft of client assets had never happened; how simple it had been to set up fake bank accounts, write fabricated SEC demands, and siphon off millions to a new company.

Peter pushed a sheet of paper across the table's silky finish. It was the dissolution order which had authorized the liquidation of the Ledbetter & Bloom partnership. The signatures of both partners were scrawled across the bottom of the paper.

"You're telling me David signed this?" Jacob asked incredulously.

Peter shook his head. "It's fake. I assume Garrett scanned a copy of his partner's signature. I'm certain Mister Bloom never saw it."

"Why didn't you tell someone?" Jacob bristled. "You should have called the SEC. It's fraud and you knew it."

The humbled financial director stared at the table, unable to face his inquisitor. "I should have."

"Then why didn't you?" Jacob leaned across the table, eyes never leaving the wayward accountant. "Mister Lawrence, you were a director and officer of the partnership. You had a legal and fiduciary responsibility to report this. Don't you realize you could be charged as a co-conspirator?"

"Jacob, he was afraid," Trish interrupted. "He would have lost his job. A forty-year career was in jeopardy. In fairness to Peter, Mister Ledbetter is a bully. Peter was instructed to destroy all of it. If he had not disobeyed by preserving a copy," her hand swept over the pile of evidence, "none of this would exist."

Jacob sat back in his chair contemplating next actions. He glanced at his watch. It was a few minutes before 7PM. Local SEC offices would be closed for the day. He considered phoning his father for advice but knew any action would have to wait until morning.

Despite his anger at the financial controller's reluctant complicity, Jacob recognized the evidence before him proved his original premise: David Bloom was neither a thief nor a liar. It had all been a set up.

"Would you both be willing to testify against Ledbetter?" They both nodded in agreement. "Would you be willing to come in tomorrow? I want you here when I talk to the SEC." Again, they both nodded. Jacob rose from the table. "I'm going to phone Rachel. I want her to know what we have."

"Can I ask a question?" Trish inquired.

"Of course you can."

"Doesn't launching an SEC investigation take time?"

"I'm afraid so. SEC personnel will have to review all this," Jacob responded, pointing to the pile of evidence. "It will take time to formulate a case."

The PA's face looked troubled. "What happens if the accused flees the country?"

"It could make any proceedings more difficult. Why?"

"Would a case be more effective if, rather than dealing with past discrepancies, the SEC witnessed an actual criminal act in progress?"

Jacob sat down again. "Is Garrett planning something?" She nodded. "How do you know?"

"Garrett saves all confidential correspondence to an encrypted cloud storage account."

"So?"

"I set up the account. I created the passwords." Trish leaned in closer."Jacob, I've been monitoring his plans for months."

"But he hasn't acted yet?"

"Not yet, no."

"Any idea when?"

"When he's pushed."

Jacob stared at her."Pushed?"

"Jacob, all you have to do is push him. He's a coward. Ask Peter. He'll run if you scare him enough."

"Push him and you'll catch Garrett Ledbetter red-handed," Peter Lawrence agreed.

"But what's his plan?" Jacob asked, frustrated."I need details if I'm going to go after Ledbetter."

The PA pulled a second file from the dark Gucci bag. Thick lettering on the folder's cover spelled out a single word: HeavyLift.

"I don't get it."

"You will," Trish replied, placing the folder in front of him."It's all in here."

When she explained, Jacob realized he was being given a noose with which to hang Garrett Ledbetter.

He excused himself to ring his wife. After the short recess, the three of them got back to work, hatching a plan to catch Garrett in the act.

***

Garrett Ledbetter always had a Plan B. In this case, it was a highly-leveraged heavy equipment leasing company headquartered in Alberta, Canada.

HeavyLift served the northern nation's burgeoning mining industry with rental and lease services offering hundreds of moving vehicles. Its heavy equipment inventory, valued at over fifty-million Canadian dollars, included articulated trucks, dozers, compactors, graders, excavators, backhoes, paving equipment, track loaders, pipelayers, and related moving stock. Founded in 1995, it had forced surprising growth by leveraging excessive bank borrowings to finance an ever-increasing pool of equipment. When Canada's mining industry rebounded in 2014, and finding traditional banks no longer receptive to new borrowings due to its dicey balance sheet, the company's principals sought more capital by advertising for private equity investors.

At the time, Garrett had seen the company's small ad in the *Wall Street Journal* and ordered a prospectus. What interested him wasn't the company's balance sheet, which showed dismal net worth, but rather its heavy borrowings. It was for that reason the shares in HeavyLift were so cheap.

Garrett conducted more research. He learned the purchase of the business's rolling stock was financed almost exclusively through a single lender: New York's Chase Bank. Garrett had a grudge against Chase. Prior to the founding of the partnership with Bloom, the bank had turned him down for one personal loan too many. Smelling unrealized potential in HeavyLift and perhaps a chance to get even with Chase, in that year Garrett had ordered Ledbetter & Bloom traders to quietly purchase a small stake in the company.

Since that first purchase, Garrett had ordered the firm's traders to buy a few more shares here and a few more there. The small holding was easily buried in the end-notes of the partnership's annual accounts. Garrett doubted that anyone, not even David Bloom, was aware of the equity position except for the employees who actioned his occasional purchases. In the course of day-to-day rapid-fire trading, even those employees soon forgot.

On the day ex-partner Bloom embarrassed himself at a wedding reception, Garrett decided to hedge his bets by putting Plan B into play. From his hospital bed, in between treatments for a broken nose and bruised face, he ordered his traders to purchase all available HeavyLift stock. When the trade was accepted by the private company's board, Ledbetter & Bloom owned sixty-seven percent of the business.

His next move took place the day before he ordered the liquidation of Ledbetter & Bloom. Garrett phoned HeavyLift's president with a cash offer that overvalued the market price of company shares. The president knew he would be a fool not to accept, and it did not surprise Garrett when he did. Cash between the old partnership and HeavyLift changed hands within hours. Ledbetter & Bloom was now sole owner of an Alberta-based heavy equipment operation.

Late on the same day, Garrett used his revised position as Senior Partner to cut a very sweet deal. Ledbetter & Bloom agreed to an unanticipated bid from a Bermuda-based holding company to purchase the entire shareholding of HeavyLift for pennies on the dollar. The holding company was, of course, secretly owned by Garrett. And other than Garrett, only Peter Lawrence was aware of the transaction and then only because Garrett had needed his help to form the Bermuda-based offshore company in the first place.

When he was finished, HeavyLift was Garrett's personal property which included its lousy balance sheet, fifty-million Canadian dollars-worth of rolling stock, and excessive borrowings still owed to Chase. Though it had personally cost him nothing, it had cost Ledbetter & Bloom stakeholders a million bucks in write-offs, a small creditor line item accrued in the now-defunct partnership's balance sheet. The secretly-rigged trade was already buried in a web of financial records and would remain so now that the partnership was wound up. It made no difference to Garrett because the prize of HeavyLift was his.

HeavyLift was a loaded gun ready to fire. All Garrett had to do was pull the trigger. He viewed the heavy equipment company as a personal Golden Parachute: an escape pod to be used if things ever blew too hot. As with so many past ventures Garrett had formulated, he had prepared with careful diligence. Which is why on the day he had ordered Peter Lawrence to 'push the button' which sank the old partnership, while also commencing trade in Ledbetter & Associates Financial Services LLC, Garrett had actioned the final pieces of the HeavyLift puzzle.

He had been courting the Ukrainian investor for the past two years and had primed the pump with glowing testimonials of HeavyLift's financial potential, half of which were lies. However, on the day Garrett's new City-based financial services company started operation, and for the first time in the two-year dance, he sent the would-be purchaser financial disclosures that were full and transparent. Garrett emphasized the gross value of HeavyLift's rolling stock and significant bank borrowings, and enclosed a recent audit which proved the existence of all equipment assets.

The would-be investor had been chomping at the bit for twenty-four months. Garrett had strung him along with a bevy of lies, knowing his deceptive Ukrainian counterpart expected nothing less. But now, the time had come for the kill even if Garrett really didn't need the money.

After all, Garrett's interest in the sale of HeavyLift was all a game. He was convinced that his ascension to true wealth would come through his new financial services company, Ledbetter & Associates Financial Services. As sole owner, he was no longer burdened by an ineffective business partner. Thus, he had already laid the groundwork for significant riches. Which is why earlier that day he had scoffed when his ex-partner's wife had presented Jacob Ryan's short financial analysis.

To Garrett, Jacob's hypotheses were rubbish. No, he thought, when he first scanned the young lawyer's work, he would not have been content to sell the old partnership for ten million dollars as Jacob had surmised. Nor would he have sold even for twenty million. As sole owner of a new company, Garrett had his eye on a sum that would prove transformational.

Garrett was convinced that with a bit of effort, he could turn Ledbetter & Associates Financial Services into a $10 billion assets-under-management company. Based on the old partnership's past performance, and considering ever-increasing market confidence, he did not believe it would take too long—five years, perhaps less. When he hit that heady AUM number, Garrett would execute an exit strategy of stunning proportions. He would find a buyer. But not for ten million. Not even for twenty or thirty million.

Two hundred million dollars. That was Garrett's target. That was real money. And when it happened, it would all be his.

However, this morning's visit from Laura Bloom had upset his plans. Though she had underestimated his intent, her threat of informing the authorities was unsettling if not explicit. Garrett did not know if she was blustering. But if she found the guts, and luck, to get the attention of the SEC, IRS, or New York State agencies, Garrett realized he could suffer disastrous consequences.

Garrett also recognized that Jacob's involvement could prove catastrophic. As an employee of an effective legal firm and son of the senior partner, he could muster a strong offense to dig too deep into hidden discrepancies.

Sitting at his desk, the flamboyant businessman picked up Jacob's brief financial analysis for what must have been the hundredth time. He realized the young lawyer's numbers held nothing new. They were all based on the financial spreadsheets he had given to Rachel, numbers that were fabricated from a mountain of lies. Yet he also recognized that Jacob's analysis had provided deep insight to a woman he believed to be ignorantly ineffectual.

He had underestimated Laura Bloom.

Her ungrateful phone call the previous evening had caused him to lose sleep. Her visit that morning, with its unvarnished threats, was more disturbing. He had tried to bully her. He had tried to quash her. But the woman's obstinance had seen right through his thin tissue of lies. Though he knew an audit of the old partnership would find nothing, he did not relish the prospects of a visit by the SEC and their vicious bloodhounds. He knew they always found something no matter how clean a business's books.

He could not help but wonder how clean Peter Lawrence had left the books at now-defunct Ledbetter & Bloom? He had a sudden urge to talk to Peter and could not help but wonder at the whereabouts of his financial controller. Trish had said he was on a day's leave. When Garrett came back from a late lunch following the unsatisfactory meeting with Laura, he had stalked to the financial controller's office only to find the door locked. Peter's personal assistant confirmed his boss was out for the day. When Garrett tried phoning Lawrence on his private cell phone, he would not pick up.

Where was Peter Lawrence?

Then there was Trish. Her resignation letter sat in front of him. He had read the first paragraph. He would not give her the satisfaction of reading more.

Laura then Peter then Trish. To Garrett, it was all too much of a coincidence.

He knew what he was considering was an over-reaction. He knew himself well enough to know he was predisposed to feelings of paranoia. He realized that if he acted, he could be bypassing a once in a lifetime two-hundred-million-dollar future. But he also feared that if he did not act, he could lose everything. He could also spend much of the rest of his life in a Federal Penitentiary, which would pose a true inconvenience.

As he mulled over possible actions, the desk phone rang on his direct line. Few people had the number. When Garrett answered, the abrupt conversation forced his hand.

The tough voice identified itself as George Pandopolous. He stated he was with the New York office of the Securities and Exchange Commission. A discrepancy had been reported. In no uncertain terms, he informed Garrett of an investigation for suspected trading irregularities at Ledbetter & Bloom, now in liquidation. The IRS and FBI had been notified. Pandopolous stated the call was a courtesy: he was phoning to instruct Mr. Ledbetter to make himself available tomorrow morning at 0930 in the SEC's New York offices. If he did not show up, a warrant would be issued for his arrest.

It never dawned on Garrett that the SEC seldom traded in such convivial conversations. Often, they announced their suspicions by breaking down the door of an unsuspecting trader.

Not for the first time in Garrett's life, fear overcame prudence. He executed Plan B.

Following the SEC phone call, Garrett called the unscrupulous Ukrainian investor. Hiding the high-stakes pressure he was now under behind a smooth greeting, Garrett stated he was willing to part with Can$50 million in HeavyLift rolling stock for a mere twenty million Canadian dollars. The fact they both knew Chase Bank was still owed over forty-million was beside the point. Garrett never had any intention of paying back the bank. Neither would the Ukrainian. Following any sale, Garrett was certain the heavy equipment would disappear into the desolate hills of Canada's mining community, sold for cash to unknowing buyers on the cheap but for a handsome profit to the Ukrainian businessman.

At such a steep discount, Garrett believed the Slavic investor would not resist. Nor did he. Thirty minutes later he phoned back. They haggled a bit. An hour later, still smarting from his morning meeting with Laura Bloom and the threatening SEC phone call, Garrett took heart when the Russian phoned again to confirm a deal. The final price: CAN$12 million. Garrett had already prepared contracts. He filled in the blanks and emailed them using a secure VPN Internet provider. When the signed copy was returned moments later Garrett saved it to his encrypted cloud account where he always saved private correspondents. The digitized communiqué between buyer and seller agreed that the transaction would be fully executed upon receipt of payment.

Sitting in the office he had stolen from his naïve ex-partner, Garrett looked at his watch. It was 10:24PM EDT. Suspecting enough time had elapsed, his clumsy fingers tapped on a computer keyboard. Once again using secure VPN, he accessed his private company's Bermuda-based bank, and an offshore account that this time was all too real. His broad face broke into a healthy grin at the sudden appearance of the Canadian $12 million deposit.

Garrett Ledbetter leaned back in his seat, gloating at the result.

Fuck Laura Bloom and her ridiculous plans to thwart his financial future, he thought. Fuck Trish O'Sullivan and Peter Lawrence for their disloyalty. Yes, he could kiss goodbye the prospect of selling his new financial services company for some mind-boggling amount. But Garrett was practical enough to know that a few million in the bank now was worth far more than nothing in the future, which was possible if the SEC found anything.

For now, Garrett had twelve million Canadian dollars tucked away in his personal account. He was sole owner of a Bermuda-based off-shore company which, he believed, had even greater prospects. When he walked through the door of his yet to be used Caribbean offices, as he knew he would soon, he would start to plan an even greater coup because as he studied the bright offshore bank balance, an exciting new opportunity occurred to Garrett.

There was no reason why he couldn't move the entire operation of Ledbetter & Associates Financial Services from New York's miserable weather to the sunny freedom of Bermuda. By changing a name here, an address there, he was certain he could wrangle a new trading license. And there wasn't a thing the SEC or IRS or Laura Bloom or Jacob Ryan could do about it.

The eventual sale of his company for two hundred million dollars seemed once again within reach. He relished the thought.

Smiling once more, Garrett glanced again at his watch. Only a half-hour had passed. A good thing too because he had some packing to do, a flight out of the United States to book, some Caribbean beaches and bars to visit, and some good-looking gents to meet.

He turned to his computer, accessing a secure Internet connection. He saved a copy of the overseas bank transaction to his encrypted cloud account. Next, he booked a one-way flight to Bermuda's L.F. Wade International Airport which he also filed to encrypted storage. Finally, he printed out the ticket and turned off the computer. Gathering his coat and briefcase, he strode to the door.

Garrett Ledbetter took one last look around the office he had embezzled. He would soon forget the details of his betrayal because that was how life worked. A man could choose to forget so he could move on to a new day and a new reality, thereby again knowing happy freedom.

One last thought occurred to him. He must remember to phone his private banker. He had a check to cancel which would save him a cool one-hundred and seventy-five thousand. What better way to return Laura's threat than with a surprise parting shot?

With a smile on his face, Garrett turned his back on the past and stepped out the door to a future of endless possibilities.

***

Two miles away, Trish O'Sullivan sat at Jacob's computer monitoring the activity of Garrett Ledbetter's encrypted cloud storage account. Peter slouched, sweating, at a small table, drinking a cup of tepid tea. A few hours earlier, the three of them had moved into Jacob's cramped office. An hour later another man, Doug Williams—a retired SEC official, a man as big as a New York Giant's tackle, and a sometimes consultant to Ryan, Willowby & Latham—joined them. Following a detailed briefing he made a phone call.

"My God is he good," Trish whispered to Jacob. "Where did you find him?" They all listened as Williams bullied their unseen opponent. When he hung up, the hired gun grinned.

"It's done. He fell for it. Now I got to get home," Williams said in a gruff Brooklyn accent. "My grandkids are visiting."

"Hang on just in case he needs another push," Jacob pressed. "Please, Doug."

Williams spent the time grousing as they waited.

At 9:35PM by Jacob's watch Trish, still sitting in front of the computer screen, sat straight up in her chair. "Well, look what Mister Ledbetter is up to."

She printed a multi-page document. Jacob started reading the signed contract spelling out the details of the HeavyLift sale. At 10:49PM, two more documents showed up. Again, Trish punched the print icon. A copy of Garrett's off-shore bank transaction spit out of a printer onto a side table, together with details of a morning flight to Bermuda.

"It worked," Jacob cheered. "We got the bastard by the balls."

Williams turned to him. "Now can I go home?"

"One more favor, Doug, and I'll buy you a case of Bud. Who do you still know at the SEC?"

The older man scratched his enormous balding head. "Nancy Griffiths. She still works there and we're good friends."

"Good enough to phone her at home?"

"Now?" Williams frowned. "It's almost eleven."

Jacob punched him on the arm. "Come on, Doug. Don't you think she'd like to be the cause of a morning stir at JFK?" He turned to the others in the room. "What do you think, people? Want to go too?"

"I'm in," Trish chimed. "I want to see his face."

"Me too," Peter chipped in. "Garrett has it coming. But Jacob…"

"Don't worry. I won't tell the SEC a thing." Jacob placed a reassuring hand on the financial controller's shoulder. "We'll figure it out, Peter. You've done good."

Jacob turned back to the retired SEC man. "So, Doug, what about it? You want to be on the side of truth and justice and make that call, or do you want to go down in history as a soulless scumbag?"

Williams gazed back at the three expectant business people. "Ah shit. I guess truth and justice wins any day. But you owe my grandkids big time."

***

I am afraid in the night.

From the bed, I gaze upon blank walls and barred windows of my prison. Ghosting light from a distant dawn filters into the ward turning fellow men into specters of sleeping indifference.

4AM and I have not slept.

When Bollocks came in for night-check I feigned sleep beneath thin blankets, the touch of his inquisitive torch on my face. Its warmth reminded me of distant lighthouses. When it was gone, I was adrift and have been all night.

In my bed, rivers of twisting thought wash over me. In hours, a tribunal of people I do not know will decide my life. Before that, I am certain I will learn of my daughter's failure with the insurance company. I am frightened by the knowledge of Dolores's abandonment.

I yearn to hold someone's hand. To hear words of reassurance. To be held like a six-year-old. Like my mother did, who before she was ill always reassured me with the strength of her love.

Earlier today, Cutes said my psychosis has evaporated on the tide of drugs but the knowledge gives no comfort. I cannot confess this to anyone but

—I miss my dog—my mother's love and father's strength—an Island lad's youthful first love—the solid reality of a beaming lighthouse—

I want to go back. Even if they are nothing but illusion, I would give anything to again live my mad dreams.

Lying on this strange bed on an early morning before a tribunal's ugly sentence I roll over, eyes closed tight and pray:

Lord, if they do not let me free,
Let me go Mad, Lord, Mad.
So I might find the light of dreams,
And rest in their love again.

Then I realize what would happen if my prayer is answered, and in the night

I shake with terror.

31

<u>0752hrs Irish Summertime</u>

Breakfast. Men grouse as they eat. I nibble at the corner of scrambled egg but they taste of bitter anxiety.

Whale Man reaches across the table. Hope rises again within addled psychotic eyes as he grips my hand too tight, wishing me luck. "Go get 'em brother. We're counting on ya. Rose-Marie sends luck." His face is filled with an unspoken promise: If brother can do it, I can too.

Ol' Fella rocks and rocks not touching food at all, still wearing torn pajama top, distant look in somber eyes. His loneliness so consuming he does not see me.

My head is also full but not with loneliness. Instead, a thousand hot conflicting 'What ifs?' careen through my brain's billion nervous neurons.

What if:

I don't get out or I do get out and let down Rachel and

I never again see Dolores or

Cutter wins and I lose or

I keep my cool but lose my sanity or

I get out and don't have anywhere to go but what will Laura do and what has she already done and/or what has Garrett done to me and how can I strike back: but

does it matter does any of it matter because no one gives a shit, not really, do they?

Not even me?

Unsteady, I get up and join the hopeless queue for meds. Meeting Bollocks and two paper cups at the door. Swallowing, determined not to gag. Seeing the smirking face I want to slap.

"Good luck today, Bloom." He leans close so no one else will hear. "You don't stand a chance."

He's right. I wish I had a knife.

0952hrs Irish Summertime

Rachel Bloom had been waiting in the Insurance Company reception area since 8AM. She glanced again at her watch. It would take two hours to drive back to Bantry. The tribunal was at three. Which meant at the absolute latest, she must leave Cork City by 1PM.

She had little more than three hours to get the fire report. If, of course, it existed at all.

Rachel had already stalked up to the reception desk a dozen times, reminding the young Irish woman she was still waiting. On each occasion she was told the senior manager she must see was still not available.

Rachel clung to hope. That morning Harrington had phoned, then Jacob. The Irish solicitor was now armed with a pile of evidence which proved beyond doubt that her father was innocent of theft. He would meet her at the Unit. She promised she would do everything in her power to be there on time.

But he needed more than a promise. Harrington needed that report.

Sitting again in an uncomfortable reception chair, surrounded by other waiting customers, Rachel held mounting frustration in check, determined that Jacob's success would be followed by her own.

1103hrs Irish Summertime

Cutes wraps the cuff around my arm, deep eyes filled with concern.

"One-forty-nine over eighty," she pronounces, frowning at the digital readout of my daily blood pressure. "Your heartrate is up to eighty-nine beats per minute."

"Don't tell me to relax. It's patronizing."

She smiles. "Okay, so I won't tell you to relax. But you have to relax."

I can't smile back. "What if I fuck it all up?"

"You won't. Do you want to do some breathing exercises?"

I nod like a helpless kid. She begins.

As I breathe in, I do not tell her that again—I hear—

the Goddam ticking.

1118hrs Irish Summertime

Anne Tenbrooke left her Dublin clinic for the drive to Bantry at eight AM sharp. During a sleepless night she had tussled over the recommendation she would make to the tribunal that afternoon. The psychiatrist had suspected she would come to a decision about David Bloom by morning but had not. Instead, the war in her head continued as she drove the late-modeled Porsche two-seater west onto the M7 motorway. The battle continued as she turned south on the M8, driving through thinning traffic and past the verdant green fields of Ireland's heartland.

In County Tipperary, she stopped at a small restaurant in the tourist town of Cashel. The weather held and in the late-morning sunshine Anne sat at a flimsy outdoor table sipping tea. As she mulled through her thinking, she watched visitors flock toward an ancient fortress which was also one of Ireland's famous tourist attractions.

She was still certain David Bloom's involuntary admission had been made without merit. She was confident the patient's consulting psychiatrist had acted inappropriately. She knew if she was David Bloom, she would consider legal action due to the malpractice he had endured, even if in the circumstances it was unlikely to succeed.

And yet, there was still the other troubling consideration. One that pointed to Bloom's continuing mental illness. One that could place him in jeopardy should he be released. A mental decline, she reminded herself, that was the fault not of Bloom but of his present psychiatrist.

Still unsure of what to recommend to the tribunal, Anne's intelligent eyes looked up at the ancient Rock of Cashel which towered high on its stony promontory. Within its strong castle walls, the Kings of Munster had deliberated justice as far back as the 12th Century. She wished she had the counsel of such wise royal deliberators. Still uncertain, Anne climbed back into the tiny car and again headed south.

Still thinking of the Kings of Munster and the justice they served, it was only as she passed Cork City and turned southwest down the narrow hedge-lined backroads toward Bantry that she realized what she must do.

Anne had spent her entire professional life fighting for the rights of the mistreated mentally ill. David Bloom had been mistreated. He had been stripped of his human rights due to a broken system. For that reason and that reason alone, at the tribunal she would recommend the immediate release of this patient.

As for the other consideration, the one she had discovered due to a simple hunch and a single phone call to local Garda personnel; the one that proved beyond a shadow of a doubt that David Bloom continued to suffer from mental illness, no matter whose fault it was; the finding that could result in the patient's continuing involuntary admission by proving David Bloom still suffered from serious psychosis; on that point:

Anne Tenbrooke decided she would not say a word. She was certain that with the right diagnosis, the right medication, the right support back in the arms of his loved one, David Bloom would recover.

Now a half hour from Bantry, she passed the crossroads of Bealnablath where Michael Collins, a founder of the Irish Republic, was ambushed and killed by the British in the late summer of 1922. Seeing his monument, a reminder of horrific bloody engagement, she could not help but wonder if David Bloom might also be ambushed.

Anne Tenbrooke realized that if Paul Cutter had also discovered the same damning information she had unearthed, David Bloom did not stand a chance.

1233hrs Irish Summertime (0733hrs U.S. EDT)

Jacob waited at a kiosk on the crowded floor of JFK's Terminal 2 departures area, sipping a cup of coffee. Late the previous evening, following the extended meeting with the welcome informants, he had scanned and emailed a file of vital documents to the Irish solicitor. He was confident Harrington would use them to argue the release of David Bloom, involuntary mental health patient.

Much earlier that morning, he had also messaged Rachel and again reviewed her plans. He could picture his wife sitting in the Insurance Company reception area, ready for a fight. Jacob grinned. He would not want to be the claims manager. The poor fellow had no idea what would hit him when confronting the anger of Rachel Bloom.

Maybe they had enough now to force his father-in-law's release. But the young lawyer wanted more. He demanded justice.

Jacob looked across the crowded terminal. Trish and Peter sat in a waiting area, partially hidden by the travelling public. The suited financial controller had his head down in a newspaper. Trish, dressed in a pair of jeans and fashionable sweater, sipped a bottle of orange juice. When she met his eyes, he could see her nervous determination.

A hundred feet in the other direction, a small team of men and women dressed in black huddled together near the Delta Air Lines check-in counter. To any outsider, they looked like business associates discussing a pending sales trip. Jacob knew otherwise.

He glanced at his watch. The Bermuda flight was scheduled to depart in just over an hour. His quarry was late. Jacob couldn't help but wonder if the betraying business partner had changed his mind.

He looked again toward the revolving entry doors. At the door nearest to him, a young family of five struggled with suitcases through the tight entrance. Just behind them, Jacob saw a tall unmistakable man who was dressed as elegantly as if it was any ordinary day at the office. Impatient, the businessman waited as the anxious parents shepherded their excited children into the crowded departures area.

Garrett Ledbetter swaggered around the travelers, a thin smile on greedy lips as if party to a well-kept secret. What he did not know was a hundred other people also knew his secret.

Jacob threw his coffee cup into a garbage can. Just as he had planned with the SEC and their FBI attack dogs, he strode toward the target.

"Garrett Ledbetter?"

The businessman, disloyal ex-partner, liar, and thief was forced to stop because Jacob's solid figure stood in his way. Garrett laid on a grin of surprise.

"Jacob! What are you doing here? How are you, boy? How's Rachel?"

"She's in Ireland with her dad."

"That's great, delightful stuff. Sorry Jacob, I can't talk. I'm late for a flight." Garrett tried to push past. Jacob stepped in front of him.

"You mean the one for Bermuda? Delta flight 437, isn't it?"

Ledbetter's smile disappeared. "How did you know that?"

"Oh, I know all sorts of stuff, Garrett. And now, so does the SEC."

Ledbetter found himself surrounded by black suits. Jacob stepped toward the accused man, looking him in the eye.

"Garrett, I want a confession regarding false accusations you've made regarding your business partner, David Bloom. These people are here to help."

As the FBI and SEC agents took Garrett Ledbetter into custody, Jacob joined Peter and Trish to watch the parade. Trish waved as her ex-boss was frog-marched outside.

"He doesn't look too well," Trish deadpanned.

Jacob grinned. "He's going to look a whole lot worse when the SEC is finished with him."

1235hrs Irish Summertime

The insurance claims manager didn't know what hit him. One minute he was extending a hand toward a lovely, well-dressed young American woman and the next minute she was in his face.

"I want that Goddam fire report and I want it right now."

The reception area was filled with customers. The claims manager, a heavyset middle-aged man named John Curry, wished he'd stayed in bed. When he tried to calm her, the young woman stormed to the middle of the packed, sunlit waiting area.

"Hey listen, everyone. See this guy?" she bellowed, pointing at Curry. The insurance company's customers looked. "He's a liar. So is his employer. They're a bunch of corrupt assholes. How can any of you do business with these people?"

The Irish customers, unused to American brashness, shifted uncomfortably.

"Please, miss, that's not necessary," Curry pipped as he hurried to her, trying to stem the tide. "Why don't we find an office?" When he tried to place a mollifying hand on her shoulder Rachel Bloom pushed it away.

"I'm not going anywhere, mister. I've been waiting over four hours for you. I waited all day yesterday for you. You either give me what I want or I'm suing your fat ass."

She pulled out an official-looking letter and thrust it toward him. Curry was forced to take it. It was another demand from Jacob which he had drafted late last night. This one was even more threatening. Written on Ryan, Willowby & Latham letterhead, and signed by his father, it informed the insurance company that because its previous communiqué had been ignored, legal proceedings would commence forthwith. The New York law firm representing David Bloom would sue for breach of contract, personal injury, defamation, and unspecified damages. Bloom's local legal counsel would file with the Cork Circuit Court later that day.

"My father is suffering," Rachel roared."You could help him but you choose not to." She stepped closer as the small crowd watched with growing sympathy."Now which is it? Do you want to extend a professional courtesy by giving me the report now or face a lengthy, expensive, months'-long court case during which, as part of discovery, we'll get it anyway? My father is seriously ill. Are you going to help him or not?"

When Curry scanned the letter, Rachel had the satisfaction of seeing him break into a cold sweat. Finished, he looked up. The crowd of customers scowled at him. An older woman, dressed in a long grey skirt and old flowered blouse, stepped toward Rachel.

"Oh ya poor gersha, what did they ever do to you?" Then she faced the manager, her aging apple cheeks blistering with anger.

"John, are ye not going to help the young one?" she boomed with sharp familiarity.

"Mary, it's complicated. We're trying."

"Well yer not trying hard enough. And don't ye be stopping by the house anytime soon for a cup of tea, do you hear me John Curry, not if you're mistreating such a lovely looking girl." The old woman turned to the rest of the crowd."I've known this young man since he was in short pants and don't listen to him. Too rich for his own good. They all are." Then, turning back to Curry:"Now which is it? Will ye help the poor girl or do I take my business elsewhere?" Rachel heard the crowd's murmuring support.

"Wait here," Curry said, embarrassed."I'll talk to my manager."

"I'll give you five minutes," Rachel responded, glancing at her watch."Five. Do you understand that, mister?"

Nodding, Curry backed away from the temperamental American and angered customers. Though he thought the letter was probably only bluster, John Curry knew what he would recommend to his employers. Local opinion and chattering mouths could make or break an Irish company. They could not afford to take the chance. Holding up a fire report, particularly one that had no evidentiary cause, simply wasn't worth the risk.

Four minutes later, with the report gripped in her hand and the approval of Irish customers tolling in her ears, Rachel was out the door.

As she climbed into her rental car, Rachel couldn't help but glance at the envelope resting in the passenger's seat and wondered at its contents. Then she remembered her dreams. She prayed the report would exonerate her father, not crucify him.

1425hrs Irish Summertime

In his office, Doctor Paul Cutter told the receptionist at Castletownbere Hospital he would hold and put the phone on speaker. The chirpy hold music did not match his mood.

Cutter was angry. He was defensive. He was anxious. And he knew it.

For the past few days he had prepared diligently for the Tribunal of David Bloom. During that time he had reviewed in detail all of the patient files. He had reread his rationale for past diagnoses and treatment decisions. He examined his notes on the patient's self-harming behavior during his stay in the Unit. He summarized the various episodes of Bloom's psychosis. He reread his reasoning for the patient's renewal order.

He was not sure how to handle Bloom's stay in hospital due to the sepsis he had contracted as a result of prescribed drug therapy. It was a blot on his argument and Cutter knew it.

For that reason and despite his preparation, he was still not satisfied that he could make a decisive argument for the continued confinement of his patient. More to the point, he worried he would leave himself open to professional criticism. Needing to plug some holes, and on a hunch, he decided to take additional action.

Yesterday, he had rung a colleague from medical school, a man who now worked as a palliative care specialist at the remote Beara Peninsula hospital. Cutter was chasing a query. A suspicion regarding his patient's continuing lack of mental capacity. Something Bloom had said to Cutter early in his treatment. A remark that went almost unnoticed but had resurfaced in the young psychiatrist's thinking.

If he was right, he knew no matter what any other member of the tribunal might argue, they would be forced to accommodate this patient's best interests by denying release.

Yesterday, his colleague had taken a day's leave. Cutter had phoned again that morning but his university friend had still not shown up for work.

Cutter glanced at his office clock: 1428. The tribunal would start in a half hour. The young doctor knew his last-minute detective work was cutting it fine.

The hold music was replaced by the receptionist as she came back on the line. Dr. Cutter's colleague was now in. She would connect him immediately. When Danny O'Neill picked up, Cutter got right down to business.

"Danny I'm in a bit of bother. I'm looking to track down a person of interest, someone who lived on Bere Island. I was hoping you could help." Cutter listened intently. "That's right. Timeline somewhere between the late-eighties or so and present." He listened again. "Danny, I know it's a pain, but I need that information right now. Like in the next twenty minutes."

Dr. Cutter ignored his colleague's grievances until he was asked a final question. "What's that? The name? Sure, you need a name."

Cutter gave it to him.

1428hrs Irish Summertime

It is early but I have already dressed for combat. I examine myself in the bathroom mirror. The suitcoat hangs perfectly, hiding my growing fear behind tailored armor. My balding head is shaved close with a borrowed Mach 3.

I want to throw up.

I have the Unit's toilet to myself. I do not want company. As I adjust my tie I observe hands that belong to someone else. Unfamiliar hands. Misshapen hands. Hands that shake and I cannot control.

Then deep inside. The silent wail of horror as the room tilts like a Fun House ride. Oh not now. Please not now.

Dolores, come to me. Whatever I have done forgive me. I need your loving strength.

<u>1437hrs Irish Summertime (0957hrs U.S. EDT)</u>

Laura walked through her home's front door following the early morning meeting and decided to have a Bloody Mary. Rarely did she imbibe in a morning drink but this was a cause for celebration. Striding to the kitchen, getting out the rarely-used ingredients, and mixing her cocktail on the expansive island, she recalled the conversation she'd had with her new lawyer which concluded only a half-hour earlier.

The attorney—Megan Whitfield—was everything Laura had been looking for and more. Old enough to possess deep experience, yet young enough to have the energy required for the argumentative rigors of divorce, they had spent two hours getting to know each other, mapping a strategy that would secure Laura's future.

When they finished, the energetic professional looked her new client right in the eye. "Laura, are you certain you're up for this? It will be a journey of emotional exhaustion that takes a great deal of courage. Are you sure?"

"Don't worry about me," Laura insisted "You wouldn't believe what I've survived. Divorce isn't my first choice. But I've learned—if I don't stand up for myself, no one will."

"Even if we have to humiliate your husband?"

Laura hadn't thought of that. "If I'm asked and what I have to say is true, I'll say it."

"Even if your husband's lawyer fights back with fire?"

"I've already fought men who thought they were mental giants."

"What happened?"

"I won."

As Laura sipped her Bloody Mary, thinking again of the meeting and a victory that would certainly be hers, her eye caught the glint of a blinking red light. Someone had left a message on her telephone's answering machine.

Taking the drink with her, Laura strode to a side-counter. Her hand touched the telephone's messaging button.

It was from the bank manager asking her to call him. His few words were urgent.

Two minutes later she had him on the line. Following a perfunctory exchange of greetings, he informed her of the stopped check. He told

Laura the one-hundred and seventy-five-thousand-dollar deposit to her checking account would never see the light of day.

Laura Bloom dropped her glass. The tomato juice-based Bloody Mary, mixed with shards of a fine crystal tumbler, spread like blood across the cold marble floor.

Alone, she began to cry. She found herself wishing she could talk to her husband. She couldn't understand how it had all gone so very wrong. Now, it was too late to do anything about it.

1438hrs Irish Summertime

"Oh God, oh it's so good to see you."

I hold my girl tight, shocked by the sudden visit. We stand again in the garden, the sun playing bright on her auburn hair, surrounded by the fragrance of blooming roses.

"I can only stay a minute."

"How did you get in?"

"The Nurse. She knew how much you wanted to see me."

"Cutes? She's fabulous. She reads my mind."

"I thought I was the only one to read your mind." Dolores gazes at me with delight. "You have a new suit. It's handsome on you."

"Rachel got it for me."

"I wish I had brought you something."

"You did. You brought you."

We sit on the warm bench. I can't take my eyes off her.

"I'm sorry I haven't visited more often. It's been difficult. I wasn't well."

"You were sick?"

"Not anymore." Dolores smiles as bright as a sunbeam.

"You're here now. Nothing else matters. You contacted the solicitor just like you promised, didn't you."

"I had help."

"You mean Rachel? Did you meet her? She never said anything. We'll have all the time in the world for you to meet when I get out of here."

"Davy, I've been thinking." She takes my hand. "When you do get out…"

"And I will."

"Come home."

I can't believe her words."You want me back? But you told me…"

"I've been a fool. I need you. I wish we could move back time. I wish we could start over again."

"We don't have to start again because you're here. Time doesn't matter."

"Doesn't it?" She holds me, brushing away tears."It's almost time. I have to go. Good luck today, Davy." She holds my face in angelic hands."Promise. When you get out you'll come home to me."

"I promise. I'll come home."

<u>1458hrs Irish Summertime</u>

I stand in the hospital's fetid hallway, dressed in the gifted suit too hot for spring and wait. Harrington, at my side, explains as tribunal members stride toward the loaned Room of Judgement.

"That's the tribunal solicitor, there. The older man in the dark blue coat. He'll act as chairman. And the tribunal psychiatrist, he's the bearded man in pinstripes. The woman coming down the hall now, the woman in the pink skirt, she's the lay member. A teacher, I'm told."

Sweat pops deep in my armpits. Despite the wool I am cold. Shuddering.

Think of Dolores, I tell myself. *Remember how good she felt in my arms. Remember what you've promised. The hope for tomorrow she brings.*

He glances at me."Are you okay?"

"Where's Rachel?"

"She's coming. I told you. She phoned." He takes control of my barely contained terror."David, this is not a court proceeding. You are not on trial. What I must do—what we both must do—is clearly establish that you are not a threat to yourself or others. We will fracture the very foundations of your involuntary admission."

I eye the fat briefcase he holds."With what's in there?"

"With what's in here and what Rachel is bringing." He pokes at my sweating forehead."Also with what's in here."

My fear crystalizes, cold as ice.

Tenbrooke strides down the hall absorbed in a document she holds, reading as she walks. I think she will not look at me. She looks up. Meeting my eye.

I see her honest smile. She nods to me then to my solicitor as she enters the room. Harrington grins when she is gone. "That's good."

"What? A smile?"

"Damned right a smile. If she didn't smile I'd be worried."

"You're not worried?"

He checks his watch again. "I wish your daughter would show up."

Then she's here. Running down the hall, her pretty face red with exertion. She thrusts a fat envelope into Harrington's waiting hands. Then she's in my arms.

"It's going to be all right, Dad. It's going to be fine."

My face fills with questions.

"Yes. It's the fire report." But she has more news. "Dad, Garrett was arrested. You never stole anything. Garrett did."

I breathe deep. I don't know how to thank her and my son-in-law. I wish I could share the news with Dolores. I feel lifted up in the brightness of her light.

Harrington has the fire report open. It's thick, fifty pages long. I look at my watch. It is exactly 3PM. The tribunal chairman looks out the door, seeking Harrington's attention. They are ready.

"We just received some information relevant to the hearing," my lawyer growls and holds up the document. "I request ten minutes to read this."

The chairman agrees. He notes they are also waiting for a final attendee to turn up. He's rung. He's late. I hear a name but am too nervous to make it out.

"Who are we waiting for?" I ask when the chairman leaves. Harrington is deep into the text of the report.

"Doctor Cutter," he utters, continuing to read. I push down the urge to run.

At my side, Rachel waits for Harrington to reach a conclusion. "You're coming in with me, aren't you?" I ask her.

She grasps my hand. "Oh, Dad. I can't. Don't you remember?"

"No family or friends, David. Only you, me, Cutter, Doctor Tenbrooke, and the tribunal members," he says, absorbed in the text. He turns a page and grunts.

"What?" Rachel asks.

"It doesn't reach a conclusion."

"What?"

"The cause of the fire has not been determined." Harrington turns to me and I hear false confidence. "They can't prove you did it, David. That's how I'll argue. You were not a threat to yourself or others and never have been."

But I know what he really means. If they can't prove I did it, we can't prove I didn't.

A man in a dark expensive suit wearing round glasses hurries down the hall. Unlike Tenbrooke, Cutter will not look me in the eye. Nor does he look at Harrington or my daughter. He wears a cocky piss-ant smile as he enters the room.

"Just keep your cool, Dad. Remember, don't listen to him."

Harrington preaches final encouragement. Rachel hugs me with final words of love. I cannot hear them. I hear only the pressure of blood pushing through a heaving mind.

As I leave Rachel to step through the door, I sense distant ticking. My hour is come. I pray it will not be as terrible as the 10PM of my past.

I pray I get out to do what I have promised. I pray I go home to Dolores.

32

Harrington:"We question the veracity of the involuntary admission. We are not convinced the process was lawful."

My solicitor speaks first. He attempts to get me out on a legal technicality. There is a chance, however slight, that my admission was executed unlawfully. Many involuntary patients play this card. Most lose.

Chairman responds, not unkindly:"Mister Harrington, the tribunal has reviewed Mister Bloom's admission. Everything is in order. The detention was lawfully executed."

Lawfully?

I grin as I remember that day. Across the table, Chairman tries to read my mind.

If this is not a trial, it feels like it.

Three tribunal members sit like judges on one side of a long table wedged into the nondescript airless room. Tenbrooke is seated to my left, at the end. She listens, waiting her turn to speak. Opposite and to my right, boy Cutter has his pugnacious nose in a thick folder which I know is mine. Like a prosecutor, he ignores me with acute dispassion.

As if a defendant with legal counsel, Harrington and I sit facing the tribunal. They will witness my every reaction.

Breathe. Be calm. Remember what Rachel said.

Rebuffed, Harrington consults a heavy folder holding his planned argument. He stands, taking the posture of a courtroom litigator.

Tribunals are supposed to be inquisitorial; a humane discussion which leads to a determination of what is best for the patient: freedom or continued involuntary admission. But with so much at stake, tribunals can descend into an adversarial circus right out of an old television courtroom drama. I will witness this at first hand because I smell blood.

Harrington:"Then let me summarize why my client's original detention is as fundamentally flawed today as it was on the day he was admitted against his will."

He paces as he argues. His voice large. Logical. I hear only snatches because I am busy hiding my soul from Members who watch me for signs of madness.

Let me be as still as Prince. Let me be a hunting dog silently pointing his prey.

"He was accused of uncharacteristic theft… violence due to alcoholism … mental incapacity."

He lays out facts like fat dominos. I am dumbstruck by the insane details of Garrett's betrayal: the discovery that my purported theft never took place; the knowledge that all accusations against me are lies.

I glare at Cutter.

Why wouldn't you listen to me? You rat. You fucking ass.

The Psychiatrist Member. Inches from me. Studies my reaction with inquisitive eyes.

Don't let him see your anger. Breathe. Listen to your lawyer.

Harrington:"The man accusing Mister Bloom of theft has himself been arrested by American authorities for fraud. My client suffered undo emotional trauma due to this repugnant betrayal. Subsequently, he engaged in a violent act by striking his business partner. I assure you, if I had been the target of such betrayal I would have also lashed out."

He waves a fist-full of paperwork at the tribunal."Here it is. The truth."

Fine words, Harrington. But my God. What did Garrett do to me? He has cost me a career. My family. My freedom. I'll murder the man.

Harrington:"As to Mister Bloom's purported alcoholism?" He holds up a sheaf of lose papers. They flutter in his hand."These are affidavits signed by people who know my client. They include his personal assistant and financial director. Affidavits from his daughter, son-in-law, friends, and neighbors. All attest to a simple fact of general knowledge: for years this man has been abstinent. He does not take a drink. Not one."

Harrington never mentioned affidavits. Even Rachel believes me now.

Harrington:"We must also remember Mister Bloom's grief. The recent death of his father greatly affected him, compounding the traumatic loss of his mother by suicide during this man's younger years. But there were more harmful factors at play." He strides back to the table, extracting a bound document, holding it high."Parental alienation."

What in God's name is parental alienation?

Psychiatrist Member:"Mister Harrington, this is hardly relevant."

Harrington:"The World Health Organization seems to think it is." He points to the cover and the WHO logo so all can see."Doctor, are you familiar with parental alienation?"

Psychiatric Member:"Of course I am." He takes off his glasses."I admit my depth of knowledge isn't too deep."

Harrington:"Then let me remind you." He reads from the document."Bernet et al, two-thousand-and-ten, considers a primary feature of parental alienation to be where a child whose parents are engaged in a high conflict divorce or separation allies himself or herself strongly with one parent while rejecting the relationship with the other previously loved parent without legitimate justification." He stares at the psychiatrist."I repeat: without justification." Harrington places the document before the tribunal.

He's talking about Rachel.

Harrington:"My client's estranged wife, hurt and desperately seeking revenge, manipulated this man's only daughter, whom he loves with all his heart, to turn against him. The daughter believed her mother's accusation that Mister Bloom was a thief and a liar. She believed her mother's accusation that Mister Bloom was an alcoholic. So much so that his daughter barred him from her wedding. So much so that she was convinced to sign an admission order. Yet as we have already shown, there was no justification for these attacks on Mister Bloom's character."

Psychiatrist Member:"But his daughter is hardly a child. Certainly, she is old enough to make up her own mind."

Harrington:"Perhaps. But a strong-willed parent can cause untold damage. I know. I've seen it. Can I ask you, do you have children? Yes? Can you imagine the pain and instability you would suffer should your only child stop talking to you for no legitimate reason? To bar you from her wedding? To accuse you of horrendous acts with no justification? By happy chance, his daughter has rejected her mother's lies. She now knows the truth. Yes, Mister Bloom's behaviour was, for a time, questionable. However, we have already discussed the reasons for such behaviour.." He addresses the Chairman. "What my client suffered was unconscionable. It would drive me to distraction, as it would any loving parent."

Christ, what did my family do to me?

Harrington: "Together with all the other issues he faced—pressures and betrayal at his place of work; a home that was anything but loving— my client faced stresses in his life which most could not have coped. Yet for the most part he did."

My mother. My father. Laura. Oh God, I have lost so much. But remember Rachel and Dolores. They have come back to me. Hold onto that.

Harrington: "Let's now address the fundamental reason why Mister Bloom was involuntarily admitted: the assumption he was a threat to himself or others. In Mister Bloom's case it is believed he purposely started a fire with the intention of taking his own life." He picks up the fifty-page report. "Mister Bloom's purported harm against himself cannot be proved."

Listen to this. Here, Harrington reaches for a truth they must believe.

Harrington: "The report finds that in all probability the fire was started accidentally; the cause will never be precisely known due to extensive damage. The report reasons that in all likelihood my client was not the cause."

I was not the cause! Believe it!

Harrington: "Mister Bloom swears he did not start the fire. The fire report does not prove that he did. For that reason alone, we cannot assume he was or has ever been a threat to himself. Mister Bloom categorically denies trying to harm himself. Furthermore, he admits to becoming confused during the fire's chaos. He thought someone was in the house with him. At personal disregard to his own safety, he reentered the blaze in an attempt to save a life."

Oh, Dolores. Why aren't you with me to hear this?

Harrington: "Mister Bloom should not be punished for such self-sacrifice. Instead, he should be applauded as a hero."

I wonder what the Members are thinking? Do they believe us? Will they believe Cutter instead? See how Chairman listens. Are those tears in Lay Member's eyes?

Harrington:"Mental health law is clear regarding involuntary admission. The patient must be shown to be a threat to himself or others. If he or she is not a threat, then the patient must be released with immediate effect."

He's summing up. Look like an innocent victim.

Harrington:"We have clearly demonstrated that Mister Bloom is a victim rather than a perpetrator of theft. Confronted by the gravity of such betrayal, he acted as any normal person would. We have also demonstrated that he is not an alcoholic. We have shown that he was never a threat to himself or others. For those reasons, we ask the members of this tribunal to agree that Mister Bloom's detainment was unnecessary. Doctor Cutter's renewal order must be denied. It follows that my client must be released immediately."

Hold tight to what Harrington says. Believe it. You are a good man, David Bloom.

Chairman:"Mister Harrington, may I make one observation?"

Harrington:"Of course."

Chairman:"If the fire report does not prove what started the fire, then how can we be certain Mister Bloom did not?"

It is Tenbrooke's turn. She does not stand. Her words rise on wings of conviction.

Tenbrooke:"I have interviewed David Bloom twice. In my opinion this man has been the subject of careless, over-zealous, and inappropriate treatment by his Consulting Psychiatrist."

Oh see how her eyes burn at the mention of Cutter. Do not watch as he squirms beneath her reproachful gaze.

Tenbrooke:"...suffered incorrect diagnoses followed by improper medication. ... I agree with Mister Harrington. The assumptions that this man was a threat to himself or others has never been proven. ... Parental alienation is appropriate to bring up in this case. His wife, now estranged from him, inappropriately manipulated his daughter into seeking the admission order for suspect motives.... Mister Bloom should have been evacuated to hospital for appropriate medical care rather than suffering an admission which only exacerbated his condition. The Consulting Psychiatrist should have come to a proper diagnosis."

Chairman:"Which is?"

Tenbrooke:"Post Traumatic Stress Disorder. I interviewed first responders. They are adamant that Mister Bloom would have perished within minutes had he not been pulled out of the fire. The Consulting Psychiatrist should have taken the trauma of Mister Bloom's exposure to a life-threatening situation into consideration."

She has been talking to Cutes! She agrees with my good Nurse.

Tenbrooke:"It is my professional opinion that David Bloom did not suffer from Hypo-Mania, at least not in the context Doctor Cutter describes. Nor is he schizophrenic. As to the psychotic episodes, may I point out they were triggered by the patient's trauma. The episodes have since subsided due to appropriate drug therapies. I reiterate: David Bloom is not a threat to himself or others."

Look at Lay Member. She is convinced! See the secret smile she wears?

Lay Member:"Doctor Tenbrooke, just to make sure I understand. Are you saying that Doctor Cutter misdiagnosed Mister Bloom? That his time in the Psychiatric Unit together with the wrong drugs he was given actually made his condition worse?"

Tenbrooke:"I am. Unfortunately, Mister Bloom is not alone. Many involuntary patients are mis-diagnosed. Many should never have been brought into a psychiatric treatment environment in the first place. Mister Bloom has suffered a similar fate. He has endured a regime of treatment which can only be described as unnecessarily cruel."

See Cutter wince. Oh, how she cuts him!

Lay Member:"And it is your recommendation that Mister Bloom should be released?"

Tenbrooke:"Provided he continues correctly prescribed drug therapies and seeks appropriate psychiatric follow-up when he gets back to his home in New York, to which he has already agreed. Isn't that correct, Mister Bloom?"

It is not exactly a lie. But I have promised Dolores. I nod, confirming I agree with this kind doctor's advice.

Tenbrooke:"Then yes I do. I recommend Mister Bloom's immediate release."

Oh, feel it! Freedom. Dolores, I am coming home to you. Thank you, Dr. Tenbrooke. But… down the table. Cutter. Look at him.

…why does he squint at me like I am a lamb for the slaughterhouse…

Chairman:"Mister Bloom, what do you think of all this? Why don't you tell all of us why you should go home?"

Don't snivel. Don't shake. Don't lose control. It is time to stand and be a man.

"Yes I had some problems. Yes I was uncooperative. Yes at times I was hostile. Wouldn't you behave like that if you were locked up against your will for no reason?"

Take your time. Look at Harrington's confidence. I must feel that confidence.

"I was minding my own business. Then my world fell apart. Wouldn't you act a little… off? Unlike yourself? Even seem a little… crazy? Mister Harrington has already told you what I faced. I wonder how any of you would have coped. Then, of course, the fire. It was an accident. And no, I was not trying to commit suicide. All I want now is one thing. Please let me go home."

Lie but only a little.

"As I've already promised Doctor Tenbrooke, I'll go to a doctor when I get back. I'll take whatever medication I'm given as long as I agree it will help me. I plan to stay with my daughter, at least in the short term. Please. Give me back my freedom."

For God's sake be strong. Remember, you're not doing this just for you.

"But I'm not the only one to be mistreated, am I? How many others has this system tried to destroy? Every night I hear the nightmares of my fellow patients. I watch their loneliness and hopelessness. Yes, many of these people need help. But have you forgotten we are human beings? You treat us like animals. You lock us up. We don't talk to you because we don't trust you. We know you won't listen. Particularly this man, this trained zookeeper. Instead of listening to me, Cutter almost killed me. He stripped me of my human rights for no reason at all. Just this one time, listen to me."

Be brave. Look Cutter in the eye.

"My name is David Bloom. I am as sane as you are. Release me at once."

See how Cutter will not look at me. See how the Members shift as they consider my damning words.

Psychiatrist Member:"Mister Bloom, thank you for your comments. But I must ask you… in your opinion, are you a threat to yourself or others?"

"Again? I have answered that question many times."

Psychiatric Member:"I don't mean to give offensive. But are you?"

"No. And I never have been. Let me go home."

Chairman:"Thank you Mister Bloom. Please take a seat."

Sit. Breathe. I did it. Rachel and Dolores. They'd both be proud of me.

Chairman:"Doctor Cutter?"

Cutter! My choir boy rises. The rat gazes at me and turns his fawning, defeated smile to the Members.

Cutter:"…reviewed all patient notes, original and subsequent diagnoses, and the patient's medications. The choice of Clozapine was … incorrect for this patient. But may I remind the Members that this drug has been used successfully to treat patients with similar psychiatric issues."

Won't he shut up? He prattles on and on trying to justify inept actions. Harrington touches my leg. He reminds me I must not react to the coward's words.

Cutter:"… while I understand why Doctor Tenbrooke has said what she has said, may I point out that she was not present at the patient's admission nor for one-on-one sessions nor for any of his time in treatment? I have spent hours with David Bloom. With every respect to Doctor Tenbrooke, I am the only one with the insight to know what is best for my patient."

Sure you do, you fucker. You liar. You dick of a psychiatrist.

Cutter:"…Mister Bloom's insistence on not eating. His insistence not to take medication. His adamant refusal of prescribed treatment. He was a threat to himself. I had no other viable course of action available to me. I must say here and now: Mister Bloom is still at risk."

Lying ass. Look at Harrington. See how he smirks. Cutter is digging his own grave. He won't get a job as a busboy.

Cutter:"For all of these reasons, I ask this tribunal to agree with my decision for a renewal order."

Nice try fuck-face. You haven't got a chance. Look at Chairman. He is not convinced.

Chairman:"Doctor Cutter, I respect your position as Consulting Psychiatrist. I agree that you are more aware of Mister Bloom's mental capacity than any of us, and the likelihood that he may still be at risk. But…"

Oh see how Cutter pales beneath the Chairman's humane gaze.

Chairman:"…we must also consider Doctor Tenbrooke's opinion. We are not here to question your professional judgement. We are here, as you know better than most, to do what is best for this patient."

Cutter:"Then perhaps we should ask the patient. It is my opinion he is still experiencing issues that could prove harmful to himself and others."

What the hell. Why is he looking at me like that?

Chairman:"If you believe it is in the patient's interests. Of course."

My interests? He doesn't give a fuck about my interests!

Cutter:"Mister Bloom. David. When was the last time you experienced…well, we've discussed this before. Tell us about your visions."

"He can't question me."

Harrington:"Yes he can, David. Just answer."

"I've told you. I saw some stuff. It's gone now."

Cutter:"All of it?"

"Yes, all of it. Doctor, you will be glad to know I don't even see pink elephants anymore."

Lay Member giggles. She gets it. Go on, Cutter. Throw me another one.

Cutter:"So the dog is gone."

"Yes."

Cutter:"You don't see or hear your mother anymore."

"No."

Cutter:"You feel you are mentally capable. That you are ready to reenter the world."

"Doctor Cutter, I'm as sane as you are."

That stops him. Oh see that prick-grin of his. He doesn't know what to do!

Cutter:"Of course you are."

Chairman:"Doctor Cutter, thank you for your comments. Doctors Cutter and Tenbrooke. Mister Bloom and Mister Harrington, thank you for your cooperation. Now if you'll excuse us, the Members will consider your statements."

Look at Cutter, the poor bastard. The fight knocked out of him as he heads to the door. His career in tattered defeat.

Harrington taps me on the arm, his look one of profound congratulations. We rise, the tribunal ended. We will leave so they may deliberate but I already know their verdict.

Cutter:"Mister Chairman, I apologize. Could I have one more question?"

What? Another one?

Chairman:"If it is salient."

"I thought we were finished."

Cutter:"Just a question, Mister Bloom. Do you remember, when you first came here, during our very first discussion, we talked about your mother?"

The bastard. Leave my mother out of it.

"What's my mother got to do with it?"

Cutter:"Years ago, you were made to believe you had been responsible for your mother's death. Do you remember we discussed it?"

Fuck off, you prick. Why is the room turning? Hold on. Hold on…

Cutter:"Do you remember you became upset? You couldn't continue talking about it. Instead, you asked if—" *Why is he glancing at his notes?*"—Dolores Foley had phoned."

"I don't remember."

"That's what you said. It's all here in your patient notes."

Oh look at the rat trying to look wise for the Tribunal.

Cutter:"Dolores is a good friend of yours, isn't she?"

"Yes."

Cutter:"In fact, you were hoping to marry her."

"It's none of your business. That was years ago."

Cutter:"Your proposal was common knowledge in the small community of Bere Island. But it never happened because you were forced to immigrate. I'm sorry."

"So am I."

Cutter:"David, when did you see Dolores?"

I sense it. Ambush. Be careful.

"I said she's none of your business."

Cutter:"Maybe not. But it seems a small question. When did you see your friend?"

"I don't know. Over a week ago. Right before you tried to kill me. We met in the garden."

Cutter:"The Unit's garden?"

"What other garden is there?"

Cutter:"What did you talk about?"

"About getting the fuck out of here."

Cutter:"I see. And have you talked to her even more recently?"

What is this ass getting at? Be careful. Tell the truth. I'm safe if I tell the truth.

"An hour ago. Right before this…hearing…started. She came to wish me luck. Nurse Healy let her see me."

Cutter:"Nurse Healy did?"

"Yes."

Cutter:"Which means you talked to Dolores after you started taking your current medication. The Lexipro?"

"You know I started the Lexipro a few days ago. I met Dolores an hour ago."

Cutter:"And the Lexipro has stopped all of your visions? It has cured your psychosis?"

"Yes."

Why is he staring at me like that? Why is Harrington on edge? Why does Tenbrooke look like she's going to die?

Cutter:"Mister Bloom. Nurse Healy finished her shift at one o'clock. That's almost three hours ago."

"So?"

Cutter:"She could never have approved such a visit because she wasn't here."

So what? Big deal. So Dolores made a mistake. It was another nurse. Christ.

Cutter:"But let's assume you did have permission to meet your friend. Did you meet again in the garden?"

"Where else is there? I'd never bring her into the Unit."

What is this scumbag up to? Why does he address the tribunal so seriously?

Cutter:"Members of the Tribunal, prior to the start of this meeting Mister Bloom was in his ward getting dressed. Then he went to the toilet. Following that, he was brought to this meeting room by his solicitor. He never left the unit. He never went to the garden."

"You're wrong. I met Dolores!"

Cutter:"Mister Bloom, I'm afraid there's more."

More? What could be more? What's that piece of paper he holds up?

Cutter:"This is a palliative care treatment summary for a woman who was admitted to the Castletownbere Community Hospital. Mister Bloom, as I'm sure you know, palliative care assists patients who are terminally ill."

Where the hell is he going with this? Why won't Harrington look at me?

Cutter:"I must warn you it concerns your friend, Dolores Foley."

"Keep your fucking mouth off Dolores."

Cutter:"The report I hold, this one here, states that Miss Foley, a resident of Bere Island, attended the hospital following unsuccessful surgery for cervical cancer."

What cancer? Dolores never had cancer.

Cutter:"I'm afraid she didn't survive. David, Dolores Foley is dead."

What? When? The bastard is fucking with me.

"You're lying. You prick."

Cutter:"It's the truth, David. Here, look at it. It's official. Dolores Foley died on the twenty-eighth day of July, 1997 from complications following surgery."

"You liar!"

Harrington:"David sit down!"

"You want me to go nuts, don't you? You're fucking with my head!"

Chairman:"Mister Bloom, take your seat! Mister Harrington!"

"Get your hands off me! I'm going to kill you, you fucker. Dolores is alive!"

Why does he torture me with lies?

"I love her. I'm going home to her. I promised. Let me out!"

Harrington:"David! David!"

Chairman:"Someone call security. Get a nurse in here!"

"You fucker you goddam fucker this time I won't take it do you hear me you goddam fucker

"Leave me alone get off me leave me alone leave

"Prince get him kill him kill him now prince just do it just leave me alone oh

please just leave me alone just leave me just leave me"

Bollocks? Here? Get off me! A syringe? It hurts! What do you inject into me?

"No no no no no no!"

The ticking of my dead mother's clock.

It comes for me on the light of a beaming lighthouse.

And Dolores says:

Sleep now, David. Go to sleep. I'll wake you when you come home to me.

When you come home.

SECTION FIVE

BANTRY PSYCHIATRIC UNIT

PATIENT: DAVID BLOOM

CONTINUING TREATMENT

To: Chief Executive Officer, Mental Health Commission, Dublin 4
From: Dr. Anne Tenbrooke, Consulting Psychiatrist
Ref: Objection to Care of David Bloom and Withdrawal from Panel Membership

A Chara,

I write to object to the continuing care of David Bloom, involuntary patient, Bantry Psychiatric Unit. A Renewal Order has been imposed which, I believe, places this patient at even greater risk than that which he suffered upon his initial admission.

As of this date, Mr. Bloom is being held in seclusion. I understand this is necessary following an altercation involving the patient. However,

Mr. Bloom's behavior is a direct response to the <u>damaging</u>, <u>inappropriate care</u> he has received throughout his confinement.

As I stated at Mr. Bloom's Tribunal: the symptoms he presented when admitted to the Unit were due to the stress, indignation, and humiliation he suffered at admission; his involvement in a life-threatening fire contributed to his agitation. Yet no mention in his file, or by his consulting psychiatrist, is ever made of Post Traumatic Stress Disorder.

Parental alienation, initiated by Mrs. Bloom and resulting in rejection by his daughter, aggravated emotional distress and instability. This was compounded when his daughter, manipulated by his estranged wife, sought involuntary admission. Mrs. Bloom's motives should have been questioned due to the breakdown in the matrimonial relationship.

Subsequently, the patient was prescribed inappropriate medication based on debatable diagnoses. Mr. Bloom continues to be in a very vulnerable position.

While I am forced to agree that Mr. Bloom must remain at the Unit for the shorter-term due to his current condition, I must go on record as follows:

His outrage and lack of cooperation during treatment is understandable. His current psychological decline is the culmination of a serious breach of judgement on the part of his consulting psychiatrist. It is my strong opinion that if correct medical and psychiatric treatment had been prescribed following the fire, Mr. Bloom would have recovered. Placing him involuntarily into psychiatric care was never necessary. Continued detainment will result in additional harm to Mr. Bloom.

But even more damning is the knowledge that his current condition can also be attributed to Ireland's inexcusable Mental Healthcare strategy.

In 2006, the strategic document 'A Vision for Change' recommended an integrated approach to address the biological, psychological and social factors that contribute to mental health problems. Yet today, many years later, most of these recommendations have not been adopted by relevant authorities. Due to this lack of change, mentally ill patients in Ireland and globally, including Mr. Bloom, are betrayed daily by ill-considered therapies that often exacerbate their conditions.

Until global mental healthcare practices are changed; until we learn to listen to the patients we are supposed to serve; until we admit that psychiatrists do not possess the only valid insight into a patient's condition and stop acting as if we are omnipotent gods, we will continue to endanger the very people we are tasked to heal.

For all of the above reasons, I withdraw my name from the list of Independent Psychiatrists appointed to Commission Tribunals. I do so because I object to existing practices, and no longer desire to serve in such a capacity.

Yours Sincerely,

Dr. Anne Tenbrooke

Anne Tenbrooke printed out the words she had written with so much care on her Dublin office laptop. She read them once then ripped the letter in two.

She believed that despite their best intentions, few at the Mental Health Commission would read her furious call to action much less listen. And even if they did, the Commission did not have the power to change anything. Change in the approach to mental healthcare was up to the Irish government and relevant agencies, as well as governments around the world. However, elected officials and the bureaucracies that protected them used any excuse to ignore the plight of the mentally ill. Call it ignorance. Call it an abuse of power. Whatever it was called, Anne had had enough.

As she locked up her office for the day, Dr. Tenbrooke wondered about David Bloom. She wondered if she had wasted her life by jousting at immovable mental healthcare legislative windmills, as well as inept psychiatry that hid behind impenetrable layers of professional stupidity, and brutal by-the-book psychiatrists who thought they knew it all despite their threat to peoples' lives. What she did know was that despite her best efforts, she had failed this patient.

It gave her no comfort to think that so had everyone else.

33

"Dad?"

"David?"

"Daddy? Can you hear me?"

A daughter and nurse stood at the door's security window, straining to see into the cell-like Seclusion room. The patient did not respond to the questions spoken through the crude two-way sound system. His silence was nothing new. He had not responded in over twelve hours since being dragged, screaming, through the heavy steel door.

David Bloom sat unmoving on a padded steel chair bolted to the floor. Leather restraints had been removed from the patient's wrists and ankles because immobility no longer required such precautions.

His head was cocked at an improbable angle staring, unseeing, at the single steel-meshed window recessed high into the wall above him. Threatening cloud swept across the limited horizon of his vision. God alone knew what intensity of thought flowed through the repository that had once been a rational mind. God had to know because Rachel knew she did not.

Every few minutes, his left hand trembled. Muscle spasms shook his back and neck. His trousers were soaked. Urine pooled at naked feet, yellowing the blue carpet-tiled floor, a stinking ocean that would be mopped up by Unit staff when they got around to it. In the last two hours he had urinated on himself a half-dozen times.

Other than the chair and a mattress covered in a blue sheet, the man she once knew as David Bloom—father, husband, human being—was the only object in the room. But for the shaking, he was as inert as the furniture.

In the next room, one as oppressive as her father's, screams of psychotic outrage hurled abuse at unseen tormenters. The enormous patient, a man who had tried to defend a brother-in-arms following the discovery of an old man's suicide, and the attack on a consulting psychiatrist, screamed for justice. In howling words, he begged Rose-Marie to open the channels of communications so he could enlist the aid of righteous avengers. His pleas went unanswered; his screams descending into painful sobs heard only by two visitors who were powerless to help.

When the screams subsided, Rachel turned to the nurse. "What do I do?"

"Get some rest. I'll ask Doctor Cutter to let you come back tomorrow."

"Will he be different?"

"Come with me. I have something for you."

As Nurse Healy took her elbow, Rachel could not help but again look into her father's eyes. What remained of his humanity gazed at a sea of distant something she could never fathom.

It was then, knowing she had lost him forever, that Rachel began to cry.

***

PATIENT NOTES

Patient: David BloomConsulting Psychiatrist: Cutter
Revised Diagnosis: Acute Schizophrenia
Revised Medication: Ziprasidone (intramuscular injection, 15 mg).
Continuing treatment for EPS, e.g. acute dystonia, akathisia, and bradykinesia

The patient has entered a phase of intense psychosis. Sensory awareness is limited. He has been placed in seclusion to prevent further harm to self or others. He is monitored on a 24-hour basis, per guidelines.

All vital signs, except for EPS characteristics and frequent urination, are normal.

I will reevaluate this patient's treatment upon release from seclusion. Based on the current psychotic episodes, as well as depression which he has experienced throughout his stay in the Unit, ECT—Electro-Convulsive Therapy—will be considered. ECT has resulted in significant benefits to patients presenting similar psychiatric distress.

P. Cutter, Consulting Psychiatrist

Dr. Cutter printed out the latest patient notes and signed them. As he did, he glanced at his right hand. Bloom's teeth had penetrated the skin, the hand swathed in bandages. He must remember to take a course of antibiotics, and arrange a blood test, as precautionary measures.

Again, he read through the notes. The young psychiatrist had never attended an ECT treatment. From his training, he knew patients were given a general anesthetic. The brain was stimulated by passing electricity through electrodes placed on the subject's head, thereby inducing a brief seizure. Following six to eight such treatments, an anti-depressant effect was delivered which may result in improvement.

Or not, of course, depending on the patient.

Cutter thought it prudent to give it a try. After all, he had a duty of care for mental health patient David Bloom.

His left hand toyed with a pen as he reviewed the morning's necessary actions. Following the brutal series of incidents, he had ordered a rapid response to restore order. Garda had secured the area. The old man's body was in the morgue. The two violent patients secluded. The cafeteria, damaged by some residents who took part in useless outbursts, had been cleared, the perpetrators reprimanded.

With his Unit now back to controlled normality, his flock safe, Cutter concluded with the matter of Bloom. He placed the patient notes, together with the renewal order he had executed, in the patient's thick file and closed it. He glanced at his desk clock. The day was already half gone. The psychiatrist knew he could at last turn to other pressing issues.

Opening the file of a patient involuntarily admitted only an hour ago, the young psychiatrist smiled to himself. Efficiency was the name of the game if he was to serve his patients well.

If nothing else, Dr. Paul Cutter knew himself to be efficient.
***

Mary Healy had never endured a day as bad as this one. She had expected some trouble if the tribunal agreed with Dr. Cutter's renewal order. But she had not expected this.

Yesterday, the nurse had arrived back at the Unit at 4PM for the start of her second shift. When she learned of the tribunal's decision, and David Bloom's violent reaction, she was too late to intervene. Her male colleague had already rushed to assist.

When David was brought back to the Unit, he was already sedated and placed in the ward. The hulking male nurse kept a sharp eye on him, fearing he would make trouble. In that case the patient would be restrained. But Bloom had not stirred for the entire evening.

Nurse Healy had looked in on him just after midnight. She found him awake, sitting up in bed, typing on the borrowed laptop. When she whispered a quiet hello, he answered with a silent smile. He did not seem disappointed. He did not display any signs of anger or agitation. Though the life in his eyes had dimmed due to the drugs injected into him, she was unsurprised when he pointed to two empty beds motivated by caring concern.

The small community had taken David Bloom's tribunal ruling hard. Most were convinced he would be released. Liam and the older patient seemed particularly upset. It was their beds that were empty.

She had rushed to the courtyard. There, she found the two missing patients sitting together on a bench. The old man had a comforting hand on Liam's immense robed shoulder. The younger patient had been crying. When she asked how she might help, the older man said they were almost finished and promised to go back to bed. Nurse Healy later blamed herself because she had not detected the depth of the old man's depression.

The nurse was scheduled to go home at 1AM. Instead, still concerned, she worked another shift. She spent the next few hours at the Nurse's station. She made periodic bed checks, as was her routine. All seemed in order.

At six in the morning, Dr. Cutter had walked in. He was early. David was already up and dressed. He had wandered into the courtroom at the exact moment of Cutter's arrival. Mary was on her way to the cafeteria when she saw them together. At first, she worried her patient might assault the doctor, repeating his attempt at the tribunal. She was relieved when she saw the two men shake hands. She could not hear the conversation but based on his calm deportment, David seemed to apologize.

He went to the toilet. Cutter entered his office. When she heard David's yell, Mary ran into the Men's Room.

The old man—the patient David called Ol' Fella—hung dead by his neck. He had used the long cord of an old robe tied from an unused fitting at the top of a partition. It had been enough.

David gripped the old man's hand, staring into open dead eyes. Even in death, they were filled with tears of desperate hopelessness.

That is when David Bloom went crazy.

She heard the growl of an enraged animal. Unable to contain him, he bolted past her, shouting at the top of his lungs. His scream woke other patients. Liam stumbled from the ward. At the same time, the male nurse ran toward pending trouble.

When the Unit's Consulting Psychiatrist opened his office door, he was greeted by the fist of David Bloom.

"You fucker, you Goddam stupid miserable fucker. You killed him didn't ya. Ya killed Ol' Fella!"

For the first time in her career, Mary Healy was overwhelmed.

The male nurse went for David. Liam went for the male nurse. The scrum of bodies fell like warriors into the psychiatrist's office. The big patient punched whatever came into range. David was sprawled on top of Cutter, jaws locked on the psychiatrist's bleeding hand.

The male nurse took care of Liam with a chopping thrust that caught the patient in the neck. David was next; grabbed around the waste. Crimson blood flowed down the doctor's wrist and arm, staining his white shirt the color of rage.

Nurse Healy reacted as additional nursing staff rushed in. As she herded upset patients to the courtyard, she saw Liam being carried, unconscious, down a narrow hallway by a team of men. David Bloom followed. It took three male nurses to lift his cursing, struggling body, transporting him to an isolation room of supposed safety.

As they lifted him, David Bloom caught her eye. For the last time, Nurse Healy saw within them the silent scream for help. Once again she could not hear him.

She cursed herself for it.

***

"Where do you think he's gone? Will he ever come back?"

His daughter and nurse sat together on a garden bench. The spring weather had turned. It rained a fine mist, masking colorful flowers in an opaque shroud.

"I don't know."

"Isn't there anything I can do for him?"

"Nothing. At least not now."

"It was Cutter's fault wasn't it." The name was uttered like a curse. "Won't he be held responsible?"

The nurse shook her head. No.

"But he was to blame! Won't he even receive a reprimand?"

Again the nurse shook her head.

"We'll sue him. We'll sue the Health Board."

"You can try."

"You don't think it would work."

"If it was a medical case, you could sue for malpractice. Mental health cases are more difficult. I've never heard of anyone winning a case like your father's. Ask your solicitor. He'll say the same thing."

The nurse opened a plastic bag, withdrawing a laptop computer. Mist dappled its surface.

"Your father kept a journal. He wrote in it almost every day."

"Have you read it?"

"Some."

"What's in it?"

"What he went through. He wanted people to understand. No one would listen."

"You listened."

"It took a long time. Too long."

She slipped the laptop back into the bag and gave it to her patient's daughter.

"You asked me where your father is. I think he's gone someplace he can be happy."

"Where?"

"He's gone home." In the falling mist, Rachel saw Nurse Healy's wistful smile."I wish we could go with him."

***

I can no longer trust. Not the doctor. Not my wife. Not my daughter. Not my business partner. Not what I see or hear. Not even myself.

Especially not myself.

"David."

Oh I know what's going on. Cutter was right. I am broken for all time. From this chair, I see dark clouds. Swirling beyond the concrete glass of my caged time capsule. I hear only the ticking of an eternal, damning clock. So it should because I am a fool.

"David, look at me."

They are dead. Mam, Dad, dog, Dolores. I was crazy to think I could see them. Touch them. Make them listen. At least now I know:

It is finished.

"Is that all you've learned?"

Oh, God yes. I have learned nothing at all. I will sit here, a shattered mute because there's nothing to be done. Christ, there's only one option left.

"Die? Is that what you want?"

Yes. They would not treat a dog like they have treated me. Let me die.

"David, that's not what you've learned."

Leave me alone. Whoever you are, go away.

"You say you can't trust? You can trust me, David. You can trust Rachel. Isn't that what you've learned? Isn't it time you learned to trust yourself too? You know what to do."

Who pulls me from the chair? Why does she make me stand? Go away. You're dead.

"Look. There. At the window. What's out there, David? Tell me."

Storm clouds and darkness. Enough darkness to choke a man.

"Is that all you see? Look again. Beyond the darkness."

I don't see shite. Nothing's there.

"Yes there is. Look closer."

Oh…yeah. Yes. Oh my God! Look at it.

Light! Look at the light!

"Reach for it. Fly to me."

I don't know how to fly.

"Yes you do."

The lighthouse beam. It fills the room with light.

"Reach higher. Hold onto it. Feel its warmth?"

I can't.

"Higher. Isn't that what you've learned, David? That you can reach higher than anyone? Touch the glowing river, David. Let go and fly."

I fly! Dolores, I fly!

"Come home to me, David. Please. Come home."

***

My dearest Rachel,

If you're reading this, something has happened which prevents me from giving this to you, myself. If Nurse Healy gives it to you, thank her for me. She's a good woman.

Honey, all my life I've tried my best to support and protect you and your Mom. I like to think I tried my best. But it wasn't good enough. I learned I wasn't made of steel. The ghosts of my past caught up with me and I failed you both. For that I have only deep regret. Someday I hope you'll both forgive me.

If you read this, I could be dead. Or maybe I'm beyond hope. Whatever has happened, please don't worry about me.

I've come to believe the passing of time isn't the one-way street people believe it is. Those we love are still here, I think. Perhaps it is their love that makes them all too real to me.

Maybe Cutter is right. Maybe I am crazy. I don't think so but read what follows and I hope you'll understand.

Some things we experience are true and eternal. They remind us of both the good and bad inside us. My love for you, for instance. A good thing. The ticking of a grandfather clock. Bad. But they are all truths. If I can make peace with them I know I will find myself again, even though I lost my way a long time ago. If I can do it, I think I will also find a bit of happiness.

Don't be sad, daughter. If nothing else I've learned the people we love are always with us, which is why I will always be with you.

Find the ring I gave to Dolores. If you do, you'll find me too.

With all my love, Dad

***

Frank McQuill entered the Seclusion area for the fourth time that day. He lugged a steel bucket filled with a mixture of water and disinfectant, and an old mop. He hated the chore. Forty years of cleaning up the piss of crazy patients was forty years too much.

Frank didn't know Bloom. He didn't care about Bloom. The fact that Bloom was now nothing but a vegetable bothered Frank not at all. All Frank wanted to do was mop up the piss as quick as lightning, stroll into town for a couple of pints, and call it a day.

The old janitor selected a key from the set he wore on a chain attached to his white boiler suit. When he made it to Bloom's door, he jammed the key in the lock. As was his custom he took a look through the security window. Long experience warned him to be wary. He knew fellows who had been almost killed by secluded patients. Frank was often accompanied by a nurse just to be on the safe side. In Bloom's case, it wasn't necessary. The vegetable hadn't moved in hours.

A small man, Frank had to stand on tip-toe to see clearly. "Huh," he said to no one when he peered through the security window. "Where is the fecker?"

Bloom's chair was empty.

Frank unlocked the door and entered the room. "What the fuck..."

The old man turned on his heal, running like a madman to report what he'd found. He didn't lock the door. Not that he had to. David Bloom was no longer in the room. At least, not the important part.

***

It was 3PM when Rachel finished reading her father's journal. She skipped dinner, still wrapped in the troubling, improbable words he had written. At 7:59PM, she decided to make it an early night and went to bed.

Ten minutes later she received the urgent phone call, asking her to return to the Unit.

34

Her father stood motionless, arms raised high toward the prison window as if in rigid benediction, his face transformed by the fire of soul-consuming rapture.

"What is he hearing?"

"We don't know."

"Can't you do anything?" Rachel rounded on the young psychiatrist. "Look at him, for God's sake. Help him. That's your job, isn't it?"

Cutter considered the frightened young woman beside him. "Your father is experiencing specific psychotic episodes associated with acute schizophrenia."

"How do you know?"

"Because he conforms to pre-established diagnostic stereotypes. Studies by worldwide clinicians would agree with such a diagnosis eighty percent of the time."

"What about the other twenty percent?"

"Unfortunately, we can never be certain."

Paul Cutter didn't see it coming. Rachel Bloom slapped him as hard as she could.

"My father was right. You really are a prick." She spun from the stunned psychiatrist to face her father. "Dad, wait for me. I'm coming."

Back in the car, Rachel glanced at the dashboard clock. It read 8:47PM. She remembered what her father had written. She would go to the house. She must get there by 10PM if she was to ever find him again.

She also knew her hope was as mad as the schizophrenic patient who had once been her father.

Accelerating through an evening town empty of traffic, the car swept west along the winding coastal road of Beara Peninsula, toward an island home that waited for her.

***

I stride upon a river of gold which streams high above the landscape of my youth.

Odd how a lighthouse beam can assume the solidity of a boat deck, or a young man's passion. Below, we light an evening Bay swept into whitewater by the coming storm. To the south, I see a Whiddy Island tug struggling to reach anchorage. Its twinkling lights remind me of a boyhood spent watching trawlers head into safe harbor. Or a Christmas tree decorated with so much care.

I want more of that twinkling past. Even in the face of my mother's madness I yearn for it.

To the north, I spy the mountainous spine of a peninsula. To the west an island breaches the horizon. A lighthouse towers white from its rocky nest. Its steady light rises like the sun to guide me home.

Within the corners of my heart I hear,

"How are things in Glocca Morra?"

When she arrived in Castletownbere, Rachel was forced to wait as the old man who was her skipper made the ferry tight against the dock. She glanced at her watch. It would take twenty minutes to cross the harbor and straight, another fifteen to get to the house.

The wind was getting up, the water blown to chop. Backing her car onto the ferry, Rachel could see the storm approaching through setting sunlight, covering the sky in a fist of darkness. As the boat pulled out into the harbor, she tingled with the anticipation of homecoming or the horror of death.

She did not yet know which.

I find my black dog waiting outside the front door. Prince dances at my homecoming. This time I know what to do. I kneel to him.

'You gotta help me fella. You gotta make him listen. Do you remember what we did before?' I open the squealing door.

I am expecting the interior to be razed by fire. Instead, it is as clean as the day I left it in my youth. I smell the welcome of old baking and glance at the ticking grandfather clock. It is 6:14PM.

Rachel entered the house through a wide-open doorway singed by fire. She turned on the flashlight, sweeping its beam through choking shadows.

"Dad?"

She did not expect a reply. But she did not think she was crazy to try. Not after reading the words he had written.

She stepped across rubble-strewn floors and into each room, searching. The place stunk of smoking aftermath. She coughed, clearing her throat.

"Dad?"

The front room was gutted, the ceiling fallen in. In the kitchen, a carbonized table frame stood in the middle of the room. An old Belfast sink hung from the wall. A pot of dead flowers lay shattered on the floor.

She backed into the entryway.

"Dad? Are you here?"

The stairs were gutted. But somehow, despite the damage, the stairway return was untouched. There, standing tall, proud, undamaged, was the grandfather clock.

Its unmoving hands read 10PM.

Time moves. Hands sweep as the clock ticks. 7PM.

Davy walks downstairs in fresh T-Shirt.

"Remember, Prince? Talk to him. Make him listen." Our dog bolts. Barking, barking furiously in the face of my youth.

"Davy, look at me. Look!"

Within a glowing lighthouse beam, he looks past me.

"Davy! Here!"

He must see! He saw me before, didn't he?

He walks by me, patting our dog, and out the door.

"Davy! You'll kill her!"

"Dad?"

Rachel peered again at the clock. Its hands remained unmoving."-Dad?" She could swear she had heard him; the echo of faint warning shouted in darkness. Rachel headed down the gutted hallway, toward the back rooms.

If he was in the house, she would find him.

"How are things in Glocca Morra?"

I rush to the kitchen. She sits in danger as she has always sat. Kitchen table. Whiskey tumbler in hand. Open bottle at an elbow. Blooming flowers on the windowsill.

"Please Mam. Listen to me. Don't please don't."

"Maud is that you I hear?"

"You hear your son. I know you do. Wait for Davy to come home."

"I think it's time to go see Maud, don't you Prince?"

"Goddammit, no!"

On the stairway the clock strikes 9PM. I rush past it with silent footfalls, following my mother up the stair. I am filled with fear that I am wrong. That what I saw before is impossible and I cannot change anything. That I am only experiencing the imaginings of a sick mind. I am terrified knowing: if I do not succeed my mother will die again. And I am condemned to spend eternity within revolving madness.

The back room was untouched. In the flashlight beam, Rachel's eyes swept across old furnishings. He was not there. She could chance walking up the charred stairway, past the grandfather clock that had somehow survived the singeing flames, to explore the upstairs rooms. But she understood it was unnecessary.

Her father was not home.

"I'm a fool," Rachel stated and laughed at herself. She had hoped to find her father. Yet she knew he was locked up in a Bantry Psychiatric Unit a lifetime east of where she stood. She understood that in clinging to desperate hope, she had fallen into the same pit of mad illusion her father had created. One that may have helped him cope but which had ultimately failed. Now, it had also failed her.

Outside, the gale rose in a song of vicious wind. She turned to the broad picture window. In the distance, the beam of the lighthouse swept gold across the descending storm.

Rachel took a seat at an old oak table, pondering her journey. For weeks, she had worked to build a new reality, one in which she might save her father. One which would prove him sane. One which matched the loving memory of the man she had known all her life and hoped to find again.

Hail hit the window like gunshot. As Rachel watched, she realized that in reaching for the memory, she had denied what was real. No matter whose fault it was, her father was mentally ill. In his sickness, she had lost him and would never get him back. *That* was the reality. Now she had to deal with it. It was time to stop searching. It was time to go home.

Rising from the table, she stepped out of the room. It was only when she walked into the hallway that she smelled it: the house was filled with the scent of baking.

We bang at the locked bathroom door but make no sound. All we hear is mad wailing. Soon she will make the cruel cut. In moments our father will come home with his unending 10PM accusation.

Lightning. The storm is rising.

"Davy?" I hear her whisper.

Dolores. She holds our ring. "I said you'd find me. Isn't that what I promised?" She walks into my arms. "Don't cry. I'm here"

"No you're not. No one is here. No one is real." I sob like a child.

"Yes we are. What did I say? Trust yourself." She pulls my face toward her. "You came home. Things will be different now."

The ticking of a clock. The blinding light of life. Time falls

I fall within it

Through the thunderous lightning of life

Past those I love, will always love

Onto the steady beam of a lighthouse

The glowing light parting into two quick-moving streams. A fork in my road.

I have a choice to make. Left or right?

A life already lived? Or one filled with unknown glowing possibilities; one that could take me back to a life I never had the chance to live?

As I fall, I decide.

Rachel ran into the kitchen. Nothing had changed. The fire's aftermath still littered the room.

Except on the windowsill.

In an unbroken flowerpot, glorious blooms of bright pinks and mad yellows grew tall against the rain-swept window. She was certain it was not there before. She was certain the pot lay smashed on the floor, the plant dead.

Outside, lightning filled the sky. Thunder roared. Within its crackling voice she heard the ticking of a clock. She hurried back to the entryway. The grandfather clock still stood untouched on the stairs. Its hands pointed steadily to 10PM.

As she watched, they moved.

I land at the entryway to my life.

Prince barking, barking madly as the door opens. The boy who was myself re-enters the house in a rush.

He holds Dolores by the hand. "I shouldn't have left. Help me find her."

I realize. It is not I who have changed anything. It is Davy.

I step toward them. As I do—I hear the loud crunch of footfall. I know: finally, I am home.

Davy hesitates. He turns, peering at me. I know he hears my presence. As if he is a human sonar, his probing signal detecting opportunity across distant time.

"Come on," he says to our girl. I follow toward unknown outcomes because none of this has happened before.

Rachel watched the hands move backwards from 10PM. Three minutes. Fifteen. An hour. Revolving anticlockwise in a mad sweeping rush. Counting back the days and years toward alternative endings that had never existed.

The room filled with its ticking.

As we rush into the kitchen, I feel it.

The division of my being. The one who lives in a cruel present, secluded in a mental ward, wrapped in a body that reaches to nothing, instructed by a sick mind.

And the other.

Standing in an old home, a middle-aged soul intertwines with the youth of his past as we rush to save our mother.

David or Davy no longer exists. Instead, having bent the glowing hands of time, we seek to become as one.

"Mam?"

We see guilt in our mother's eyes. She reaches to a high cabinet and its open door. We make out a whiskey bottle secreted deep within its shadows. The one we did not find. The one she has not touched. The one she will never touch.

Mam's lips quiver. Then she is in our arms, sobbing.

"Oh, Davy, Davy. I'm so glad you're home."

We hold her at arm's length, seeing the sweet face, the loving eyes. We take her hand, noting the elegance that is also present in a daughter's. In doing so, the hand that is Davy's and the hand that is mine merge to become much more than ours.

We are someone completely different.

I reach for Dolores. She takes my hand, the golden ring glittering on her finger. Two hands holding a single heart. I will never let go of that heart again.

"Mam," I promise, "I'll always come home."

The hands stopped. Then the minute hand crept forward. It was again exactly 10PM. The clock struck ten times, its solid voice echoing through the ruined house. The hands moved on, second by minute, hour by day, onward toward endless, mad possibilities.

"Dad, be at peace," she whispered.

When Rachel turned to go, she noticed what rested on the stairs at her feet. She knew it wasn't there a moment ago. Curious, she bent down, picking it up.

When she did, the room filled with light.

35

Jacob held his wife tight as she sobbed. She stood back from him because she was not yet finished with her story.

"I'm not crazy, Jacob," she said through her tears.

"I never said you were. Rachel, you're jet lagged. You've been through too much. Why don't you go up to bed?"

"Not yet." She took a breath and went on.

"When the clock struck ten, I thought I was crazy. I mean the whole thing was mad. You should have seen the house. The clock should have been cinders."

"There's an explanation."

"Is there?" she whispered. "When I looked down at my feet, I found it. It wasn't there before, but I did. Then I picked it up and…

"What did you pick up?"

"I picked it up and Jacob, the room filled with light. It was ten o'clock at night, the lights weren't working, and the sun had set. But the room filled with light."

"You were upset."

"No I wasn't. That's when I heard it."

"What?"

"A dog barking so I went outside." She looked straight at him. "Jacob, nothing looked real. It was as bright as morning. Brighter than that. It was like something out of a Van Gogh painting. The dog barked again. It was Prince, I'm sure it was. I could see a tractor plowing a field. There was a woman working in a garden. Then I saw a teenage boy. He was with a young woman. He walked up and looked right at me. Jacob, he took my hand. I could feel it. Then he said something."

"What did he say?"

"He said, 'No matter where I am, I'll always love you.'" Rachel's faced filled with awe."Jacob, it was Dad."

"And the girl. Was it Dolores? Is that what you think?"

Rachel showed him her hand. A golden Irish Claddagh ring glittered on her right ring finger. She slipped it off, giving it to her husband.

"This is what you found on the stairs."

"It's the ring Dad gave to Dolores."

Her husband did not dismiss the idea as crazy. As he studied it, she felt comforted by his practical analysis of the facts.

"It looks new yet from what you say it has to be over thirty years old. There's not a mark on it. It doesn't look like it was in a fire."

"It wasn't. Dolores made sure of it. Look inside."

Jacob turned the ring over. Inside he could see the small engraving. *D+D forever*.

"You think I'm mad don't you?"

He slipped the ring back on her finger."I'm not going to answer that."

"But you do."

"Life is a funny thing, Rachel. Who knows what's mad? Who can say what's real? Maybe you have to be mad to know the difference."

"Just like Dad."

He smiled."Just like Dad."

A week later, Rachel took the ring back to her father. He had been released from seclusion but due to ongoing acute schizophrenia had been moved to an isolation room.

He stood as straight as a lighthouse beam. He still reached toward the ceiling. He still smiled in rapturous, eternal bliss. Only Rachel and a nurse with whom she had shared the secret knew why he smiled.

His daughter coaxed his hand toward her. She placed the ring in his palm, wrapping his fingers tight around it.

"I love you, Dad. Where ever you are, be safe. Be happy."

For the rest of his natural life, and an eternity after that, David Bloom lived just as his daughter wished.

He was happy.

—END—

Acknowledgements

Unlike *Dolphin Song*, I have very few because this book hurt so much to write that I could not share it with anyone, not even Carmel Murray, the love of life.

To my GREAT FRIEND, absent now: Irish filmmaker, writer and director LIAM O'NEILL who read every word and hoped to make a television series before he died in May, 2020: rest easy my friend; this message of hope (and doom) is finally being broadcast.

To my grandparents, whom I will not identify: Hector and Clara (whom this novel is dedicated to) suffered their own indignities.

To Anne Tracey, my beloved friend.

Most importantly: to those on the Front Line – the doctors, lawyers, nurse practitioners, wrongly admitted patients (who are often at the wrong end of an Involuntary Mental Health Assessment), and their relatives and friends who knock their heads against a mental health system THAT REFUSES TO CHANGE despite contrary professional opinion…

I dedicate this book to their struggle. I pray for them. I hope you do too. They need it.

Amen.

At last, the secrets of Newgrange, Ireland's astounding Megalithic tomb, revealed! Its secrets discovered not by an archaeologist, but by an untidy Maths teacher, Barnabus, and two of his students:
When Jonathan and Cathy leave school on an April day to find their missing teacher, this brave couple did not know what lay in store for them on the other side of the sun: adventure, excitement, a crash course in Newtonian Astrophysics and a relentless and all-powerful universal enemy, Borgnoff.
First released in 1994, this novel quickly climbed to the top of the Irish Times Young Adult bestsellers list. Reader comments conclude that Tom Richards has written an utterly compelling science fiction novel, an unputdownable read for all whose imaginations can still travel to the other side of the known universe.

(Look out for Hotfoot and Hotfoot II, Lucky's Revenge, to be published later in 2022. Combining football – soccer to you American readers – with a Faustian tale, this zany story focuses on Larkin's Lot, an inept football team, and their run-in with Lucky Lucy, the Devil himself disguised as a football coach. Hotfoot went to Number One Young Adult Bestseller in 1995. Its re-release lets another generation of young readers enjoy this fantastic tale.)

Late-Summer, 2022

Misplaced Lovers

The sequel to Dolphin Song (sort of!)

The PREMISE

Grace Upendo (32) is a Sexually-abused Black African. Full of fear and unwilling to reach out to those who could help heal her scarred heart, she finally meets the man of her dreams, **Sean Hope**. But when Sean understands how damaged she is, and despite his great love for her, he comes to realize that to heal her he must leave her.

When Grace finally gains the courage to escape from **Jester Jones**, an abusive Australian sailboat owner, she begins a frightening voyage of new discovery through stormy seas to an uncharted island only 150 nautical miles from Brisbane. There, in this land of lakes, streams, stunning wind-swept beaches and tall trees, she begins to find new hope. On the island an adventure begins with a magical play, MISPLACED LOVERS. Its cast of characters, all animals and insects and talking bees, too, even include a talking two-headed Kangaroo. But when they begin to stage a raucous play based on Shakespeare's *Midsummer Night's Dream*, Grace soon discovers she cannot understand it. Filled with confusion, she is taken to Fish School by a pod of talking Dolphins. There, beneath the churning waves, she finally learns her lesson: she can talk to the magical animals and even the two-headed 'Roo! Having found the key, she is taken ashore and finally asleep, she dreams of a door. Behind it is the 'Roo, the talking Kangaroo, who turns out to be Sean, her misplaced lover.

A combination of Shakespeare's Midsummer Night's Dream and Peter Pan, and written in Iambic Pentameter, Misplaced Lovers combines a sense of fun to the tragedy of misplacing – and again finding – your one, true love. Out soon. Look for it on **www.tomrichards.ie**